Lieutenant Phillip Hazard was
intrigued when he was introduced to
the two ladies who were to journey
to Constantinople aboard his ship,
Trojan. The Baroness von Mauthner,
a thin elderly woman with a lined
face and birdlike eyes, seemed an
unlikely travelling companion for the
pale, heavily veiled and elegantly
dressed girl who was presented
simply as 'Mademoiselle Sophie'. Why
was so much secrecy attached to their
journey, and to Sophie's real identity?
The answers to these questions
were surprising . . .

Vivian Stuart

The Valiant Sailors

CORGI BOOKS
A DIVISION OF TRANSWORLD PUBLISHERS LTD
A NATIONAL GENERAL COMPANY

THE VALIANT SAILORS

A CORGI BOOK 0 552 09053 0

Originally published in Great Britain
by Robert Hale

PRINTING HISTORY

Robert Hale edition published 1966
Corgi edition published 1972

Copyright © Vivian Stuart 1966

Set in 10 on 11 point Baskerville

Corgi Books are published by Transworld
Publishers Ltd.,
Cavendish House, 57–59 Uxbridge Road,
Ealing, London W.5.

Made and printed in Great Britain by
Cox & Wyman Ltd., London, Reading and Fakenham

**NOTE: The Australian price appearing on the back
cover is the recommended retail price.**

AUTHOR'S NOTE

With the exception of the Officers and Seamen of H.M.S. *Trojan* and her passengers, all the characters in this novel really existed and their actions are a matter of historical fact. Their opinions, too, are in most cases widely known and where they have been credited with remarks or conversations – as, for example, with the fictitious characters – which are not actually their own words, care has been taken to make sure that these are, as far as possible, in keeping with their known sentiments.

The author thanks the Navy Records Society and its Council for permission to reproduce maps from the Society's publication No. 83, Russian War, 1854. Edited by D. Bonner-Smith and Captain A. C. Dewar, R.N.

This book is dedicated to Admiral of the Fleet the Earl Mountbatten of Burma, *as an expression of the author's admiration and respect for 'the most valiant sailor' of her lifetime, under whose command in Burma it was her privilege to serve.*

PROLOGUE

On 30th November, 1853, a small frigate squadron of the Turkish Navy, overtaken by a severe storm, was compelled to put into the Bay of Sinope for shelter. Sinope, a little town situated midway between Constantinople and Trebizond and a hundred and fifty miles south of the Russian naval base at Sebastopol on the Crimean peninsula, had been in Turkish hands since 1471.

Despite the fact that war had been declared between Turkey and Russia a little over a month before, the Turkish Commander, Vice-Admiral Osman Pasha, anticipated no danger to his small fleet in spite of his present close proximity to Sebastopol. Both the Tsar and the Sultan had announced to the world that, whilst reluctantly compelled to settle their differences by force of arms, each intended to confine himself to the defensive.

In consequence an unofficial truce existed between the two opposing navies which had hitherto been scrupulously observed by both sides. In spite of this, however, under cover of fog, six Russian line-of-battle ships, each mounting between 80 and 120 guns, entered the harbour and attacked the Turkish ships at anchor. Within an hour all these had been sunk or set on fire.

The Russians were armed with shell-firing guns – the *canonobusier* advocated by the French General Paixhans, in 1824, which had never before been used in any naval action, and the Russian Vice-Admiral Nachimoff, his prey completely at his mercy, used them ruthlessly for target practice.

Having destroyed the frigates, the Russian gunners directed a murderous fire at the few survivors who were attempting to swim ashore. The Commander of the Russian fleet did not call a halt to the slaughter until close on 4,000 Turkish seamen had perished, after which he turned his guns on the town. It was soon ablaze, the shore batteries reduced to heaps of rubble and the garrison in headlong flight.

News of the disaster reached England, via Berlin, on 12th December and it roused a storm of public feeling, culminating in repeated demands for the British Mediterranean Fleet – then in the Bosphorus – to be sent into the Black Sea in order to protect Turkey from further unprovoked attack. This was not done immediately, however, for the British Prime Minister, Lord Aberdeen, was still seeking to avert a war with Russia.

Eventually, on the 3rd January, 1854, the Allied Fleets, numbering eighteen sail-of-the-line with escorting frigates and steamers, entered the Black Sea, their purpose to afford protection to the Ottoman territory and flag.

H.M.S. *Britannia*, a 120-gun three-decker, flew the flag of Vice-Admiral James Whitley Deans Dundas. His recently appointed second-in-command, Rear-Admiral Sir Edmund Lyons, transferred from the *Terrible*, 21 – the steam frigate in which he had travelled from England – to H.M.S. *Agamemnon*, 91, a fine new steam-screw second-rate, launched less than a year before and sent out, at the Rear-Admiral's own request, to receive his flag. In addition to these ships, the British Fleet included *Trafalgar*, 120: *Rodney*, 92: *Albion*, 90: *Vengeance*, 84: *Bellerophon*, 78, all under sail, *Sanspareil*, 90, converted to steam-screw and eight frigates. Vice-Admiral Hamelin, commanding the French Fleet, flew his flag in the 120-gun *Ville de Paris*, his second-in-command, Rear-Admiral de Tinan, in the 16-gun paddle steamer *Gomer*. A second French squadron, under Rear-Admiral Bruat, was later to join his command.

Based on Sebastopol were an estimated fifteen Russian sail-of-the-line, seven large frigates – 60's and 54's – seventeen smaller frigates and corvettes and upwards of sixty steamers of various kinds, with a further twenty or thirty gunboats on the Danube.

The clouds of war grew darker and more threatening as the world waited expectantly for vengeance to be taken on the perpetrators of the Sinope massacre, but the Russians kept prudently to their own territorial waters, avoiding any chance of an encounter with the British and French Fleets, which were thus left in virtual command of the Black Sea. Such fighting as there was took place on land, between Turk and Russian and, during the spring of 1854 – apart from some spasmodic fighting in Asia Minor – the main theatre of war was the Danube basin. There, the Turkish Commander-in-Chief – a shrewd, battle-hardened Croat, who had adopted the Turkish name of Omar Pasha – established his headquarters at the mountain stronghold of Shumla and, supplied through the Black Sea port of Varna, prepared to meet Prince Gortschakoff's expected attempt to cross the Danube and march on Constantinople.

The key to the Turkish army commander's defensive strategy was the fortress of Silistria, the most vital as well as the most strongly held of his chain of fortresses on the Bulgarian bank of the Danube, sixty miles to the north of Shumla. This he determined to defend, until the help he had been promised arrived from his British and French allies and, in particular, from their Fleets.

Queen Victoria opened the British Parliament on 31st January, 1854. In her speech from the Throne she emphasized that – although her endeavours, in cordial co-operation with the Emperor of the French, to restore the peace between Russia and Turkey had been unremitting – she believed it necessary to make a further augmentation of Britain's naval and military forces.

During February, battalions of the Guards and the 1st Royal Fusiliers entrained for Portsmouth, where troop transports were waiting to take them to Gallipoli and Constantinople. The British people, clamouring for war, cheered them enthusiastically as they marched through the streets, with bands playing and colours flying. It was announced that Lord Raglan, Master-General of the Ordnance, was to command the Expeditionary Force of 30,000 men which, in

9

the event of war, would be sent to Turkey. Vice-Admiral Sir Charles Napier was appointed Commander-in-Chief of the British Fleet destined, when war broke out, to serve in the Baltic. There was intense activity in naval dockyards and ports; ships, newly commissioned and being fitted out for service with either the Baltic or the Black Fleets, were manned and prepared for sea in record time.

Among these ships was the steam-screw frigate *Trojan* of 31 guns and 300 horse-power, built at Sheerness in 1851 and now commanded by Captain Thomas North, a post-captain in the Royal Navy. Having undergone a refit in the dockyard at Devonport and completed her sailing and gunnery trials, the frigate was lying at Plymouth in readiness for immediate departure when, on 17th March, orders reached her from the Admiralty.

The first part of his instructions caused Captain North no surprise. He was to take on board a draft of Royal Marines and another, of seamen and boys from the *Impregnable*, and proceed with all possible speed to join the flag of Vice-Admiral Dundas in the Black Sea. This he had expected but the final paragraph with which his orders concluded caused him to swear, loudly and ill-temperedly, to himself. He was directed to receive, in addition to the seamen and Marines, two female passengers of importance and was to dispatch his First Lieutenant to London at once, so that he might escort *Trojan's* two passengers to the ship.

Sealed orders concerning the destination of these passengers would be awaiting the First Lieutenant at the Admiralty and he was to call for them as soon as he reached London. . . .

Frowning, Captain North rang the bell at his side. To the sentry who answered it, he said curtly, 'Pass the word for Lieutenant Hazard. He's to report to me immediately.'

CHAPTER ONE

I

PHILLIP HORATIO HAZARD, First Lieutenant of Her Majesty's steam frigate *Trojan*, was not ill-pleased by the unexpected opportunity to visit London before his ship sailed. He concluded his official business at the Admiralty in time to dine with his parents at their house in Kensington Gore, where his arrival was warmly welcomed. Since he was not required to assume responsibility for the *Trojan*'s two female passengers until noon the following day – when, he had been told, they would meet him at Paddington Station – he was able to spend some pleasant hours in the bosom of his family which he had not anticipated and, in consequence, greatly enjoyed.

After taking affectionate leave of his mother and young sisters, he drove to the station with his father, a retired rear-admiral who, in spite of a heavy cold, insisted on accompanying him thus far on his journey. As their cab clip-clopped its slow way through the crowded streets, the Admiral talked enthusiastically of the impending war with Russia.

'I envy you, Phillip. 'Pon my soul, boy, I wish I were coming with you. Why, I remember in '98 . . .' his faded blue eyes were lit by a fugitive gleam of excitement as, for his son's benefit, he recalled some of the epic naval engagements in which, during his long and distinguished career, he had taken part.

Phillip listened dutifully. He had heard most of the stories before and, as a child, had listened to them enthralled, for they had inspired all his boyhood dreams. But he was in the Navy himself now – at twenty-seven a man, not a boy, with nearly fourteen years' seagoing experience behind him – and the oft-repeated tales of past glories had long ago lost their magic for him. He had been stripped of his youthful illusions and, although he would have changed the life he led for no other, he was unable to share his father's unqualified enthusiasm for a war in which, all too soon, he would be actively involved.

He could not regard any war . . . how had the old man put it? *As offering a splendid chance of advancement to an ambitious young officer* . . . he smiled ruefully to himself. Under the command of a man like Thomas North, he would be as well to curb his ambitions, in any case. . . .

The Admiral broke off in mid-sentence. As if guessing the trend of his son's thoughts, he said with an abrupt change of tone, although without apology, 'But that's all past history, is it not? We should talk of the future, of *your* future, Phillip . . . because I'm depending on you to acquit yourself well. You have a name to live up to, don't forget. I named you after the greatest naval commander this country ever bred, although your mother, more's the pity, insisted on Phillip as your first name. Phillip, after that uncle of hers, who was a poet . . .' he shook his head disgustedly.

'Yes, sir,' Phillip acknowledged, his voice flat.

Ignoring the interruption, his father went on eagerly, 'I'd like to hear that you've been given your own command before this war's over . . . it would mean a great deal to me. I regard you as my only son, Phillip, you know that, I think. Your brother Graham is lost to us but you . . .' the stern old face relaxed suddenly in a smile of singular warmth and affection. 'You are the source of much pride to me.'

'I am glad of that, sir.'

'Your own command, Phillip,' the Admiral urged. 'That is what you must aim for . . . your own command. I had mine when I was your age, so it is not too much to expect, is it, with a war to help you?'

'No, perhaps not, Father. Except that I . . .' Phillip bit back the words he had intended to say. He wanted to talk to his father about North, to seek his advice but he knew suddenly that he could not expect the old man to understand, in the circumstances ... to understand or even to sympathize. They were of different generations, he thought regretfully, and they saw everything through different eyes now – the navy, the war, the conduct of his brother Graham, perhaps even life itself. There was a gulf between them, which neither could hope to bridge during the few minutes left to them and this precluded his asking for advice.

'Except that you ... ?' his father prompted. 'Except that you what, Phillip?'

'It was nothing, sir, nothing at all,' Phillip evaded. 'I shall do my best, you may be sure.'

To his relief, the cab turned into the station entrance and came to a halt behind a line of other vehicles. A porter opened the door. Phillip hesitated and then alighted, to stand bareheaded in the open doorway, studying his father's lined face and red-rimmed, fever-bright eyes with a pity he was careful not to betray.

'Don't wait, sir,' he begged, 'because it will not improve that chill of yours if you do. Railway stations are draughty places and my train is not due for another forty minutes, at least.'

'And you have these female passengers of yours to meet, have you not ... the mysterious Baroness von Mauthner and her charge?'

Phillip inclined his head. 'I was instructed to meet them here, as I told you, and escort them to the ship.'

'It's deuced odd, when you come to think about it,' Admiral Hazard observed. 'Giving passage aboard one of Her Majesty's frigates to two foreign females in time of war ... but I suppose their Lordships know what they're about. You haven't any idea who they are, have you?'

'No, sir, none,' Phillip was compelled to admit. 'I have been told very little about them. Simply the Baroness's name and that she is elderly and her ward young. It is to be hoped that I shall recognize them, when they arrive.'

'Well, I must not keep you from your duty,' the Admiral said. He blew his nose with unnecessary violence. 'Remember what I've told you, Phillip.'

'I won't forget, sir.'

'And you'll write . . .' the old man was seized with a fit of coughing. He added gruffly, when he could get his breath, 'Your mother will be anxious for news of you. Women don't see wars in quite the same light that we do, of course, and they worry. Your mother more than most, I sometimes fancy.'

'I shall write as often as I can, Father,' Phillip promised, 'to you both . . .' he had a momentary vision of his mother's small, sweet face and forced a smile. 'Good-bye, sir. I'm very glad I was able to see you both again before sailing.'

'Yes, I am glad, too. Godspeed, Phillip. Take care of yourself.' A thin hand gripped his and then abruptly released it. Phillip nodded to the cab driver, anxious for his father's sake as well as his own, to keep their parting to its usual brief and unemotional level. They were accustomed to partings, after all, and there had been many before this one.

Admiral Hazard, following the family tradition, had sent him to sea as a naval cadet at the age of thirteen and had himself been appointed to his first ship – H.M.S. *Captain*, 74 – when he was barely eleven but in time, as he had just proudly recalled, to serve under Nelson's command at the Battle of Cape St. Vincent. But now he was approaching his sixty-eighth year and, with indifferent health, was beginning to show his age, Phillip thought, conscious of an unexpected pang as the cabby, in obedience to his signal, whipped up his horse and the cab started to move away. If the duration of the war with Russia should prove to be longer than the five or six months predicted by the experts, this might well be the last time that they would see each other, he realized. The last time, perhaps, that he would feel that thin old hand clasp his and listen to the rasping injunction to remember that he had a name to live up to . . . he smothered a sigh.

'Carry yer bag, sir?' A porter was hovering at his elbow but Phillip shook his head. Reminded of the reason for his presence at the station, he picked up his small grip and went to stand by the entrance to the booking hall, looking about him speculatively. No one even remotely resembling the two ladies he had been commanded to meet appeared, as yet, to have arrived but, consulting his pocket watch he saw that – thanks to his father's passion for punctuality – there was still plenty of time before the departure of the Plymouth train. To make assurance doubly sure, he went on to the platform and, having ascertained that they were not on the train, he left his bag in a vacant first class carriage and returned to his vantage point by the booking office.

He was, as instructed, in uniform and he hoped, on this account, that the ladies he sought would pick him out from the crowd of other travellers and make themselves known to him, should he himself fail to recognize them. He frowned, as two ladies muffled in furs walked past him without any sign of recognition. As he had explained to his father, he had been told very little when he called at the Admiralty. The confidential nature of his mission had been impressed on him and was emphasized by the sealed orders he had been given to deliver to his Captain. These, presumably, concerned the two ladies who were to be the *Trojan*'s passengers but, being sealed, were not for his eyes and he could expect no details, unless Captain North chose to confide in him, which ... Phillip's firm young mouth compressed. Which would not assist him in his present search and was, in any event, unlikely since Captain North had already demonstrated a marked preference for keeping his own counsel.

As his father had observed, the whole affair was more than a little odd, he thought, glancing again at his watch. Ladies, it was true, were not infrequently carried as passengers aboard naval vessels in peacetime, and many captains brought their wives with them when cruising or on being posted to a new station. Often they invited female relatives and friends as guests, on a cruise of short duration – this was one of the privileges of command and was officially permitted by the Board of Admiralty. But at a time like this – when a declaration of war was expected almost hourly and when H.M.S. *Trojan* was under orders to proceed to the seat of war – the reason for their Lordship's decision to allow two

15

ladies of importance to take passage in her was difficult to imagine.

Indeed, it passed his comprehension. He had welcomed the news no more enthusiastically than Captain North had welcomed it yesterday, when the Admiralty's instructions had reached them . . . the only occasion, in fact, when he and his commander had seen completely eye to eye about anything, Phillip reminded himself wryly. Admittedly he had found consolation in the prospect of being able to bid his family farewell, while the Captain had been annoyed at having to dispense with his services for twenty-four hours but . . . he started to pace restlessly up and down, still keeping a watchful eye on the station entrance.

His father had urged him to seek a command of his own, he reflected, and expelled his breath in a deep sigh of frustration. There was nothing he wanted more, heaven knew, but this was the first appointment he had held in his present rank and his chances of a command were slight. He had been gratified when promotion to First Lieutenant of a frigate had been offered him, although it had meant leaving the *St. Jeanne d'Acre*, a 101-gun ship-of-the-line – at this moment on her way to the Baltic with Admiral Napier's Fleet – and her much loved commander, Captain the Honourable Henry Keppel, under whom he had been serving at the time. Now, however . . . Phillip permitted himself a tight-lipped smile. Now he regretted the change, although he had not told his father so, and regretted it with increasing bitterness with each passing day.

He had served under Captain North for nearly two months and relations between them were still as strained and unhappy as they had been after the first day, when the newly appointed Captain had arrived on board the *Trojan* to read his commission to the assembled ship's company. From the outset, they had found themselves opposed, both professionally and personally. No doubt the fault for this was largely his own, Phillip thought, forcing himself to review the situation objectively. He had resented North's appointment to command of the *Trojan* and, perhaps, had failed to hide his resentment . . . but he had reason, surely, to feel resentful?

It had been he, not North, who had put the ship in commission. He had done so, he recalled, when she was lying in an uncovered dock with her masts out and no copper on, her engines being overhauled, her rudder in a shed repairing and ten foot of water in her hold. Since no captain had then been appointed, it had been left to him to supervise her fitting-out and manning, to wrangle with the foreman shipwright, the dockyard engineers and painters – even to plead with the Admiral-Superintendent, on occasions – so that his ship's needs might be satisfied. He had entered her crew, had stood over the sailmaker and the carpenter and their mates, watching the progress of their work with a critical eye, passing nothing that failed to reach his own exacting standards of perfection.

During those weeks of preparation, while *Trojan* was masted, rigged, armed, stored and provisioned, she had been *his* ship. As he had watched the masts and yards rise and the rigging take shape and listened to the powerful hum of her newly tuned engines, he had come to love her as other men love a woman, with all the pride and the passionate devotion that was in him. He had been fully aware than she was *not* his ship, of course. He had neither expected nor hoped to be given command of her – a 31-gun frigate was a post-command and he was too junior – but he had hoped that a captain who was worthy of her might be appointed when the time came. A man of the calibre of Henry Keppel, perhaps, and instead . . . Phillip's hands clenched convulsively at his sides. Instead, their Lordships had given *Trojan* to Thomas North.

He frowned, endeavouring to analyse his feelings concerning North, to justify them. It was not only that he disliked the man. Other things being equal, he could have overcome his dislike or, at least, contrived to conceal it, for he was not by nature rebellious or inclined to criticize his superiors. In North's case, however, his feelings went deeper than mere personal dislike – he mistrusted his senior's professional capabilities, his seamanship and judgment and doubted his fitness for command. Worse still, he could not escape the uneasy conviction that, when the real test came, Thomas North would be found wanting. His fears on this score were probably more instinctive than reasoned but, for all that ... Phillip halted his restless pacing. For all that, they haunted him and he could not erase them from his mind.

The advent of war with Russia had, he knew, made heavy demands on the manpower reserves of the British Navy. Many more ships than were normally required had had to be put into commission and officers and seamen found to man them. Inevitably a number of officers, who had been on half-pay for many years, had received seagoing appointments ... and Captain North was one of these, a man approaching fifty, whose last command had been that of a 6-gun brig on the West Africa Station. His ship had paid off in 1841 and he had been on shore ever since, either not wishing or being unable to obtain another command, while his name rose slowly higher on the Navy List.

He ranked now as a post-captain but he had never before commanded so large a ship or so many men. He had no experience of steam and *Trojan* was fitted with an auxiliary screw-propeller and engines of 300 horsepower. In addition to her seamen and marines, she carried a full complement of engineers and stokers, of whose particular functions Captain North knew nothing ... and concerning which, on his own admission, he had no desire for enlightenment.

'Engines, Mr. Hazard, are auxiliary to sail and, in my view, they always will be,' he had stated, his tone dogmatic and brooking no argument. 'I shall thank you to remember this, even if you do chance to hold a certificate to prove that you have successfully completed a course of study in the use of steam-power. In *my* ship the engines will, no doubt, serve their purpose when it is a question of entering or leaving harbour but, at all other times, they will be auxiliary. There is a qualified *engineer*' – he made the word sound offensive – 'in charge of the engines, leave them to him. You will best please me by working up the seamen's divisions to the peak of efficiency I'm accustomed to and am entitled to expect of a smart crew and a competent first lieutenant. I'll tolerate no slackness aloft, Mr. Hazard ... no slackness at all!'

'There will be none, sir,' Phillip had assured him. 'The men are shaping well and—' but Captain North had not allowed him to go on.

He had interrupted coldly, 'Do not be too sure of that, Mr. Hazard. We have a great many raw hands and half-trained coastguards to lick into shape and very little time in which to do it. I shall require all officers to assist in training by their personal example and I shall hold you, as First Lieutenant, responsible for setting that example. My standards are high – a good deal higher than you've been used to, I've no doubt – and it is evident to me that discipline on board this ship leaves much to be desired. In the absence of an experienced senior officer you have permitted too much laxity ... particularly where the officers are concerned. Well, we must put that right, Mr. Hazard ... we must tighten up discipline and I shall see to it myself. For a start, I intend to grant no requests for shore leave until I am satisfied that all officers have earned the privilege ... which includes yourself, is that clear?'

It had been made abundantly clear ... Phillip gritted his teeth in futile bitterness as he remembered. These had been almost the first words his new Captain had addressed to him, after having inspected the ship and her company, and he had found fault with everything he saw, with all that had been accomplished prior to his own appointment. There had been other speeches on similar lines and, each day, a carefully compiled list of minor complaints and criticisms, given to him in writing ... always with the suggestion that his standards were not high enough.

Yet Captain Keppel's standards had been high, he thought angrily. There had been few smarter ships than the *Jenny d'Acre,* as her seamen affectionately called her. Certainly there had been none better disciplined than the lovely

44-gun frigate *Maeander*, which Captain Keppel had previously commanded and in which – first as Mate and then, on promotion, as junior lieutenant – he himself had served a three-year commission. *Maeander*, lying with lower yards and topmasts struck, could get her royal yards across in under six minutes, Phillip recalled, with nostalgic pride. Quite recently, *Acre*, with a raw crew and a gale blowing, had reefed all three topsails in a little over three ... a considerable feat, in such conditions, which had earned her a *'Well done, Acre,'* from the flagship, whose own hands were still struggling with hers. But then Harry Keppel had always found occasion to praise, to express appreciation of work well done and to encourage his men ... unlike North who, it seemed, could only criticize and condemn.

North held himself aloof and was a stickler for formality, insisting that both officers and men show him the deference due to his rank, at all times and without relaxation. He liked to think of himself as a 'taut hand', and he punished with extreme severity, paying meticulous attention to petty details which most captains would have deemed unworthy of their notice.

His gig's crew, for example, had undergone the most rigorous 'smartening up' exercises, the Captain supervising their training himself. In the course of a single week, he had put four different midshipmen in charge and had expressed dissatisfaction with each one. His coxswain and steward – both tried and trusted long-service men – went in mortal terror of him and had begged to be relieved of their duties, and two of the gig's crew had deserted, one an A.B. with an exemplary record, who had been commended for gallantry.

The same pattern was repeated, on a larger scale, throughout the ship. Soon there was scarcely an officer whose leave had not been stopped, on the Captain's instructions, for failure to put his heart into his work. No one escaped the caustic lash of North's tongue and the senior watch-keeping lieutenants and warrant officers were no more immune to punishment and public reprimand than were the midshipmen and boys. In the sacred name of discipline, seamen were sent to the gratings for comparatively minor misdemeanours and officers constantly humiliated ... Phillip's cheeks burned, as the unpleasant memories came flooding back into his mind. He resumed his measured pacing, back and forth, in front of the booking office, lost now in his own thoughts and no longer consciously watching the station entrance.

Discipline in the British Navy had always been severe and even harsh, at times, as he knew only too well. A high degree of discipline was essential when the lives of hundreds of men and the safety of their ship often depended on instant and unquestioning obedience to orders. Provided that it was enforced justly and combined with efficient command, few rebelled against the severity of naval discipline or doubted its necessity. A commander whose seamanship won the respect and trust of his men could drive them relentlessly without incurring their active resentment. But the men's trust was not easily given and ... Phillip frowned. North's command was *not* efficient and his seamanship had so far inspired little confidence.

On their first brief shakedown cruise after *Trojan* completed for sea, he had permitted two grave errors on the part of the elderly Master to pass, apparently without being aware of either and his handling of the ship under sail had been, to say the least of it, hesitant and uncertain. It had continued to be unimpressive and there had been an almost uniform look of strained bewilderment on the faces of the old hands, before the cruise ended. Even the younger men, whose pride in their ship had been intense, were uneasy when her sailing trials took place and, matched against other ships of the Fleet, she had made a poor showing.

Trojan's steaming trials had also been disappointing, her newly fitted engines constantly breaking down. North, cursing the shipwrights and engineers and his own First Lieutenant with equal vehemence, obtained permission to return the ship to the dockyard basin, so that an addition might be made to her false keel and an overhaul of her engines put in hand. All this had held her up for longer than expected, delayed her sailing for gunnery exercises with the Channel Squadron and necessitated turning the crew over to a hulk once more, with all the resultant inconvenience and extra work.

Phillip sighed in remembered frustration. The men were not deceived by these excuses for their ship's mediocre performance ... they had begun to sense, in the uncanny way seamen always did, that all was not well and they were uneasy. By the time Captain North declared himself ready to put to sea again, it was mid-February and the Channel Squadron, under Rear-Admiral Sir Armar Lowry-Corry, was exercising off the Portuguese coast, their crews already approaching a high state of efficiency. *Trojan* was instructed to rejoin and the spirits of her men rose, But, after a stormy passage through the Bay of Biscay, during which all three top-gallant masts went over the side and the main topmast was found to be sprung, she had done little more than salute the Rear-Admiral's flag when orders were received to return to Spithead.

It was rumoured that Her Majesty the Queen would hold a review of the battle squadrons before their departure for the Baltic, now generally believed to be imminent. Excitement ran high, as the long line of ships came-to off the Spit and dropped anchor, their guns booming out in salute to the flag of the Commander-in-Chief, Sir Charles Napier, then flying from the main of the *Princess Royal*.

There had been talk of Cronstadt and Sweaborg, Phillip recalled, with eager speculation as to the chances of being in action against the Russian Fleet, and he and his shipmates had joined in the discussion with as much enthusiasm as any. Next day, however, *Trojan* was detached from the Baltic Fleet and, designated as an addition to Rear-Admiral Sir Edmund Lyons' small steamer squadron in the Black Sea, was sent to Cork, to ferry troops from some of the Irish garrisons to Plymouth. To the chagrin of her officers and men, she had returned to Plymouth and was lying there, awaiting orders to proceed to Constantinople, when the

Royal Review took place at Spithead on 10th and 11th March. Immediately afterwards, the Fleet weighed for Copenhagen.

He had been as disappointed as the rest of the ship's company, Phillip thought, to have missed so great and historic an occasion as that which had marked the Queen's visit to Spithead. Yet, in spite of this, he had been secretly relieved that *Trojan* had not been sent to the Baltic, where there was the prospect of early action. He was not satisfied with the progress made in training by the crew and Captain North's handling of the ship, which had been at its worst during the storm they had encountered on their way to Lisbon, still worried him more than he cared to admit, even to himself. In addition, his superior's insistence on the continued need to tighten up discipline was the source of even greater anxiety to him, since this, he was wretchedly aware, was likely to have an adverse effect on the morale of every soul on board.

Morale, Phillip reflected, was of supreme importance in a fighting ship, as he had learnt by experience. Although at the start of any commission, a new and untried crew had – as Captain North had put it – 'to be licked into shape', no amount of coercion could weld the men into an effective and reliable fighting unit if their morale were lowered beyond a certain point. Discipline, harshly applied for its own sake, was useless when men reached the state the *Trojan*'s men had reached. Once pride in their ship had been lost, there had to be some relaxation of discipline, some concession offered to human dignity and feelings, some attempt made to restore confidence. A wise commander, recognizing the danger signals, would have made concessions but North was either blind to these or, if he had noticed, chose to ignore them. Far from relaxing the pressure, he seemed obstinately determined to increase it. His only answer was to punish with greater severity and the result was little short of disastrous.

A happy, hardworking ship's company had become, after a few weeks under North's command, sullen and discontented, hating him and the ship. The men muttered among

themselves and grumbled ceaselessly and, of late, there had
been an alarming increase in the number of desertions . . .
particularly during their short stay in Irish waters. Worse
still, Phillip reminded himself, the discontent was not
confined to the lower deck. Three officers had recently requested transfers and several others were, he knew, considering the advisability of doing so although, as yet, no
transfers had been granted. He himself had been tempted
more than once to follow their example but . . . he glanced, a
trifle impatiently, at his watch and was surprised to see that
only fifteen minutes had elapsed since he had taken up his
position by the booking office.

He drew a long, unhappy breath. This had been the problem he had hoped he would be able to talk over with his
father, only to find when he attempted to broach the subject
that the words had stuck in his throat. He knew, he supposed
wearily, what his father would have said, what advice he
would have given, had he been asked . . . *Trojan* was his
ship, the men his men and he had a duty towards them. He
could not leave them, no matter how great the temptation.
Yet, as he paced up and down in front of the station entrance
and attempted to see the events of the past week in their
proper perspective, Phillip – for all his long training and love
of the Service – would have given everything he possessed to
be able to walk away. At that moment he would gladly have
left North and the *Trojan* and her two tardy passengers to
whatever fate destiny had in store for them.

Like the seamen who had deserted, he thought, he had
lost pride in his ship and faith in his commander. Like his
brother Graham, perhaps, he had lost faith in himself . . .

2

'Excuse me, sir, but are you the officer from 'er Majesty's
ship *Trojan* . . . Lieutenant Hazard?'

Phillip turned, startled out of his abstraction, to find a
stocky young footman, dressed in buff livery, standing in his

path. 'Yes,' he acknowledged, 'I am Lieutenant Hazard. And you, I take it, have brought – er—' he had to search his memory for the name. 'The Baroness von Mauthner here, with her ward?'

The footman touched his cockaded hat. 'Yessir, that's right.' He gestured to where a large private carriage stood beneath the station portico, with a little knot of porters starting to gather round it in response to the coachman's imperious signal. The carriage was dusty, the horses mud-spattered and steaming and the footman added, in answer to Phillip's unvoiced question, 'Come a fair lick we did, sir, fearing as we might be late for the train. The ladies is both there, sir, with his lordship. I've bin sent to get their tickets.' He hesitated. 'Have you got yours, sir, or will I get it for you? His lordship has given me money and he said as I was to ask you.'

'No, it's all right, thanks . . . I have mine.' Phillip took out his watch. There was still plenty of time, he thought, as he dismissed the footman and walked across to the carriage, from which the porters were now unloading luggage under the supervision of a tall, good looking grey haired gentleman of about fifty, whose face seemed vaguely familiar, although he could not recollect where he had seen it before. He was about to introduce himself when the grey haired man turned and, taking him by the arm, led him out of earshot of the porters.

'Ah . . . Lieutenant Hazard, is it not, of H.M.S. *Trojan*? I am sorry that we are so late . . . we had to drive up from the country, you understand. But I will take you to meet your charges as soon as these porters move the baggage out of our way. Er . . . they gave you full instructions at the Admiralty, I suppose? You know what you have to do?'

'Yes, sir. I was given full instructions.'

'Excellent . . . always very efficient, the Navy. I'm Melgund, by the way, George Melgund of the Foreign Office – I used to know your father, I believe. Some years ago, when he was commanding the *Hogue*, it was. No time for social chit-chat now though, is there? You have a train to catch.'

'The train isn't due to leave for about twenty minutes,

sir—' Phillip began, only to be interrupted by his new acquaintance, who pointed to a luggage-dray whch had just drawn up behind the carriage and said grimly, 'We shall need twenty minutes to get all this baggage loaded on to the train, believe me, Mr. Hazard. There's a deuced mountain of it, trunks, portmanteaux, hat boxes, jewel-cases, hampers . . .' he shrugged. 'I don't know what your Captain's going to say when he sees it all but I'll warrant he won't be too pleased, eh?'

Captain North would *not* be pleased, Phillip thought, with cynical satisfaction, as a large trunk was lifted from the dray, two hefty porters staggering under its weight. He had placed his companion now . . . Lord George Melgund was a very distinguished member of the diplomatic service, who had been at Rio when the *Maeander* had called there, on passage to the East Indies. With the Minister, Lord Howden, he had entertained the officers royally on their brief visits ashore, in particular those from the midshipmen's berth . . . he smiled, remembering.

Lord George stared at him for a moment with furrowed brows and then echoed his smile. 'We've met before, have we not, Mr. Hazard? Where was it, d'you know?'

'In Rio de Janeiro, I believe, sir.'

'Ah, yes, indeed! In '48 . . . you were one of the youngsters Captain Keppel brought ashore with him. Wonderful place, Rio, I've never forgotten it. They sent me to St. Petersburg after that, quite a contrast, as you may imagine. Pity we've no time for a chat, Hazard, but' – Lord George waved a hand in the direction of the carriage – 'duty calls and you must not miss that train, whatever happens. Ah, John . . .' he broke off as the young footman returned. 'Got the tickets? Good, let me have them. Then see to loading the luggage in the guard's van, will you? And while you're about it, get hold of the stationmaster and make sure he's reserved a compartment . . . look sharp, man! We haven't all day, you know.'

'Very good, m'lord.' The footman departed on his errand, followed by the laden porters and Lord George started to move towards the carriage, his hand still on Phillip's arm.

'Regarding your passengers, Mr. Hazard ... you have not been told anything about them, have you, or who they are?'

Phillip shook his head. 'No, sir, I have not.'

'But your Captain – what's his name? Captain North has orders from the Admiralty concerning them, has he not?'

'I was given sealed orders to deliver to Captain North, sir, when I called at the Admiralty yesterday afternoon. I have them here.' Phillip tapped his breast pocket. 'My instructions are to escort the Baroness von Mauthner and her ward to the ship, sir, and to do so as discreetly as possible.'

'H'm, yes, I see. Well, I'll tell you all that you require to know about them. The Baroness von Mauthner is Austrian and she is travelling in her own name. But her companion ...' Lord George lowered his voice. 'Her companion is travelling incognito, for reasons I am not at liberty to explain. You will address her as Mademoiselle Sophie, Hazard, and this is the name by which she will be known whilst she is on board your ship ... Mademoiselle Sophie.'

'She is French then, sir?' Phillip suggested, conscious of relief.

'She speaks French,' Lord George evaded. 'English, too, quite fluently. And there is a maid as well but she need not trouble you ... she's a sensible Bavarian woman called Anna Hofner. Not the kind who's likely to cause any stir among your bluejackets.' He smiled. 'Well, come along, my boy, and I'll present you.'

Phillip followed him to the carriage. A thin, elderly woman, with a lined, rather sallow face and bright bird-like dark eyes was the first to emerge. Lord George offered her his arm. He said in German, 'This is Lieutenant Hazard of the Royal Navy, Baroness. He will escort you to your ship and see you both safely aboard. The Baroness von Mauthner, Hazard.'

Phillip bowed. The Baroness subjected him to a careful scrutiny before she acknowledged the introduction with a stiff little inclination of the head. 'Ach, yes, ze naval officer.'

Her English was gutteral and heavily accented. 'Sank you, Lieutenant Hazard, we shall be grateful for your escort.' She turned away from him and, relinquishing Lord George's arm, leaned into the dark interior of the carriage, to say something which Phillip could not catch to its remaining occupants. There was a momentary delay and then a girl stepped out, so heavily veiled that little could be seen of her face, save that it was small and pale. She was elegantly and fashionably dressed in a fur-trimmed travelling coat, dark haired and slender and her voice, as she responded politely to Lord George's introduction, was pleasant and without accent. The maid followed her from the carriage, a plump woman in sober black, who curtsied awkwardly and then moved away, clutching a small jewel case and looking about her apprehensively, as if fearing that it might be wrested from her by one of the passers-by. Taking pity on her, Phillip offered to relieve her of her burden but she flushed scarlet and shook her head.

'No, I sank you, Herr Leutnant. I must keep ze case myself, if you please.'

'We had better take you to the train, Mademoiselle,' Lord George said firmly. He had addressed the girl, Phillip noticed and, as the little party started to make their way to the platform, he walked at her side, hat in hand, treating her with marked deference. Mademoiselle Sophie talked to him easily and naturally and, when they reached the train, thanked him with great charm for his kindness to her. The top-hatted stationmaster materialized from nowhere to bow them into a reserved compartment and Phillip glanced inquiringly at Lord George.

'Shall I travel in the next compartment, sir?' he suggested. 'I left my bag farther down the train but it will not take me a moment to fetch it.'

The Foreign Office representative hesitated. 'I rather think that would be best, Mr. Hazard,' he began. 'If the ladies wish—' Baroness von Mauthner nodded in emphatic approval but, to Phillip's surprise, Mademoiselle Sophie gestured invitingly to the reserved carriage.

'We have caused Lieutenant Hazard the inconvenience of a journey to London on our account,' she pointed out. 'And, since we are to be travelling companions on a much longer journey, it is only right, is it not, that he should sit with us? Please, Mr. Hazard ... we should enjoy your company. Send for your bag, won't you, and join us? There is plenty of room.'

Lord George looked as if he were about to demur and then changed his mind. A porter was dispatched for his bag and Phillip handed both ladies into their seats. The guard was waiting, whistle to his lips, eyeing the stationmaster expectantly, and Lord George Melgund took courteous leave of the two ladies and returned to the platform, motioning to Phillip to follow him.

'You'll be off in a moment, Hazard,' he said. 'So it only remains for me to wish you *bon voyage*. Remember, my boy ... discretion! This is no ordinary young woman, as no doubt you have realized. As I said, I am not at liberty to disclose her identity to you but – treat her with circumspection, that's my advice to you.' He wrung Phillip's hand. 'Good-bye and good luck.'

'Good-bye, sir. You may rely on me to heed your advice ... and thank you, sir.'

Phillip climbed back on to the train and the stationmaster, with a murmured apology, slammed the carriage door and waved to the waiting guard. Lord George stood back, the whistle shrilled and the train started to move slowly away from the platform. Phillip seated himself opposite the *Trojan*'s two passengers a trifle uneasily, wondering again who they were and why so much secrecy should be attached to their journey and to Mademoiselle Sophie's real identity. She had removed her veil, he saw, and was much younger than, at first sight, he had judged her to be .. seventeen, perhaps, eighteen at most. His curiosity aroused, he studied her covertly.

She was not beautiful in the accepted sense, he decided, but her face was possessed of unusual character and charm. Her eyes were lovely, dark and wide-set, with very long black lashes and she had a small, sensitive mouth, now curving into a shy smile as she looked up to meet his gaze. He reddened and she asked, a faint note of challenge in her huskily attractive voice, 'I puzzle you, Mr. Hazard?'

'A little,' Phillip confessed and she laughed aloud, the laugh a delightful sound, musical and genuinely amused.

'Believe me,' she assured him, 'all this mystery is not of my choosing, Mr. Hazard, and I am not responsible for any of it. The truth is that I have been forgotten – or perhaps overlooked – and . . .' Baroness von Mauthner flashed her a warning glance and Mademoiselle Sophie broke off, biting her lower lip. 'I talk too much,' she apologized. 'I . . . how do you say this in idiomatic English? I am letting my tongue run away with me.'

'You speak English beautifully, Mademoiselle,' Phillip told her, with sincerity. 'And your accent is perfect.'

The girl looked pleased. 'You think so, Mr. Hazard . . . you really think so?'

'I do indeed, Mademoiselle.'

'You are very kind. But' – she shrugged her slim shoulders – 'I have been in this country for nearly a year, for no other purpose than to learn to speak your language. My mother believes that . . .' again the Baroness glanced at her pointedly and she left the sentence unfinished, making a wry little face at her mentor and saying, in rapid French, 'You are a dragon, Madame. Not just a watch-dog, but a veritable dragon!'

Phillip's French was of the schoolboy variety, rusty from lack of practice, but he understood the words and observed, with some astonishment that, although the tone in which Mademoiselle Sophie addressed her guardian was the reverse of respectful, it called forth no reproof.

The Baroness answered mildly, also in French, 'That is what I am here for, is it not? I know what I must do, my little one, for your protection . . .' Phillip could not follow the rest, for her accent was by no means as good as her ward's and she spoke very fast, scarcely pausing to draw breath. He guessed, however, that it concerned himself, when Mademoiselle

Sophie protested indignantly, 'But he is an English naval officer, Madame! And all English officers are completely trustworthy.'

'Perhaps,' Baroness von Mauthner conceded, without conviction. 'But he has not been told anything, has he? Lord Melgund said that he had not, he warned me before we boarded the train . . .' she turned to Phillip, her bright dark eyes searching his face suspiciously. 'Do you speak French, Lieutenant Hazard?'

Phillip drew himself up. 'A little, Baroness,' he admitted stiffly.

'You have understood what we were saying?'

'A word here and there, that was all. But I assure you that nothing you say in my presence will go any further . . . I have had my instructions. And, of course, if you wish to converse in private, I can leave this compartment at the next stop and—'

'Do not be offended, Mr. Hazard.' Mademoiselle Sophie leaned towards him and laid a small, gloved hand on his arm. 'I told you that all this secrecy was not of my choosing, did I not? In any case, it was impolite of us to converse in a foreign language in your presence, and I ask your forgiveness most humbly. Please . . . are we forgiven? Tell me that we are!'

'Of course you are, Mademoiselle.' Phillip's momentary indignation faded instantly. 'There is nothing to forgive, I promise you. Speak in any language you wish in my presence.'

'I prefer to speak in English.'

'I am glad. I find it easier to understand than French.'

They both laughed and the girl said eagerly, 'Tell me about your ship, will you not? I have never set foot on board a British naval vessel in my life and I should like to know what to expect. The *Trojan* is a steam-ship, is it not?'

'Yes, she is a steam-screw frigate, Mademoiselle.'

'She . . . a ship, then, is feminine?'

'To a sailor, yes, Mademoiselle.'

Her dark eyes sparkled. 'And she – this *Trojan* of yours –

she is large? How many guns does she carry and how many sailors?'

Phillip smiled, gratified by her eager interest. '*Trojan* is a fifth-rate of 1,570 tons, Mademoiselle. She mounts thirty-one guns on her main and upper decks and carries a crew, at full strength, of three hundred men. But we shall be taking out drafts of seamen and Marines for distribution among the Fleet, so there will be nearer four hundred men on board when we sail.'

'So many men!' Mademoiselle Sophie exclaimed, in a tone of wonder. 'The sailors sleep in hammocks, do they not, below decks? Are they not very overcrowded?'

'They sling their hammocks on the lower deck,' Phillip explained, 'where there are no guns. And, although fourteen inches is the regulation distance between one hammock and the next, the overcrowding is not so bad as it seems, because the men are not all there at the same time. The hands are divided into watches and, when the watch below turns in, the duty watch is on deck . . .' he started to go into details but the Baroness interrupted tartly, 'The *officers* have cabins, have they not? Cabins with bunks in them?'

'Some of the officers do, Madame,' Phillip spoke dryly. 'The junior officers – that is to say the mates and mid-shipmen and cadets – mess and sling their hammocks in the cockpit, which is on the starboard side of the steerage, on the lower deck. *They* are overcrowded, I am afraid. There are fourteen of them and the gunroom, which would be their mess in a ship-of-the-line, is used by officers of wardroom rank in a frigate.'

'And where is that?' Mademoiselle Sophie wanted to know. 'The gunroom, I mean?'

'On the after part of the lower deck, Mademoiselle, but it is well lighted by the hatchway and skylights whereas, in the midshipmen's berths, lamps are necessary day and night.'

'And the Captain also has his meals there?'

'No, the Captain's day and sleeping cabins are on the main deck, Mademoiselle, and I imagine that you will be invited to take your meals with him.'

'The main deck, Mr. Hazard? That is the deck above, is it not?' Mademoiselle Sophie looked at him in some bewilderment. Phillips searched in his pockets and finally brought out a pencil and a used envelope, which had contained a letter from his mother. 'I will draw you a rough plan of the ship, if you wish,' he offered, 'so that you will be able to find your way about without difficulty.'

He returned the letter to his pocket and set to work, Mademoiselle Sophie watching him with absorbed interest, as his pencil moved deftly across the scrap of paper. 'It – she, I mean – has more decks than I had thought,' she observed, as the sketch progressed.

Phillip nodded. 'We speak of a three-decker,' he explained, 'but this only refers to the number of gun-decks. A first-rate line-of-battle ship has three decks of guns and, in addition, of course, the hold and the orlop, which are below the waterline, and the quarterdeck and poop. A frigate like the *Trojan* has only one gun-deck although, as I told you, guns are also mounted on the upper deck and she has two 68-pounder guns on the quarterdeck. But you will see from this, Mademoiselle' he passed her his quickly sketched diagram – 'that, in fact, she has five decks, or levels, including the hold and quarterdeck. A three-decker has seven.'

She studied the sketch, her smooth brow pensively furrowed and then, after thanking him politely for going to so much trouble to make everything clear to her, passed the sketch to her companion. 'See, Madame, this is very interesting and really not difficult to follow. Here is the cockpit, where the poor young officers have to sleep in their hammocks ... and the gunroom. Oh, and the Captain's cabin also, with the quarterdeck above.'

'I am concerned only with the position of *my* cabin,' Baroness von Mauthner stated coldly, in French. She added, in English, her tone still cold, 'Zat is to say, Lieutenant Hazard, if I am to be found a cabin in zis so crowded ship of yours.'

'I am sure that the Captain will have allocated suitable accommodation, Madame,' Phillip answered politely. 'For both yourself and Mademoiselle.' He refrained from mentioning that his own cabin would almost certainly be one of those earmarked by Captain North for the use of the *Trojan*'s passengers and, when Mademoiselle Sophie retrieved her sketch and asked him to show her which cabin was likely to be hers, he pointed to it without a qualm.

'Tell me more, Mr. Hazard,' she begged. 'Please . . . it is all so very fascinating. Have you served in a three-decker?'

Phillip inclined his head. For the remainder of the journey they talked – of the ships in which he had served, of British naval customs and then of his own career. Mademoiselle Sophie was an intelligent and interested listener, asking innumerable questions and leading him on to tell her about himself. He was usually reticent and ill at ease in the company of any strange young woman but he found himself relaxing under the spell of this young woman's charm and friendliness and conversing with her without any feeling of constraint. In response to her eager prompting, he told her of the voyages he had made and the places he had visited and she listened entranced, the beautiful dark eyes seldom leaving his face.

'Borneo, China . . . Australia and South America too! Oh, but you are fortunate to live such a life, Mr. Hazard. I envy you. Is he not fortunate, Madame?' She appealed to Baroness von Mauthner.

The Baroness sighed. She had taken no part in their conversation and clearly disapproved of it, Phillip thought. Once or twice she had attempted to dissuade her charge from talking to him but Mademoiselle Sophie patted her hand gently and assured her, in French, that it was doing no harm. 'We pass the time, Madame, that is all. Would you have us sit in silence?'

'That might be wiser, in the circumstances,' the Baroness returned repressively. But she did not press the point and finally, to Phillip's relief, dozed off and slept peacefully until the train was in sight of its destination. Then, rousing herself guiltily, she peered out of the carriage window. 'We are nearly there, I think. Come, it is time to remember who you

are, my little one, and put an end to this ... this foolishness.'

'It is not foolishness, Madame,' Mademoiselle Sophie protested. 'And I do not forget who I am.' But she reached
obediently for her veil and began to drape it once more
about her face. She said softly, almost apologetically, to
Phillip, 'It has given me much pleasure to talk to you, Mr.
Hazard. I ... thank you for making our journey so interesting and enjoyable.' Then, as if this were his dismissal, she
turned away from him, still fumbling with the veil and
lapsed into silence which Phillip, his conscience pricking
him, did not attempt to break.

Had he, he wondered uneasily, treated her as cir-
cumspectly as Lord George Melgund had warned him he
must? Who was she, this girl with the husky, accentless voice
and the beautiful, intelligent dark eyes, whose real identity
had to be kept so carefully hidden? He sighed, conscious that
he, too, had found the journey in her company interesting
and enjoyable. But ... his spirits lifted. The journey had
only just begun, it was not ending here and there would be
other opportunities of seeing and talking to her in the future.
He might offer to take her on a tour of the ship, perhaps, or
even to escort her ashore, when they called at Gibraltar and
Malta ... he glanced across at her, in mute and anxious
question, but the dark folds of the veil she had donned now
formed a barrier between them. Mademoiselle Sophie did
not look up, did not seem to be aware of his gaze and the
Baroness said, an edge to her voice, 'We have arrived,
Lieutenant Hazard, have we not?'

CHAPTER TWO

I

THE train drew into the platform and came slowly to a halt. Phillip alighted and was about to go in search of porters when he noticed a naval captain, in frock coat and sword, standing beneath one of the hissing gas lamps and looking about him with an air of expectancy. By the ticket barrier a party of blue-jackets waited, under the command of a midshipman, two of them on the ropes of a handcart which, as the train halted, they started to haul in the direction of the guard's van. He recognized the midshipman first, then one of the seamen and finally, with a sense almost of shock, realized that the resplendent figure in the gold-laced frock coat was that of his commander come, it seemed, in person to receive the passengers he had been so reluctant to accommodate on board the *Trojan.*

Captain North strode briskly along the platform towards him, as he assisted the two ladies, in turn, to alight. Brushing past him without apology or greeting, the Captain removed his cocked hat and bowed ceremoniously over Mademoiselle Sophie's hand.

'Good evening, ladies . . . Mam'zelle, Ma'am . . .' his tone was deferential and he smiled at them both, Phillip observed, with every appearance of pleasure. 'I am Captain North of Her Majesty's ship *Trojan,* at your service. Permit me to take you out to my ship. I have a closed carriage and a boat waiting and my men will look after your luggage.'

He offered his arm to the Baroness von Mauthner, who eyed him with the first sign of approval she had so far displayed and laid her hand on his braided sleeve.

'Sank you, Captain . . . you are most kind.'

'It is my pleasure, Ma'am. If you are ready, Mam'zelle...'
with Mademoiselle Sophie walking demurely on his other
side, Captain North ushered them past the ticket barrier and
towards the waiting carriage. He said, over his shoulder, to
Phillip, 'Take charge of the working party, Mr. Hazard, and
see that the luggage is brought on board and stowed, if you
please.'

The request was peremptory and Phillip reddened but he
managed a dutiful, 'Aye, aye, sir.' Then remembering the
orders he carried, he took the envelope with its heavy
Admiralty seals from his breast pocket and, waiting until
Captain North had handed both ladies into the carriage
with due ceremony, he stepped forward. 'Excuse me, sir—'

'Well, what is it, Mr. Hazard?' North turned impatiently.
They were standing in a draughty spot and the wind whipped
his sparse grey hair into a disarray which accorded ill with
the magnificence of his new full dress uniform. He passed a
hand over it, eyeing his First Lieutenant with disfavour,
and clamped his hat on his head. Phillip held his ground.

'I was instructed to deliver these orders to you, sir.'

Captain North grunted. He accepted the proffered envelope, glanced at it indifferently and thrust it into his own
pocket. 'I received instructions from the Port Admiral this
morning,' he stated curtly, 'which, I imagine, duplicate
these. Very well, you may carry on, Mr. Hazard ... and look
lively with that baggage, will you? It is my intention to get
under way as soon as it's on board.'

'You intend to get under way tonight, sir?' Phillip questioned, mildly surprised.

'That was what I said, Mr. Hazard ... are you deaf? You
heard me, did you not?'

'Yes, sir, I heard you but ... the draft from *Impregnable*
sir. I understood that—'

'The draft from *Impregnable* joined this forenoon,' the
Captain told him. 'Which reminds me ...' he spoke lightly,
as if it were a sudden afterthought but his cold grey eyes
were narrowed and watchful as they met those of his First
Lieutenant. 'Yours is rather an uncommon name, isn't it ...

Hazard? An honoured name in naval circles, I understand
. . . with one unfortunate exception.'

Phillip stiffened. He knew that look, knew from painful
experience that, when North pretended to be casual, he was
usually at his most venomous. 'I do not think that I quite
follow you, sir,' he said cautiously. 'Perhaps you—'

The Captain waved him to silence. 'Oh, come now, I feel
sure you do. Let me refresh your memory, Mr. Hazard. You
had a brother in the Navy, had you not . . . an elder brother
who was court martialled and dismissed the Service a few
years ago? I cannot recall all the somewhat sordid details
but' – he frowned, as if in an attempt to remember – 'there
was something about being drunk on watch, as the result of
which and his negligence his ship went aground and was lost
. . . that was one of the charges brought against him, was it
not? Yes, it is coming back to me now – the ship was the
Comet and she ran ashore entering the River Plate.'

Phillip felt sick with impotent fury but, aware that North
was endeavouring to provoke him into an outburst, he was
silent, not trusting himself to speak. Where, he wondered
bitterly, had the Captain raked up the unhappy story, from
whom could he have heard it? And why should he have
chosen this moment to taunt him with it, unless in the hope
of catching him off his guard and forcing an admission from
him? He remained obstinately silent. The fact that the story
had, at least, an underlying basis of truth made him the more
determined to admit nothing and he waited, his expression
carefully blank, for his tormentor to continue.

Nothing loth, Captain North went on, 'You are no doubt
wondering why I should have brought this matter up now.
Well, there is a man in the draft from *Impregnable* whose
name, by an odd coincidence, is Hazard . . . George Arthur
Hazard, according to his papers, rated A.B. He claims that
he's not a relative of yours but you must concede that it *is*
something of a coincidence, Mr Hazard, and I felt that – in
fairness to you – I should speak to you about it at once.'

The colour drained slowly from Phillip's cheeks. This
could not be happening, he told himself despairingly, it was

38

impossible, a nightmare from which, quite soon, he would awaken. Yet in his heart, he knew that it was by no means impossible, for was it not just the sort of impulsive, foolishly quixotic idea his brother Graham might have had? To volunteer for the Navy because there was to be a war and therefore men would be needed, men who – if they volunteered – would not be too closely questioned ... yes, Graham was quite capable of reasoning along those lines. He ... the German maid, Anna, passed him with a murmured apology and Phillip stood aside, grateful for the interruption. Summoning the remnants of his shattered self-control, he opened the door of the carriage for her and assisted her to enter it, her grateful smile helping to restore his equanimity.

'Thank you for calling my attention to this matter, sir.' He had himself well in hand when he turned once more to face his commander, but it still cost him an effort to steady his voice. 'However, my brother's name is Graham, so it seems unlikely that this man can be he. And if you will forgive me, sir, the court martial evidence was—'

Captain North cut him short. 'I'll be obliged if you will make certain of his identity when you return to the ship, Mr. Hazard. You will find your namesake in the master-at-arms' charge ... he was in possession of liquor when he came aboard and appeared to be drunk. Which is in character, is it not? There was a sneer in his voice and he smiled, obviously enjoying his subordinate's discomfiture. 'I hope for your sake, of course, that he is *not* your brother.'

'For my sake, sir?'

'Naturally. It would be extremely bad for discipline if he were.' The Captain's smile faded and his lean, angular face assumed an expression of grave concern. 'The man was drunk ... I have had to sentence him to six dozen lashes, Mr. Hazard.'

'Yes, sir,' Phillip managed woodenly but he was conscious of a sick feeling in the pit of his stomach. Six dozen lashes, expertly laid on, could scar a man for life and, if the recipient of such a flogging were not in good physical condition, then ... he swallowed hard, his mouth suddenly dry.

'See the man as soon as your duties permit,' Captain North ordered. 'And report to me when you have done so.'

'Aye, aye, sir.'

The Captain turned on his heel. Without troubling to acknowledge his First Lieutenant's salute, he curtly bade the coachman drive on and climbed into the waiting carriage.

Phillip watched him go, staring after the slow-moving vehicle until it disappeared from sight in the gathering darkness. Gradually his anger subsided. It was useless, he knew, to lose his temper under the sting of North's taunts and insults and he was thankful that he had not done so. But, if this seaman should prove to be his brother Graham ... he sighed, afraid to envisage the probable consequences. That they would be unpleasant he did not doubt and he found himself hoping fervently that George Arthur Hazard was no more than he had claimed to be ... an able-seaman whose surname happened, by chance, to be the same as his own. Since Hazard was originally a Devon name, this was not beyond the bounds of possibility but ... Phillip sighed again, with weary resignation. Then, thrusting the thought of his brother to the back of his mind, he returned to the station in search of the working party he had been ordered to supervise.

Back on board the *Trojan* after a long, cold pull out against the wind in the twelve-oared cutter laden with luggage, he found steam up and learnt, from the officer of the watch, that preparations to get under way were already well advanced.

'The Captain wishes you to report to him immediately, sir,' Lieutenant Laidlaw informed him. He added, his homely young face the picture of concern, 'He's sent three times to inquire if you had returned, sir, but I had to tell him you hadn't. My orders are to weigh anchor as soon as I've got the cutter inboard.'

'Very well, Mr. Laidlaw. You can pipe the watch to stations for leaving harbour when you've winched up that baggage and stowed the cutter,' Phillip instructed. 'But there is a great deal of baggage and it will have to be carefully handled . . . that is what delayed me. So put a couple of good men on the winch.'

'Aye, aye, sir. Shall I report your return aboard to the Captain?'

'No.' Phillip gestured to his sodden frock coat, which had received a wetting when crossing the so-called 'Devil's Bridge' between Drake's Island and Mount Edgecumbe, with the wind against the tide. 'I'll report to him myself as soon as I've changed. Has my cabin been turned over to the passengers, do you know?'

Young Laidlaw nodded. 'Yes, sir, it has. Your gear has been shifted into Mr. Fox's cabin, sir.'

Phillip went below. There was no opportunity to visit the arrested seaman or even to make inquiries about him . . . that would have to wait, he decided. In the cramped forward cabin which he had now to share with Martin Fox, the senior of the three watch-keeping lieutenants, he had scarcely divested himself of his shore-going uniform when he heard the shrilling of the boatswain's mates' pipes, followed by a thud of feet on the deck above as the duty watch went to their stations. He was donning his seaboots when the midshipman of the watch came breathlessly to report that the ship was ready to proceed to sea.

'You are late, Mr. Hazard,' Captain North observed coldly when, in turn, Phillip made this report to him. 'Punctuality is the first essential in an efficient officer and it is your duty, as I have had repeatedly to remind you, to set an example for your juniors to follow. You had a few pieces of luggage to bring out to the ship from Mutton Cove and a midshipman and the cutter's crew to help you do it. You were aware that I was anxious to get under way as soon as possible but you delay sailing by over an hour! It is most reprehensible in an officer of your experience.'

'Yes, sir,' Phillip acknowledged, tight-lipped. He offered neither excuse nor apology for his lateness and, for an uncomfortable moment, feared that the Captain was going to insist on an apology but – warned by his expression, perhaps – North thought better of it and did not do so.

'Very well, Mr. Hazard,' he said, after a perceptible hesitation, 'you may carry on. Weigh and proceed under engines until we are clear of the Sound. If this wind holds, you should be able to make sail before we round the Eddystone ...' he issued a string of detailed navigation orders and ended, with an abrupt change of tone, 'Muster the ship's company aft at three bells. I shall inform all hands of our destination and of what will be expected of them when we reach it. It is to be hoped that there will be less slackness when the men realize that they are to have the chance of action – and of prize-money – very soon.'

'Yes, sir.' Phillip's voice did not betray his feelings but the Captain glanced at him sharply. 'I intend to make Gibraltar by Wednesday morning, if I can,' he went on. 'So I shall want the ship under all the sail she can carry, day and night. But the engines will only be used when I deem it necessary, Mr. Hazard ... we have to conserve our coal. Under no circumstances will steam be raised unless I order it and the officer of the watch is to obtain my permission before shortening sail, except in an emergency. Is that clear?'

'Quite clear, sir.' Was it, Phillip wondered, on the passengers' account that Captain North was so anxious to reach Gibraltar by Wednesday morning ... would they, perhaps, be leaving the ship there? He waited but North volunteered no further information. Instead, his tone curt, he said, 'I take it that you have not forgotten the seaman I put under arrest ... the seaman who calls himself Hazard? Because I shall require a report from you when you have seen and' – the Captain paused significantly – 'identified him, Mr. Hazard.'

'I have not forgotten, sir. I'll see him as soon as I am able to leave the deck, sir.'

'Then that will be all. I trust that it will not be necessary to remind you to put the best men you have on look-out and at the wheel during the hours of darkness? Good ... then set topsails immediately and I shall want her under every stitch of canvas she can carry when the screw is raised.'

'Aye, aye, sir.' Phillip stiffened to attention, thankfully accepting his dismissal. To young Lieutenant Laidlaw, patiently awaiting his return to the quarterdeck, he said crisply, 'Hands to cat the bower anchors, Mr. Laidlaw. And handsomely, if you please. We are to be in Gibraltar by Wednesday morning – without the assistance of our engine – and the screw is to be raised when we drop the pilot.' He glanced at the elderly Master, standing within earshot, the pilot beside him. 'By Wednesday morning, Mr. Burnaby . . . those are the Captain's orders. Perhaps you'd be so good as to step into the chartroom. I should like to check our course with you.'

Both officers stared at him incredulously but, wise now in the ways of their commander, neither offered any comment. Burnaby exchanged a wry smile with the pilot and followed Phillip to the chartroom. . . .

2

Trojan slipped from her moorings and ran quietly down Plymouth Sound under her screw. She was a graceful ghost in the light of the newly risen moon, her tall masts and the black and white chequered paintwork, which marked the line of lidded gun-ports along her main deck, reflected briefly in the ruffled surface of the water as the breeze freshened.

Phillip glimpsed the reflection, as he left the chartroom with the Master and felt the strengthening breeze on his cheek. He walked over to where the officer of the watch was standing, the pilot at his side.

'Hands aloft to set tops'ls and jibs, Mr. Laidlaw,' he ordered. The boatswain's mates put their calls to their lips and the pipe echoed throughout the ship as Laidlaw passed on the order and the topmen of the watch went surging up the rigging in instant response. Few were in need of the Boatswain's stentorian shouts or the urging of the ropes' end 'starters' carried by the petty officers . . . they swarmed hand

43

over hand up the shrouds with scarcely a check, each man setting to his task with a will.

Indeed, all hands were working with a new zest and spirit, Phillip observed, as if – although as yet they had not been told – they had guessed their destination and its purpose. Mast was competing against mast and, as the afterguard was piped to the braces to trim the newly-set canvas, there was a roar from the maintopmen, who had sheeted home a few seconds before those on the fore- and mizzentops.

Phillip frowned, as he watched them make their agile descent to the deck, hoping that, when the time came for the Captain to make his official announcement regarding their destination, he could confine himself to the few words that were necessary.

If only North would appeal to the men's patriotism and loyalty, he thought, instead of making impossible demands on them and issuing threats, then this new spirit and keenness might be fostered and kept alive, and pride in their ship reborn.

Beside him and evidently sensing his unspoken thoughts, the white haired Master said reflectively, 'These are good men, Mr. Hazard – and there'll be none better by the time we reach the Black Sea if they are handled the right way. But if they are driven too hard . . .' he broke off, his shrug expressive. 'I've seen it happen before. A taut ship isn't always the best fighting ship, in my experience.' He tucked his rolled charts under his arm. 'Well, I'd best take these to the Captain now. If he gives me half a chance, Mr. Hazard, I'll try to warn him. But I doubt if he'll give me the chance.'

Phillip doubted it also but he nodded, smiling.

'Thank you, Mr. Burnaby. You'll do you best, I am quite sure.'

'My best may not be good enough, Mr. Hazard, either for this or . . .' Burnaby tapped his charts. 'Or to get us to Gibraltar in under five days. Wednesday forenoon, the Captain said, I believe . . . well, the *Banshee* made Spithead to Lisbon in three and a half days, under sail and steam, did she not? If we could use our screw we might do it and I shall tell Captain North so. Perhaps he'll listen, if he's all that anxious to get there.'

'Yes, perhaps,' Phillip agreed noncommittally but again he doubted it . . . North seldom took advice from anyone.

The ship's bell had just struck three times when Captain North came on deck. The news that they were on their way to join the Black Sea Fleet was received by the assembled ship's company with prolonged and enthusiastic cheering. The cheers were, however, swiftly subdued when the Captain subjected them to a lengthy harangue on the vexed question of slackness and lack of discipline. The men listened attentively but apprehensive murmurs followed his announcement that dawn to dusk training exercises were to be the daily prelude to the ship's arrival in Constantinople. Deaf to the murmurs, North addressed Phillip, his voice flat.

'You will turn out hands at seven bells in the Middle Watch to wash decks, Mr. Hazard, and the ship's company will go to breakfast one hour earlier than usual. Colours will be hoisted at six bells in the Morning Watch and training exercises are to commence immediately after Divisions . . .' he paused, looking about him but not a man moved in the packed ranks facing him, although there was a concerted gasp of dismay as the fact that they were to be turned out of their hammocks at three-thirty in the morning gradually sank in. 'This will continue,' the Captain told them sternly, 'until I am satisfied, not only with the standard of proficiency attained in sail and gun drill but also with the general standard of discipline of the entire ship's company.'

There was a stunned silence then, the silence of shock and the men's faces were glum with foreboding, Phillip saw when, at last, he received permission to dismiss them.

Apparently quite indifferent to the effect his words had had on officers and men alike, North went below to take supper with his passengers but Phillip – lacking all desire for food since hearing them – remained on deck. Normally, as First

45

Lieutenant, he was not required to stand a regular watch but he had plenty to occupy him when *Trojan* cleared the Sound and headed into the crowded shipping lanes of the Channel, her screw raised and all possible sail set before a blustering north-easterly wind. Even when the ship had settled on her course and most of the coastal traffic had been left astern, he continued to put off his visit to the seaman called Hazard. For a time his conscience troubled him but he quietened it with the thought that – if the man were, indeed, his brother Graham – their reunion in such circumstances was likely to be, for them both, the source of more pain than pleasure.

The watch changed; Martin Fox relieved his immediate junior, Anthony Cochrane, who had kept the six-to-eight, and Phillip walked the deck with him, exchanging news and replying, as informatively as he could, to Fox's questions concerning their passengers and his own brief trip to London. As if by mutual consent, they avoided all mention of the Captain's recent announcement although, Phillip knew, the subject was uppermost in both their minds.

Martin Fox was a tall, powerfully built young man, and a fine athlete, possessed of more than ordinary good looks and an exceptionally even temper. Although a year or so younger than Phillip himself, their friendship was of long standing, dating back to the old *Maeander* days and it had stood the test both of close association and subsequent lengthy separation. Usually they talked to each other freely and without constraint when opportunity offered and they were alone together. This evening, however, each had imposed a guard on his tongue as if fearing that, were it removed, he might be tempted to say too much.

When the subject of the passengers and speculation as to their identity had been exhausted, they talked in general terms of the coming war and of their personal hopes and ambitions, their conversation occasionally interrupted by a shouted warning from the masthead look-out and the necessity to alter course in order to pass clear of other craft. At four bells, Sean O'Hara, the midshipman of the watch, brought them two mugs of steaming cocoa, and, when he had finished his, Phillip's conscience began once more to trouble him and he announced his intention of going below.

'There is a prisoner I must see, Martin – I have to make a report on him to the Captain before I can turn in. But ... you know about that, I imagine?'

'No.' Martin Fox sounded puzzled. 'I was not aware that we had any prisoners, Phillip. My optimism was clearly misplaced ... who put him under arrest? Did you?'

'The Captain. I thought you would know – in fact, I was a trifle surprised that you did not mention it to me earlier but then' – Phillip's smile was wry – 'I decided that you must be trying to spare me.'

'To *spare* you? I don't understand.'

'Frankly, nor do I. You were acting First Lieutenant in my absence ... the arrest should have been reported to you.'

Fox shrugged. 'It was *not* reported to me, Phillip. But you know North ... everyone else must go by the book but he is a law unto himself. Besides ...' he broke off, frowning. 'I must be careful what I say or this prisoner of yours will not be the only one in irons! What was his crime?'

'Drunkenness. The man joined with the draft from *Impregnable* this morning and was found with liquor in his possession, it seems. The Captain has ordered him six dozen lashes and—'

'Wait a minute, Phillip ... I inspected the draft from *Impregnable* and they were all sober when they came aboard.' Martin Fox frowned. 'Oh, well, I suppose the Captain caught him when he made Rounds. Why are you worried about it, in any case? Heaven knows' – his tone was cynical – 'this will not be the first time Captain North has ordered six dozen lashes for a trivial offence. It should not surprise you.'

'It doesn't,' Phillip answered grimly. 'But on this occasion they will flog a man whose name is the same as my own.'

'A relative, you mean? But—'

'Possibly my brother. I do not know, I haven't seen him yet. I should have, of course, I should have gone to see him

47

hours ago. But' – Phillip spread his hands in a despairing gesture – 'I have been putting it off. I . . . well, I suppose I am afraid of the truth, Martin.'

'I should not blame you if you were.'

'Nevertheless I must go to him. It is no use procrastinating, is it? If this man is my brother, there is very little I can do for him . . . you remember his story, don't you? He was court martialled and dismissed the service when he was a lieutenant in the *Comet*.'

'Yes, I remember, Phillip.' Fox was frowning again. 'I'm trying to remember the faces of the *Impregnable* men but there were so many of them and when one simply inspects them . . .' he sighed. 'I honestly cannot recall anyone who looked at all like you. I'm sorry.'

'We do not resemble one another very closely. Graham is seven years older than I am.'

'He joined under his own name?'

Phillip shook his head. 'Under the name of George Arthur Hazard, according to Captain North.'

'Does the Captain know?' Martin Fox asked. 'That he may be your brother, I mean?'

'Oh, yes, he knows.'

'And he's using it against you, I suppose?' Phillip was silent and Fox said explosively, 'He can't go on like this, Phillip – he can't! Did you see the men's faces when he told them they were to be turned out at seven bells to wash decks?'

'I saw them,' Phillip admitted. He glanced up at the tautly stretched canvas above their heads. The wind had shifted again and it was rising, causing the ship, under the press of sail she was carrying, to shudder as the gusts caught her. 'You had better obtain the Captain's permission to shorten sail, Mr. Fox,' he suggested formally. 'Or we shall be in for a very uncomfortable night, which our passengers might find distressing. That wind has shifted aft a point whilst we've been talking and it seems to be rising. If I were you, I should man the braces but I shouldn't trim her until you've sent word to the Captain . . . and received his reply.'

Lieutenant Fox met his gaze in swift comprehension, as he braced himself to meet the sudden roll of the ship. 'Aye, aye, sir,' he answered, with matching formality, 'Goodnight, sir.' He added softly, 'And good luck! I hope to heaven that man is *not* your brother.'

Phillip thanked him and went below.

The prisoner was confined in the midships part of the hold, in a small, dark space between the chain-cable locker and the engine room. He was in irons, apparently asleep despite the extreme discomfort of his position, under the guard of a Marine sentry, who stiffened to attention at Phillip's approach. By the dim light of a single lantern hanging from the bulkhead above him, it was impossible to make out more than the shadowy outline of his face but this was enough. Stifling a sigh, Phillip motioned the sentry to withdraw out of earshot and took down the lantern, setting it on the deck beside the prisoner's huddled shape. He dropped on one knee, shaking his brother urgently.

'Graham ... Graham, wake up, old man. It's me, Phillip.'

'So you've come! Phillip, you fool ... I was hoping against hope that you would have the sense to stay away.' Graham roused himself and struggled, swearing under his breath, into a sitting position. He was dishevelled and unshaven, his eyes bloodshot, blinking in the glare of the flickering lantern as he went on harshly, 'For God's sake, I denied even knowing you when the Captain questioned me! And you have got to deny it, too, it's the only thing to do. Why in the world did you come down here? You must realize that it can help neither of us.'

'Yes, I realize that but ...' Phillip eyed him unhappily. 'The captain ordered me to see you. I am to report to him when I have done so.'

'I was afraid of it! He suspected, of course, the moment he heard my name – but he can prove nothing, unless you admit I'm your brother. You must not do that, Phillip ... your life will not be worth living if you do. And as for mine ...' Graham Hazard's swollen lips twisted into a mirthless smile.

49

'I call myself George these days. It's a name my shipmates can get their tongues round more easily than the one our dear father chose for me. How is he, by the way? You saw him, did you not, when you were in London?'

'Oh, yes, I saw them both, Mother and Father. And the girls. I spent last night at home . . .' Phillip enlarged on this and his brother's expression softened a little as he listened.

'I am glad you saw them. I wish that I could but . . .' he shrugged and his voice became harsh again. 'My name is never mentioned within the family portals, I suppose? I still do not exist, so far as my father is concerned . . . the only Hazard who ever disgraced the name! All right, lad' – he laid a hand on Phillip's arm – 'I will spare you the embarrassment of replying to that question. I know the answer, in any case.'

'Do you, Graham?' Phillip hesitated, studying him intently. 'Is that why you decided to rejoin Her Majesty's Navy.'

'Perhaps – I honestly don't know. There is to be a war and there was talk of it in the taverns I used to frequent. Seamen from the Fleet came in and they talked, too . . . there was an old warrant officer who bought me drinks.' Graham sighed. 'I joined on impulse, really . . . funds were running low and I had nothing better in prospect at the time. Needless to tell you, I now regret it!' He lifted his manacled wrists, holding them out in front of him to emphasize his words. 'I had gone back to the sea before this, Phillip, as it happened. It's the only trade I know and there is something in breeding, I imagine.'

'Yes, I imagine there is.' Phillip was conscious of an intense and almost overwhelming pity for this strange, ill-fated brother of his. As a boy, he remembered, he had worshipped Graham, had envied him, too, when he had come home on his first leave, a tough, experienced seaman after three years on the China Station, and with a midshipman's white patch on his collar. He had seemed to be happy in the service, had been making a fine career, earning glowing reports, gaining promotion to lieutenant before he was quite twenty . . . so much so that their father, Phillip recalled painfully, had held him up as an example to be followed, when he himself left school. But now ... he looked down at his brother's rough, calloused hands and bit back an exclamation of shocked surprise. They were seaman's hands, and the callouses were not of recent origin.

'Were you in the merchant service, Graham?' he asked flatly. Graham nodded.

'Yes, for the last four and a half years, on and off. I made two voyages to Australia in the *Wanota* – a lovely frigate-built Indiaman, Phillip, of 1,140 tons, commanded by Captain James Quilhampton. I did not do so badly either ...' he smiled reminiscently. 'Believe it or not, I was Third Mate of the *Wanota* eighteen months ago. Then I transferred to the *Lady Peel* as Second and ran into trouble ...' his smile faded but he did not offer an explanation of the trouble and Phillip, seeing his mouth tighten, wisely did not pursue the point or question him as to its nature. 'I shipped home before the mast in the *Tudor* and I'd taken my discharge when ... well, when that mad impulse seized me. I was mad to join the Navy again ... raving mad. For heaven's sweet sake, look at me!' Angrily Graham beat his manacled fists against the bulkhead and the sentry, alarmed by the sound, came running to ascertain its cause.

'Sir ... Mr. Hazard, sir, is the prisoner misbehaving? Will I put him under restraint?'

'No,' Phillip answered shortly. 'The prisoner is giving me no trouble. Return to your post.'

'He may be giving you no trouble at this moment, Phillip. But wait ...' Graham's tone was bitter. 'You'll come in for plenty if it's ever known that we are brothers. Tomorrow morning, in case you have forgotten it, I am to receive six dozen lashes for drunkenness and—'

'Were you drunk, Graham?'

'Does it matter?'

'It matters to me. *Were* you?'

Graham Hazard shifted uneasily. He avoided Phillip's anxious scrutiny and said, with simulated indifference, 'I

51

had brought a bottle of whisky on board with me and I'd had a tot out of it ... that, according to your Captain, merits a flogging. But if it really matters to you, I was not drunk – I very seldom am these days, and you may believe that or not, as you please. It's the truth.'

'Then why bring whisky on board with you?' Phillip demanded.

'Why? As a precaution against cold nights on watch and because I've a cough that troubles me,' Graham answered. 'It is an old merchant navy custom and I assure you, no one was ever flogged for it in the *Wanota*.'

'This is the Royal Navy,' Phillip reminded him. 'And you know the regulations.'

'Oh, yes. I realize it was a stupid thing to do ... stupid to allow myself to be caught with the stuff, I mean.'

'Who actually caught you?'

'The Captain. He was making Rounds, smelt the whisky on my breath, I can only suppose, and ordered a search of my kit ... with the result you know. He put me under arrest and I have been in this noisome hole ever since. But ...' Graham's thick, fair brows met in a thoughtful frown. 'I have been aboard this ship long enough to hear some very ugly talk concerning this Captain of yours, Phillip. No one has a good word to say for him, not even his own coxswain.' His frown deepened. 'His name's North, is it not?'

'Yes, it is. But you—'

'Thomas North?' Graham persisted. 'Who commanded the *Guillemot* brig on the West African coast about twelve years ago ... is that who he is?'

Phillip inclined his head. 'Why – do you know him?'

'I know *of* him ... and what I know isn't to his credit, I can tell you. The *Guillemot* was a hell-ship and her commander would have had a mutiny on his hands if he had not lost more than half his crew from yellow fever. Eventually, in sheer desperation, the officers got up some sort of petition and North was relieved of his command and sent home. There would have been an inquiry – or possibly a court martial – if the Admiral had had his way, but all the witnesses were sick and *Guillemot* was at Accra, unable to put to sea for lack of seamen to man her.'

'Are you sure of this, Graham? Because if it's true—'

'I can vouch personally for the truth of it, my dear Phillip,' Graham asserted. 'Because I was serving in the flagship at the time – H.M.S. *Thalia*, Rear-Admiral Sir Patrick Campbell. He sent a confidential report on North to the Admiralty – to Admiral Dundas, if I remember rightly. I do remember hearing him say that North would never be given another command, if he had anything to do with it.'

'I see,' Phillip said tonelessly. He did not doubt that his brother was right – Captain North had been behaving very much in character since assuming command of *Trojan* and the leopard, it seemed, had not changed his spots. Probably this particular leopard was incapable of doing so . . . he expelled his breath in a long, pent-up sigh.

'*Do* you see?' Graham challenged. 'Do you see why you cannot admit that I'm related to you? North is a sadist, with a record that won't bear a close examination. For pity's sake, Phil – for *my* sake, if not your own – you've got to lie to him. Otherwise . . .' he spread his hands helplessly.

Phillip saw, only too clearly, and what he saw did not bear thinking about. An ex-officer, dismissed the service and disgraced – his own First Lieutenant's elder brother, serving as a seaman on the lower deck and already under sentence for having brought liquor aboard . . . of course North would take full advantage of the situation, would exploit it to the full. He could not allow that to happen, since Graham would suffer for it, even more than himself.

'Very well,' he agreed wearily, 'I will deny our relationship, although I don't imagine that North will be deceived for a moment. However, as you pointed out a little while ago, he cannot prove anything . . . your merchant service papers are in the name of George Arthur Hazard, I take it?'

'Yes, they are . . . all quite legal and above board. I even answer to the name of George more readily than I do to my given name. Odd, is it not? To be honest, I prefer it . . .

53

although, for no reason that I can possibly explain, I clung to the name of Hazard, George Arthur Hazard, A.B. Hardly a "name to live up to", is it, Lieutenant Hazard, sir?'

Phillip got to his feet. He said, having to make an effort to steady his voice. 'I shall do the best I can to convince Captain North that it's your correct name, Graham. I will also endeavour to have your punishment reduced.'

'And how,' Graham asked cynically, 'do you imagine you'll be able to do that? I hardly think that Thomas North will listen to any pleas on my behalf, do you? Even if you are willing to plead for me, Phillip . . . and you'll be a fool if you do.'

'I can get the Surgeon to examine you. If he decides that you are not fit to receive the full number of lashes, then the Captain will have to accept his decision.'

'But I am – perhaps unfortunately – very fit,' Graham stated, with a wry grin.

'Our Surgeon is opposed to flogging. He is also a good fellow and one I can trust,' Phillip assured him. 'So don't worry.' He patted his brother's muscular shoulder. Then, bracing himself for what, he was fully and wretchedly aware, would be an ordeal, he went to make his report to the Captain.

To his relief, North was not alone. He sat at his table, from which the food had now been cleared, enjoying a glass of port with Mademoiselle Sophie and the Baroness von Mauthner and, as Phillip entered the cabin, he broke off in mid-sentence, frowning at the interruption.

'Well?' His tone, as always when he addressed a subordinate, was brusque to the point of rudeness. 'To what do I owe this intrusion, Mr. Hazard? I left orders that I was not to be disturbed unless the matter was urgent.'

'You also left instructions, you may recall, sir, for me to report to you when I had seen the prisoner.' Phillip reddened but he held his ground, conscious of Mademoiselle Sophie's sympathetic gaze and of the warmth of the smile with which she had greeted his unexpected appearance.

'The prisoner?' North exclaimed impatiently. 'What are you babbling about, Mr. Hazard? *What* prisoner?'

'A seaman from the *Impregnable* draft, sir, whom you put under arrest this morning.'

'Ah, yes, of course ... you are referring to Able-Seaman Hazard are you not? The fellow who came on board drunk ...' Captain North settled himself more comfortably in his chair. He glanced at his guests, to make sure that he had their full attention and permitted himself a faint smile but Phillip, sensing instinctively what was to come unless he could prevent it, put in quickly, 'The man is an ex-merchant seaman, sir, who chances to have the same surname as I have. That is all I have been able to find out about him, sir, and we do not appear to be related.' He added, greatly daring, 'Except that he knew you when you were commanding the *Guillemot* ... er ... that's all, sir. I am sorry to have interrupted your meal.'

He bowed to the two ladies, came briefly to attention and, before the Captain had recovered from his momentary surprise, turned his back on all three of them and swiftly stepped outside. Mademoiselle Sophie called after him, bidding him good night in her shy, charming voice but Phillip scarcely heard her and his hands were shaking as he closed the door of the cabin firmly behind him.

He had won a small victory, he thought, with a feeling of heady, unaccustomed elation ... a very small victory but the first since Captain Thomas North had assumed command of *Trojan*. He had not allowed himself to be publicly humiliated and – whether or not the Captain believed him – he had denied his relationship to his brother Graham, before two unimpeachable witnesses. It would not end there, of course, he had no illusions on that score but ... North had been shaken by his mention of the *Guillemot*. His florid face had paled and, for an unguarded instant, there had been alarm in his eyes and he had not been able to think of a reply having, no doubt, imagined that the story of the *Guillemot*'s near-mutiny was safely buried in the past.

He had mentioned it on impulse, Phillip thought, but it

had had an unexpectedly telling effect on his commander, had silenced him, as nothing ever had before. Now, if he could succeed in getting his brother's sentence reduced, he would have consolidated his first small victory and ... there would be others, if he had the courage to fight for them. Up till now he had accepted North's right, as Captain, to order his ship as and how he saw fit to do so – he had never questioned that right because his training, and the rigid discipline it imposed, permitted no questions of a superior officer. As First Lieutenant it was his duty to enforce any order his commander issued, however harsh or unjust, however much he might personally regret or disagree with it, however unfortunate the consequences might be.

But, he told himself, there must be no repetition of the *Guillemot* tragedy, whatever the cost to himself or anyone else. He had to avoid such an outcome where *Trojan* was concerned ... that surely was his first duty? From the deck above he heard the twitter of the boatswain's mates' pipes and the watch being called to take in sail, followed by the familiar thud of bare feet on the planking overhead. '*All the sail she can carry, day and night,*' North had ordered ... Phillip smiled grimly to himself in the darkness as he made his way to the gunroom in search of the Surgeon.

CHAPTER THREE

I

In accordance with their commander's instructions, the hands turned out to wash decks at seven bells in the Middle Watch. It was still pitch dark and blowing hard from the north-east, the ship running at nine knots under double-reefs, and rolling heavily in a wind-tossed expanse of cold black water. The wretched seamen shivered and grumbled in low voices among themselves as they started on their unwelcome task, doing what they were ordered to do sullenly and without heart.

Phillip, who had turned up with them, blew on his frozen fingers and paced the weather side of the quarterdeck, speaking no more than he could help and endeavouring to shut his ears to the grumbles, which the boatswain's mates made little attempt to suppress. He sent the men to breakfast as soon as he reasonably could and was glad enough of his own, washing down the unappetizing mixture of minced salt-beef and ship's biscuit with two scalding, well-sweetened cups of strong tea. He had hoped for a brief respite but, no sooner had the first pale light of dawn appeared in the eastern sky than the Captain – from the comfort of his sleeping cabin – sent word to the officer of the watch to make sail.

Young Duncan Laidlaw, who had the watch, attempted to set lower topsails and shake out the reefs in her upper canvas but the ship pitched and plunged like a wild thing, heeling so far over to starboard that her main deck guns were awash and the topmen had difficulty in regaining the comparative safety of the upper deck.

They experienced still more when the sails had to be taken in again and Phillip had himself to struggle aloft when the

57

fore-upper-topsail broke loose and the topmen, daunted by the violently flapping canvas and fearing to lose their footing, failed after several half-hearted attempts to secure it. Under his breathless urgings, as he lay out along the yard, they managed eventually to do so but he was exhausted and soaked to the skin when he returned to his post on the quarterdeck.

The wind abated shortly afterwards and, within another hour when Captain North made his appearance on deck, *Trojan* was running close-hauled under all the sail he had ordered and logging a brisk $12\frac{1}{2}$ knots. Having checked her position and the night's run with the Master, he said abruptly to Phillip, 'We have a man to flog before Divisions, have we not, Mr. Hazard?'

'Yes, sir.' Fearing that his sudden pallor might betray him, Phillip averted his gaze from the Captain's but North went on relentlessly, addressing his bent head, 'You flinch from witnessing this particular flogging, no doubt?'

'No, sir.' Recovering himself, Phillip faced him with simulated indifference. 'I have no reason to flinch from it.'

'Are you sure of that? This man, after all, bears the same name as yourself, does he not?'

'Yes, sir, he does. But as I informed you when I made my report on the man last night, this would seem to be merely a coincidence. He is an ex-merchant seaman.'

'Very well, Mr. Hazard, if you insist on these rather unconvincing evasions, there is nothing more I can say. Pipe hands to witness punishment and let us waste no more time. As I intend to commence training exercises aloft with a minimum of delay, you may inform the officers that they will be excused ceremonial dress on this occasion.' The Captain eyed his second-in-command coldly. 'For what are you waiting, Mr. Hazard? I gave you an order, did I not?'

Phillip did not move. 'There is just one matter, sir . . .' his lips were dry and he passed his tongue over them nervously. 'That is to say I—'

'Well?' North challenged irritably. 'What is it? Speak up, man, for the love of heaven!'

'After I had seen the prisoner last night, sir, I was concerned about his physical condition. I therefore asked the Surgeon to examine him, with a view to finding out whether he was fit to receive the punishment you had ordered. In the Surgeon's opinion, sir, he is *not* fit to receive six dozen lashes. He—'

'On what authority,' the Captain put in wrathfully, 'did you have this man examined by the Surgeon, Mr. Hazard?'

Phillip continued to meet his commander's angry gaze, his own unwavering. All fear of the consequences had left him now ... he had committed himself, had defied North and there was no turning back. In any case Surgeon Fraser had promised to back him up and he had expressed some concern over Graham's persistent coughing. 'On my own authority, sir,' he answered quietly.

'*Yours*, Mr. Hazard?'

'Yes, sir. As First Lieutenant, I am responsible not only for the discipline but also for the well-being and fitness of the ship's company and I do not consider, sir, that I exceeded my authority. It is laid down in Regulations and Instructions for the Medical Officers of Her Majesty's Fleet, sir, that whenever a seaman is sentenced to be flogged the Surgeon, having examined the man may, at his discretion, advise reduction of the sentence or its postponement if—'

'That will do, Mr. Hazard.' Captain North cut him short. 'I am familiar with the regulations, I do not require you to remind me of them. I consider that you have grossly exceeded your authority and, I can promise you, this is not the last you will hear about it. Although, of course, in spite of your evasions ...' his tone was acid, 'one need not look very far in order to discover what impelled you to do so in *this* case. Blood is thicker than water, it seems ... but you will not save your brother from the flogging he deserves by enlisting the Surgeon's aid, let me assure you.'

'But, sir, you—'

'I'll thank you to attend to your duties, Mr. Hazard,' the Captain interrupted, losing patience. 'Pass the word for the

Surgeon to report to me immediately. Then have the prisoner brought up and pipe all hands to muster without any more delay.'

'Aye, aye, sir.' Phillip passed on these orders, his voice expressionless but his mind in a fever of anxiety. Everything depended on Angus Fraser now, he thought . . . so long as the Surgeon refused to allow himself to be browbeaten, so long as he kept his word, all would be well. He watched the small, stout figure of the Surgeon emerge from the companion-hatch on the upper deck and come hurrying aft in search of the Captain, and unable from his own position on the lee side of the quarterdeck to hear what passed between them, waited tensely.

Angus Fraser was a man of forty or so, who had been in civilian practice for the past ten or eleven years, a gruff, taciturn Scot of considerable professional competence. His previous naval service had been in his youth, as an assistant surgeon and, on his own admission, he did not like the Navy and found its discipline unnecessarily harsh. He had accepted his recall from the half-pay list with resignation, though not without complaint, regarding it as his unwelcome but unavoidable duty to serve his country in the event of war and making no secret of the fact that he did not expect to enjoy the experience. He was outspoken in his criticism and, on more than one occasion, had stated uncompromisingly that he disapproved of flogging for minor breaches of discipline but this was the first time he had been called upon to give active expression to his views and . . . Phillip sighed.

Whilst surgeons and their assistants ranked officially now as wardroom officers, in practice they had little power outside their own, strictly limited sphere and few cared to risk anything in the nature of a trial of strength with the commanders of the ships in which they had served. Fraser had seemed willing enough last night to support him in his humanitarian act of defiance, he recalled. Indeed, he had voiced his opinion of North in bitterly critical terms but he was a civilian at heart . . . a man of peace, wanting no trouble and anxious only for the war to end, so that he might return to his family and his quiet country practice as soon as he could.

Would he, Phillip wondered, when it came to the point, dare to stand up to North if the Captain chose to assert his superior rank and make an issue of the affair? Had he the right, in these particular circumstances, to expect Fraser to keep his promise? Miserably aware that he had not, he looked across to where the two men were standing. They were still talking, North very red of face and obviously angry, but the Surgeon, although pale by contrast, appeared quite calm and his hopes rose momentarily as he watched them.

'Hands to witness punishment!' the Boatswain shouted, at the pitch of his powerful lungs, from the upper deck. 'All hands muster aft to witness punishment!'

Martin Fox appeared from below and Phillip left the quarterdeck to join him. The pipes shrilled and the men came crowding up from every part of the ship, to fall in in their allotted lines, the divisional officers in front, facing their men, and the Marines, in their scarlet uniforms, to the right of the blue-frocked seamen. Fox said in a tense whisper, before taking his place with his own division, 'Don't weaken, Phillip ... whatever happens, you must not weaken.'

'I know it,' Phillip assured him grimly. 'That is what he wants, isn't it?'

'You must leave this to Fraser,' the younger man warned. 'He has the right to intervene ... but you have not. And the Captain will *know* he's your brother if you attempt to do so.'

Phillip nodded, stony faced. The warning, he was aware, was kindly meant and he would be well advised to heed it but ... he called the ship's company to attention, his voice harsh with strain.

Graham was brought on deck, stripped to the waist, his wrists pinioned in front of him. He walked past the assembled men without faltering, his cheeks white beneath their coating of tan but his face betraying no emotion. Two boatswain's mates triced him to the grating which had been rigged under the mizzen-stay and one of them picked up the cat-o'-nine-tails and stood, balancing it carefully in his big red hands, stolidly awaiting the order to begin. On the prisoner's other side a Marine drummer also waited, drumsticks raised, both face and eyes devoid of expression. The Boatswain, a massive Welshman named Williams, glanced expectantly at Phillip.

'Six dozen lashes, is it, sir?'

The Captain answered him. He, too, had crossed from the quarterdeck, the Surgeon at his heels, and he advanced until he was within a few feet of the bound and helpless prisoner. '*Six* dozen lashes,' he confirmed, with icy emphasis. 'To be laid on well. Bo'sun's mate, you know your duty!'

Angus Fraser stared down at the deck beneath his feet, saying nothing and Phillip's heart sank. Obviously he had done all he could be expected to do and he had failed ... it was no use hoping that he would attempt to intervene further. A cough, after all, was scarcely sufficient to justify his risking North's displeasure and Graham had claimed that he was fit. . . .

The drum rolled and the burly boatswain's mate stepped forward, swinging the whip behind his head, to bring its knotted thongs hissing expertly across Graham's naked shoulders. The first stroke drew blood, raising a line of ugly red weals on the tautly stretched skin. The petty officer raised his whip again and the second and third strokes, following swiftly on the first, wrung a strangled gasp of pain from his victim. But, as blow succeeded blow, Graham stoically controlled himself. The tails of the lash cut viciously into the bare flesh of his back and shoulders but he endured the savage punishment in silence, broken only once by a groan he could not suppress.

Phillip, with difficulty, fought down his rising nausea. He had been compelled to witness other floggings in the past and, although none had failed to sicken him, the majority had, at least, been administered to men who deserved them ... to persistent offenders and to those guilty of crimes which demanded harsh retribution. He had deplored the necessity for flogging but, since this had been part and parcel of naval discipline throughout his training, he had never previously questioned its necessity. Indeed, it was only since serving under Captain North's command that he had seen such punishment meted out for minor offences and now, as he stood rigidly to attention in front of the ranks of motionless seamen and Marines, he had to exercise an iron restraint to prevent himself crying out in futile protest against the injustice his brother was suffering.

For this was injustice, he thought bitterly. North would never have ordered a search of Graham's kit nor, in all probability, would he have sentenced him to so severe a flogging had his name been anything but Hazard. He might, perhaps, have listened to the Surgeon's pleas had he not suspected that the seaman he had put under arrest was, in fact, an ex-officer and the brother of his First Lieutenant.

Now he was seeking confirmation of his suspicions and Phillip's throat ached with the effort it cost him to remain silent. The only way in which he could hope to allay Captain North's suspicions was, he knew, by pretending indifference and by treating the brutal spectacle he was being forced to witness as if it were merely another flogging, inflicted on a man who meant nothing to him. As Martin Fox had warned him a short while ago, he could not afford to weaken . . . he had somehow to make the lie he had told seem convincing. If he failed to do so, then this persecution of his brother would be continued. North would use Graham in order to bring him to heel, would use him ruthlessly and unscrupulously, as he was attempting to do at this moment . . . Graham would be the trump card he would keep up his sleeve, to be produced should his First Lieutenant be tempted to rebel against him in the future.

Phillip's resolution hardened. He willed himself to stand rigidly to attention, to show as little emotion as the wooden-faced seamen at his back but the strain was becoming almost unendurable . . . his hands clenched fiercely at his sides as he struggled for control.

His brother's back, he saw, was reduced to a bloody pulp

but still the lash bit into it, cutting the bruised and tortured flesh to ribbons. There would be scars, he thought, scars which would mark Graham to the end of his days ... he shivered, feeling his brother's pain as if it were his own and wishing, sick with shame and disgust, that it might have been.

At the end of the first three dozen lashes, the boatswain's mate paused. His relief took the cat-o'-nine-tails from him and was moving into position to continue the flogging when Angus Fraser thrust past him and went to the prisoner's side.

'Wait ...' his voice broke the silence, sounding unnaturally loud but, Phillip heard thankfully, authoritative and determined. The Surgeon bent over Graham's slumped body, lifted his head and put out a hand to touch his face.

'This man is barely conscious, sir,' he said, over his shoulder, to the Captain. 'In my professional opinion, he should not be subjected to further punishment.'

'Unconscious, is he, Doctor? Then he must be revived. Bo'sun's mate ...' North jerked his head. The two petty officers hesitated and then the man with the whip set it down and picked up a bucket of seawater which stood in readiness by the rail. He sluiced its contents over Graham's head and face, as the Surgeon reluctantly moved aside and, his face without expression, reached for the cat again.

'All right to go on, sir?' he asked the Surgeon tonelessly, as Graham gasped and spluttered back to consciousness and then was seized by a violent fit of coughing.

Once more it was North himself who replied to the question. 'The sentence,' he declared, an edge to his voice, 'is six dozen lashes. This man has received only three dozen and he is now conscious. Carry on, bo'sun's mate.'

The dreadful punishment continued and the Captain stood with folded arms, a curiously repellent smile playing about his lips as he watched. He was still smiling when he turned, after a while, to glance in the direction of his First Lieutenant. That smile, with its hint of derisive triumph was suddenly more than Phillip could stomach. He took a pace forward, white with anger but, before he was able to utter a single one of the damning words he had planned to fling into the smiling face of his commander, an interruption came from a totally unexpected quarter.

'Captain North, I beg you to put a stop to this!'

A small, elegantly dressed figure emerged from the companion-hatch and Phillip came to a standstill, staring at her in shocked dismay. He had neither seen nor heard Mademoiselle Sophie's approach, had not suspected her presence until she spoke and he wondered for how long she had been there. What, he asked himself, what in the name of heaven was the Baroness von Mauthner thinking of to allow her innocent charge to wander about on deck unaccompanied? That she should have witnessed so terrible a spectacle filled him with outraged horror and he signed urgently to the boatswain's mate to put down his whip, hoping that – when she realized what was going on – Mademoiselle Sophie would retire below.

She did not do so. Instead she crossed the deck with regal dignity and without hesitation, her head held high, and an astonished gasp went up from the massed ranks of seamen and Marines as they caught sight of her, most of them goggling at her in bewilderment, as if she were a vision from another world. Indeed, Phillip thought, as bewildered as the rest, she might have been a vision with her queenly bearing and the calm assurance with which she walked straight up to the startled North and addressed herself to him.

'Captain North . . .' her clear young voice did not falter and, if she was aware of the sensation her arrival had caused, she gave no sign of it.

The Captain removed his gold laced cap. 'Forgive me, mam'zelle, but you should not be here,' he began. 'You . . .'

Mademoiselle Sophie silenced him with an imperiously raised hand. 'I had imagined myself on board a Russian ship,' she told him icily, 'where it is a commonplace occurrence for a sailor to be beaten to death. But the Russians are savages, in your view, are they not? And you are about to go to war with them?'

'That is so, mam'zelle. But you . . .' North was visibly disconcerted, his face flushed and he stammered in his agitation. 'You must understand, you must realize.'

'I understand,' she stated accusingly, 'that this is a British ship and your men all volunteers – not conscripts, Captain. Yet it would seem that there is little to choose between your method of maintaining order and discipline and that of the Russians, which you affect to despise.'

'Mam'zelle, I assure you, we flog only when it is necessary,' North defended. 'We . . .' but Mademoiselle Sophie ignored him, her gaze going to the limp figure which hung, unconscious and bleeding, from the grating. For the first time since she had come on deck her voice shook and there were tears in her eyes as she said, 'Oh, that poor, poor man! You have all but killed him, Captain North.'

'Cut him down,' North ordered. 'And take him below.'

Boatswain Williams and his two mates obeyed him with alacrity and, accompanied by the Surgeon, they hustled the unconscious Graham down the hatchway and out of sight.

Phillip expelled his breath in a tense sigh of gratitude and relief and saw that his own feelings were reflected in the faces of the men grouped about him. No one moved, however, and they were silent, but suddenly the tension was over, the intolerable strain which they had all had to endure was, miraculously, at an end. The small, erect figure of Mademoiselle Sophie still drew every eye and she said, as if she had only then become aware of this, 'I will go below now, Captain.'

'Certainly, mam'zelle.' Red of face and obviously much put out by the turn events had taken, Captain North continued to treat her with exaggerated, almost servile respect, Phillip observed, and his bewilderment returned full force when he saw the Captain offer her his arm. 'Permit me to escort you.'

'Thank you. But that poor man, will he. . . .'

'The Surgeon will take care of him, mam'zelle.'

Her dignity impeccable, Mademoiselle Sophie laid her hand on the Captain's sleeve and they walked across the

66

deck together. The men stared after them, their faces, as before, Phillip noticed, reflecting his own curiously conflicting emotions. He waited with them and, when the Captain returned, once more called them to attention. Divine Service, always brief save on Sunday mornings, was concluded with more than its usual brevity, North reading the prayers in a rapid, toneless voice and, all too obviously, impatient to have done.

When it was over and the men dismissed, he turned to Phillip, his eyes blazing with barely suppressed fury. 'Now, Mr. Hazard, we will exercise these lubberly scum! We will exercise them until they are sorry they were ever born and sorrier still that they volunteered to serve in this ship. Beat to quarters!'

'*Now*, sir?' Phillip's jaw dropped.

'Devil take it, Mr. Hazard, are you hard of hearing? *Now*, of course now! I want the ship cleared for action and the guns loaded and run out . . .' he issued a string of orders and, without waiting for Phillip's dutiful, 'Aye, aye, sir,' spun round and made for the quarterdeck, bellowing for the officer of the watch.

After that, life for the ship's company of the *Trojan* became a nightmare. As the ship worked up into the Bay of Biscay in the teeth of a rising gale, the men were driven relentlessly and, despite the storm, North showed them no mercy. Evolutions aloft were followed by gunnery practice and, if any exercise was not carried out as smartly as the Captain demanded, it had to be repeated, sometimes more than once. The watch below were called to quarters twice during one bitter, wind-torn night, battle lanterns lit and the guns loaded and run-out. Decks were scrubbed and holystoned at seven bells in the Middle Watch and then – because the Captain chanced to find a discarded swab-tail beneath one of the main deck guns, the whole process had to be gone through again, before he would permit the men to go to breakfast.

The pumps were manned and three fire drills ordered the day before the ship reached Gibraltar and, during the

Second Dog Watch, lower yards and topmasts – struck owing to bad weather – were sent up and struck again in a gale-force East wind, one man falling from the rigging and being lost in the heavy seas.

Cape Spartel, on the African coast, was sighted soon after dawn on Wednesday morning but the strong easterly wind blowing through the Straits of Gibraltar made further progress difficult. After several fruitless tacks from Cape St. Vincent to Tangiers and then back to Tarifa, under double-reefed topsails, the Captain ordered the screw lowered. Rolling unpleasantly *Trojan* began at last to make headway against the wind but both officers and men were exhausted and many, even among the hardened seamen, suffering from seasickness when, just after noon on Wednesday, 23rd March, Europa Point came into sight off the port bow.

The ship ran in under her engines and dropped anchor off the Quarantine Mole. Shortly afterwards a launch came out, bearing the Governor and a number of Port Health officials and – the quarantine regulations being waived in deference to the Governor – the Captain and the two passengers were taken ashore in his launch. But there was neither rest nor shore leave for the weary, disgruntled men . . . coaling commenced immediately and was continued next day, from first light to mid-afternoon.

Phillip, begrimed with black dust and suffering from prolonged lack of sleep, had many things to worry him, even when the last barge had pushed off from the ship's side on its way back to the coaling station on shore. He was anxious – and with reason – about morale in general and his brother's state of mind in particular.

Graham was making a slow and painful recovery from the effects of the brutal flogging he had received and the change in him was both noticeable and alarming. His cough troubled him constantly and he slept badly, if at all. In addition, he was morose and bitter, reluctant to see or talk to anyone. When he could be prevailed upon to do so, his conversation was invariably about Captain North and he repeated, over and over again, the story of the ill-fated

Guillemot, offering this as a warning to any who would listen.

Surgeon Fraser, who had contrived to smuggle him into his own small cabin until he should be fit to resume his duties, expressed concern on his patient's account but, although assiduous in his efforts to restore Graham to physical health, could suggest no way in which his self-inflicted mental torment might be alleviated.

'You could, perhaps, endeavour to talk to him, Mr. Hazard,' he said, without much conviction. 'More important still, you might encourage him to talk to you because this might help him. He has a grievance, of course, which is only to be expected in the circumstances but, in addition, he appears to have what amounts to an obsession concerning Captain North. And that, as I'm sure you realize, could be dangerous. If, when he returns to duty, he should air some of the views he has expressed to *me* all too freely, on the lower deck, it might cause trouble. The men are in an ugly mood and there will be some among them, I fear, who may pay too much attention to what he tells them.'

Phillip shared the Surgeon's fears since he, even more than Angus Fraser, was aware of the increasing discontent among the men, for he had daily evidence of it. But it was not easy to find time to spend with his brother and when, usually at the expense of his sleep, he did manage to steal half an hour, Graham – although willing enough to unburden himself on the subject of Captain North – obstinately refused to heed his warnings.

'It is I, my dear Phillip, who am warning *you*, don't you understand? This Captain of yours is not fit to be entrusted with the command of a coal barge, much less with that of a thirty-gun frigate! He is a sadistic murderer and if you give him even half a chance, he will drive the ship's company to mutiny, as he drove the poor devils in the *Guillemot.* Oh, I may be skulking down here in the Surgeon's cabin all day but I know what's going on . . . the watch below isn't getting any time below, is it? North calls all hands at any hour of the day or night when he happens to feel like it, does he not?'

'Yes,' Phillip conceded, 'he does. But he's entitled to ... the drills *are* slow and he has to have the ship ready to go into action by the time we join the Fleet.'

'The drills are slow,' Graham pointed out unanswerably, 'because the men won't put their hearts into them, Phillip. And they never will, whilst North is in command ... you know that as well as I do. For God's sake, he's driving them without mercy! He's driving *you* as hard as he's driving anyone and you're his First Lieutenant. Phillip, how much sleep is he letting you have? No, don't answer – you're get-even less than the men, judging by your appearance. You should look at your face in a mirror sometime ... it will shock you.'

He was right, Phillip thought wearily. But there was little he could do to help, either himself or the men, so long as North remained the officially appointed Captain of the *Trojan* ... but he continued, nevertheless, to worry a great deal.

One, at least, of his anxieties was removed when, just as daylight was fading on the evening of the second day, the Governor's launch brought Mademoiselle Sophie and the Baroness von Mauthner back on board. He had imagined and even begun to fear that, when they had failed to return after their night on shore, they might be leaving the ship to continue their journey overland and his relief at the sight of them surprised even himself. He was unable to see very much of them when they were on board – his duties kept him too occupied and Captain North, very pointedly, invited no one to share the meals he took with his two female passengers – but the knowledge that Mademoiselle Sophie was there was, Phillip found, the source of a certain bitter-sweet pleasure to him.

Trojan weighed anchor at seven bells in the First Watch and, as Friday 25th March dawned, she entered a grey, stormy Mediterranean, her immediate destination Malta. To Phillip's surprise – although this decision was, no doubt, the result of instructions he had been given in Gibraltar – the Captain did not order the screw raised on leaving harbour.

The wind was still unfavourable and the ship proceeded under her engines throughout the night, with only her top-sails set and it was not until well into the following morning, when the weather improved with a fresh wind from the S.S.E., that North instructed him to dispense with engines and make all possible sail.

The rest of the voyage to Malta – apart from more frequent use of the screw – followed much the same pattern as that from Plymouth to Gibraltar. Keeping in sight of the African coast, the ship made good progress. After the first day, the weather was better but that was the only difference ... the training exercises were not. The Captain had stated his intention to concentrate mainly on gun-drills and this he did, until the unfortunate guns' crews were dropping on their feet, when it again became the turn of the seamen's divisions to exercise aloft.

North put them through every evolution in the sailing manual, timing them with a stop-watch and roaring his displeasure when the time taken for a particular exercise failed to come up to his expectations. In sheer desperation, in the end, the men improved on their times, realizing that – unless they could manage to do so – they would continue to be put through the same evolutions twice and often three times in the course of each watch. The resentful murmurs increased and many of the seamen became careless, risking life and limb in their efforts to satisfy the exacting demands of their commander.

Carelessness led, inevitably, to accidents. When reefing topsails in a squall the second day out, the Captain of the Maintop, a fine old seaman named Challoner, fell from the main rigging and was lucky to escape with head injuries and a broken arm. Within a few minutes of his being carried below, he was followed by another maintopman – an ex-coastguard – William Davis, who was less fortunate. He struck one of the quarterdeck guns, a few feet from where Phillip was standing with the Captain, and was killed instantly.

Next day while engaged in the exercise of sending up

lower yards and topmasts and crossing topgallant yards, two other men missed their footing and both went overboard. A boat was lowered with all possible speed to go to their assistance but one of the men, a non-swimmer, drowned before it could reach him, despite the gallant efforts of his shipmate to keep him afloat. But, as soon as the boat returned, Captain North ordered the whole exercise repeated. . . .

Head-winds again necessitated the use of engines for eight out of the next twenty-four hours but *Trojan* made a fast passage, sighting the island of Gozo from the masthead at daybreak on Tuesday morning, 29th March. Just after seven bells had struck in the Forenoon Watch, she steamed into Malta's Grand Harbour, saluted the flag of the Admiral-Superintendent and secured to a buoy off the dockyard, having made the passage from Plymouth in a total of eleven and a half days. This was better than Captain North had estimated or even hoped for but, typically, he offered no word of praise or appreciation to his hard-worked ship's company.

There were a great many ships in the harbour and dockyard, both French and British, the majority of these troop-transports on their way to Gallipoli or Constantinople, and Valetta was crowded with the soldiers of both nations, waiting for ships to take them on to their destination. But, despite the evident congestion, North made it clear that he intended to brook no delay. Coal, water and stores had all to be taken on board and Phillip was ordered to begin coaling at once . . . the Captain, as before, taking both passengers ashore with him to stay at the Governor's country house in St. Antonio – a village four miles from Valetta – until the worst of it should be over.

He sent for his First Lieutenant before leaving the ship.

'I shall make arrangements with the Admiral-Superintendent to ensure that I am given the priority to which my orders entitle me,' he said curtly. 'The rest is up to you, Mr. Hazard. I expect to be under way again within twenty-four hours or by tomorrow evening at the latest, so you will have to do the best you can. Coal and water must be loaded but if we have to leave without some of our stores, it cannot be helped, you understand? And there will be no shore leave . . . I don't want to have to send out patrols to hunt for drunken seamen or have any of my crew picking fights with the army when they're the worse for liquor. Is that clear, Mr. Hazard?'

'Aye, aye, sir,' Phillip acknowledged. With something in the region of a hundred and fifty tons of coal to load, compliance with the Captain's orders would mean working for most of the night but, he supposed wearily, it would have to be done. He came to attention, his fingers to the peak of his cap, as the pipes of the boatswain's mates twittered in ceremonious farewell and the Captain went over the side to his waiting gig.

Mademoiselle Sophie, already seated there with the Baroness, smiled up at him shyly from the sternsheets but he was only dimly aware of her presence and scarcely noticed the smile, his mind busy with calculations as the gig cast off and he dismissed the side-party.

CHAPTER FOUR

I

By four-thirty the following afternoon the passengers had returned to the ship and, thanks to prodigious efforts on the part of her crew, the coal, water and stores required for the last stage of her journey had all been taken on board and stowed. *Trojan* was ready to proceed to sea and, with steam up, Phillip called away the Captain's gig, dispatching it to pick up North who was still closeted with the Admiral-Superintendent on shore.

There was a long and unexplained delay and darkness had fallen by the time the gig was reported pulling back to the ship. Anthony Cochrane, who was officer of the watch, prepared to summon the side-party to receive their commander with due ceremony but, as naval custom decreed, he hailed the approaching boat before doing so. The reply from the midshipman in charge was also according to custom.

'Aye, aye ... *Trojan*!' he shouted back, his repetition of the ship's name indicated that her Captain was on board but his voice, which had recently broken, was oddly strained and high-pitched when he added the request for a boatswain's chair to be lowered.

'A bo-sun's chair!' Cochrane exclaimed, turning to Phillip with raised brows. 'Why in the world does the youngster want a bo'sun's chair, do you suppose? The passengers are back. Unless, of course ...' he smiled, with more than a hint of malice, 'unless the Captain has wined and dined too well on shore, perhaps!'

'That is not one of his vices,' Phillip objected, his tone short.

'*If* it's not, then it's the only vice he doesn't possess. I'm

74

sorry, sir ...' meeting his senior's reproving glare, Cochrane's smile swiftly faded. 'But that does happen to be true, you know.'

He knew, only too well, Phillip thought bitterly, but he could not admit it to Anthony Cochrane, could not encourage the younger man openly to criticize their commander.

'Carry on, Mr. Cochrane,' he returned repressively. 'You've been asked to rig a bo'sun's chair, have you not?'

'Yes, sir.'

'Then rig one. And call the side-party ... I'll see you at the entry port.'

'Aye, aye, sir. But ...' young Cochrane's irrepressible smile was again widely in evidence as he added, in a subdued whisper, 'Is it too much to hope that he's been taken ill, do you think?'

Phillip affected not to hear him although, in his heart, he found himself echoing the unlikely hope. North's health had hitherto been excellent and it seemed too much to expect but ... he hurried below to the main deck entry port, peering down into the darkness at the gig. There was a slumped figure, wrapped in a boat-cloak, in the sternsheets, he saw, and his hopes rose as the gig came smartly alongside and secured to the midships chains.

From the deck above, two of the hands carefully lowered the boatswain's chair and, with the assistance of the coxswain and one of the boat's crew, the Captain climbed into it and suffered himself to be drawn slowly upwards. Even from that distance, his florid face looked pinched and drawn and he leaned forward, legs dangling, holding his boat-cloak about him, as if in considerable pain. The boatswain's mates put their calls to their lips and the side-party came to attention but North ignored them, omitting to return his officers' salutes. Reaching the level of the entry port, he said thickly, 'Give me an arm, one of you. Come on, come on ... can't you see I'm hardly able to stand upright, devil take it?'

'He *is* ill!' Lieutenant Cochrane breathed incredulously, as if doubting the evidence of his own eyes. 'Heaven be praised ... he really has been taken ill!'

75

Phillip stepped forward and offered his arm and the Mate of the watch went round to the Captain's other side. Between them, half supporting, half carrying him, they managed to get North below to his cabin, where he sank groaning into a chair.

'Are you unwell, sir?' Phillip asked. 'Shall I call for the Surgeon?'

'What the devil does it look like?' the Captain demanded furiously. 'Of course I'm unwell, Mr. Hazard ... and of course I want you to call for the Surgeon! At once, do you hear? He'll have to give me something to ease this infernal pain.' He smothered another groan as the Mate, in response to Phillip's request, went in search of the Surgeon, and added, his voice slurred and indistinct, 'You're to take the ship to sea. There must be no delay, my orders are to ... report to ... the British Ambassador in Constantinople ... as soon as possible before ... April the fifth. I ... use the engines, if you have to, Mr. Hazard, for as long as you have to. There's a ... *gregale* blowing up, you'll ... need the screw to get out of harbour.'

'Aye, aye, sir.'

North attempted to enlarge on his orders but was silenced by a sudden spasm of pain. 'Where the devil is the Surgeon?' he gasped, when the spasm eased. 'Why can't the damned fellow bestir himself?'

The Surgeon, together with his assistant and the Captain's steward, entered the cabin at that moment and Phillip thankfully relinquished North's care to them. 'I'll be on deck, Doctor,' he said, 'if you have any news as to the Captain's condition to give me.'

Angus Fraser eyed his patient gravely. 'Get him into his cot,' he instructed his assistant and then, turning to Phillip again, he went on, 'According to Midshipman Booth, the Captain was in this condition when he went on board the gig and the Admiral was very concerned about him ... wanted him to stay on shore and go into hospital, but he refused. His illness came on him very suddenly, I gather. Has he told you anything, Mr. Hazard?'

'Only that I am to take the ship to sea,' Phillip answered. 'Which I had better see about at once. You'll let me know how the Captain is, won't you, as soon as you can?'

'I shall report my findings to you in person, Mr. Hazard,' the Surgeon promised. 'When I have examined him thoroughly ... that will take time. So ... within about an hour, shall we say? I hope to have made a diagnosis by then.'

He was as good as his word. *Trojan* was steaming on her new course against a moderately strong headwind from the N.N.E., when, a little under an hour later, he came on deck.

'Captain North has a high fever,' he stated and went into technical details, which Phillip only partially understood. 'It appears to be an acute gastric infection, picked up on shore, I can only suppose. He is in considerable pain from stomach cramp and is very nauseated but I do not think that his condition is unduly serious. I have given him opium to ease his discomfort and I believe he will sleep now.'

'For how long,' Phillip inquired cautiously, 'do you expect the Captain to remain incapacitated, Doctor?'

Angus Fraser met his gaze, his own curiously blank.

'For at least a week, Mr. Hazard,' he answered positively and added, lowering his voice, 'He will have to keep to his cot for a week and not leave it, under any circumstances, you understand. Which should give you ...' his voice sank still lower, 'a chance to restore morale by permitting the men some rest, should it not? Because you'll be in command ... the Captain will be in no state to give you any orders.'

'I see.' Phillip's heart lifted. 'Yes, a week should give me time. Indeed, Doctor, it will give me ample time.'

'I'm glad to hear it, Mr. Hazard. By the bye, your brother is now fit, I believe, to return to light duties. But I do mean light duties – he isn't fit to return to the Maintop Division. That cough of his still troubles him a good deal and ...' the Surgeon hesitated and Phillip glanced at him inquiringly.

'Your brother is not as strong as he likes to make out, Mr. Hazard. But he's qualified in navigation, he tells me, so that

77

Mr. Burnaby might be able to make use of his services. What do you think? It is a possible solution, is it not ... and it would keep him away from the lower deck.'

Phillip nodded. Putting Graham to work under the Master would also enable him to be usefully employed in a manner unlikely to attract North's notice, when he resumed command. Fraser's suggestion was an excellent one, he decided and Burnaby would almost certainly welcome it, since his other assistants, although competent enough, were young and inexperienced. He smiled. 'Thank you, Doctor – I'll have a word with Mr. Burnaby at once. I'm sure he'll be agreeable, so perhaps you would be so good as to tell my brother to report to him?'

The Surgeon departed and Phillip, having obtained Burnaby's consent to the arrangement, crossed over to where Martin Fox, the officer of the watch, was standing.

'Well?' Fox asked eagerly. 'What news of the Captain?'

Phillip told him and saw the dawn of relief in his eyes. 'Then we have a week's respite ... oh, thank God! No night quarters, no clearing for action in the Middle Watch and no washing decks in pitch darkness! The watch below will be able to get their heads down and you and I, Phillip, will be able to make up for some of our lost sleep. That is, of course ...' he turned, his expression suddenly anxious, to look into Phillip's face, '*If* you intend to use your week of independent command as I hope you do?'

'You know I do, Martin.'

'Heaven be praised! Will you tell the men?'

'No.' Phillip shook his head. 'There is no need, they will know soon enough. The gig's crew will have spread the news of the Captain's illness in any case.'

'Yes, I suppose they will. One other question, Phillip ...' Fox was smiling. 'What of our passengers?'

'What of them?'

'Well, they will no longer be taking their meals with the Captain ... should we not invite them to partake of our gunroom hospitality? I don't know about you but I've scarcely set eyes on them since they came on board, much less been

78

given an opportunity to exchange any social pleasantries with them. And I should like to, I don't mind admitting.' Fox's smile widened. 'The one who calls herself Mademoiselle Sophie made a lasting impression on me when she intervened on your brother's behalf. It took a great deal of courage to do what she did, Phillip. And in addition, she is very good looking, is she not?'

'Yes, she is good looking,' Phillip agreed flatly.

'Then will you invite her – will you invite them both to dine with us in the gunroom tomorrow afternoon?'

'I don't know if I should, Martin. You see—'

'But my dear fellow, it can do no harm, surely?'

The echo of Mademoiselle Sophie's own words to her guardian on the train returned and Phillip frowned. Had she not said, when the Baroness von Mauthner had reproached her for talking to him too freely, that 'it was doing no harm'? Remembering their conversation and the eager interest with which she had questioned him about the ship and his career, his expression relaxed.

'All right, Martin,' he decided. 'We will invite them both to take dinner with us in the gunroom tomorrow. As you say, they will be unable to take their meals with the Captain while he is indisposed ... but we shall have to offer them something better than the usual gunroom fare. And behaviour, I must warn you, will have to be very circumspect if they accept the invitation.'

'It shall be,' Martin Fox assured him. 'But as a matter of interest, though ...' he eyed Phillip searchingly.

'Well? What interests you, in particular?'

'Who *are* they, Phillip – do you know? I mean, it is obvious, from the way the Captain treats her, that Mademoiselle Sophie is a person of considerable importance, isn't it? And that "Mademoiselle Sophie" is not her real name ... could it be Princess Sophie, do you suppose? Or the Archduchess Sophie, perhaps?'

'I honestly cannot tell you,' Phillip answered, with truth. 'I know no more about her than you do, Martin.'

'Well, it is an intriguing situation,' Fox said. He smiled.

'And rather a romantic one, too. Long may the Captain's indisposition last! And, before you reprove me for lack of respect, let me point out that I shall be by no means the only member of the ship's company to express *that* wish.'

Undoubtedly he would not, Phillip was forced to concede, his own feelings very similar.

The news spread fast. Long before the watch changed, everyone on board was aware that the Captain had been taken ill and was likely to be confined to his cabin for the next seven days. The men's relief was in their eyes, as it had been in Lieutenant Fox's, and in their tired faces, now suddenly wreathed in smiles. Every order was instantly obeyed, sail set and taken in with a speed and skill not previously apparent and, washing decks next morning just before sunrise, the hands sang at their work. Even the gunnery exercises, which Phillip ordered after Divisions, were undertaken smartly and in a spirit of keen but friendly rivalry between the crews. In the final test – three rounds of quick-firing in a series of broadsides – one minute ten seconds was the time recorded for the starboard side main deck guns, with the port side less than five seconds behind them.

This so far surpassed anything achieved at gunnery practice hitherto that Phillip sent for the gunnery officer, Henry Sutherland – a young Mate, recently promoted to the acting rank of Lieutenant – and offered his congratulations. Sutherland, who had suffered frequently under the lash of North's tongue during the past eleven days, when his guns' crews had fallen short of the Captain's expectations, flushed with pleasure and stammered his thanks.

'I had begun to fear that it was I who had failed, sir,' he confided. 'I lack experience, I know, and I thought it must be for this reason that the men were making such a poor showing. But today ... today they were good, weren't they?'

'They were very good indeed, Mr. Sutherland,' Philip assured him. 'In view of which we'll give all hands a "make and mend" this afternoon ... and you may tell your guns' crews that it is they who have earned it. Mr. Fox ...'

'Sir?'

'Send hands to dinner at eight bells and then have "make and mend" piped for the watch below.'

The pipe was received with subdued cheering, for it meant that, for the first time since they had left England, the watch below would have no duties to perform and would be free to smoke in their messes, sleep if they wished and write letters home.

The gunroom dined at two o'clock at sea and Mademoiselle Sophie, accompanied by the Baroness von Mauthner and escorted by one of the gunroom stewards, presented herself at the appointed hour, to be received with respectful enthusiasm by the members of the mess. They all stood until their guests were seated and their behaviour, Phillip observed approvingly was – as Martin Fox had promised – exemplary.

Each officer who possessed a private store of food had contributed something to the feast and the cook, given such an abundance of provisions, had excelled himself. The soup, although basically the usual concoction made from stewed salt 'junk', had been appetizingly flavoured with spices and, as alternatives to the inevitable curried beef of uncertain age or boiled salt pork, there were potted lobster and shrimps, sardines and pâté, and boiled rice, instead of mashed ship's biscuit.

The Baroness von Mauthner, obviously suspicious at first of the invitation and what acceptance of it might imply, was considerably mollified when she found that, in addition to the young officers she had expected, there were a number of her own age. At table, she sat between Surgeon Fraser and the paymaster, John Oliphant, a man of sixty, who had travelled widely in India, having served at one time in the Bombay Marine.

Seated opposite her, she had the reassuring sight of the Master's snowy white head and, not far away, the balding one of the Captain of Marines, Alexander Murray, who was in command of the draft of Marine artillerymen. After a while, mellowed by the good food and wine and enjoying the conversation of her neighbours, she ceased to watch her charge as closely as she had at the beginning of the meal and Mademoiselle Sophie took full advantage of her temporary freedom from supervision.

Phillip had placed her on his own right hand, at the far end of the table from the Baroness, with Anthony Cochrane on her other side and Laidlaw and Sutherland opposite. Within a few minutes, she was talking to them gaily, her dark eyes sparkling and the lovely, sensitive mouth curving into a smile as she looked from one to another of the faces grouped about her. The young officers fell swift victims to her charm and she accepted their homage shyly, asking them eager questions and listening to the answers they gave her with the same rapt attention that, Philip recalled, she had displayed during their train journey, when he had told her about the voyages he had made.

Seeing her enjoyment and watching for the reappearance of her smile, he was glad that she had come, glad that Martin Fox had been so insistent in his suggestion that she should be asked to do so. Up till now, he thought, the voyage could not have offered her much in the way of entertainment . . . just the Captain's company and the confines of the screened-off portion of his day cabin allocated for her use, with an occasional walk on deck, with the Baroness, under his escort. She was very young to be kept thus a prisoner and forced to hold herself aloof from the sort of young, high-spirited companionship in which she was now so obviously delighting . . . too young, surely, and too eager for life for it to be anything but a hardship?

He sighed, wondering again who she was and why their Lordships of the Admiralty should have sent her with the *Trojan* to Constantinople . . . why it should be necessary to convey her there so urgently and what was to be her fate when she eventually left the ship and went ashore. Could she be of royal birth, as Martin Fox had half-jokingly suggested . . . a princess or an archduchess, hiding her real identity behind the name of Mademoiselle Sophie? It was possible,

Phillip supposed since, if she were, this would explain why she was so closely guarded and why a British frigate had been put at her disposal by the Admiralty. It would also explain why he himself had been sent to escort her from London but ... he frowned and, abandoning speculation, gave himself up to the pleasure of watching her and listening to her laughter. Soon, he reflected, she would be gone and it was highly improbable that he would ever see her again, whoever she was and whatever the mystery surrounding her ...'

At a little after seven bells, he went on deck to relieve Martin Fox, who had the Afternoon Watch.

'Well?' Fox asked, when the formalities of handing over the watch had been completed. 'How fares the gunroom reception for our royal passengers?'

'It is an unqualified success,' Phillip told him. 'Go and see for yourself ... you deserve to, since the idea of holding it was yours. The port is still being circulated and my chair, beside the chief guest, is vacant ... so I suggest you delay no longer.'

'Aye, aye, sir!' Fox acknowledged, smiling. 'That is an order I'm only too delighted to obey. And with your permission, Mr. Hazard, I intend to offer myself as escort to our young lady of mystery when it is time for her to take her evening stroll on deck. Since the Captain is still indisposed and your duties are, in consequence, very arduous, it would seem incumbent on me to volunteer my services. But, of course, if you....'

Phillip shook his head. 'Volunteer away, Mr. Fox, with my blessing. But you may find you have a rival ... I've told young Laidlaw that I'll keep the First Dog and won't require him and I do not think he plans to spend the evening on make and mend. Also, remember if you please, you will have to escort mademoiselle's duenna as well and I do not advise you to try to elude her, in the circumstances.'

'Of course, sir, I wouldn't dream of it. I seek only to solve the riddle of mademoiselle's identity, in any case ... a mystery always intrigues me. But ...' Fox prepared to go below, 'I will let you know what I'm able to discover.'

Dusk was closing in when he returned to the quarterdeck and the Baroness von Mauthner was with him, her hand resting on his arm. 'Ah, Lieutenant Hazard!' Seeing Phillip, she accorded him an unusually affable greeting. 'I have to thank you,' she went on, lapsing into French, 'for your most generous hospitality. Your officers are most charming and I have spent a very entertaining afternoon in their company ... mademoiselle also. And you are very thoughtful to have arranged for Lieutenant Fox to take me for my evening promenade ... I had feared, you see, that in the absence of your Captain I might have to forgo it.'

'It is a pleasure to serve you, madame,' Phillip told her, in English. He was careful to avoid Martin Fox's eye as he added, 'Mr. Fox will, I know, always be happy to offer you his escort, any time you wish, until the Captain recovers. You have only to ask.'

'You are mos' kind, Mr. Hazard ... really mos' kind.'

'Not at all.' Phillip continued to regard them both gravely. 'But where is Mademoiselle Sophie? Is she not taking an evening walk also?'

'Mademoiselle Sophie is fatigued,' the Baroness explained. 'I have taken her to her cabin, so that she may rest a little. But now I must continue my own promenade or my kind escort will become impatient. *Au revoir*, Lieutenant Hazard.' She gave him a gracious inclination of the head and departed on the arm of her escort, Phillip hiding a smile, as he glimpsed the expression on Martin Fox's face.

After evening quarters, when he had the men standing to their guns, he again dismissed the watch below and, for the first time since leaving Plymouth, heard them dancing and singing to a fiddler for over an hour before they turned in. It was a happy sound and Phillip listened to it with gratitude and relief, remaining on deck to do so, although he had been relieved by Anthony Cochrane, who had taken over the watch. He had been leaning, lost in thought, on the quarterdeck rail for some time when he heard the faint tip-tap of a woman's footsteps and turned, in surprise, to see Mademoiselle Sophie crossing the deck towards him. She was heavily muffled in a dark cloak and, as she reached him, put a finger to her lips to enjoin his silence.

'Mademoiselle ...' Phillip's voice was low. 'What are you doing here?'

She looked up at him, smiling. 'I came for a breath of air before retiring, Mr. Hazard. For that and ... to thank you for this afternoon. I enjoyed myself so much. You would not believe what a pleasure it was for me to meet your officers, to talk to them, to ... to laugh with them. I so seldom have the opportunity to ...' she broke off, biting her lower lip. 'I liked them – they were all so kind to me and they have such good manners.'

'I'm glad you liked them, mademoiselle. But ...' Phillip looked round uncertainly, expecting to see the Baroness. 'You've come up here alone?'

'I ... yes, I am alone,' Mademoiselle Sophie lowered her gaze. 'The Baroness von Mauthner is asleep, I did not want to disturb her. But I heard your sailors singing ...' she gestured in the direction of the forecastle. 'So I came. I ... it is all right for me to come to this deck in the evening, is it not? The Captain permitted it and I did not think that you would mind.'

'I do not mind, mademoiselle. But—'

'But you are in command of the ship whilst the Captain is indisposed, are you not?' she challenged, looking at him then.

'Yes,' he affirmed, 'I am in command. But I am responsible to the Captain, responsible for carrying out his orders and ... I don't think that he would approve of your being here by yourself, mademoiselle.'

'You would tell him?'

He shook his head. 'No.'

'Then,' she asked composedly, 'why should it matter, Mr. Hazard? So long as you do not tell him.'

He sighed and she went on quickly, her smile returning and the dark eyes bright, 'I think perhaps you are doing other things of which you do not intend to tell the Captain, Mr. Hazard ... and I think also that everyone is pleased and

85

thankful because of this. They are all much happier when *you* are commanding the ship – why, the sailors are singing, are they not? I have never heard them sing before, not once. And the Baroness and I have had a most delightful day.'

Phillip flushed scarlet. 'Mademoiselle, I assure you—' he began but she interrupted him. 'In my opinion, for the little that it is worth, I consider it a pity that you cannot command it – her, I mean – all the time, Mr. Hazard!'

There was no adequate answer to such a statement and he found himself echoing her smile. 'To express such opinions on board a British ship-of-war is tantamount to mutiny, Mademoiselle Sophie! I cannot listen to you ... indeed, if I were to adhere strictly to my duty, I should order your arrest and hold you, under heavy guard, in your cabin until the Captain is able to deal with you.'

'And then, I suppose' – her tone was unexpectedly bitter – 'he would order me to be flogged, like your brother.'

Phillip was silent and Mademoiselle Sophie added gently, 'I did not intend that as a reproach, Mr. Hazard.'

'Are you sure?'

'Yes, I am quite sure,' she answered promptly. 'I have seen enough of your naval discipline – and of Captain North – to realize that you could do nothing to help your brother. That was why I intervened ...' he attempted to express his thanks but again she cut him short. 'I ran no risk,' she told him, 'and I knew that Captain North would listen to me, that he would take heed of what I said. The only thing that frightened me a little was that I had to show myself in front of all those men, that I had to walk past them all. I hesitated, I ... waited, hoping that the Surgeon would succeed in having the flogging stopped. But when he did not, then I was left with no choice – I *had* to show myself.'

'Then you saw it all?'

'The flogging? Yes.' She shuddered. 'It was horrible! I ... how is your brother, Mr. Hazard? I have inquired for him almost daily but no one could tell me.'

'He is recovering, mademoiselle,' Phillip said, conscious of shame. 'The Surgeon cared for him well and he is now fit for light duty. I have arranged, since he is a competent navigator, for him to assist the Master. In a day or so, if you would care to receive his thanks, I know that he would welcome the opportunity to tell you himself how much he appreciated your courageous intervention on his behalf.'

'I should like to talk to him, Mr. Hazard, I ... tell me about him, will you not?' She asked a number of questions, which Phillip answered as explicitly as he could, and he saw her face soften in pity as she listened. To his relief, however, Mademoiselle Sophie did not pursue the subject.

'I must go,' she said, looking at the tiny gold fob watch pinned to her dress. 'It is late and, as you say, the Captain would not approve of my being here at this hour by myself. But I am glad to have had this talk with you, Mr. Hazard.'

'I am glad also,' Phillip assured her, with sincerity. He offered her his arm. 'Permit me to take you below.'

'You are not busy?'

'No, not at the moment. I have, in any case, to make Rounds very soon, which will necessitate my leaving the deck. So ...' she accepted his proffered arm, smiling up at him again. 'Then thank you, Mr. Hazard. I should be grateful for your escort.'

Phillip took leave of her outside her cabin, feeling a warm glow in his heart when she asked him, with charming diffidence, if she and the Baroness might again take their mid-day meal in the gunroom.

'Of course, mademoiselle ... nothing would give us more pleasure.'

'You are very kind ... it will give me a great deal of pleasure, too. Good night, Mr. Hazard. À demain!'

'À demain, Mademoiselle Sophie ... good night.'

2

The next morning, Friday, Phillip exercised both watches aloft after Divisions and was well satisfied with the manner in which the men worked.

There was a fresh south-westerly breeze and *Trojan*, under a press of sail, ran briskly through the Cerigo passage. Logging 11 knots, she passed between the two Greek islands of Zea and Therima in brilliant sunshine, with scarcely a cloud in the sky. The weather appeared to be set fair but the glass was falling and the wind showing a tendency to shift and, from previous experience of the Greek Archipelago at this time of year, Phillip knew that the lovely scene could very quickly change to one of grey, storm-wracked desolation. He was uneasy and, as a precaution, ordered steam to be got up. Within twenty minutes of his issuing this order, however, the Chief Engineer came on deck in a state of some distress, to inform him apologetically that a piston had broken right across and that it would be necessary to disconnect the screw, while repairs were effected.

'How long will your repairs take, Mr. Forgan?' Phillip asked, careful to keep his feelings hidden.

The Chief Engineer mopped his heated brow with a scrap of cotton waste. 'At least four to five hours, Mr. Hazard,' he answered. 'But . . .' he gestured to the blue, cloudless sky. 'Let's hope you won't need the engines until we enter the Dardanelles. I can guarantee you'll have them then.'

The glass continued to fall throughout the morning and, before going below for dinner at two o'clock, Phillip studied the chart with the Master. The Doro passage had yet to be made and he warned Martin Fox, who had the Afternoon Watch, to give Cape Kafirevs a wide berth and to call him, should there be any deterioration in the weather. Although the sun was still shining as brightly as ever, some instinct led him, as an added precaution, to order double breechings rove on the guns, further securing these with tackles.

'Keep as much sail on her as you can,' he advised, 'but if it looks squally, shorten sail at once. I don't like the way that glass is behaving.'

The message he had been half-expecting all morning reached him just as he was finishing his meal. Martin Fox sent the midshipman of the watch to inform him that the wind was increasing and veering to the east and a heavy sea getting up. Having warned both passengers to remain in the gunroom, Phillip left them in the Surgeon's care and hurried back on deck, to find the sky ominously overcast and a squall in the offing. The watch, under Fox's instructions, were aloft taking in sail and sending down topgallant yards, when the main-mast look-out hailed the deck.

'Land on the port bow, sir!'

Phillip frowned. He stepped aft to the binnacle and nodded to Fox, who swiftly ascended the main rigging and, a few moments later, called out a confirmation of the look-out's warning. His description of the rocky point, towards which *Trojan* was being driven, was far from reassuring and a check of the chart showed Phillip that the ship was already nearly a mile off her course ... unless the Master had made an error in his reckoning. The whole sky was now as black as night and the surface of the water – so deceptively blue and calm, less than half an hour before – was being whipped to fury by the rising wind.

When Fox rejoined him on the quarterdeck, Phillip gave his orders. Both wind and sea were setting the ship on a dead lee shore and, with little sea-room in which to manoeuvre, he knew that he dared not attempt to lie-to until the squall passed. He would have to wear her round, under as much sail as she would carry, so as to claw her off-shore. With the screw to help, it would have been a comparatively simple matter to bring her head round but, under sail alone, there was bound to be some risk with this strong, shifting wind and he knew that he would have little margin for error. But ... his mouth tightened. It had to be done and he put a second man on the wheel, hesitating over his choice and finally deciding to entrust the task to his brother Graham, who had emerged from the chartroom at that moment.

'Keep her full but ease her a spoke or two when she sends,' he said and added, 'Be careful or she'll take the wheel out of your hands! When I give the word, luff all you can.'

'Aye, aye, sir,' Graham acknowledged, his face without expression. Phillip turned to Martin Fox.

'Mr. Fox ... hands to wear ship, if you please.'

'Aye, aye, sir. Bo'sun's mate . . . pipe "hands to wear ship". Man the main and fore braces.'

'As soon as she comes round, Mr. Fox, I want the main course on her,' Phillip decided. 'But wait for my order and have a reliable man standing by the mainsheet with an axe, in case we need to relieve her in a hurry.'

Martin Fox's brows lifted but he offered no criticism of this decision. Phillip stood by the compass. He felt oddly calm, aware that he had done all he could in the circumstances when, without warning, the sails lost wind and began to flap with a sound like thunder and he yelled to Graham to put up the helm. When her close-reefed topsails filled again, *Trojan* had broken off two points and the rocky shore loomed closer, marked by a line of foaming breakers a bare quarter of a mile to leeward now.

'How's her head, quartermaster?' Phillip asked, having to shout to make himself heard.

'Nor' nor' east, as she was before she broke off, sir,' Graham answered.

There was no time to be lost; the watch were at their stations for wearing, the after-guard of seamen and Marines standing by the braces and Phillip took up his position on the starboard hammock-netting, grasping the main-mast backstay to hold himself upright, as a deluge of water broke over the forecastle. He raised his arm, brought it down smartly and saw the men at the wheel brace themselves. A strong gust of wind struck the ship with alarming violence just as her head was coming round and he was flung off his feet, only saving himself by clinging to the backstay. The deck about him was strewn with struggling seamen, striving as he was to regain their footing as he yelled, at the pitch of his lungs, to Graham to put the helm up again. He and the quartermaster obeyed but for several seconds, which to Phillip seemed endless, the frigate lay like a log, shipping water fore and aft and heeling so far over that her lee channels were awash.

Then she righted herself and, rolling heavily, responded at last to her helm. The port watch of hammocks, hammock-netting and rails, together with a number of half-ports and a water cask vanished over the side but she came round, head to wind, as Graham and the quartermaster spun the wheel. Phillip, hoarse with the effort of making his voice heard above the roar of the wind, waved urgently to Martin Fox. The men at the braces took the strain, the yards came round and, with the mainsail set and the wind right aft, *Trojan* heeled and lurched her way to safety on the other tack, the rocky shore a boiling tumult of white water, now slowly receding.

Even now she was not out of trouble for, with the mainsail on her, she lay in the trough of the foam-crested breakers, forcing her way through them as if lacking the power to rise above them and a tremendous sea breaking over her, so that even the quarterdeck was awash. Phillip regained his vantage point in the hammock-netting, peering apprehensively aloft and watching the swaying masts, with a silent prayer that they would hold. Then, when he was satisfied that she had weathered the rocky point, he shouted to the man he had stationed at the mainsheet to use his axe. Relieved of her main course, the frigate steadied and lifted herself buoyantly to meet the next wave. The danger over, Phillip breathed a fervent 'Thank God!' as Martin Fox staggered across to join him, bent double against the tearing force of the wind.

'Just for a moment there,' he exclaimed breathlessly, 'I swear I could see the keel, Phillip!'

'So could I,' Phillip confessed ruefully, his voice all but drowned by the eerie howling of the wind in the rigging and the creak of straining timbers. He yelled hoarsely to the quartermaster to put the wheel amidships and added, 'You had better find out how much damage has been done, Martin, as soon as you're able to make your way for'ard. And you'd better relieve the men at the pumps, too ... we've shipped quite a lot of water, I'm afraid.'

'I'm afraid we have,' Fox agreed, with a shudder. 'I wouldn't want to go through anything as close as that again in a hurry, I can tell you.' He flashed Phillip a wry grin. 'I wonder what the Captain thought of it?'

They did not have to wait very long to find out. An irate message from Captain North demanded an explanation and Phillip dispatched a reluctant midshipman of the watch to make matters clear to their commander. By the time the youngster returned, the storm had passed over and Phillip shrugged off the reproof North sent back with him. The wind dropped as swiftly as it had risen and, within less than an hour, had shifted again to the S.W. Phillip ordered the watch aloft to reset sail and after a further hour, with most of the damage she had suffered set to rights and her engine repairs completed, *Trojan* was once more running free under all sail and the sun had reappeared.

The sunset that evening was magnificent. Both Mademoiselle Sophie and the Baroness von Mauthner – whose meal in the gunroom had been so rudely interrupted – ventured on deck to admire it and the beautiful prospect of the Archipelago spread out before them. Phillip pointed out landmarks to them, identifying some of the nearer islands and, on the pretext of showing her their position on the chart, took Mademoiselle Sophie to the chartroom, where Graham was at work.

She greeted him sympathetically but, in the presence of the Master and two cadets who were under his instruction, no conversation of a personal nature was possible. Graham himself, to Phillip's surprise, seemed in any case anxious to avoid speaking to her. She said, when they returned to the quarterdeck, 'He is a strange man, your brother, is he not?'

'Strange, mademoiselle?' Phillip shrugged. 'Yes, perhaps he is ... certainly he is a very embittered one. He has reason, of course, to believe that life has treated him badly. Apart from the unhappy termination of his naval career – which, no doubt, was his own fault – my father has disowned him and still refuses, to Graham's distress, to have anything to do with him. He was deeply attached to the old man and to my mother, too, of course ... and this hurt him more than anything, I believe. My father is a retired rear-admiral and at one time he and Graham were very close to each other ... so much so, indeed, that I was often rather jealous.'

'That is why he has joined the Navy again as an ordinary sailor?' Mademoiselle Sophie suggested. 'In the hope of regaining his father's respect?'

'He does not admit that this is his reason but I imagine it must be, yes.'

'Poor man!' Her dark eyes filled with tears. 'He has not made a very auspicious start, I fear. Tell me ... was it by chance that he was sent to H.M.S. *Trojan* or did you arrange that he should be sent because it – she – is your ship, Mr. Hazard?'

'No.' Phillip shook his head emphatically. 'I was not even aware that my brother was serving in the Navy, mademoiselle. Had I known ...' his tone was regretful, 'I should have done everything in my power to have him entered in any ship but this one, I assure you. However, he is one of a draft of seamen intended for distribution among the Fleet, so that I shall probably be able to arrange for his transfer soon after we join. In the meantime ...' he sighed.

'In the meantime,' Mademoiselle Sophie said, with a smile, 'you are endeavouring to keep him out of the Captain's sight, are you not?'

'Yes, mademoiselle,' he admitted. 'It isn't difficult while the Captain is indisposed, of course, but when he resumes command ...' he spread his hands in a gesture of resignation and, impulsively, she caught at his arm.

'Perhaps this may be an unkind and ... and *mutinous* thing to say but I hope ...' Mademoiselle Sophie's voice dropped to a whisper, 'I hope that Captain North may remain indisposed for quite a long time. As I told you last night, the sailors are happy when you are in command ... everyone is happy, there is a different atmosphere throughout the whole ship. You make a very kind Captain, Mr. Hazard.'

Phillip's colour deepened. 'I am only a lieutenant, mademoiselle, and besides—'

'But, Mr. Hazard ...' she halted and stood looking up at him, an odd challenge in her eyes and her soft young mouth again curving into a smile. 'This afternoon when that dreadful storm overtook us, we might have met with disaster had you not acted so quickly and efficiently. Lieutenant Fox told me what happened, so you cannot deny it. He was full of admiration for your seamanship and has done nothing but sing your praises ever since. And Lieutenant Cochrane said that had the Captain been in command—'

'I think, mademoiselle,' Phillip put in hastily, 'that you had better not tell me what Mr. Cochrane said ... it is almost certain to be mutinous.'

Mademoiselle Sophie met his gaze gravely but her eyes were sparkling. 'Well, perhaps he *was* a trifle indiscreet,' she conceded. 'But Mr. Cochrane is an exceedingly nice young man and he, too, admires you very much. Indeed I cannot find anyone who does not admire and respect you.'

'I am deeply gratified to hear that, mademoiselle,' Phillip assured her, 'but all the same I—' she ignored the interruption and went on, her tone pensive, 'On the other hand, Mr. Hazard, it is impossible to find anyone at all who has a good word to say for Captain North.'

'Mademoiselle, I beg you ...' scarlet with embarrassment, Phillip stammered something unintelligible, even to himself. Then, observing the approach of the Baroness von Mauthner on the Surgeon's arm, with the Captain of Marines and Anthony Cochrane on her other side, he thankfully led Mademoiselle Sophie across the deck to join them.

'Ah, Lieutenant Hazard!' the Baroness said, in her harsh, heavily accented English. 'It would seem, according to zese gentlemen, zat we owe our preservation from ze storm to you. I should like to express my sanks.'

'Lieutenant Hazard does not like to be thanked,' Mademoiselle Sophie informed her demurely. 'Not even for having saved our lives.'

The Baroness regarded Phillip in some bewilderment.

'But zis ees not a liddle sing, eet ...' she broke off with a shrug. 'Zen ve must respect his wishes ... tell me, Mr. Hazard, ven shall ve reach Constantinople?'

'On Monday morning, all being well, madame,' Phillip replied. He flashed her a grateful smile and then excused himself, conscious of Mademoiselle Sophie's eyes following him, a trifle reproachfully, as he descended the hatchway to the lower deck. Regretting his churlishness, he waited for her after the evening meal but she did not, as he was hoping she would, come on deck for her accustomed promenade and his disappointment was quite unreasonably keen. . . .

For the next two days, *Trojan* continued on her course in perfect weather and with a fair wind, exchanging numbers with several British ships and a Turkish and two French steam corvettes, with which salutes were punctilliously exchanged. The wind headed north during the late afternoon on Sunday and, aware of the strong current in the fifty-mile length of the Dardanelles, which made the Strait impassable to sailing vessels against a northerly wind, Phillip ordered steam up and the screw lowered. At sunset the ancient Castles of Sestos and Chanak-Kalessi were sighted and an hour later *Trojan* entered the Dardanelles, the mountains of Sintros and Lemnos, purple in the distance, offering a last glimpse of the Greek Archipelago.

As the light was fading, Mademoiselle Sophie came up to the quarterdeck. She came alone and, walking over to where Phillip was standing by the taffrail, held out her hand to him.

'I have come to bid you farewell, Mr. Hazard,' she told him and added, a catch in her voice, 'All things come to an end, do they not?'

Phillip accepted the proffered hand, holding it lightly in his own and Mademoiselle Sophie made no attempt to withdraw it. 'We shall all be extremely sorry to see you go,' he said lamely, conscious that this was an understatement.

'I shall be sorry to leave, too, Mr. Hazard.'

'You will leave when we reach Constantinople, mademoiselle?'

'Yes.' She bowed her dark head. 'So I understand. The Baroness von Mauthner received a note from the Captain this afternoon and it seems that everything has been arranged for our departure. A boat will be sent to take us ashore as soon as the ship drops anchor.'

'I see.' Phillip looked down at her bent head. It scarcely reached his shoulder and he stifled a sigh, aware that he would miss her and aware, also, with a sudden quickening of his pulse, of how strong an attachment he had formed for this strange, lovely girl – half-child, half-woman – whose real name he did not even know. He had sternly repressed his feelings up till now, had refused to admit that he had any feelings where Mademoiselle Sophie was concerned but he knew, when she raised her small, pale face to his, that they existed, whether or not he was prepared to acknowledge their existence. 'Will you stay in Constantinople?' he asked huskily, hoping against all reason that she would answer him in the affirmative and that this would not be the last time he would see her.

But she shook her head. 'No, I do not think so . . . for a few days, perhaps, that is all.' There was regret in her voice and, emboldened by this, he ventured to ask another question. 'When you leave Constantinople, where will you go, mademoiselle?'

'To my Mother's house,' Mademoiselle Sophie answered bleakly. 'And then I am to be married.'

Phillip stared at her, shocked out of the controlled calm he had imposed on himself. 'You are to be *married*?' he exclaimed, unable to conceal his dismay. He had imagined many things but not this and her announcement came as a completely unexpected blow to him.

'Yes,' she confirmed. 'It was arranged a long time ago, when we were both children. That was when we were betrothed.'

'When?' he demanded harshly. 'When is the marriage to take place?'

She continued to look up at him, meeting his shocked and unhappy gaze quite steadily, her face curiously devoid of expression. 'I do not know when, I . . . they have not told me. Perhaps not for some time. I . . . I hope not for some time, Mr. Hazard.'

'But . . . do you not love the man to whom you are betrothed, mademoiselle?' Phillip asked, making an effort to speak gently.

'*Love him?* But . . .' Mademoiselle Sophie drew a quick, startled breath, as if his question had taken her by surprise and her hand moved restlessly in his. His fingers tightened about it. 'Why, yes,' he prompted. 'Surely it is usual to have some regard, some feeling of affection for the man who is to be your husband?'

'In England, perhaps,' she conceded reluctantly. 'Not in . . . that is, not in my country, Mr. Hazard. I . . . I scarcely know the man to whom I am betrothed. I have only set eyes on him once in my life and that was when I was a child. I told you . . . it was all arranged a long time ago.'

Phillip stood looking down at her in uneasy silence. He felt deeply sorry for her and sensed that, although she, too, said nothing, she had sought consolation from him and needed more than his pity. Yet there was so little he could say without betraying himself, so little consolation he could offer to one in her position and in these circumstances. She was not an ordinary young woman of his own class and he could not, in honour, take her into his arms as, for a moment, he felt tempted to do, promising her his love and devotion . . . once she left the ship tomorrow she would, in any event, be beyond his reach. He would no longer be able to serve and protect her, however much he might desire to do so, and even to suggest that he could would be to deceive her, as well as himself.

He hesitated and then raised the hand he held to his lips. 'Mademoiselle, I can only offer you my sincere good wishes for your future happiness and prosperity. It has been both an honour and a source of great personal pleasure to me to have made your acquaintance.'

'Has it, Mr. Hazard?' Her voice sounded tired and she eyed him sadly as she withdrew her hand from his. 'I, too, have derived much pleasure from our acquaintance. I . . .' she managed a wan little smile, 'I hope that we may meet again one day. It seems improbable but I shall continue to hope for it just the same. So I shall say, "au revoir", Mr. Hazard, not good-bye.'

'Au revoir, mademoiselle,' Phillip responded. 'And a safe journey to your destination.' He walked with her to the main deck but, reaching it, she bade him come no further.

'It is perhaps better if I go alone, lest the Baroness see us together. I had told her that I was going to rest for a little while in my cabin but the maid, Anna, is in there packing and . . . I could not leave the ship without bidding you farewell. Also there is something I . . .' Mademoiselle Sophie opened the bead-trimmed reticule she carried and took from it a small package, carefully wrapped and sealed, which she put into Phillip's hand. 'I would like you to have this as a souvenir and a . . . a token of my gratitude for all that you have done to make this voyage so pleasant an experience for me. But please . . .' her smile returned, with all its familiar warmth and charm. 'Do not open the package until we have left the ship. Good night, Mr. Hazard . . . and may God have you in His keeping wherever you may go.'

She slipped quietly away, leaving Phillip gazing down at the tiny package in his hand, the muscles of his face stiff.

CHAPTER FIVE

I

SHORTLY before daybreak on Monday, 4th April – the seventeenth day of her passage from England – *Trojan* steamed into the Sea of Marmora. It was a misty morning, with a heat haze lying low over the water and Phillip set course for the Bosphorus, keeping the screw down and hugging the northern coastline so as to avoid the full force of the current.

Constantinople was sighted from the masthead some three hours later, appearing suddenly out of the mist and, a little later, the domes and minarets of the city's three hundred mosques could be seen from the deck, as the sun at last broke through the obscuring haze. The vision grew in enchantment as it came nearer and brightly coloured buildings, magnificent cypress groves and extensive gardens began to appear on both European and Asiatic shores, with the Bosphorus a gleaming silver ribband running between them. Passing the ruined Castle of the Seven Towers, *Trojan* rounded Seraglio Point and came to, within sight of the Mosque of St. Sophia at the entrance to the Golden Horn, her guns booming out in salute to the Turkish Sultan and Flag.

Mademoiselle Sophie and the Baroness paid a brief visit to the quarterdeck and, as Phillip prepared to take the ship into harbour, the watch below crowded up on to the forecastle, the men eager for a glimpse of the legendary Turkish capital. Every officer not on duty made an excuse to come on deck with the same intention and Phillip turned a blind eye to them, listening sympathetically to the excited comments of the naval cadets and midshipmen, for whom this was an experience they would probably never forget.

To his dismay, however, as the ship was nosing her way into her anchorage and the passengers went below, Captain North appeared unexpectedly on the quarterdeck. He still looked far from well, his angular face fine-drawn and lacking its usual florid colour but, although walking with obvious difficulty and discomfort, he announced his intention of going ashore immediately the ship dropped anchor. In reply to the polite inquiries which greeted his arrival, he returned testily, 'I have my duty to perform, whether sick or well and, it would seem, I am resuming command none too soon.' He glanced about him sourly, taking no pleasure in the glittering scene and, to the little groups of junior officers exclaiming in wonder at all they saw, he growled an ill-tempered order to go about their business. 'You are not tourists ... you are officers of Her Majesty's Navy and I'll thank you to remember it. Is the First Lieutenant unable to find you employment? Mr. Hazard, what are you thinking of to permit my quarterdeck to be used for sightseeing in this unseemly manner?'

The young officers reddened and moved hastily away, so as to leave the starboard side of the quarterdeck to their commander, who bellowed after them, 'Since you are so anxious to gape, gentlemen ... up to the cross-trees with you! You may do your gaping from there until such time as I see fit to bid you return to the deck, is that clear? Well, Mr. Hazard ... are you gaping too? Call away my gig immediately, if you please.'

Too angry to trust himself to reply to the rebuke he had received, Phillip murmured a clipped, 'Aye, aye, sir.' He called away the gig as soon as the ship was secured and, when North had departed alone and with due ceremony for the shore, he went back to the quarterdeck with Anthony Cochrane, who had the watch.

'One of these days, Mr. Hazard,' Cochrane said as, the watch set to the task of squaring yards and drying out sails, they paced the deck together, 'I fear I may forget that I am an officer in Her Majesty's Navy and then I shall tell Captain North precisely what I think of him. He will not find my opinion of him flattering, I can promise you!'

'Keep a guard on your tongue, Mr. Cochrane,' Phillip reproved him wearily. 'At any rate in *my* hearing. Your remark is insubordinate but I shall endeavour to forget it.'

'But, sir . . .' Cochrane protested indignantly, his Scottish accent very pronounced and his pleasant young face brick red. 'Captain North does not treat any of us – including yourself – as officers, does he? And he speaks to us, when he deigns to address us at all, as if we were dogs! It was quite unnecessary to masthead those youngsters . . . they were off duty and were doing no harm, we both know that. If I am insubordinate, it is because *his* attitude makes me so and because he—'

Phillip cut him short. 'That will do, Mr. Cochrane,' he said sharply. 'You are under Captain North's command and you will kindly remember that it is unbecoming in a junior officer to criticize his superior . . . no matter what provocation he may be offered. You'll be getting yourself into serious trouble if you don't have a care what you say.'

Cochrane was silent for a moment and then he challenged, his tone bitter, 'But you'll admit that he offers us considerable provocation, will you not, sir? And that although few of us have ever been here before, this' – his gesture took in the tantalizingly lovely view on all sides – '*this* is all we shall be allowed to see of Constantinople, if the Captain has his way. Even if we remain at anchor here for a week!'

'Distance lends enchantment . . .' Phillip quoted dryly. 'The city is not quite so beautiful, when you see it at close-hand, as it appears to be from here. The sanitation, for example, leaves much to be desired and the scavenging dogs – which here take the place of dust carts for the disposal of refuse – present a singularly unlovely spectacle to European eyes.'

'Yes, but even so, Mr. Hazard,' the young watchkeeper argued, 'one has surely an obligation to find out these things for oneself as, presumably, you did on your first visit here?

And of what crime are we guilty, that we should have our shore leave stopped at every port at which we call?'

There was no answer to his last question and Phillip turned away from him, frowning. From where he stood, he could see the floating bridge which spanned the Golden Horn at Tophana and served to connect the suburbs of Galata and Pera with the main section of the city, known to the Turks as Stamboul. In memory he saw much more, saw the narrow, precipitous streets of Pera – the Christian residential quarter – the shuttered houses with their quaintly shaped rooftops, the cypress-shaded cemeteries, the fountains and the brilliantly coloured gardens. He remembered the breathtaking beauty of the panoramic view from the Tower of Galata at sunset, as he had seen it years ago when, as a young midshipman, he had paid his first visit to Constantinople.

There was so much to see and marvel at in the Turkish capital, he thought nostalgically, in spite of its poor sanitation and the filthy, half-starved dogs ... there were the mosques, the palaces, the ruined Greek temples and the magnificent cemetery at Scutari, on the Asiatic shore of the Bosphorus. And there were the bazaars, a source of endless fascination to the European visitor ... he could still recall with what eagerness he had explored the roofed-in bazaars of old Stamboul and stared goggle eyed, at the displays of silver and brass ware, Oriental silks, embroidered shawls and finely woven carpets.

But ... Cochrane was almost certainly right in his contention that, even here, North would permit no shore leave. *Trojan's* officers and men would see none of these things if their commander had his way. They would not wander through the cool, colonnaded interior of the far-famed St. Sophia or the Mosque of the Sultan Achmet, or stare up at one of the city's thousand slender minarets, as the *meuzzin* called the Faithful to prayer from the narrow balcony which encircled its graceful, tapering spire. *Trojan's* bluejackets would be given no opportunity to bargain for souvenirs in the bazaars, no chance to slake their thirst at any of the bars on shore or enjoy a welcome change from their monotonous diet of salt junk, ship's biscuits and pease pudding. There would be no reception at the British Embassy for the senior officers, no picnics in the Valley of Sweet Waters for their juniors ... not even a brief excursion across the Bosphorus to Scutari, in a hired *caique*, to seek out relatives and friends among the newly arrived British Army drafts.

Indeed, Phillip reflected glumly, they might as well be on their way to the Black Sea as lying at anchor in one of the most picturesque harbours in the world. They had come to fight a war and he was suddenly impatient to begin the fight, eager to come to grips with the enemy and to have done with the time-wasting preliminaries, the incessant training exercises which were the prelude to war. He felt curiously depressed and as bitterly rebellious as the young officer he had reproved, only a few minutes before, for his outspokenness. It seemed a very long time since he had allowed himself to dream of escorting Mademoiselle Sophie ashore at Gibraltar and Malta ... now, within the next hour or so, in all probability, she and her guardian would leave the ship, their destination secret, so far as he was concerned, and he was unlikely ever to see her again.

He bit back a resentful sigh, conscious that his depression stemmed, in part at least, from the imminence of Mademoiselle Sophie's departure and Anthony Cochrane, misunderstanding the reason for his sigh, said apologetically, 'I am sorry I allowed my tongue to run away with me, Mr. Hazard. Perhaps you will be so indulgent as to forget that I spoke to you as I did.'

'Certainly, Mr. Cochrane, I shall be happy to do so.' Phillip made an effort to banish the thought of Mademoiselle Sophie's departure from his mind but Cochrane unwittingly reminded him of it, asking innocently whether he knew at what hour the passengers would be leaving the ship. He shook his head.

'I have not been told. Mademoiselle Sophie mentioned the possibility that a boat would be sent for them but, since no boat has yet arrived, I can only suppose that the Captain has gone ashore to make arrangements for their departure. They will definitely leave us today, I understand. But we are ready ... I had the winch rigged before you came on watch and the baggage is stacked below.'

'Where will they go when they leave us, sir?' Cochrane asked. 'Do you know?'

Again Phillip was compelled to admit that he had not been told and young Cochrane suggested diffidently that both ladies might be invited to partake of a farewell luncheon party in the gunroom.

Phillip was considering his suggestion when the midshipman of the watch reported the return of the Captain's gig. 'We no longer have time for our farewell party, Mr. Cochrane,' he said regretfully, as the gig came rapidly nearer.

'No, sir,' Cochrane conceded. He crossed to the starboard rail, his glass to his eye and focussed on the approaching boat. 'One moment, though, I rather think ...' he broke off, turning to face Phillip again with a grin. 'Perhaps we have, sir – the Captain isn't aboard.'

'Isn't he?' Phillip strode across to join him at his vantage point, hearing the 'No, no' in response to his hail which confirmed the watchkeeper's claim. 'Perhaps,' Cochrane added jubilantly, 'he has been taken ill a second time! Dare we hope for it, Mr. Hazard?'

It would have been hypocritical to reprove him and Phillip did not do so. But Midshipman Booth, who was in charge of the gig, shattered the insubordinate hope when he returned on board. He delivered a note from the Captain which Phillip read with puckered brows, although its meaning was abundantly clear ... the British Ambassador to the Sublime Porte, Lord Stratford de Redcliffe, would be coming in person to the ship to welcome her two distinguished passengers and later escort them ashore.

'*His Excellency,*' the note concluded, '*will be accompanied by Lady Stratford de Redcliffe and will be visiting H.M.S.* Trojan *unofficially and in his private capacity. Therefore, at His Excellency's own request, the cus-*

tomary honours will not be paid and no Salute will be fired.
His Excellency will, however, be received by a full side-party
and a Marine guard of honour and the ship's company will
muster in white frocks. All officers to wear frock coats and
swords . . .'

Phillip passed the note to Anthony Cochrane, whose smile
faded as he digested its contents. 'When, sir?' he asked, his
voice flat.

'Mr. Booth . . .' Phillip turned to the waiting midshipman,
'Did the Captain tell you at what hour His Excellency would
be coming aboard?'

'No, sir, he didn't say. But I don't think they'll be long, sir
. . . the Ambassador's boat is what they call a State caique, I
believe, and if that's the rum looking craft I saw as I left the
jetty . . .' the tall young midshipman gave a rueful shrug.
'Well, they were calling away her crew, sir, and rigging her
awning then. And the cox'un, who's been here before, told
me she belonged to the Embassy. His Excellency uses her to
travel between Therapia and the city, he said, sir.'

'In that case,' Phillip said, consulting his watch, 'we have
no time to lose, have we, gentlemen? Mr. Cochrane. . . .'

'Sir?'

'Pipe all hands to muster, if you please. And then hail the
masthead and tell Mr. O'Hara to keep a sharp lookout for
the Ambassador's barge. The rest of the youngsters can come
down and make themselves useful on deck. Mr. Booth, take
the gig round to the port side and secure to the main chains.
Mr. Lewis . . .' he gave his orders crisply, sending Lewis, who
was midshipman of the watch, scurrying below with instructions to inform Mademoiselle Sophie and her guardian of
the Ambassador's impending arrival and then to escort them
both on to the quarterdeck.

The youngster had scarcely departed on his errand than
the whistles of the boatswain's mates started to shrill, and
the watch below – due, in any case, to muster in twenty
minutes – came swarming up on deck in answer to the pipe.
For a time, all was confusion; then the petty officers formed
them up in their divisions, the divisional officers taking their

places in front of their men, most of them breathless from their hurried dash below to don frock coats and swords.

The Marine guard of honour, under Captain Murray, marched smartly into position, their booted feet thudding rhythmically on the spotless planking of the deck, as a small party of seamen lowered the accommodation ladder into place. Phillip descended to the entry port, buckling on his sword; the white-gloved side-boys came to attention and the boatswain's mates of both watches ranged themselves in two lines, facing each other, between the main deck guns.

They had not long to wait. A hail from Midshipman O'Hara, from the masthead, announced the approach of the Ambassador's *caique* and Phillip glimpsed young Booth's 'rum craft' skimming through the blue water of the harbour, propelled with considerable speed and skill by five pairs of dark skinned oarsmen. The *caique* was a large vessel, high prowed and resplendedly gilded, with a canopy covering its after-end, beneath which he was able to make out the figure of Captain North, seated beside an elegantly dressed lady in a picture hat ... evidently Lady Stratford de Redcliffe, the Ambassador's wife. The barge came alongside; the bowman, a slim youth in a scarlet *fez*, his white robes girt by a broad scarlet sash, reached deftly for the chains with his boathook and the craft lost way, as two of *Trojan*'s seamen, stationed at the foot of the accommodation ladder, drew her towards it.

The boatswain's mates put their pipes to their lips and the Marine guard of honour presented arms as, preceded by his wife, the British Ambassador ascended the ladder and stepped on to the deck, doffing his top hat in acknowledgement. He was a tall, upright man, Phillip saw, despite his seventy years, clean shaven and with a strong cast of countenance, his white hair thinning a little and worn a trifle longer than current fashion decreed. He had recently been raised to the peerage and, as Sir Stratford Canning, had had a very distinguished career in the diplomatic service of his country, mainly in Turkey where, if rumour were to be believed, he exercised considerable influence over the Sultan and his ministers. It was said that he had become arrogant and over-bearing with advancing years but, if this were so, Phillip thought, there was singularly little sign of arrogance in his manner now. Indeed, Captain North, thrusting himself past the side-party with scant regard for their alignment, so as to be in a position to receive the Ambassador and his wife when they reached the quarterdeck, was displaying far more arrogance than either of his guests ... Phillip saluted, his face expressionless, and stood aside to give the Captain precedence.

North ignored him and, making no effort to present him, led the way up to the quarterdeck where, dressed for departure, Mademoiselle Sophie and the Baroness von Mauthner were waiting. He did not witness their meeting with the British Ambassador but, a few minutes later, the whole party descended once more to the entry port, Mademoiselle Sophie on His Excellency's arm, North bringing up the rear with Lady de Redcliffe and the Baroness. He called the side-party to attention and himself stood at the salute, as the Marine guard of honour again presented arms and the boat-swain's mates blew shrilly on their whistles.

Reaching him, Mademoiselle Sophie hesitated momentarily, flashed him a swift, shy smile and then passed on, her small hand still resting on the Ambassador's deferentially extended arm. Phillip's last sight of her was as she took her seat beneath the *caique*'s white canopy, with Lady de Redcliffe at her side. She did not look up, did not wave as the be-fezed bowman released his boathook from the midships chains and she was talking gaily to her hostess when the *cajees* bent to their oars and sent the barge skimming at its usual rapid pace across the calm surface of the Golden Horn.

She had gone, Phillip told himself, his heart heavy and there could be little doubt – in view of Lord Stratford de Redcliffe's deference to her – that she was of royal birth. His fingers closed about the tiny package she had given him, which he had carried in his pocket ever since ... she had asked him not to open it until she had left the ship, but he was free, now, to do so. He was in the act of taking it from his pocket when the Captain called to him impatiently and he let it slide back once more into its resting place.

'Yes, sir?'

'For the Lord's sake, Mr. Hazard, where are your wits?' North demanded. 'Dismiss the ship's company ... they are still at attention, while you are woolgathering. And then see to the passengers' baggage without delay. It is to be sent to *Furious* at once.'

'To *Furious*, sir?' Phillip stared at him in some bewilderment. H.M.S. *Furious* was, he knew, a 16-gun paddle frigate commanded by Captain William Loring and forming part of the steamer squadron under Admiral Lyons' command in the Black Sea, and he had not been aware of her presence in Constantinople.

'She's coaling, Mr. Hazard,' the Captain explained irritably, 'and due to weigh for the Bosphorus this afternoon. If you get the luggage loaded smartly and send the cutter away with it at once, you may be in time to catch her. If not, then the cutter will have to go after her to Beicos Bay ... which is a pull of about ten miles, I believe, so perhaps you'll bestir yourself.'

'Aye, aye, sir.' Phillip knew better than to ask questions, when his commander was in this mood and he was turning away to carry out the order he had been given when North called him back.

'Pass the word for the Surgeon,' he said. 'I am going below and I am still far from well, unhappily ... so you will have to carry on. Prepare to coal ship first thing tomorrow morning. We shall sail for Kavarna Bay to join the Black Sea Fleet as soon as our coaling is completed.'

'Aye, aye, sir.' Phillip glanced at the ranks of motionless men, still standing to attention in their divisions and asked, his voice expressionless, whether shore leave might be granted to the watch below.

'Shore leave, Mr. Hazard? To this undisciplined rabble?' North's eyes were blazing. 'We shouldn't get half of them back.'

'But, sir—'

'That will do, Mr. Hazard. No shore leave is to be granted, in any circumstances, to anyone ... and that includes the officers. Is that clear?'

'Perfectly clear, sir.' From force of long habit, Phillip controlled himself. It was, in any case, only what he had expected, he thought bitterly ... and what Anthony Cochrane had predicted. But at least the ship was not to remain at anchor in the Horn for a week, which he supposed was something.

'We are not on a pleasure cruise,' North snapped, 'and the sooner this ship's company realizes it, the better. War is about to be declared at any time ... it may even, according to His Excellency, have been declared in England already. He hinted that it had, which I imagine means that he has been informed by telegraph, but he has to await the official dispatches before the news can be made public ...' his tone was expansive as if, Phillip thought, it gave him considerable pleasure to suggest that he had enjoyed the Ambassador's confidence during his brief sojourn at the Embassy. 'I shall be spending the night ashore,' North added. 'At Missiri's Hotel. ... His Excellency has invited me to dine with him. But now I am going to try to get some sleep and I'll thank you to see that I am not disturbed unnecessarily.'

'Very good, sir.' Phillip dismissed the ship's company and, having sent word to Surgeon Fraser that he was required in the Captain's cabin, he ordered 'make and mend clothes' to be piped for the watch below. To Martin Fox, who had taken over the deck from Cochrane, he entrusted the unloading of Mademoiselle Sophie's baggage.

Fox gave the necessary orders. He asked, as he and Phillip watched the baggage being winched up from the hold, 'But why is *Furious* to receive this luggage, Phillip, do you know? Are our passengers to be transferred to her also?'

Phillip shrugged. 'One must presume they are, although the Captain did not say so. And, as I've frequently assured you, Martin ... I don't know any more than you do about our passengers.'

'You still have not found out the real identity of our beautiful archduchess or her destination?' Fox pursued. 'Oh, come now, Phillip, you must have some idea! Did she not confide in you when you walked the deck with her last night?'

'No, she did not,' Phillip returned shortly. 'The extent of her confidence was the information that she expects to marry soon after she reaches her destination ... wherever that may be.' Again he fingered the little package which Mademoiselle Sophie had given him and finally, after some hesitation, he took it out of his pocket. 'She presented me with this, though, as a parting gift,' he confessed, reddening. 'With a strict injunction that I was not to open it until she had left the ship. Do you suppose that it may contain a clue to her identity?'

'Open it and see, my dear fellow!' Fox urged. 'That is the only way to find out, is it not?'

'You will keep it to yourself, if the package should contain such a clue?' Phillip asked cautiously.

'Of course I will, Phillip ... what do you take me for?' Fox laid a hand on his arm. 'I meant no affront to you – or to Mademoiselle Sophie – when I remarked on your walking the deck together. I happened to see you, that was all.'

'And you happened to draw the wrong conclusions,' Phillip accused wryly but Fox shook his head.

'No,' he denied, 'certainly not. She is shortly to be married, you say ... and I know you to be the soul of honour, Phillip my friend. Besides, it is evident, is it not, that our mademoiselle must be of royal blood? If I ever doubted that, Lord Stratford de Redcliffe dispelled my doubts this morning. He accorded her the most obsequious bow when he greeted her and his wife was about to drop her a curtsy when His Excellency drew her attention to the fact that the entire ship's company was standing watching her, so she changed her mind and merely bowed too. But the intention was there and people like the de Redcliffes don't bow the knee to just anyone. I'm quite sure.'

'No, I suppose not.'

'I am still curious to know who our mysterious arch-duchess really is.' Fox smiled. 'Open the package like a good fellow, I beg of you, and don't keep me in suspense any longer.'

'Very well but . . .' Phillip broke the seal on the tiny package. 'She told me that it was a souvenir and it may only be that . . . we may learn no more about her when we have opened it.'

'Nevertheless open it, for pity's sake or I shall be unable to contain my curiosity!'

Phillip prised open the wrapping, bringing to light a small leather-covered case. There was a ring inside the case, he saw, of heavy gold, set with a single, very fine emerald, obviously of considerable value and he stared at it in some dismay. He had expected a trinket, not a gift worth a small fortune and he was about to say so when Martin Fox leaned forward and took the ring out of its velvet-lined case. He held it up to the light and, as he examined the stone, his lips pursed in a silent whistle.

'It is a signet ring,' he said. 'But for heaven's sake . . . look at the device on the stone!'

Phillip peered over his shoulder, unable at first to make out what the device was intended to represent. 'Well, what is it?' he demanded. 'I can't see anything very startling about it . . . apart from its value, that is. Is it some sort of bird?

For answer, Martin Fox laid the ring on the palm of his hand. 'It is a double-headed eagle,' he stated flatly. 'The Imperial Russian Eagle . . . our mademoiselle is a Grand-Duchess, Phillip! Which at least explains the secrecy, does it not? And the haste with which she had to be conveyed here. Also . . .' he frowned thoughtfully, 'her destination.'

Phillip looked up, startled. 'You mean . . . Sebastopol?'

'Perhaps. Or Odessa. Wherever she's going, she has to reach her destination before the declaration of war. Hence the *Furious* . . . didn't you say that she would finish coaling this afternoon and get under way immediately afterwards?'

'Yes. But she's to call at Beicos Bay?'

'Which faces Therapia ... where the Ambassador has his summer residence, Phillip! My guess is that *Furious* will stay in the Bosphorus only long enough to pick up Mademoiselle Sophie and the Baroness ... then she'll weigh for the Black Sea. If the declaration of war is imminent – as it evidently is – then there will be British consular representatives and British residents to be brought here from Russian ports. No doubt that is why the *Furious* is being sent to ... well, wherever she is being sent, to Sebastopol or Odessa.' Fox's expression relaxed. 'Of course, that *has* to be the explanation!'

'Has it?' Phillip demurred.

'My dear Phillip, there's no other explanation.'

'But what was Mademoiselle Sophie doing in England if she is a member of the Russian Royal Family?'

'Several members of the Russian Royal Family were in England last summer,' Fox pointed out. 'Don't you remember? They were received by the Queen, it was reported in the Court circulars. Let me think ... yes, I remember. There was the Tsar's eldest sister, the Grand-Duchess Marie, widow of the Duke of Leuchtenberg, who stayed in Torquay with her children. There were also the Crown Prince and Princess of Wurtemberg – the Crown Princess was the Grand-Duchess Olga of Russia, another of the Tsar's sisters – who came on a State visit to London last July. They stayed at the Russian Legation and were attended wherever they went by the Russian Minister, Count Brunow. I can't recall exactly when they left but I do remember that the Duchess of Leuchtenberg remained in Torquay until the end of October, because my mother was there and she wrote and told me she had seen them. I believe they all crossed in the *Vivid* to France early in November.'

And Mademoiselle Sophie had been left behind, Phillip thought ... had she not hinted at something of the kind, when she had first talked to him on the train? What had she said, before the Baroness had warned her to be careful? '*I have been forgotten or overlooked*' ... and then, when he had complimented her on the excellence of her English, she had told him that she had been in England for nearly a year, for the purpose of learning the language. Yes, it all fitted neatly enough and, as Martin Fox maintained, it was the only explanation. Mademoiselle Sophie, the gentle, charming child he had admired so much was, he realized regretfully, a member of the Russian Royal Family . . . a niece, probably, of the Emperor Nicholas or, at all events, closely related to the despotic ruler of Russia. He had had three brothers as well as the sisters Martin Fox had mentioned . . . The Emperor Alexander, whom he had succeeded in 1825, the Grand-Duke Constantine and the Grand-Duke Michael, all of whom were dead. But they could have had children, Phillip supposed, and Mademoiselle Sophie might be one of them. Whoever she was, in the coming war she would be on the other side, the enemy side, cut off from him by more than time and distance . . . he caught his breath sharply.

Fox said, as if reading his thoughts, 'They are not pure Russian, you know, any of the Tsar's family . . . they all intermarry with Prussian, Austrian or Germanic royalty. The present Tsar's mother was a Wurtemberg princess and his wife is a sister of Frederick William of Prussia, is she not?'

Phillip shrugged despondently, 'That does not alter the fact that Mademoiselle Sophie is about to return to Russia and that we are about to go to war with the Russians, does it?'

'No, it doesn't,' Fox eyed him with a sympathy he did not voice and went on, with an abrupt change of tone, 'The cutter is loaded. Shall I call her away?'

'If you please.' Phillip returned the ring to his pocket. The cutter was under the command of Midshipman O'Hara, he recalled, who was an intelligent and trustworthy young man . . . 'Ask Mr. O'Hara to find out where *Furious* is going, if he can.' He sighed. 'For my own peace of mind, I should like to know her destination, Martin.'

'Yes, of course,' Martin Fox acknowledged. He crossed to the rail and, cupping his hands about his mouth, summoned young O'Hara to the quarterdeck.

Five minutes later, Phillip watched him take the cutter smartly away. He was back within an hour with the information that *Furious* had received orders to proceed with all possible speed to Odessa and, under a flag of truce, to take off the British Consul and any British residents who desired repatriation before war broke out. There was no mention, however, of *Trojan*'s passengers, whose baggage, according to Midshipman O'Hara, had been received and loaded aboard the paddle frigate without comment.

Trojan remained in the Golden Horn for a further forty-eight hours. Then, having coaled and taken on water and stores, she was ordered to Beicos Bay, where a further unexplained delay kept her at anchor for some six hours. There were a number of other British warships in the Bosphorus, including the steam-screw frigate *Niger*, 14, whose Captain, Commander Leopold Heath, had his wife with him at Therapia. Phillip, during one of Captain North's periodical absences on shore, contrived to visit *Niger* and dine with her First Lieutenant, from whom he obtained a good deal of useful information regarding conditions in the Black Sea.

North returned on board during the afternoon of Thursday, 7th April, declaring himself fit to resume command and finally, in company with H.M.S. *Highflyer*, a 26-gun steam-screw frigate commanded by Captain George Moore, *Trojan* was ordered to proceed to Baltchik Bay, off the port of Varna on the Bulgarian coast of the Black Sea, to join the Fleet. The two frigates weighed anchor at six that evening and, by three-thirty the following afternoon, sighted the combined British and French Fleets, lying at anchor in the bay.

They made a brave and impressive sight, Phillip thought as *Trojan* – following the movements of *Highflyer* – prepared to salute the flag of Vice-Admiral Dundas, flying in the three-decker *Britannia* of 120-guns. He counted seven British sail-of-the-line, including *Britannia* ... *Trafalgar*, 120; *Queen*, 116; *Albion*, 91; *Rodney*, 90; *Vengeance*, 84 and *Bellerophon*, 80. In the distance he also recognized *Aga-*

memnon the fine new steam-screw two-decker of 91 guns, in which the flag of Rear-Admiral Sir Edmund Lyons was flying, returning to the Fleet anchorage in company with the 70-gun *Sanspareil*, also steam-screw. There were a number of frigates, both sail and steam, and among these Phillip noticed the beautiful Symondite, *Arethusa*, 50, coming in under a fine press of canvas from the N.E., and the paddle steamers *Terrible*, 21; *Tiger*, 16; *Sampson*, 6; and *Inflexible*, 6.

Highflyer saluted the flag of Admiral Dundas and then, on running in and shortening sail, made the signal 'Where to anchor?' To this the flagship replied 'Where convenient.' She had run in under her screw but Captain North, without giving any reason for so doing, had ordered *Trojan*'s screw raised, stating that he was finished with engines ... with the intention, Phillip could only suppose, of demonstrating his seamanship.

It was, in the circumstances, a disastrous decision. *Highflyer* steamed slowly between the two lines of British ships, her hands aloft furling sail, and she came-to under perfect control at the end of the second line. *Trojan* had, perforce, to follow her but there was no room to haul to the wind and, with *Agamemnon*, *Sanspareil* and *Arethusa* also coming in, a signal from the flagship ordered *Trojan* to take a berth alongside *Tiger*, for which North had obviously not been prepared. Phillip, without waiting for orders, yelled to the topmen to sheet home top and top-gallant sails and, as the frigate ran the gauntlet between the two lines of anchored first- and second-rates, he watched apprehensively from the weather hammock netting, aware that the gap between them was narrowing.

From the quarterdeck, North issued confident instructions to the quartermaster which the unfortunate man, sweating profusely, did his best to obey. *Trojan*, lacking steerage way, cleared *Rodney* and *Bellerophon*, not without difficulty but, swinging, carried away *Albion*'s jib and flying jib-boom and snapped off her own close to the cap. It was an inauspicious beginning and called forth a rebuke from the flagship and an acrimonious signal from Captain Lushington of *Albion* when, finally, *Trojan* came-to and dropped anchor in her allotted berth. North, white to the lips with fury, blamed everyone but himself for his ship's unfortunate display. He put the wretched quartermaster under arrest and was in the process of dressing down both Phillip and Burnaby, the Master, who had the watch, when a second signal from *Britannia* ordered him to report aboard immediately. Burnaby called away his gig, while Phillip went to the forecastle with the Boatswain and Carpenter and a working party, to salvage as much as he could of *Trojan*'s damaged jib-boom and rigging.

He received a visit from *Agamemnon*'s acting First Lieutenant, who was an old friend and who brought with him Admiral Lyons' Flag-Lieutenant, Frederick Maxse. Having entertained them both in the gunroom, he was invited to dine on board *Agamemnon* the following day. He accepted the invitation with pleasure but added the cautious proviso that he might be unable to obtain Captain North's consent to his absenting himself, since all *Trojan*'s officers were under suspension of leave.

'So it is like that, is it, Phillip?' his friend Thomas Johnson suggested shrewdly and, when Phillip flushed uncomfortably, laid a consoling hand on his arm. 'All right, you need not answer my questions, old man. One hears rumours, even in the Black Sea, you know.'

'Rumours, Tom? What sort of rumours?'

Lieutenant Johnson exchanged a significant glance with his companion and the Flag-Lieutenant said quietly, 'Not particularly pleasant rumours, Mr. Hazard. The one I heard came from one of our senior officers, when your Captain's name cropped up a few days ago. Didn't he command the *Guillemot* brig on the West African Station, about eleven or twelve years ago?'

'Yes,' Phillip confirmed shortly, 'he did.'

'Then I need say no more. However ...' Lieutenant Maxse smiled engagingly, 'if it would make it any easier for you to accept our invitation, I can ask Admiral Lyons to endorse it. I'm sure he will ... he can't do enough for me at the moment, because he's about to replace me as Flag-Lieutenant with a nephew of his. Cowper-Coles of the *Sybille*, who is due here from the West Indies ... but in any case, you served with his son Jack at one time, Tom tells me, and that is a certain passport to the Admiral's table. So don't worry about obtaining your commander's consent, I'll see to it that you receive an official summons and we'll look forward to seeing you aboard *Agamemnon* tomorrow at noon.'

'Thank you,' Phillip acknowledged gratefully. 'I shall also be looking forward to the occasion.'

The official invitation to dine with Admiral Lyons on board *Agamemnon* was duly delivered that evening and North, returning in an evil temper from his visit to the Commander-in-Chief, gave his consent to its acceptance with a bad grace. But he gave it and Phillip was satisfied, despite the tirade of criticism and abuse to which he was subsequently compelled to listen and he made no protest when blame for the damage to *Albion* was attributed to his failure to wait for his commander's order to take in sail. It was, he decided philosophically, a small price to pay for the concession he had won.

He won another when, next morning, instructions came for the drafts of Marine artillerymen and seamen – to whom *Trojan* had given passage from England – to be distributed among other ships of the Fleet, in order to bring their complements up to strength. Captain North left this task to him, and Phillip contrived to send his brother Graham to the *Tiger*, to act as replacement for Captain Giffard's Second Master, who had had to be put ashore in Constantinople owing to illness. The appointment, although necessarily of uncertain duration, carried with it temporary promotion to warrant rank and Graham was delighted. They bade farewell to each other with some regrets but Phillip was thankful that he had managed to effect his brother's transfer when, within less than an hour of his departure to join his new ship,

North asked for him with the avowed intention of returning him to duty with the Main-top Division.

At seven bells in the Forenoon Watch, correctly attired in frock coat and cocked hat, Phillip set off in the duty boat for *Agamemnon*. . . .

CHAPTER SIX

I

HAVING, under the proud guidance of her acting First Lieutenant, inspected 'the finest steam-screw ship-of-the-line in the British Navy' from poop to engine room, Phillip was warmly received by Sir Edmund Lyons in *Agamemnon*'s spacious and well appointed after-cabin.

Here a party of about a dozen senior officers – most of them commanding ships of first or second rate – had gathered, at the Admiral's invitation, to dine with him. An excellent meal was served and Phillip began to enjoy himself, finding the atmosphere friendly and informal, despite the presence of so many officers of post-rank. A number of Admiral Lyons' guests, he realized, had served under his command as midshipmen in the *Blonde* and *Madagascar* frigates in the 'thirties. Among them were his Flag-Captain, Thomas Symonds, Captain Colpoys Dacres of the *Sanspareil*, Captain Thomas Mitchell of the *Queen*, Captain Stephen Lushington of the *Albion* and Captain de Saumarez Brock, who was attached to *Britannia*. Their friendship with their old commander had endured over many years and it was evident, as the meal progressed and conversation became general, that they all held him in the highest esteem and were looking to him – rather than to the Commander-in-Chief – for leadership in the coming war.

This was, perhaps, not surprising since Sir Edmund Lyons, Rear-Admiral of the White, had an exceptional record. He had been chosen for his present appointment, Phillip knew, because of his extensive knowledge of the area and, in particular, of the Black Sea. Although only second-in-command to Vice-Admiral Dundas, he had been

designated his successor before leaving England. An extremely
talented and courageous man, Lyons possessed the unusual
distinction of having made a brilliant career in the diplomatic service, after having served – with equal brilliance – in
the Navy until he was forty-five. He was now sixty-four, to
Admiral Dundas' sixty-nine, and had been British Minister
to the Court of King Otho of Greece from 1835 until the
summer of 1849.

It had been in this capacity, Phillip recalled, that – as a
young midshipman – he had first made his host's acquaintance. The Embassy in Athens had been open house to all
British naval officers, however junior, who had called there
during Sir Edmund's term of office and he still remembered
the many kindnesses he had received, in those far-off days,
from both Sir Edmund and Lady Lyons. Since then, in the
company of their younger son, Jack – Captain Edmund
Moubray Lyons, now commanding the steam-sloop *Miranda* in the White Sea – under whom he had served for a
time, he had met the Admiral on several occasions. The last
occasion had been nearly four years ago, when Sir Edmund
had spent a few months on leave in London at the termination of his Athens appointment, but he seemed to have
changed very little.

He had aged, of course, and his hair had turned white in
the intervening years but he had lost none of his driving
energy, none of the strong personal magnetism and charm
for which he had always been noted. Indeed, Phillip
thought, listening to a discussion he was having with Captain Brock, the Admiral appeared to possess more energy
than ever and his understanding of the present complex pol-
itical situation in the Balkans was – as befitted a man who
had spent the better part of fourteen years in Greece – im-
pressively well informed.

As if sensing his thoughts, Tom Johnson, who was seated
beside him, touched Phillip's arm. 'Our Admiral is a remark-
able man,' he observed softly. 'One of the most brilliant
commanders under whom it has ever been my good fortune
to serve. Who else could have returned to the Navy as he has,

after nearly twenty years ashore, as smoothly and efficiently as if he'd never been away? Who else could prove, as he's proved, time and again, that he's lost none of his professional skill, forgotten none of his early training? It is almost impossible to believe that his last active command was that of the *Madagascar*, which he relinquished when he went to Athens in 1835! His seamanship is as good as it ever was, which is saying a great deal, and I'd be prepared to wager that his knowledge of steam-power – both theoretical and practical – is at least as comprehensive as yours or mine. And we've both taken a course in steam, which the Admiral hasn't.'

'I'd concede you your wager,' Phillip answered smiling.

'It's a pity he ever left the Navy,' Lieutenant Johnson went on. 'Imagine what he might have achieved, if he had not ... a career which might well have emulated Nelson's. He was said to have the "Nelson touch", wasn't he, in Java in 1811 whenn he took Marrack Fort with two boatloads of bluejackets? And consider his early record, Phillip ... he was a commander at twenty-one and a post-captain before he was twenty-three. Nelson himself did not win promotion any more rapidly than our Admiral. He never talks about it, of course, but I've often wondered why he left the service because he obviously loves it.'

Phillip murmured a non-committal rejoinder. He knew, from what Jack Lyons had told him of his father, that as a young Post-Captain, Edmund Lyons had cherished a secret ambition to follow in the footsteps of England's most famous naval commander to whom, in his youth, he had borne a strong physical resemblance. But with the ending of the Napoleonic War, the need for economy had compelled the British Admirality to make a drastic reduction in the number of ships to be kept in commission. As a result, in common with a great many other brave and able officers, Captain Lyons had been placed on half-pay and his youthful dreams doomed to frustration.

Phillip sighed reminiscently, his own father's wrathful speeches on this subject fresh in his mind. The Navy List of 1816 had contained the names of two hundred admirals, eight hundred and fifty captains, nearly nine hundred commanders and upwards of four thousand lieutenants ... small wonder therefore that, in spite of his fine record, it had taken Edmund Lyons almost fourteen years to obtain another command. He had married and brought up a family when at last he was appointed to the *Blonde*, a 46-gun frigate, in which he had played a distinguished part in the blockade of Navarino in 1828. The following year, *Blonde* had been chosen to convey Sir Robert Gordon to Constantinople as British Ambassador, charged with a delicate diplomatic mission to the Porte and fate had taken a hand in deciding her commander's destiny.

Whilst there, Lyons had made so favourable an impression on the Sultan that he had obtained permission to embark on a cruise in the Black Sea. The *Blonde* was on record as the first British warship to pass through the Bosphorus – with the full knowledge and consent of the Turks – since the signing of the Treaty of Unkiar Skelessi, twenty years before. With the enterprise that was typical of him, Lyons had visited and drawn careful plans of the harbour defences and fortifications of Sebastopol and Odessa and he was said also to have conducted an extensive survey of the Black Sea coast ... one of the reasons, presumably, for his recall to the Navy and his present appointment as second-in-command of the British Fleet in the Black Sea.

The wheel, Phillip reflected, had turned full circle, so far as Admiral Lyons was concerned. It was evident, from what he was saying now, that he was aware of this and that he meant to turn his previous experience of the Black Sea to good account in the near future, if afforded the opportunity.

'The capture of Sebastopol and the destruction of the enemy Fleet based there is and must be our aim, gentlemen,' the Admiral stated. 'To me, the mere idea of our *not* striking a successful blow at Sebastopol is painful ... it haunts me in my solitary evening walks on the deck of this splendid ship. I am convinced that, if we do not leave our mark on the Black Sea this time, we shall have to do the work again before many years elapse. It is, of course, a question of men and money, as was the campaign which ended at Waterloo. But in my considered view – which is supported by Captain Drummond of the *Retribution*, in his report on its defences to the Admiralty – it will require a combined assault, by both land and sea, to take Sebastopol.'

'When, Admiral?' someone asked.

'This summer, I trust,' Admiral Lyons answered. 'That is the course I am urging on Sir James Graham and their Lordships. The measures already taken will be sufficient to ensure the safety of Constantinople and the Dardanelles ... even if the Turks are driven back from the Danube, they will have gained us time. And Omar Pasha is still holding out whilst inflicting heavy losses on the enemy ... a state of affairs which, he has assured me, will continue with the minimum of help from us. But the little knowledge I have of human nature leads me to believe that the Emperor of Russia will not knuckle under until he has been dealt some hard blows ... and certainly one of the hardest blows would be the destruction of his Fleet and the arsenal at Sebastopol.'

'You mean, sir,' one of the Captains asked, 'that we should launch an attack on Sebastopol – a combined naval and military attack – rather than go to the support of the Turks in the Danube provinces?'

The Admiral gravely inclined his head. 'Precisely ... and with as little delay as possible, we should effect a landing of the British and French Armies on the Crimea coast, covered by the Fleets.' He went into details, illustrating his points in time honoured fashion, by moving glasses and cutlery about the table in front of him, and his Captains crowded round him, listening with absorbed interest. 'We cannot take Sebastopol with our Fleets alone,' he said. 'On the other hand, once war is declared, there will be a great deal we can do, while we are waiting for the land-based forces to come to our support. By means of an effective blockade of the Russian ports and of raids on the coasts of Circassia and the Crimea – or even an attack on Odessa – I believe that we may compel the Russian Fleet to leave harbour and do battle with us. My plan would be this. . . .'

Phillip's spirits rose as he listened to the Admiral's cultured voice, expounding one bold, brilliantly conceived plan of action after another. He began to understand and share the admiration his brother officers felt for this white haired sailor-turned-diplomat, who had now returned to his old profession and whose enthusiasm for the task he had undertaken was so infectious. Admiral Lyons' whole heart, it was clear, was still very much with the Navy . . . as Tom Johnson had said, he might never have been away. He was very much at home here, in *Agamemnon*'s stern cabin among his ships' Captains, energetically discussing the finer points of naval and military strategy with men who respected his views.

Coffee was being served when, excusing himself to his other guests, the Admiral rose and came to take a chair at Phillip's side. 'Don't move, Phillip my boy,' he admonished, as Phillip made to get to his feet. 'This is an informal gathering and I just wanted a few words with you before you return to your own ship. You've seen my son Jack quite recently, I believe?'

'Yes, sir . . . *Miranda* was fitting out at Devonport at the same time as ourselves. I had the pleasure of dining with Captain Lyons several times, sir.'

'I'm delighted that he's been given another command. Tell me how you found him, will you?' There was pride in the Admiral's voice and a brightness in his eyes as he made this request and, aware of the strong bond of affection that existed between Jack Lyons and his father, Phillip did his best to comply with it explicitly and in detail. The Lyons family consisted of two sons – the elder, Bickerton, was in the diplomatic service and had remained in Athens after his father left – and two daughters, both of whom were now married. Lady Lyons, to whom they had all been devoted, had died the previous year in Stockholm, Jack had told him, and Phillip ventured diffidently to express his sympathy.

'I feel her loss very deeply, Phillip,' the Admiral confessed. 'But I was fortunate, we had a wonderfully happy life together . . .' he sighed and returned to the subject of Jack Lyons' new command. 'We've both chosen steam-screw. And you are First Lieutenant of *Trojan* are you not?'

'Yes, sir.'

'Steam is going to be the thing of the future, I am convinced. Though with regret . . . it will be a sad day for the Navy when engineers take the place of seamen. But that day will come, Phillip, however little we want it to . . . the writing is on the wall. You made a fast passage out here, I'm told?'

'Yes, sir. We had passengers on board who . . .' Phillip hesitated, uncertain of how much he ought to say about *Trojan*'s passengers in the hearing of others.

'I've also heard about your passengers,' the Admiral assured him. 'By this time, let us hope they have reached Odessa in safety . . . and before the declaration of war. *That* had not reached Constantinople when you left, I gather?'

'No, sir, not officially,' Phillip began, 'But—' he was interrupted by one of *Agamemnon*'s lieutenants, who came up to the Admiral, cap in hand, to announce that the *Furious* had been sighted.

'Good!' Admiral Lyons rose from his chair at once. 'Send a boat across to her as soon as she drops anchor, I'm anxious to learn how she fared on her mission. Do you hear that gentlemen? *Furious* is back from Odessa.'

Phillip drew in his breath sharply. He, too, was anxious to learn how *Furious* had fared and he postponed his departure, following the Admiral and his other guests on deck when, not long afterwards, the boat sent from *Agamemnon* was reported to be returning. The First Lieutenant of *Furious* was on board and his account of what had happened was given to Admiral Lyons in person, creating something of a sensation among the other listeners. The frigate, it seemed, had reached Odessa at daybreak on the morning of 6th April and had stood-in to the harbour, showing her British colours and a flag of truce.

'Captain Loring ordered me to take a boat ashore, also under a flag of truce, sir,' the First Lieutenant explained. 'I brought the – er – the two passengers with me, together with a letter addressed to the British Consul. We secured alongside the Quarantine Mole, sir, at about five-thirty and were met by an official of the Port Health authority. When I made my mission clear to him, sir, he told me – in very bad French – that I was too early but he promised that the Harbour Master would come out to us at six o'clock and that he would undertake delivery of the letter to the Consul. The passengers went ashore at their own request, sir, and when they had done so, I ordered my boat's crew to pull away from the Mole, sir, to wait for the Harbour Master.'

'And *did* the Harbour Master come out to you at six o'clock?' the Admiral asked, with interest.

The First Lieutenant shook his head. 'No, sir, and nor to the best of my knowledge was the Consul informed. I waited with my boat for nearly an hour and then I received a signal to return to the ship. Captain Loring came in to meet us and, as we were pulling back to the ship, sir, six successive shots from cannon were fired at us from one of the shore batteries. The last three, which were shells, were aimed at *Furious*. The direction of the shots was good, sir, but none had sufficient elevation and neither we nor the ship were touched.'

'But the fire was deliberate?'

'Oh, yes, indeed, sir . . . quite deliberate.'

'You were showing your British colours, as well as the flag of truce, were you not?'

'*Furious* was sir, all the time,' the young officer answered promptly. 'My boat showed a flag of truce only. And we did not return their fire . . . when I returned to the ship, the Captain gave orders to stand-off out of range. A Russian gun-boat came in close for the purpose of observing us, sir, and we gave chase. She escaped into Dnieper, after we had pursued her for about ten miles. After that, sir, the Captain deemed it expedient to rejoin the Fleet, in order to make a full report of what had occurred to Admiral Dundas and yourself. Captain Loring is aboard *Britannia* now, sir.'

'And the Consul?'

'We had to leave him, sir.'

'I see ... thank you,' Admiral Lyons acknowledged. He turned to the officers grouped about him, his expression grave. 'Gentlemen, I must see the Commander-in-Chief immediately. The British flag has suffered unprovoked insult and aggression and I believe that the threat of an attack on Odessa would be fully justified, the instant war is declared. I say threat advisedly for, if we threaten Odessa with the steam squadron, Admiral Nachimoff can scarcely continue to skulk behind the protection of the guns of Sebastopol, can he? We may well find out, before we are much older, gentlemen, of what stuff the hero of Sinope is made!'

There was a loud murmur of assent, followed by excited discussion, which was interrupted by the officer of the watch, who touched his cap. 'Signal from the flagship, sir,' he informed the Admiral. 'Requesting you to come aboard. Shall I call away your barge, sir?'

'If you please, Mr. Douglas.' Sir Edmund Lyons turned to his guests. 'I'll take my leave of you, gentlemen,' he told them, smiling. 'But it will not be for long ... you may expect to be summoned on board the flagship for a council of war very soon, if I have my way. And I rather think I shall.' He laid a hand briefly on Phillip's shoulder. 'Dine with me again, Phillip.'

'Thank you very much indeed, sir.' Phillip attended the Admiral to his barge and, after watching him depart with due ceremony for *Britannia*, accompanied by his Flag-Lieutenant Frederick Maxse, there was a general move on the part of *Agamemnon*'s visitors to return to their own ships.

The following afternoon, 9th April, the *Niger* arrived with dispatches from Constantinople. Within a few minutes of these being delivered to Admiral Dundas, the long awaited signal '*War is declared*', was broken out from the flagship's masthead, the date of the actual declaration in England being given as 28th March.

The signal was greeted with enthusiasm by the British Fleet. The *Albion*'s crew were the first to man her rigging and cheer, and her example was quickly followed by the other ships. *Trojan*'s men cheered as heartily as the rest, Captain North looking on without any visible sign of excitement or pleasure. At Phillip's urgent prompting, he gave grudging permission for an extra tot of rum to be issued with the men's evening meal but, apart from this, he made no concession to the prevailing spirit of exuberant optimism by which most of the other ships were enlivened. His men did not cheer him, as many of the other crews cheered their commanders, but he did not appear to be in the least concerned by the omission and, as usual, decks were scrubbed next morning before daybreak and *Trojan*'s seamen at exercise aloft soon after first light.

A frustrating delay of two days followed – due, it was said, to the failure of the official declaration of war to reach the French Fleet – and only the little 6-gun steamer *Fury* was sent to keep observation off Sebastopol. There was a constant coming and going between various ships and the two flagships, as senior commanders consulted with the Admirals. On the morning of 11th April, the French Commander-in-Chief, Admiral Hamelin, paid a visit to *Britannia* attended by his second-in-command and numerous staff. Soon after the French Admiral's return to his own flagship, the *Ville de Paris*, Admiral Dundas summoned his Captains to a final council of war, at which they received instructions to commence a rigorous blockade of the Russian Black Sea ports, in co-operation with the French Fleet.

Trojan received orders to proceed to Odessa in company with *Retribution*, a 28-gun paddle frigate commanded by Captain the Honourable James Drummond, *Niger* – Commander Leopold Heath – and the French steam frigate *Descartes* of 20 guns. The small squadron came-to off the Russian port on the morning of 13th. News of their coming had evidently preceded them, for a large crowd of townsfolk gathered on the cliff-top to watch their arrival.

The four ships stood off, out of range of the shore batteries, and a note addressed to the Governor, Baron Osten-Sacken, was delivered, demanding an explanation of the attack on the *Furious* and reparation for the outrage offered to the British flag. A boat from *Retribution* took the note to meet one which had put out from the shore and, as they waited for this to return, Phillip ascended to *Trojan*'s main-top and, his glass to his eye, subjected the harbour and what he could see of the town to a lengthy scrutiny.

It was a warm, sunny morning and everything looked very peaceful, the crowds on shore apparently regarding the approach of a squadron of enemy warships with more curiosity than apprehension. The guns, although manned and trained on the waiting ships, were silent ... their crews evidently under orders not to provoke aggression. The town, Phillip saw, was attractively laid out with trees and gardens, the houses built of stone and the tall spire of the Orthodox Cathedral rising above the gaily painted domes and cupolas of its numerous Moslem mosques and temples.

He studied the place with mixed feelings, recalling Mademoiselle Sophie's presence there and Sir Edmund Lyons' plans for an attack on the harbour defences. These, at first sight, did not look as formidable as he had imagined they would. There was a coastal fort to the west of the town, standing high up, and several batteries at intervals along the curve of the bay, well placed for their guns to dispute entry to the port. The harbour itself was an artificial one, formed by three long stone moles which projected into the sea and divided it into two basins, both of which were crowded with shipping. Each mole was guarded by a stone parapet, split with embrasures for cannon on the seaward side. The most powerful of these lay to the north of the cliffs – the Imperial Mole – with a fort at its extremity, from which the muzzles of some twenty-six heavy calibre cannon bristled menacingly. Behind the fort lay the Imperial Harbour and dockyard, with a number of ships on the stocks, and some stone buildings which appeared to be barracks, naval storehouses and an extensive arsenal, on the town side. As his glass swept the harbour, Phillip estimated that at least two hundred vessels of various sizes were sheltering inside, the majority small trading brigs and schooners which were congregated within the Quarantine Basin, several flying the British flag.

Niger and *Descartes* made a reconnaissance of the western side of the bay and both were returning to their anchorage when a brig, lying about fifteen hundred yards from the beach, unwisely showed Russian colours before slipping her chain and making sail towards the shore. *Niger* gave chase and, hooking her skilfully, towed her outside again, passing within range of a battery of eight guns which, to Phillip's surprise, did not open fire. *Descartes* stood in, to give her British ally support but no attempt was made by the Russian gunners on shore to interfere and, still triumphantly towing her prize, *Niger* steamed out of range. *Trojan*'s men cheered her lustily and *Retribution* signalled 'Well done, Niger.'

Next morning, no reply to his note having been received from the Governor, Captain Drummond of *Retribution* announced his intention of remaining off Odessa to await any communication that might subsequently arrive from the shore. He dispatched the rest of his squadron to commence a blockade of the coast – *Descartes* to proceed to the mouth of the Dniester river, *Trojan* and *Niger* to that of the Dnieper – their instructions to intercept and capture any enemy vessels they might encounter.

Captain North, returning from a conference on board *Retribution*, appeared not ill-pleased by the opportunity for prize-taking which his new orders offered. After telling Phillip to make sail, he added, a trifle sourly, 'It is to be hoped, Mr. Hazard, that Commander Heath, in his efforts to win promotion to post-rank, will not snaffle all the prizes.'

It had rankled with him more than a little, Phillip was aware, that Captain Drummond – although a few weeks junior to him – had been put in command of the squadron on the grounds of his greater local knowledge and experience, and his temper improved visibly as Odessa faded into the distance. There could be no disputing his right to give orders to *Niger*, since Leopold Heath was only a Commander, and *Trojan*'s Captain exercised his prerogative throughout the rest of the day, until the two ships parted company ... *Niger* giving chase to a Russian transport, in tow of a tug, *Trojan* in pursuit of a schooner.

Niger's prey escaped into the river where, without a pilot, Commander Heath could not follow her, but North showed the schooner no mercy, finally driving her ashore just out of range of the Russian fort at Kinburn, with which a few shots were abortively exchanged. She was carrying a cargo of coal and, when this had been transferred to *Trojan*'s depleted hold, he ordered her set on fire, since she was too badly damaged to be worth taking as a prize. During the next three days, however, five other small vessels were taken, two empty, the rest with cargoes of linseed, salt and oatmeal. North drove his ship's company relentlessly from dawn to dusk but for once – aware that they would eventually be entitled to a share of the prize money – the men did not resent it. They worked efficiently and well and, under screw or sail, *Trojan*'s speed was more than a match for any small trading ship to which she gave chase.

On 17th April, *Sidon* arrived and Captain Goldsmith brought orders for *Retribution* and *Descartes* to join him in an attack on the batteries at the Sulina mouth of the Danube. Due to bad weather, this attack could not be made until 19th, when *Niger* joined the rest of the squadron, leaving *Trojan* to patrol off Odessa and the Dnieper river mouth. On 20th, *Sidon* again brought orders from Admiral Dundas. The combined British and French Fleets were, it seemed, on their way to Odessa, and *Retribution*, *Trojan* and *Descartes* were instructed to join at once. *Sidon* herself – having run aground and sustained some damage during the attack on the Sulina forts – was to return to Varna for repairs, accompanied by *Niger*, the latter having gallantly gone in under heavy fire and towed her to safety.

That evening the two Fleets were sighted at anchor some four miles off Odessa. A summons to the Governor to surrender all Russian ships in the harbour and to send out British, French and neutral trading vessels – under the threat of a bombardment – had apparently elicited no reply. In consequence, arrangements for an attack were already being made and Captain North, in common with the other steam frigate commanders, was sent for by Admiral Dundas as soon as the squadron dropped anchor. Speculation as to the form the attack would take was rife on board the newly arrived ships, as officers and men waited impatiently for their commanders to return from the flagship.

Phillip was conscious of oddly conflicting emotions as he, too, waited for news. Somewhere on shore, he could only suppose, Mademoiselle Sophie must also be waiting and wondering anxiously what would transpire. No doubt if she could not see the forest of masts and spars rising above the Fleet anchorage, she would be aware of the presence of the great, menacing ships, would know that the Governor had given no answer to their ultimatum. It was a trifle ironic that the ship in which she had journeyed from England was, in all probability, to be one of those which would launch the attack, he thought wryly, and he wondered if she would see and recognize *Trojan* when the time came or whether, as he hoped, she was even now being taken to a place of safety outside the town. He had no means of knowing where she was or what dangers she might be called upon to face and . . . he gazed stonily at the distant shore. In spite of a natural desire to strike a telling blow against the enemy, he was aware of a strong and growing reluctance to take any personal part in the coming attack on the town which had given Mademoiselle Sophie shelter.

By the following afternoon, however, Phillip knew that he would have to do so. North, taciturn and uncommunicative as always, had told him nothing and was again absent aboard *Agamemnon*, where Admiral Lyons was said to be drawing up the final plan of attack, when Tom Johnson appeared alongside in one of *Agamemnon*'s boats. He greeted Phillip cheerfully when he came on board. 'I can only stay for a few minutes,' he apologized. 'Frederick Maxse is aboard *Vauban* on the Admiral's business and I am on my way to pick him up. But I thought you'd like to know that *Retribution* and *Trojan* are to lead the steam squadron in, when the attack on Odessa takes place. You'll go in under engines, of course, but instead of anchoring, each ship is to deliver her broadside and then retire out of range, while the next in line takes her place.'

Phillip's brows lifted in surprise. 'We are not to anchor? These are new tactics, are they not, Tom?'

Tom Johnson grinned. 'And no doubt you can guess from whose fertile brain they sprang! Admiral Lyons knows this harbour and the only thing that worries him is the probability of heavy casualties among your men. So he's devised this plan, which should keep them to a minimum. It may be a trifle unorthodox but it's a clever strategy, Phillip. You will be able to come close-in to the batteries, but you will present a moving target throughout the attack ... out of range as you reload, of course, and only in range for the length of time it takes you to discharge your broadsides, in turn with the other ships of the squadron. Look, I got Frederick Maxse to help me make a sketch to illustrate how it's to be done ...' he took a folded sheet of paper from his pocket, spreading it out for Phillip's inspection. 'The whole squadron will wheel and circle in a radius of half a mile, do you see?'

'Yes, I do indeed.' Phillip studied the sketch minutely, impressed by its ingenuity. 'Which ships will be engaged, do you know?'

Tom Johnson nodded. 'It is to be a combined British and French operation, Phillip, undertaken by light-draught steam frigates only. As I told you, *Retribution* and *Trojan* will lead the lines, then *Descartes* and *Mogador* to maintain French honour, followed by *Terrible* and *Tiger* of ours, *Vauban* and *Caton* of the French and finally *Furious* and *Sampson*, with *Highflyer* in reserve. Your targets, you'll observe' – he jabbed an explanatory forefinger at the sketches – 'are to be the harbour fortifications and the fort and arsenal on the Imperial Mole, as well as the Russian ships sheltering behind it. And the dockyard, of course, if you can reach it ... but the town itself and all neutral vessels in the Quarantine Harbour are to be spared.'

Phillip was immensely relieved. 'I am thankful,' he confessed, with feelings, 'that the town is to be spared.'

'Well, it is certainly a more civilized conception of war than what occurred at Sinope,' Tom Johnson agreed. 'For which, as you say, we can be thankful ... again to Admiral Lyons since, according to Maxse, he is responsible for the decision. On his advice, the Commander-in-Chief has directed that the line-of-battle ships are to take no part in the bombardment, beyond supplying rocket-boats, whose fire will be directed by Commander Dixon. This means that only military targets will be attacked and those from close range, so that there will be less danger of random shots falling on the town.'

'Good,' Phillip approved. He folded the plan and returned it to its owner. 'When are we to launch the attack?' he inquired. 'Or hasn't that been decided yet?'

'The Commander-in-Chief's ultimatum expires at sunset,' Lieutenant Johnson told him. 'If the Governor rejects it and fails to give up the ships he is sheltering – including our own and the neutrals – then I understand that the attack is to begin tomorrow morning, as soon after daybreak as possible. The Admirals are hoping, of course, that word may reach Sebastopol by telegraph in time for the Imperial Fleet to sail to Odessa's defence. If Nachimoff decides to try conclusions with us, we shall be waiting for him! Well ...' he extended his hand. 'I must go, I promised I would not keep Frederick waiting. Good luck to you tomorrow, Phillip. I'm sure that *Trojan* will acquit herself well.'

'Thanks, Tom,' Phillip said, with sincerity. 'I am more than grateful to you for telling me what is in prospect. Captain North ... that is, I did not know very much, I—'

'Having met your commander, I'm not surprised,' Tom Johnson put in dryly. 'He is not very forthcoming, is he ... particularly to his inferiors in rank?'

'No, not very, I'm afraid. But—'

'I did not take to him,' *Agamemnon*'s acting First Lieutenant admitted. 'And since I had, in any case, to pass under your stern, I thought I would call on you and make sure you knew what was going on. Also ...' reaching the entry port and his waiting boat, he paused, eyeing Phillip gravely. 'Also it occurred to me that you might feel some concern for the passengers you brought from England, the two ladies whom *Furious* put ashore here recently. I reasoned that you would feel some qualms at the prospect of being ordered to bombard the city where they had taken refuge ... and, indeed, that few of your ship's company would welcome it. I hope I've been able to set some of your fears at rest because – if they are still in the town, your passengers should be in no serious danger.'

'I'm much in your debt, Tom.'

'Nonsense, my dear fellow. It was the least I could do.' Tom Johnson swung himself down into his boat and took his place in the sternsheets, a hand lifted in farewell as the boat cast off.

Phillip returned to the quarterdeck where Martin Fox, who had just come to watch, assailed him with a spate of eager questions.

'Pass the word for the Gunnery Officer, Mr. Fox, if you please,' he said formally and then, relenting, put an arm round Fox's shoulder. 'Tomorrow, Martin, we are to bombard Odessa with a combined steam frigate squadron. But between then and now, we have work to do, so beat to quarters, will you please? When Sutherland joins us, I'll explain the plan of attack Admiral Lyons has worked out, which I've just had expounded to me. It is unorthodox but I believe it will be successful ... and the town itself is to be spared.'

'And so, let us hope, will our poor little Grand-Duchess,' Fox answered soberly. He gave the necessary orders, a grim little smile curving his lips. . . .

2

It was still quite dark when, on the morning of 22nd April, orders came from the steam frigate squadron to clear for action.

On board *Trojan*, the men went about their preparations

with grim purposefulness, mingled with a certain apprehension common to both the experienced and those who had never seen action before. Hammocks were sent up and stowed in the nettings during the Middle Watch, the decks sanded and, after an early breakfast eaten by the light of lanterns – for which only the hardy few had any appetite – the galley fires were damped down. Mess tables and stools were triced to the overhead beams of the deck above, bulkheads taken down and, as the ship's company were drummed to quarters, the Surgeon and his assistants took possession of the midshipmen's berth on the lower-deck shifting four sea-chests together to form an operating table.

Below decks, the felt-lined copper doors of the magazines were opened, the Marine sentries stood aside and soon a procession of powdermen and ammunition carriers converged in the darkness of the narrow alleyways in the bowels of the ship, to begin passing up supplies of powder and filled cartridges for their guns. On the main and upper decks, the guns' crews stood to their guns, six men to each, with six others to assist in running out, training and elevating the gun. The tompions were removed from the muzzles, the vents cleared, the match-tubs half filled with sand in readiness to receive the lye-soaked matches on their linstocks, when the guns' captains set them alight.

Admiral Lyons' plan of attack called for starboard broadsides to be fired in succession so, the previous evening, Phillip and the Gunnery Officer had placed as many 32-pounders from the port batteries as they could contrive to fit into the starboard side of *Trojan*'s upper deck. Since the action was likely to be prolonged, Phillip had men from the port-side guns' crews standing by to relieve those on the starboard side, and the powdermen and auxiliaries serving each gun also had their reliefs, to ensure that there should be no delay in reloading and bringing the guns to bear.

The cable was hove in and, as the squadron awaited the signal to weigh, *Trojan*'s starboard guns – including the two long 52-pounder, pivoted guns on the forecastle – were elevated to 1,200 yards range, loaded with shell and run out through the open port-lids. At four bells in the Morning Watch, the expected signal was broken out from the mast-head of *Britannia*: '*Weigh and proceed.*'

The signal midshipman, glass to his eye, read and repeated the order to the Captain, his young voice commendably steady.

'Very good.' North's voice was as devoid of emotion as the expression on his face. 'Carry on, Mr. Hazard.'

The boatswain's mates put their whistles to their lips and the links ground harshly through the hawse pipe, as the order was obeyed. In line astern of *Retribution* and followed by the eight other British and French steam frigates composing the squadron, *Trojan* steamed towards Odessa's Imperial Harbour. Phillip, standing motionless on her quarterdeck, felt the muscles of his stomach knot into a tight, painful ball and, glancing at North, saw that the Captain's normally florid countenance had drained of colour, although it retained its mask-like blankness.

Every gun which could be brought to bear on them from the shore opened fire as *Trojan* and *Retribution* approached the Mole but the first few salvoes fell short and *Retribution*, holding her course without deviation, discharged her first broadside and put her helm over. *Trojan* followed her, the roar of her guns deafening and her decks wreathed in smoke, which cleared slowly as she, in turn, put about to yield her station to the French frigate *Descartes*. One by one the ten ships of the attacking squadron discharged their starboard broadsides and, each tracking in the wake of her next ahead, wheeled in the circle which Admiral Lyons had envisaged.

The Admiral's unorthodox plan of attack proved extremely successful. The gunners on shore were accustomed to aiming at stationary targets and anchored ships and they were confused by the constant twisting and circling of their attackers, as well as by the heavy volume of fire to which their batteries were subjected. No sooner had they managed to find the range of one ship than she had passed on, making way for her successor in the ever-revolving circle. An almost continuous cannonade was maintained, each ship delivering her fire from that point in her orbit which was nearest to the enemy, then wheeling and reloading her guns the instant they were discharged and once again, in her turn, coming into the attack. In spite of this and the naval gunners' increasing accuracy, the Russians replied with praiseworthy steadiness. Those manning the 26-gun battery in the fort on the Imperial Mole pounded away ceaselessly, firing a stream of red-hot shot, shells and chain-shot ... the latter, even when it passed overhead, wreaking havoc with the spars and rigging of the attacking ships.

Within an hour the French frigate *Vauban* of 20 guns was set on fire by red-hot shot and, blazing furiously, was forced to withdraw from the circle, out of range. As boats from the Fleet went to her assistance, H.M.S. *Highflyer*, 26, took her place. A small dispatch-steamer – which Phillip thought he recognized, through the smoke of battle, as the 2-gun *Banshee* – arriving with mail from Constantinople, disputed with *Highflyer* for the honour, until she was recalled by a signal from the flagship, which she obeyed with obvious reluctance.

Some distance away from the circling steamer squadron, the 50-gun sailing frigate *Arethusa*, employed for the purpose of intercepting any Russian ships that might attempt to escape, was fired on by a coastal fort. Under all sail and brilliantly handled by her commander, Captain William Mends, *Arethusa* accepted the challenge. Sailing majestically in, she fired her port broadside, tacked and fired her bow guns, then hove about to fire her starboard broadside and finally wore round and brought her stern guns to bear. She continued her classically executed manoeuvres, to the admiration of the watching Fleet until she, too, was recalled by a signal from *Britannia*, to which she responded with even greater reluctance than *Banshee* had shown. She was enthusiastically cheered when at last she returned to the Fleet anchorage.

As the morning wore on, *Retribution* was hit but she remained in action, concentrating her fire on a battery mounted on the quay of the so-called Port de Pratique, from which a dangerously accurate rain of red-hot shot appeared to be coming. Phillip drew Captain North's attention to this battery and, receiving permission to direct *Trojan*'s long 52-pounders at it, had the satisfaction of recording several hits, which eventually silenced all but one of its eight heavy guns.

The guns on the south side of the fort on the Imperial Mole began to find the range of the circling ships, however, and despite an extension of the circle's orbit, *Retribution* and *Sampson* were hulled half a dozen times and the foremast of one of the French ships went over the side and she steamed out of action. *Trojan*, after seeming to bear a charmed life, received a direct hit from a shell, which struck the starboard side of her quarterdeck and, narrowly missing the crew of the after-52-pounder, tore up the deck planking as it exploded, three of the gun's crew being injured by flying splinters.

The men were not severely wounded but one of them cried out blasphemously in pain and Phillip, hurrying across to their aid, happened to glance back at his commander and was shocked by what he saw. Captain North had been several yards from the path of the exploding missile and in no danger from it but he was now standing as if transfixed, his gaze fixed on the charred timber it had left in its wake, his cheeks ashen and his big body trembling violently. He recovered himself almost immediately and shouted for the Surgeon but Phillip was left with the uneasy conviction that, for an unguarded moment, he had seen the real North beneath the bullying and the bluster. And if he had . . . he fought down the anger which rose in him. If he had, he thought resignedly, then God help *Trojan* should she be called upon to face any more dangerous opposition than she was facing at this moment. He knelt beside the man who had cried out and said reassuringly, 'All right, lad, we'll get you to the Surgeon . . . I don't think you're too badly hurt.'

North said nothing. When the injured men had been taken below to have their wounds dressed, he snapped an impatient order for replacements to be put on the gun and then, turning his back, abruptly vanished below. He returned to the quarterdeck, ten minutes later, his breath smelling strongly of rum. . . .

The bombardment continued, seemingly with little effect and, just before one o'clock, H.M.S. *Terrible*, 21, commanded by Captain James McCleverty, signalled that she – as the most powerfully armed of the British frigates – would endeavour to put the fort out of action by closing the range. She steamed close in to the extremity of the Mole and, although greeted by a fierce hail of shot and shell and hit a score of times, she maintained her course and gallantly held her own fire until she was within seven or eight hundred yards of the fort.

Her commander's courage was rewarded as, her four squat funnels belching thick clouds of black smoke and her paddle-wheels churning the water about her to a frenzy, she came about and brought her heavy 68-pounder Lancaster cannon to bear, firing these, as well as a shower of rockets, with deadly accuracy. The rockets landed on a shed at the rear of the Imperial Fort, which instantly burst into flames. The flames spread to the magazine and this blew up with a dull roar, the violence of the explosion shattering part of the outer wall of the fort, the rest of which was soon caught up in the general conflagration. The garrison fled in terror, as a series of explosions brought their stronghold crumbling about them, and *Terrible* was cheered to the echo by the crews of the other frigates when she returned to her station.

A signal from the flagship, relayed by *Sanspareil*, ordered the squadron to stand in closer and continue the bombardment, concentrating on the destruction or capture of the Russian ships lying inside the Imperial Harbour and the dockyard beyond. One by one they obeyed, wheeling into line ahead and running the gauntlet of the guns mounted on the Quarantine Mole, which had hitherto been unable to bear on them effectively. *Retribution*, supported by *Sanspareil*, broke off to engage the Quarantine batteries. Her attack, although it failed to silence the Russian guns, enabled a number of British and French trading vessels to escape in the confusion from the Quarantine Harbour, bravely flying their national colours.

The rest of the steam frigates pressed on towards their original objective, followed now by the rocket-boats, which were rowed or towed into position. A Russian corvette, abandoned by her crew, was the first victim, a shell from *Tiger* penetrating to her magazine and blowing her to pieces. Two new warships, together with several other ships still in the course of construction, were burnt on the stocks, and a brig, a sloop of war and an armed schooner sunk. Half a dozen others, laden with supplies, were captured and towed out into the bay by the victorious frigate squadron, *Trojan* taking an armed schooner and twenty-five prisoners.

Before long, despite the spirited resistance of a troop of horse artillery which unlimbered and opened up on them unexpectedly from the quay, the rocket-boats, ably led by *Agamemnon*'s Commander Dixon, entered the Imperial Harbour. There they destroyed a quantity of naval and military stores and munitions of war and set the dockyard ablaze. The fires spread, fanned by a strong breeze, to the lower part of the town and – due, in part at least, to the inefficiency of Odessa's fire service – took a strong hold. By dusk, when the signal came to break off the engagement and return to the Fleet anchorage, much of the town was burning fiercely and a pall of flame-tinged smoke hung heavily over the rest of it.

Phillip gazed back at the devastation they were leaving behind them, his heart heavy as distress succeeded the excitement that, during most of the action, had buoyed him up. Admiral Lyons had wanted to spare the town and its civilian inhabitants, he thought sadly, but the strong wind, for which he had not bargained, had made this impossible. The fires had spread too rapidly for the damage to be confined strictly to military targets and inevitably, whatever had been the Admiral's intention, the civilian population would suffer. He felt conscience-stricken, wondering again whether

Mademoiselle Sophie had remained in Odessa and, if she had, where she was now, conscious of a haunting anxiety and a longing – which, he knew, could not be gratified – to go ashore in search of her.

Beside him, the Captain said thickly, his smoke-grimed face relaxing in an unaccustomed smile of satisfaction, 'Well, we have dealt the Russians a blow they won't forget in a hurry, Mr. Hazard ... and at a surprising small cost to ourselves. We can repair most of the damage we have suffered in under twenty-four hours and we haven't lost a man.' He gestured to the charred ruins astern, the gesture contemptuous. 'Soon, let us hope, we shall leave Sebastopol in a similar state. I confess I am eager for that day to come.'

'I don't imagine that we shall find Sebastopol quite so easy as we found Odessa, sir,' Phillip demurred. 'We met with no opposition from the Russian Fleet today but, if we launch an attack on Sebastopol where it is based, it must be a different story, I think ... quite apart from the fact that the fortifications are said to be very formidable. I understand Captain Drummond reported them to be impregnable from the sea and—'

'Have you no stomach for such a fight, Mr. Hazard?' North put in, a sneer in his voice. 'Let the Russian battle squadrons come, I say ... and the sooner the better. We shall be more than a match for them, ship for ship.'

Phillip avoided his gaze. 'Perhaps we may be, sir,' he began, 'Although I hardly think—'

Captain North ignored the interruption. 'There is nothing to equal British naval discipline and training,' he stated, with conviction. 'You've seen proof of that today, have you not? Or has the lesson been wasted on you?'

'I do not believe so, sir.'

'Thanks to my insisting on the maintenance of proper discipline aboard *this* ship,' North went on. 'Her crew bore themselves well and did all that was required of them. I am not yet by any means satisfied with the standard of discipline we have achieved but ... it is better than it was when I assumed command. So you may send all hands to dinner as soon as the galley is functioning again, Mr. Hazard, and you may order the grog ration doubled, as a mark of my approval of the manner in which the ship's company conducted themselves today.'

'Aye, aye, sir,' Phillip acknowledged. He tried not to think of the expression of stunned terror he had surprised on his commander's face a few hours before and added a dutiful, 'Thank you, sir, I will see that the Divisional Officers pass the word to their men, sir.'

Young Lieutenant Sutherland appeared, at that moment, looking unutterably weary, to report all guns secured and to request permission to dismiss his guns' crews. North gave the required permission with a curt nod and, since he offered no praise, Phillip said, choosing his words carefully, 'The Captain has expressed his approval of the manner in which your men conducted themselves today, Mr. Sutherland. It is his wish that you inform them ... and he has ordered the grog ration doubled, as a mark of his approval.'

Sutherland's exhausted, sweat-streaked face lit up as he stammered his thanks. When he had gone, North said, with heavy emphasis, 'The fact that we have been in action is not to be made an excuse for slackness, Mr. Hazard. Let that be made quite clear ... and see that you remember it yourself. Small thanks are due to *you* for the measure of efficiency and discipline this crew has attained. But I trust I shall be able to count on better co-operation from you in the future.' Afraid to trust himself to reply, Phillip was silent, hoping to be given his dismissal. When this was not forthcoming, he ventured diffidently, 'Will that be all, sir?'

'No, it will not be all, Mr. Hazard. I shall require a full report of the damage we have sustained as soon as we drop anchor. And' – the Captain glanced skywards, his eyes narrowed – 'there will be a moon, which should give you enough light to work by, should it not?'

'To work by, sir?' Phillip stared at him in unconcealed dismay. 'But the men are exhausted, sir, they—'

North waved him to silence. 'They are seamen, not children, Mr. Hazard, and this is a ship of war,' he stated coldly.

'The duty watch will commence repairs to spars and rigging at once. Give them an hour for dinner and then put them to work . . .' he issued a string of orders and then said, his smile thin, 'I intend *Trojan* to be the first ship in the squadron to declare herself ready for sea. If she is, then the Admiral can hardly refuse my request for an independent patrol . . . and I want some prizes, prizes I don't have to share with three or four other commanders.' He jerked his head in final dismissal, his expression one that discouraged argument. 'Very well, you may carry on, Mr. Hazard. And I shall expect you to have the ship ready for sea by tomorrow afternoon, if you please.'

With the exception of a few minor replacements of burned and splintered deck planking, *Trojan*'s repairs were completed by the following evening, when the First Dog Watch was called. To her commander's chagrin, however, his request to be given an independent patrol was refused, without explanation, by Admiral Dundas. She was sent instead to Constantinople, acting as escort to some damaged British merchant vessels which had escaped from the Quarantine Harbour during the bombardment. In addition, she took a number of prize ships to be sold by auction to the Turks, returning with their crews to rejoin the combined British and French Fleets off Sebastopol on 4th May.

CHAPTER SEVEN

I

THE Fleets had been at anchor off the Russian Naval Base for a week but, prudently refusing to accept the challenge which their presence offered, the enemy line-of-battle ships remained behind the shelter of their guardian fortresses, making no move to pick up the gage of war. In an effort to provoke them to action, Admiral Dundas eventually yielded to the pleas of his second-in-command and directed him to lead a combined steamer squadron on a series of harrassing raids on the Crimean, Georgian and Circassian coasts.

Admiral Lyons divided his force, sending *Highflyer*, *Trojan*, *Niger* and *Firebrand* to Kertch Bay, at the entrance to the Sea of Azov, under the command of Captain Moore of *Highflyer*, with orders to sink, burn or capture enemy merchant shipping and to destroy military stores on shore. A second squadron, under the Admiral's personal command and including three French ships, made for Kaffa Bay on the north-east of the Crimean peninsula with a similar purpose.

Neither expedition took any prizes. *Niger*, with a Turkish pilot aboard, sighted two Russian merchant brigs on rounding Cape Takti and gave chase, only to run herself aground on an uncharted ledge of rock ... from whence it took five hours hard work on the part of the crews of her sister-ships to free her. Admiral Lyons decided to proceed to Anapa in *Agamemnon*, taking *Highflyer* and *Firebrand* with him, his intention to raid and reconnoitre the coast and, if possible, make contact with the Circassian chief, Schamyl, in order to assist his revolt against the Russians.

Trojan, to Captain North's intense disappointment, was

ordered to rejoin the Fleet with the damaged *Niger* in company. He obeyed sullenly, bewailing his ill fortune but his hopes rose once more when, on 11th May, *Trojan* was dispatched to patrol the coast off Odessa, with *Tiger*, *Niger* and *Vesuvius*. 'If we can contrive to get away on our own,' he confided to Phillip, with unusual expansiveness, 'we may yet take a few worthwhile prizes. I think we'll shape our own course to Odessa. Pass the word for Mr. Burnaby to report to me with his charts before we sail.'

The four frigates left the Fleet anchorage at noon. Captain Giffard of the *Tiger*, as senior officer, took command and just before dusk, signalled the course he intended to steer during the night. It was agreed, much to Captain North's satisfaction, that in the event of parting company, all four would rendezvous off Odessa the following day but no definite hour for the rendezvous was specified. When darkness fell North, having set his chosen course, retired for the night in a better humour than he had been for weeks.

But when day dawned a thick fog shrouded the whole coastline in mist and it was impossible to see the bows of the ship from the quarterdeck. Duncan Laidlaw had the Morning Watch and, when Phillip came on deck to join him soon after five bells, an impenetrable curtain of dank white vapour hemmed *Trojan* in on all sides. She was running under engines, in accordance with the Captain's instructions, but at reduced speed, with look-outs doubled and a man at the lead, taking regular soundings and Laidlaw asked, when he had reported these precautions, whether he ought to stop the engines until the fog cleared.

'It's a real pea-souper, is it not, sir?' he observed and Phillip, frowning, agreed that it was. The Captain's permission would have to be sought before he could order the screw raised but ... he went to consult with the Master and study the charts. They were apparently in no immediate danger of running ashore; nevertheless, with *Niger*'s example before him, he decided to take no risks and dispatched the midshipman of the watch to make a report to Captain North and ascertain his wishes with regard to the continued use of the engines. North, without coming on deck, ordered them stopped.

At eight o'clock the watch changed and Anthony Cochrane relieved Laidlaw. The ship being hove to, Phillip went below for breakfast, for once able to to take his time over the usually hurried meal, which he shared with Martin Fox. When he returned to the quarterdeck, he was startled to hear the sound of gunfire, coming from somewhere fairly close at hand and he reproved Cochrane sharply for not having informed him.

'I'm sorry, sir,' the younger man apologized. 'But it has only just started and I did not pay it much heed. We're only a few miles from Odessa and I took it for granted that the garrison were engaged in firing practice. Those aren't naval guns, surely, sir?'

Phillip listened. The swirling mist distorted all sound but the gunfire, he was convinced, was not coming from Odessa, which was still four or five miles to westward of the ship's present position. He could distinguish the crackle of musketry and the deeper, muttering roar of cannon and his brows came together in a puzzled frown, as he mentally visualized the coastline. There was, if his memory was not at fault, no fort on this part of the coast ... it was a place of high cliffs and a shelving, rocky shore devoid of habitation, and there seemed no logical explanation of the thunderous cannonade which was now disturbing the fog-bound silence.

Unless, of course, a British ship had run aground there – one of the three making, with *Trojan* herself, for the agreed rendezvous off Odessa ... he said crisply, 'Call the Captain, if you please, Mr. Cochrane. That's no garrison exercise, I'm sure.'

North, when he came on deck a few minutes later, agreed with him and, a trifle to his surprise, concurred with his suggestion that *Trojan* should approach cautiously and investigate the cause of the firing. The screw was lowered and, proceeding at a careful three knots, Phillip took the ship closer inshore, as the ship's company went to quarters and the guns were manned. After covering about a mile, the depth of water decreased so sharply that the Captain refused to proceed any further.

'Our charts are by no means accurate,' he said, 'and I'm not going to risk running on shore in this infernal fog. There's nothing to be done but drop anchor and wait until it clears.'

'But suppose one of our squadron has beached herself, sir,' Phillip objected. 'Surely we ought to make some attempt to go to her assistance?'

'How do you suggest we do so, Mr. Hazard?'

'With your permission, sir, I could run in with the cutter,' Phillip offered and, again to his surprise, North nodded, after a slight hesitation. 'I share your anxiety, Mr. Hazard,' he admitted. 'So take command of the cutter by all means and see if you can find out what is going on. But do not attempt to engage the enemy if they are merely exercising and, if *Trojan*'s help is required, return at once and report to me. I'll have a bugle call sounded at five minute intervals, to enable you to regain the ship.'

The cutter was lowered and, so thick was the all-enveloping mist that, after less than a dozen strokes of the oars, *Trojan* vanished from sight. Phillip stood in the bows and, guided by the sound of gunfire, called back directions to Midshipman O'Hara at the tiller. After rowing steadily for about a mile, they could hear voices and the thud of bare feet running across wooden deck planking, but the voices were too far away to make out what language they were speaking and a prolonged burst of cannon-fire swiftly drowned them. As they drew nearer, it became evident that some of the firing was coming from the grounded ship and Phillip knew that his instincts had not been at fault . . . a ship had run ashore and the chances were that she was British and one of his own squadron. He called to the cutter's crew to give of their best and the men responded with a will.

Within about a hundred and fifty yards of the shore, the fog dispersed and on the cliff-top, bathed in watery sunshine, he was able to make out seven or eight field guns, served by green uniformed Russian artillerymen, supported by at least two companies of infantry and a squadron of cavalry. The field pieces were firing down at the *Tiger* lying, helpless as a stranded whale on the rocky, shelving beach a hundred and twenty feet below, and within about thirty yards of the foot of the cliffs. Her foremast had been shot away and she was virtually defenceless, for, in a vain attempt to gain sufficient elevation for his starboard guns to reply to the enemy cannon, Captain Giffard had all but careened her. She now lay on her port beam, her starboard guns pointing skywards at so acute an angle that they could not be fired effectively. A single 32-pounder, mounted on her upper deck, spat brave but abortive defiance at her enemies and her colours, Phillip saw, had not been struck. The single gun, heroically though it was being fought, was no match for the eight that were ranged against it and, stretched prone on the cliff-top, marksmen with muskets and Minié rifles were picking off any member of the crew who exposed himself within the compass of their fire. An anchor, laid out astern of the grounded frigate, and two upturned boats, waterlogged and riddled with holes, bore mute witness to the efforts of her crew to warp her off the rocks.

Phillip's heart sank, as he took in the scene. Even as he watched, a shell struck *Tiger*'s forecastle, scattering a group of seamen and Marines who were endeavouring to haul a second gun into position. This was followed by a shower of red-hot shot, some of which fell on the quarterdeck, causing tongues of flame to creep ominously along the deck planking. He hesitated, recognizing – or imagining he recognized – his brother Graham among those who ran forward with a hose to fight the flames.

His first instinct was to go in and take off as many men as he could but, a moment later, he thought better of it. The cutter could not, with safety, hold more than a dozen or so and many of *Tiger*'s crew were probably wounded. Besides, his reason told him, when the soldiers on shore caught sight of her, the cutter, too, would become a target and he dared not risk that.

'Put her about, Mr. O'Hara,' he ordered urgently. 'We must get back under cover of the mist and then try to guide *Trojan* in. If she can bring her guns to bear on that battery on shore, she may be able to drive them off. It will be *Tiger*'s only chance . . . and possibly our own. So pull for your lives, my lads, before they sight us!'

A tense 'Aye, aye, sir,' from O'Hara answered him but, before his order could be obeyed, the watchers on the cliff-top had seen the cutter. There were shouts, some of the green-uniformed gunners tugged their field pieces into position so as to bear on their new target and, between *Tiger* and the cutter, the surface of the water was spattered by a hail of musket balls as the infantrymen opened fire. A shell shrieked overhead, another exploded prematurely and fell short but two round-shot, coming unpleasantly close, straddled the cutter's bows. Her crew pulled frantically on their oars, needing no urging as O'Hara put her about, and Phillip yelled to the coxswain to send up a distress rocket in the faint hope that, despite the fog, its bright orange trail might be seen from *Trojan*'s quarterdeck.

The coxswain had managed to set his rocket fuse alight and the curtain of mist, for whose concealment they were making, was drawing appreciably nearer when the field guns fired a second salvo, less accurate and a good deal more ragged than the first. All the shots passed harmlessly overhead, with the exception of a single round-shot, which struck the water some distance astern of the lurching boat. This appeared to offer no danger but it ricocheted off the surface of the water and, its approach so slow that Phillip watched it in horrified fascination, it hit the cutter amidships, smashing an oar and tearing a gaping hole in her port side, between gunwale and waterline. Miraculously only one of the two seamen, between whose straining bodies the missile made its exit, suffered any injury but the boat's bottom boards were stove in and the coxswain, still clutching his rocket and match, was flung overboard.

Water started to pour in through the cutter's shattered hull and despite her crew's attempts to plug the hole the

Russian round-shot had left in its wake, the level rose too rapidly for those who were bailing to keep pace with it. Phillip knew that it would only be a matter of minutes before she sank although, relieved of the dead weight of the men she was carrying, she might stay afloat long enough to support the non-swimmers and the man who had been wounded ... at least until the fog cleared sufficiently for *Trojan* to pick them up. He hesitated, reluctant to order them to abandon the boat, yet aware that he would have to do so very soon, if she were not to be lost to them altogether.

Faintly above the crackle of another volley of musketry from the sharpshooters on shore and the moaning whimper of the wounded seaman, he heard the distant sound of a bugle call and remembered North's promise to sound a call at five minute intervals, to guide him back to the ship. His mind made up, he stepped carefully to the injured man's side and took a firm grip of him beneath the armpits, ready to lift him into the cutter's bows. The man, a young A.B. called Lacey – a mizzen-topman, Phillip recognized – looked up at him and managed a twisted grin. His right leg had been crushed to a shapeless, bleeding pulp about which someone had tied a belt, in the hope – a vain one – of arresting the bleeding. But there was no time to attend to that now, if any of them were to survive. ...

'We shall have to swim for it, my lads,' he said, having to shout to make himself heard. 'Strong swimmers, try to get back to *Trojan*, if you think you can make it ... she's about a mile to the sou'east, and the bugle calls will give you her direction. Non-swimmers, over the side and hold on to the cutter ... she should keep you afloat, if there aren't too many of you. The rest ... make for *Tiger* and good luck. Right .. over you go, stroke oar first.'

Phillip had intended to wait until all her crew had left the sinking cutter and then, being a strong swimmer, endeavour to return to *Trojan* but suddenly he found himself chest-deep in water, the wounded Lacey clinging to him with the strength of desperation. He freed himself, with difficulty, from the choking hold and dragging Lacey after him, struck out instead for *Tiger*. A patter of what, for a moment, he imagined was rain struck the water in his immediate vicinity and then he realized, with a sense almost of disbelief, that the Russians were firing at him from the cliffs . . . using cannister. Fortunately their aim was poor and he was unscathed and although the swim seemed endless, he reached his objective at last. Two of the *Tiger*'s seamen, clinging to her midchains, helped him on board and relieved him of his limp burden.

Breathless and gasping, Phillip gained the entry port and turned to look back, hoping against all reason that a few of the cutter's crew might, like himself, have come safely through the murderous barrage of cannister and musket balls. But there were no bobbing heads, the short expanse of water was empty and one of the seamen, following the direction of his gaze, said gruffly, 'Most of them turned back, sir, when the Russians opened up on you . . . they swam back into the fog and they was trying to tow the cutter. But that gives 'em a chance, sir . . . a better chance than we've got against them murdering devils up there.' He jerked his head shorewards. 'They're just using us for target practice, I reckon, because we ain't got nothing to hit back at 'em with, and that's the truth, sir.'

Aware that it was, Phillip felt anger catch at his throat but he offered no comment and, when he could get his breath and was able to stand upright unassisted, he asked to be taken to the Captain. 'And . . . you'll see this lad of mine receives attention, will you not? He's lost a lot of blood, I'm afraid.'

The *Tiger*'s two bluejackets exchanged unhappy glances. 'Your lad's dead, sir,' the elder of the two told him. 'And Captain Giffard . . . why, he was hit some while ago, when they first started firing on us. In a bad way, he is or so they say. I'll take you to the First Lieutenant, sir, he's in command now.'

Tiger's First Lieutenant was on the upper deck, leading a fire party with reckless disregard for his own safety, as they fought to extinguish the leaping flames in which the frigate's forecastle was enveloped. Phillip's news of the presence, close at hand, of *Trojan* brought a brief smile to his smoke-blackened face. 'If we can hold out until this thrice-damned fog clears and *Trojan* can come to our aid, we may have a chance. But to tell you the truth, Mr. Hazard, I don't think we *can* hold out for much longer without heavy loss of life. I was on the point of hauling down our colours when I spotted your cutter coming in and hoped it meant that immediate help was on the way. If *Trojan* cannot get to us at once, then . . .' he shrugged despondently. 'The Captain is severely wounded, he's lost his left leg and poor young John Giffard, his nephew, has lost both legs and is dying. We've a bo'sun's mate and a boy killed and at least a dozen others wounded. And' – he gestured to the charred and shattered deck – 'you can see the state we're in. If this fire reaches our magazine, there'll be none of us left to tell the tale, will there? Tell me frankly . . . what are the chances of your Captain bringing *Trojan* in before the fog lifts?'

Phillip peered into the heavy pall of fog to seaward. *Trojan* was, perhaps, less than a mile away but without the bugle call – which had ceased – he could not tell even in which direction she lay. Those on board could have no conception of *Tiger*'s desperate plight, still less could they know how urgently their help was needed. Unless some of the cutter's crew had managed to swim back to her . . . young O'Hara, perhaps, who was a strong swimmer and a brave and resolute young man. Or the coxswain but . . . he sighed. It would be a miracle if any of them found their ship and Captain North would not risk coming any closer inshore, would not be justified in doing so, without positive evidence of the extreme danger of *Tiger*'s position and . . . a boat to guide him in. He turned to *Tiger*'s First Lieutenant.

'Captain North will not come in unless the position is made clear to him,' he said regretfully. 'But if you can give me a boat, I believe I could find my way back and—'

'I'm sorry, Hazard.' His companion wearily cut him short. 'We've no seaworthy boats. They've all been damaged and we lost one when we were trying to warp the ship off when she first went aground. We worked for three hours to get her off, you know ... and then they found us. A cavalry patrol on shore sighted us and gave the alarm. They brought up their artillery and have been pounding away at us ever since.'

'Without giving you a chance to surrender?' Phillip exclaimed, shocked. *Tiger*'s temporary commander wiped the sweat from his brow. 'We were offered the choice between surrendering with our guns intact or being blown to extinction,' he answered bitterly. 'By some arrogant young Russian princeling who appears to be in command ... look, you can see him up there, on a grey horse. Colonel Prince Andrei Narishkin or some such name. The Captain refused his terms and—' he broke off, yelling an order to his fire party as more red-hot shot tore into the blackened deck. Within a few minutes the gun's crew were driven from their gun by smoke and heat, bringing their supply of filled cartridges with them which, in obedience to their First Lieutenant's order, they dropped overboard.

The First Lieutenant said to Phillip despairingly, 'It is no use attempting to hold out any longer. I cannot watch all my men die when now we are unable even to answer their fire, can I?'

'No,' Phillip confirmed. 'You have done all in your power, all that honour demands.'

'I shall ask Captain Giffard's permission to strike our colours,' the First Lieutenant decided. 'If he is conscious ... if not, I must strike them on my own authority, so as to avoid further unnecessary loss of life. Half our guns are already overboard ... we'll spike the rest and throw them out too. The Russians shall not have them ... they've cost us too much for that.' He glanced up at the ensign still flying from *Tiger*'s main-mast and his voice was choked with emotion as he added, 'Oh, God, if only the fog would lift so that *Trojan* could see us! But it isn't going to lift in time, is it, Hazard?'

Phillip could only shake his head. Left alone, he went to join the fire party and, bearing a hand with one of the hoses, found Graham at his side, although it was a moment before he recognized his brother's face beneath its thick coating of sweat and grime. They looked at each other and Graham's cracked lips twitched into a rueful smile. 'Well, so we meet again, Phillip ... though I wish it were anywhere but here.'

'I wish that, too,' Phillip agreed.

Graham passed a hand over his filthy, perspiring face. 'Where's *Trojan*? Too far away to save us, I suppose?'

'She's less than a mile away, Graham ... but in this fog, she might as well be fifty.'

'That was what I feared,' Graham returned, his voice harsh with disillusionment as he eyed the swiftly spreading flames. 'Are we to burn to death in heroic defence of the honour of the British flag, do you know? Or shall we surrender ourselves to languish as Russian prisoners for the duration of the war? Because ...' his answer was supplied by a shouted order from the quarterdeck. The British colours were hauled down and, after a momentary delay, a Russian flag run up in their place. Firing from the shore diminished and finally, when a leaking boat put off from *Tiger* under a white flag, it ceased altogether.

When the boat returned, after a lengthy parley with the Russians, orders were issued for *Tiger*'s crew to go ashore and give themselves up. Ironically the first boatload was on its way when, with startling suddenness, the fog cleared and *Trojan* could be seen, less than a mile astern, with *Vesuvius* another mile or so further out to sea. Both ships were at anchor but with steam up and Phillip, watching them anxiously, saw a signal flutter from *Trojan*'s masthead which he read, with bitterness, as '*How can I assist you?*'

'Half an hour ago,' *Tiger*'s First Lieutenant said, his glass to his eye, 'I should have replied to that question on my knees, thanking God for our deliverance. Now ...' he lowered his glass, leaving the sentence uncompleted. 'Your cutter's there, what's left of her, Hazard, so at least some of your men must have got back to their ship. Only they weren't in time either, were they? Unhappily for us ...'

again he left his sentence unfinished and went, shoulders bowed and walking like an old man, to superintend the removal of his Captain and the rest of the wounded to the boat which was awaiting them.

Phillip stayed where he was. He saw *Niger* steaming up from the direction of Odessa and she, too, signalled an inquiry concerning the assistance that had come – tragically – so much too late. All three frigates, receiving no reply from the stricken *Tiger*, approached cautiously, their gun-ports open and their crews at action stations. Glasses were trained on beach and clifftop, as the signals were repeated. *Niger* altered course and ran out her port side guns, directing them at the cliff-top battery but did not fire.

Phillip measured the distance between himself and *Trojan* and started to strip off his already sodden jacket. He was not a member of *Tiger*'s crew and therefore, he thought, would be breaking no pact to surrender if he were to endeavour now to swim back to his own ship. He had reached the rail, his jacket over his arm, when Graham – evidently divining his intention – shouted something he could not make out and pointed urgently shorewards. To his dismay he saw that the Russian artillery men were once more manning their guns and the first of these, still trained on *Tiger*'s upper deck, opened fire with shell. A fresh rain of missiles, which included redhot shot, descended upon her forecastle, as the other cannon followed suit.

The shots were obviously intended as a warning to the other British ships to come no closer and to deter them from making an attempt to rescue any of *Tiger*'s crew, most of whom were, by this time, either already on shore or making their way there in her badly damaged boats. But . . . Phillip drew in his breath sharply. A few remained, including his brother Graham and, in the act of lowering himself over the side, he hesitated. The last salvo from the Russian battery on shore had rekindled the fire they had fought so hard to put out and two wounded men, who had been receiving attention from the assistant-surgeon, lay perilously close to where the blaze had been restarted. If they were not moved, they

156

would be cut off from the after part of the deck . . . and the boats.

Graham saw them too. He started forward and, aware that, even if it meant jeopardizing his only chance of escape, he could not leave his brother in such circumstances, Phillip dropped his jacket and followed him. He neither saw nor heard the approach of the shell which struck the deck a few yards behind him but he heard it explode and was conscious of a searing pain in his right side. He stumbled, biting back the cry which rose to his lips and striving vainly to regain his balance, and then the strength drained from him and he felt himself falling, apparently from a great height.

His last memory, before all awareness left him, was of a high-pitched scream, which he did not recognize as his own, and of hands reaching out to seize him, whose clutches he fought vainly to evade. . . .

2

From a long way away, a voice asked kindly, 'Well, how are you today, old fellow?'

Another voice, coming from nearer at hand, answered the question, 'He's not conscious, sir, and there is no change in his condition. His head injuries are severe, I'm afraid. I removed the shell splinters from his thigh yesterday evening, after they brought us here, but the wound is too high up for me to amputate. If the leg turns gangrenous, then . . .' the voice trailed off into silence but Phillip could guess the implications of that unfinished sentence and could imagine the resigned shrug that accompanied it. He had seen wounds turn gangrenous before and he wondered pityingly of whom the two men were talking.

The first voice, which sounded familiar, although he could not recall where he had heard it before, went on, 'Then he will not be sending any letters with the *Vesuvius*, I fear. How about you, Dr. Lawless? If yours are prepared, I can take them and send them aboard with mine.'

'I'm obliged to you, sir, but the Surgeon took all I had time to write about an hour ago. We understood that the *Furious* was leaving at once. I did not realize that *Vesuvius* was still here.'

Furious ... *Vesuvius*? Phillip puzzled over the names, still hearing the two voices as if from a considerable distance. He heard the first voice say, 'Commander Powell agreed to wait for news of Captain Giffard and the Governor gave his consent. I only wish the news we had to send of him were more hopeful ... his wife is in Therapia, you know. This will come as a terrible shock to her.'

'Yes, sir, undoubtedly it will. I very much fear that he cannot last much longer but ... the Surgeon is at his bedside, if you would care to have a word with him.'

'I've seen him, Doctor ... and I spoke very briefly to the Captain. All he can talk about is the kindness and consideration he has been shown since his capture by the Governor. He asked me if the men were being shown equal consideration and I was able to assure him that they were, which seemed to relieve his mind. He hasn't a thought for himself, has he?'

'No, sir, he hasn't. The Governor visited him in person this morning, as you probably know ... with the Baroness Osten-Sacken. Her Excellency brought every kind of delicacy from her own kitchens, in the hope that Captain Giffard might be persuaded to eat but ...' again the sentence was left in mid-air and as before its implications were all too plain. 'She even suggested that Mrs. Giffard might be brought here, sir.'

Phillip attempted to sit up but was unable to do so, feeling as if a heavy weight across his chest were holding him down. His efforts to speak to his two companions were equally vain. The room was dark and he was unable to see either of them, although he continued to eavesdrop on their conversation and now he identified the first voice as that of *Tiger*'s First Lieutenant. He also recalled that Baron Osten-Sacken was Governor of Odessa ... *Odessa*? Bewildered, he once more struggled to sit up but the weight on his chest held him imprisoned.

'Poor fellow, he is restless,' the doctor said. 'But at least he does not know anything.'

'Young John Giffard dead, Boy Hood, Trainer, Tanner and that lad from *Trojan* ... and now the Captain himself and, in all probability, your patient as well ...' the First Lieutenant spoke bitterly. 'It's a high price to pay, is it not, Mr. Lawless, for a trifling error caused by fog and an inaccurate chart? But at least they did not take the ship ... she's burnt out, you know, so they cannot claim her as a prize. All they managed to save were three of her guns, two of which they had to recover from under water. I saw them brought in ... the streets were lined with people, cheering insanely, as if in celebration of a major victory!'

'You're allowed out quite freely then, sir?'

'Yes, Mr. Lawless, I am. I've given my parole ... a course I shall advise all officers to take when it is offered to them, as I understand it will be in the near future. We do not know for how long we shall have to remain here as prisoners.'

'And the men, sir?' Phillip heard Surgeon Lawless ask.

'The men are to be permitted their liberty within the confines of the town. I see them daily, with the Governor's full knowledge and consent.'

'And this is the town we bombarded and set on fire less than three weeks ago! The Governor is displaying a high degree of Christian forebearance, is he not?'

'A remarkably high degree, Doctor. I confess it surprises me to receive such treatment from an enemy but His Excellency the Governor is a gentleman of the old school. I have been invited to dine with him this evening, in order to discuss the advisability of removing Captain Giffard to his residence and of accommodating our midshipmen and cadets there also. His Excellency feels that, in view of their youth, they should not remain here any longer than necessary, among the sick and wounded. There is even talk of sending them to St. Petersburg, if their captivity should be prolonged.'

'It is almost unbelievable, sir!' Lawless exclaimed. 'After all the stories one hears of Russian barbarity.'

'I gather, from what the Governor has told me,' *Tiger*'s First Lieutenant went on, 'that he is grateful for the fact that we confined our recent attack on Odessa to military targets and used only frigates to undertake the bombardment. The fire which destroyed part of the town was accidental. His Excellency knows that, and due, in part at least, to the inefficiency of his own fire-fighters, who failed to bring it under control. His Excellency told me that he was expecting us to destroy the entire town, as a reprisal for Sinope and . . .' his voiced faded suddenly and, strain his ears as he might, Phillip could hear no more. Having nothing now to distract him, he drifted into sleep.

Everything became strangely confused after that. He slept and wakened, heard voices and sometimes understood what they were saying. More often, however, he did not understand and life took on a curiously dream-like quality, in which he lost all consciousness of time, all sensation of reality. He experienced pain during his occasional lucid moments . . . a pain which was, at times, almost unendurable. But this passed and finally he was aware of little discomfort save when, borne down by the weight on his chest, he found difficulty in drawing breath. His body became numb and inert, scarcely possessed of feeling, and his mind wandered apart from it in a lost, dream world peopled by ghosts, in which there was neither night nor day.

A few of the ghosts were recognizable by voice or touch. He knew the hands of Lawless, *Tiger*'s young assistant-surgeon, for their skilled gentleness and for the relief they brought him when he suffered a bout of pain. The voice of his brother Graham sometimes penetrated the mists which encompassed his brain, although he was seldom able to make out what his brother was saying. The other voices were distant and unintelligible, often speaking in a foreign language which he could neither follow nor translate. He sensed that they were kindly and concerned but that was all and they made very little impression on him.

The only ghost, among the many that haunted his dreams, whose voice reached him and whose presence seemed real was, ironically, the one he knew with clear, cold certainty to be a ghost ... or, at best, a figment of his imagination. For Mademoiselle Sophie, Phillip told himself, could not in reality be there. It was quite inconceivable that a Russian Grand-Duchess, a member of the Imperial family of the Tsar, should sit for hours at his bedside, moving only when it was necessary to hold a cup of water to his parched lips or lay a small, cool hand on his sweat-drenched brow. Certainly it was inconceivable that Mademoiselle Sophie should speak to him, in tones of anxious affection, that she should call him by name and beseech him, her voice choked with sobs, to answer her. Still less was it likely, Phillip was aware, that – when his pain was at its worst – he should lie with her fingers entwined about his own and the salty dampness of her tears falling on their two linked hands.

Yet the dream was a source of intense happiness and comfort to him and he clung to it with all his failing strength, letting his imagination have free rein, seeing her face, hearing her voice, deriving pleasure from the illusion of her nearness to him, her concern for him. In his imagination he held long conversations with her, answered her tearful inquiries as to his progress and more than once, greatly daring, bore her hand to his lips and kissed it. He was indifferent to the murmured protests of the Baroness von Mauthner and another elderly woman – a stranger to him – the intrusion of whose presence occasionally detracted from his enjoyment of his dream. For the most part, however, he noticed no one else when Mademoiselle Sophie appeared to him and he waited eagerly for her to come, the time between one dream-visit and the next seeming endless.

Then, as suddenly as it had begun, the dream ended. Mademoiselle Sophie's visits inexplicably ceased and Phillip felt bereft. She came to him for the last time one day – or one night, he could not be certain which – and stayed for only a few brief moments, not seating herself, as she usually did, in the chair at his bedside but standing looking down at him, her face too shadowy and far away for him to be able to read the expression on it.

'Phillip . . .' he heard her voice but this, too, was indistinct, as if it were coming from a distance and, although he exerted every effort to concentrate on what she was trying to tell him, her words had no meaning for him. 'Phillip, I . . . I do not know whether you can understand or even whether you can hear me. I . . . tomorrow is my wedding day. Here, in the Cathedral, I am to be married and then I have to go away. I have no choice, you see, I . . . I have to go with my husband. First to St. Petersburg, where we shall present ourselves to Uncle Nikita for his blessing and then . . . then I do not know. We may go to Sebastopol, perhaps, or to Georgia . . . there is fighting everywhere.' She spoke with infinite sadness and Phillip put out his hand in search of hers, thinking to offer her comfort. Her fingers felt cold to his touch and they were trembling, he realized, when at last he found them with his own. She let him hold her hand for a moment or two and then withdrew it.

'We shall not meet again, Phillip,' Mademoiselle Sophie told him with finality. 'We cannot meet again, I . . . I know my duty.' Her small, lovely face, remote in its grief, was no longer the face of a child but of an adult woman, courageous and resolute and Phillip sensed the change in her, without understanding what had caused it. 'This time,' she went on, 'it is not "au revoir", this time I must bid you farewell. But you will grow strong and well again, you will live . . . for my sake, you *must* live, Phillip.' There was a catch in her voice. 'To know that you are living somewhere in the world will . . . comfort me. I shall think of you and pray for you . . . for you and your valiant *Trojan*. And one day, when you are *Trojan*'s Captain, I shall know because my heart will tell me. The heart does not forget, Phillip, however sad it is . . . and when peace comes, I shall see you with the eyes of the heart, as you set your course for England. May God be with you, now and always, my dear English sailor . . .' she stooped over him and Phillip felt her lips lightly brush his cheek.

Even when she had left him, he could not quite take in what she had said to him, could not believe he would not see her again. Her words remained locked in his memory, treasured there, although they were incomprehensible to him for a long time, because they were the last words he had heard her speak to him. Slowly his condition improved and the dream which had meant so much to him during his illness began to fade. It had, after all, he told himself repeatedly, been no more than a dream and, as his fever abated and he began to regain his strength, he had less need of illusion to sustain him. Other people became recognizable as people, not simply as voices, and the ghosts took on substance and emerged from the shadows when Phillip found that he could see and communicate with them once more.

Tiger's young assistant-surgeon was the first with whom he was able to hold a rational conversation, in the course of which he learned of Captain Giffard's death.

'It was a tragedy,' Dr. Lawless told him. 'His wife came, at Baroness Osten-Sacken's personal invitation, to be with him ... *Retribution* brought her here with all possible speed but alas, poor soul, she arrived too late to see her husband alive. We did everything we could – indeed, the Surgeon scarcely left his side but the Captain had not your robust constitution, Mr. Hazard. He succumbed to the infection caused by his wounds and was buried, with full military honours, on the second of June. The whole ship's company attended the funeral, the officers acting as pall bearers, and the garrison troops and also the townspeople lined the streets in his honour. It was a most moving ceremony.'

'The townspeople of Odessa, do you mean?' Phillip asked, in astonishment.

'They bear us no ill-will,' the surgeon assured him. 'We are permitted to wander freely about the town, officers and blue-jackets alike, and no one displays the slightest sign of hostility towards us. The officers are in great demand socially and receive frequent invitations to attend balls and concerts and to visit private houses ... the midshipmen and cadets especially were showered with invitations, before being sent to St. Petersburg. Our men are allowed a good deal more freedom here in Odessa then they would be in Portsmouth or Plymouth ... and few of them abuse it. Even the few who do are treated very leniently by the Russian authorities. Of course ...' he smiled, 'this all stems from the Governor and his good lady. They have overwhelmed us with kindness, Mr. Hazard. You, for example, are in His Excellency's residence now, occupying one of his guest-rooms.'

Phillip stared about him. 'In the Governor's residence, Doctor? I do not understand, I thought ... that is I am a little confused, you see.'

'That is not to be wondered at ... you have been very ill, Mr. Hazard,' Dr. Lawless explained gently. 'At one time we despaired of your life. When His Excellency the Governor heard of this, he had you brought here from the lazaretto, so that you might be better cared for, and he put the services of his own physician at your disposal. It is to *his* skill, rather than mine, that you owe your life ... he is a brilliant man and he has been in attendance on you ever since you were brought here.'

'Have I been here for very long?' Phillip questioned and the assistant-surgeon nodded.

'For nearly eight weeks, Mr. Hazard. You were wounded by an exploding shell, splinters from which entered your head and chest and also your right leg, high up in the thigh. Infection set in and you suffered a severe fever, which few men would have survived. But you have a remarkably strong constitution and ... you had the will to live. This and the skill of Baron Osten-Sacken's physician pulled you through, together with the care lavished on you by the ladies of the household.'

'The *ladies* of the household?' Phillip echoed, his mouth suddenly dry.

'Indeed yes, Mr. Hazard ... including the Baroness herself,' Lawless confirmed warmly. 'You were still very weak, of course, but you are making an excellent recovery. In another month or so, you should be as fit and healthy as you ever were. Even the wound in your leg is healing well.'

Phillip thanked him and ventured a few more questions, which the young assistant-surgeon answered fully and frankly. But he made no mention of Mademoiselle Sophie, adding only that Graham had done much to aid his recovery.

'He confided to me that he is your brother and he cared for you unremittingly when you were with the rest of us, in the lazaretto, you know. In fact, I understand that our First-Lieutenant intends to bring his conduct to the attention of the Commander-in-Chief at the first opportunity. He displayed great courage and devotion to duty during the attack on *Tiger* and was instrumental in saving the lives of two wounded seamen, in addition, I have reason to believe, to my own. So we are both deeply in your brother's debt, Mr. Hazard. Perhaps, as a result of the First Lieutenant's report, he may have his commission restored to him when we are released . . . let us hope so, at any rate.'

Phillip echoed this hope. 'Is there any immediate prospect of our being released, Doctor?' he inquired.

'There is talk of an exchange of prisoners,' Lawless answered. 'Although when this will take place I cannot tell you. Some of our men will be sorry when it does, after the way they have been treated here! But' – he laid a solicitous hand on Phillip's shoulder – 'you should try to sleep now, Mr. Hazard. It is inadvisable to overtax your strength when you are making such good progress. Plenty of rest and good food are what you need now to make your recovery complete . . . and to ensure that you are fit to return to duty, when our release is eventually arranged. So make the most of your convalescence in these pleasant surroundings.'

Phillip was glad enough to take his advice. For the next few days he rested, eating well and building up his strength, visited daily by the Governor and his personal physician and waited on hand and foot by his servants. He formed a great liking for Baron Osten-Sacken and his kindly, charming wife learning, somewhat to his surprise, that the Baron held the high rank of Aide-de-Camp General in the Russian Army and was in active command of some thirty thousand troops, which formed the garrison of Odessa. They talked of the war and – again to Phillip's surprise – the Governor talked to him freely, admitting the failure of the Russian Army of the Danube to take Silistria as a major disaster and making no secret of his strongly felt regret that their two countries should be opposed.

'England has not chosen her allies well, Mr. Hazard ... her cause should be Christian Russia's, not that of the heathen Turk. A war between our two great nations can only weaken both and ultimately do neither the smallest good. Had England, Russia and France been united now, instead of fighting against one another, then the "sick man of Europe" – as the Emperor aptly calls your present ally – could speedily have been disposed of and the Ottoman Empire divided between us ... to its vast betterment. Christian peoples, for so many bitter years under the barbarous and inhuman domination of the Sultan, could have been freed from slavery. The Black Sea could have been opened to the trade of all nations, once the Porte's stranglehold on the Bosphorus was challenged and broken. But as it is ...' the Governor shrugged regretfully. 'You will lose the flower of your manhood, if you attempt to wrest Sebastopol from us. And, until you do, Mr. Hazard, the war will drag on ... for the Russian peasant will fight heroically and to the death in defence of his own soil. This was a lesson Bonaparte learned to his cost, was it not?'

Phillip listened to him attentively and afterwards thought over what he had said, recognizing the logic of his argument, if not its justice. The Russians had suffered a set-back on the Danube front and were in full retreat, leaving Omar Pasha, the Turkish Commander-in-Chief, in victorious possession of Silistria and his strongly held headquarters at Shumla. The threat to Constantinople had been removed, the British and French expeditionary forces were steadily building up at Varna, on the Bulgarian coast and the Allied Fleets were in undisputed command of the Black Sea. Admiral Lyons' steamer squadron had scored signal successes in raids along the Circassian coast but ... there had been no attack on Sebastopol and the Russian Black Sea Fleet waited there, behind its formidable shore defences for the battle that, inevitably, must come. Admiral Lyons had said so and the Governor of Odessa had expressed a similar view ... Phillip stirred restlessly in his luxurious bed and longed, despite the comfort of his prison and the kindness of his captors, to return to *Trojan*'s quarterdeck so that, when the eventual struggle took place, he might take part in it.

The Governor raised his hopes, a few days later, with the news that an exchange of prisoners was being negotiated, and thereafter he made strenuous efforts to put his illness behind him. It was a painful and laborious process, for he still had little more strength than a child and his right leg, when he attempted to stand on it, crumpled up under his weight and the room whirled about him in dizzy circles when, clinging to a chair and ignoring the pain, he tried to take a few faltering steps. The Russian doctor anxiously counselled patience, even *Tiger*'s two surgeons besought him to prolong his convalescence but Phillip refused obstinately to listen to them. Only fit men would be exchanged and he was determined to be fit, at whatever the cost, when the Governor's negotiations were completed. He knew, from a chance remark dropped by *Tiger*'s First Lieutenant, that the number of Russian prisoners to be repatriated was a hundred and eighty which meant, in all probability, that about thirty of *Tiger*'s men would have to be left behind.

'You would be welcome to remain here, Mr. Hazard,' the Governor told him, sympathetically watching his agonized attempt to walk, unaided, across the room. 'You, perhaps, more than any of your brother officers merit special consideration. Indeed, if it were your wish, I could arrange for you to be transferred temporarily to St. Petersburg. There, like the midshipmen who were previously my guests here, you could undertake a course of study at the Imperial Naval Academy until you are well enough to resume active duty.'

'Your Excellency is suggesting that I should remain here voluntarily?' Reaching the chair that had been his goal at last, Phillip grasped its back with both hands, holding himself upright and facing the Russian Governor, a shocked question in his eyes. 'But why, sir . . . what have I done to merit more consideration than any of my brother officers?'

'Surely you know, Mr. Hazard?' Baron Osten-Sacken challenged, smiling. 'You have a ring in your possession, have you not . . . an emerald ring of unusual design?'

The ring Mademoiselle Sophie had given him, Phillip thought, feeling the blood rush to his cheeks. Until this moment any questions he had asked concerning Mademoiselle Sophie had been evaded or politely ignored by his Russian captors, as if they were all, from the Governor downwards, bound by a conspiracy of silence. His visitors from the *Tiger*'s crew had made no reference to the part she had played in bringing about his recovery and, for this reason, he had almost convinced himself that the vigil she had kept at his bedside had been, as he had originally supposed, a dream . . . an hallucination, born of his feverish delirium. Yet now, suddenly meeting the Governor's gaze, he was less certain, conscious that he might have been deceiving himself. And if he had, if his vision of Mademoiselle Sophie at his bedside had not been an hallucination, then . . . his heart leapt exultantly but sensing that, behind the bland smile, Baron Osten-Sacken was watching him keenly, he kept a stern rein on his emotions.

'The ring was a gift, was it not, Mr. Hazard . . . a gift made to you as a token of gratitude for personal services rendered to a member of the family of His Imperial Majesty the Emperor?' the Governor persisted, without change of tone.

But now, although he continued to smile, the shrewd dark eyes were alert and watchful beneath their heavy brows and Phillip sensed that it would behove him to tread warily. Evidently the Governor's servants had found the ring among his few possessions and had reported their find to their master. It seemed equally evident that Mademoiselle Sophie's visits

– *if* they had really taken place – would also have been reported to him, since they must have taken place beneath his roof and it was probably on this account that he was seeking reassurance. Phillip took a firmer grip of his chair-back and braced himself, feeling for the ring in his pocket.

'The gift was made to me by a lady I know only as Mademoiselle Sophie, your Excellency,' he said quietly. 'This lady travelled as a passenger from England to Constantinople on board Her Majesty's steam frigate *Trojan* of which I have the honour to be First Lieutenant. Only the Captain was informed of her identity, sir, and . . .' Phillip hesitated but Baron Osten-Sacken was silent, eyeing him expectantly, and he went on, choosing his words with care, 'The pleasure I derived from serving her was more than sufficient reward and I did very little. Therefore, if your Excellency wishes, I will return the ring, together with my personal assurance that the lady in question will continue to be known to me simply as Mademoiselle Sophie. As indeed, sir, she is known to the rest of my ship's company.' He held out the ring, still in its velvet lined case and added, meeting the tall Russian's dark gaze quite steadily, 'I have no recollection, sir, of having seen Mademoiselle since she left the ship at Constantinople.'

'I see that we understand each other, Mr. Hazard,' the Governor said. There was relief in his eyes and his smile was now unreservedly warm. 'There is, of course, no necessity to return the ring . . . your assurance is all that I require, your word as an English officer and gentleman. No doubt you are aware that Mademoiselle Sophie's nuptials were celebrated recently, in the Cathedral here in Odessa?'

'I had heard something to that effect, your Excellency,' Phillip admitted. 'And Mademoiselle herself told me, before she left the *Trojan*, that she was to be married. She did not tell me to whom and I . . . may I be permitted to know his name?'

'Her bridegroom is the Prince Andrei Stepanovitch Narishkin, Colonel of the Regiment of Chasseurs of Odessa.' Baron Osten-Sacken's voice did not betray his feelings but the smile he had worn for so long abruptly faded. 'His Highness is aide-de-camp to the Prince Menschikoff, Governor of the Crimea and Commander-in-Chief of our military and naval forces. As possibly you may have been told, it was the Prince Narishkin who destroyed the *Tiger* frigate and brought about your capture, Mr. Hazard.'

The arrogant young princeling on the white charger, Phillip recalled, of whom *Tiger*'s First Lieutenant had spoken with so much bitterness, as his field guns had reduced the defenceless frigate to a blazing wreck ... he felt a sick sensation in the pit of his stomach, the memory filling him with revulsion. So *he* was Mademoiselle Sophie's husband, he was the one to whom, as a child, she had been betrothed and who now ... he had to struggle to hide his dismayed reaction to this news but somehow, tight-lipped and white of face, he managed to do so. Alarmed by his pallor, Baron Osten-Sacken insisted on his seating himself.

'You are not strong enough to stand for so long, Mr. Hazard,' the Russian reproached him. 'Believe me, you would be well advised to remain here until your health improves.'

'I am grateful for your concern, sir. But I ...' Phillip turned in his chair to face him. 'If I merit any special consideration from your Excellency, then I would ask that I may be included in the number of officers who are to be exchanged. I am anxious to return to my own ship, sir, and to my duty.'

'Very well ... if this is what you really wish, it shall be arranged. Your anxiety to resume your duties is highly commendable but ...' The Governor shrugged his elegantly uniformed shoulders. 'I am sorry. I had promised Sophia Mikailovna – that is to say, Mademoiselle Sophie – that I would see you fully restored to health and I have done all I can to keep my promise to her. I cannot compel you to stay here against your will but I have made a similar offer – also at Mademoiselle's behest – to your brother, Mr. Hazard. He is, I understand, serving as a seaman and not as an officer in the English Navy?'

'Yes, sir, he is. But I scarcely imagine—'

'How does this come about?' Baron Osten-Sacken put in, 'When, as I believe is the case, your father is an Admiral and when your brother was apparently one of the heroes of the recent action against the *Tiger* frigate?'

Phillip explained, as briefly and non-committally as he could adding, with conviction, 'I do not think that my brother will wish to remain here either, your Excellency.'

'Do not be too certain, Mr. Hazard ... the suggestion is not that he should remain here but that he should go to St. Petersburg, in order to study at the Imperial Naval Academy. There, I assure you' – the Governor's tone was dry – 'he will be treated as an officer and use made of his services, if he should desire to offer them although not, of course, against his own countrymen. We have enlisted English and Scottish officers in the Russian Navy in the past, Mr. Hazard, and many have served with great distinction and risen to high rank.'

Notably Admiral Sir Samuel Greig, Phillip thought, known as 'the father of the Russian Navy', his sons, and Admirals Mackenzie, Drysdale, Tait and Alexander Elphinstone ... all had flown their flags in the Black Sea within the last seventy years. A British Captain, Adolphus Slade, held Flag rank in the Turkish Navy at present, with the title of Muchaver Pasha, so that it was by no means unusual for British officers to serve a foreign power but surely Graham ... he said, with confidence, 'It is extremely good of your Excellency to make this offer to my brother but, in all honesty, sir, I believe that, like myself, he will want to rejoin the British Fleet.'

'To be flogged again, Mr. Hazard?' the Governor questioned. He rose, his smile returning briefly. 'Her Highness the Princess Narishkina told me of the incident. It shocked her a good deal, I think, when she witnessed it. As your brother's decision may shock *you* but ... I will send him to you, when he has definitely made up his mind. Au revoir, Mr. Hazard.'

His assumption proved, however, to be correct. A few days

171

later, Graham presented himself in the sickroom and announced, without excuse or apology, that he intended to accept Baron Osten-Sacken's offer and was leaving for the long overland journey to St. Petersburg that night. Phillip stared at him in shocked disbelief and Graham went on, still without apology, 'Some of us have to remain behind, Phillip. I've volunteered to do so, that is all.'

'*You* of all people! I find it hard to credit,' Phillip managed at last.

'Do you ... you shouldn't. You cannot possibly imagine that I enjoy life as it is lived on the lower deck, even if you've never experienced it for yourself.' Graham spoke with unconcealed bitterness. 'For God's sake, Phillip, don't look so horrified! What has the British Navy to offer me if I do return? Service under a commander like North? An ableseaman's berth wherever I serve, with perhaps the chance of promotion to bo'sun's mate if I behave myself and touch my forelock fifty times a day to officers, whose professional competence will never match mine? No thank you ... I infinitely prefer the chance the Russians are willing to allow me.'

'*Tiger*'s First Lieutenant intends to report favourably on your conduct,' Phillip reminded him. 'You saved two lives under fire, Graham, and he will make the facts known to Admiral Dundas. He—'

'Will that get my commission restored to me?' Graham demanded harshly.

'It might. After all you—'

'Don't be naïve, Phillip. You know as well as I do that nothing *Tiger*'s First Lieutenant can say will have the slightest effect on their Lordships of the Admiralty, on whom the decision will ultimately depend. The transcript of my court martial will be referred to and the recommendation rejected ... even if Admiral Dundas can be prevailed upon to put it forward. The Navy has a long memory.'

There was truth in what he said, Phillip was forced to concede. Nevertheless he advanced every argument he could think of to persuade his brother to change his mind, but Graham was adamant. 'No,' he said, with a firmness which precluded further argument. 'I'm going to St. Petersburg, Phillip. I only came here to tell you so and to take leave of you. I hope we can part without bitterness.'

'Do you wish me to inform Father of your destination and what you intend to do?' Phillip asked, playing what he was aware was his last card.

Graham shrugged. 'That is for you to decide. I'd prefer you simply to tell him that I am a prisoner of war as, in fact, I am. It would hurt him needlessly if you told him anything else and he wouldn't find it easy to understand the reasons for my decision.'

'I do not find it easy to understand them myself.'

'Oh, come now . . . you do in your heart, Phillip.'

'Yes, perhaps I do,' Phillip confessed reluctantly.

Graham smiled at him. 'I shall have friends in high places in Petersburg,' he observed lightly. 'You know, I suppose that our "Mademoiselle Sophie" is a niece of the Tsar and that she is now married to one of the richest landowners in this part of Russia?'

'I had heard that.' Phillip's tone was stiff. But he accepted his brother's proffered hand and wished him well, although already there was a gulf between them and both were aware of it. He was more relieved than disappointed when Graham cut short his leave-taking on the plea of other fare-wells to be said, yet watched him go with deep sadness, convinced that they would be unlikely to see one another again.

Arrangements for the promised exchange of prisoners were concluded a few days later and, on 11th July, the little six-gun dispatch steamer *Fury* entered Odessa Harbour under a flag of truce to land a hundred and eighty Russian soldiers, captured by Admiral Lyons' squadron during raids on the Circassian coast. Still scarcely able to walk, Phillip was assisted on board, together with the other members of *Tiger*'s crew who were to be liberated. He was sent to Therapia to recuperate and found himself a guest of Lord Stratford de Redcliffe, at the Ambassador's pleasant summer residence on the Bosphorus.

Admiral Lyons, bringing Sir George Brown – commander of the British Light Division – with him, arrived in *Agamemnon* on 2nd August and promptly co-opted Phillip's services. A land-based assault on Sebastopol had been agreed to by the Allied commanders, the Admiral told him, and he was now faced with the stupendous task of supplying ships in which to transport the 30,000 men of the British Expeditionary Force from Varna, on the Bulgarian coast, to the Crimean peninsula and landing them there, with their guns and horses.

'Sir George Brown and I, with General Canrobert and Colonel Trochu, have made a reconnaissance of the Crimean coast, Phillip,' Sir Edmund said. 'Our object was to ascertain the position of coastal forts and gun batteries in the vicinity of Sebastopol, which might impede the landings, and to make sure that ample supplies of water were available. The Bay of Katcha seems to offer all we need for a suitable landing place . . .' he pointed to it on the chart and spent half an hour, enlarging on his plans for the disembarkation and the merits of the spot he had selected for this to take place. 'We had seven fathoms of water at half a mile from the beach, which will mean that the Fleets can enter the river mouth to cover the landings and supply the armies. Then, when the military forces converge on the town we, from the sea, can engage the Russian Fleet in harbour, if they still refuse to come out and meet us. If they attack our convoy on its way to the Katcha River, we shall have ample strength with which to counter them.'

The plan seemed to Phillip, as he studied the maps and charts, admirably conceived. Admiral Lyons had allowed for every contingency and, now that the decision to attack Sebastopol had at last been reached, he applied himself with his usual dynamic energy and efficiency to the problem of finding sufficient ships to enable the land-based assault to be put into operation. As always, Lyons' powers of organization surmounted all difficulties and Phillip, working with his small staff, witnessed the creation of an armada, seemingly by magic.

From Malta came several steamers, towing flat-bottomed boats and in Constantinople itself Admiral Boxer and his transport officers procured others and began the construction of wooden pontoons, made from Turkish long boats lashed together in pairs and planked over, to form rafts capable of carrying a battery of guns or a company of infantry. In addition to these there were, of course, the transports – both steam and sail – which had brought the Army from Malta to Gallipoli and Scutari and thence to Varna and, on paper, the makeshift fleet grew daily. During August ships left the Bosphorus for Baltchik and Kavarna Bays in a steadily increasing flow and Phillip, at a desk on board *Agamemnon* or at another in Admiral Boxer's office on shore, dealt with a mountain of paper-work. Despite lack of sleep and long hours of toil, the wound in his leg healed and he was able to walk for quite long distances, with a slight limp but unaided and without strain. He was impatient to return to active duty but, realizing that the work with which he was at present assisting was of greater value than anything he could have done at sea, he restrained his impatience.

An epidemic of cholera had broken out in Varna, taking an appalling toll of both seamen and soldiers but, in spite of this, preparations for the invasion of the Crimea went on. It was generally believed that Varna was the source of the outbreak and that, once the Allied forces left the unhealthy little town, they would leave the infection behind them.

'There are those – naming no names, Phillip,' Sir Edmund Lyons observed, 'who seek any excuse to avoid attacking Sebastopol. Nevertheless I am confident that the attack will succeed, if it is undertaken before the end of August and if our combined naval and military forces press it home with sufficient courage and vigour, from the moment of landing. But if it is delayed for even three or four weeks, then I very much fear the outcome ... and fear that embarkation *may* be delayed, unless I am on hand to ensure that it is not. So I shall return to Varna now and to the endless conferences and councils of war we hold with our allies, which seldom result in anything but faint-hearted argument in favour of caution.

Wars are not won by exercising caution . . . the bold, decisive action is the only one that can bring success.' He sighed, eyeing Phillip thoughtfully. 'Do you want to come with me, Phillip? Or will you remain here, at Admiral Boxer's elbow, where your presence will be of great value for another few weeks? Two, at the outside, if I have my way.'

'I will do whatever you command me, sir,' Phillip assured him.

'Then stay,' the Admiral said. 'I'll send for you when the embarkation begins. And, as a reward for your exertions here, during your convalescence, would you like me to have you appointed to *Agamemnon*?'

Phillip stared at him incredulously. The offer of appointment to *Agamemnon* was more than he had ever dared to hope for . . . yet, gratified though he was, he did not at once accept it. The Admiral, evidently reading his unspoken thoughts, said with a smile, 'You may, of course, return to *Trojan*, if you would prefer to do so. She is your ship, is she not?'

Yes, she was his ship, Phillip thought ruefully . . . or she had been his ship, until North's appointment had taken her from him. Under North's command, he had very little desire to return to *Trojan*, he realized . . . indeed, he shrank from the prospect. Life in Constantinople had been pleasant, in spite of the long hours he had had to work and he had enjoyed the Admiral's confidence, even his friendship, during the time he had been here. It would not be so pleasant to return to North's taunts and insults, after his happy association with Sir Edmund Lyons, he was fully aware. In addition Captain Mends – whose gallant and skilful handling of *Arethusa* during the attack on Odessa had won the admiration of the entire British Fleet – had recently exchanged with Captain Symonds and was now, as Flag-Captain, commanding *Agamemnon*. There were few men he would rather serve under than Mends . . . Phillip looked up to echo the Admiral's smile, his decision reached.

'I am sure that Lieutenant Fox is more than capable of acting as *Trojan*'s First Lieutenant, sir. So, if you will permit me, I should like nothing better than to serve under your command and that of Captain Mends, sir, in *Agamemnon*. I am deeply grateful for being given this opportunity to do so.'

'Good.' Admiral Lyons patted his shoulder, the gesture affectionate and fatherly. 'I shall be glad to have you and Jack will be pleased, when I tell him you're with me. He's done exceptionally well with *Miranda* in the White Sea . . . I must show you his last letter, which I received a few days ago.'

The Admiral consulted his watch. 'I shall have to go . . . Captain Mends will be wanting to get under way.' He returned his watch to his pocket and held out his hand. 'You have made the right decision, Phillip. Strictly between ourselves, I hear somewhat disquieting reports of *Trojan* . . . she's not a happy ship, is she? Or, come to that, a particularly efficient one, from all accounts. The Commander-in-Chief has had requests for transfer to other ships from several of her officers, I understand. And one of them – Lieutenant Cochrane – is under arrest, awaiting trial by court martial on charges of insubordination brought by his Captain . . . the Admiral mentioned this, in his letter to me delivered this morning by the *Banshee*.'

Young Anthony Cochrane, Phillip thought unhappily, had finally allowed his impulsive tongue to run away with him and had said too much. He was distressed, although scarcely surprised, by the news and, for a moment, regretted his decision not to rejoin *Trojan*. But if he had done so he could have done nothing to save Cochrane, he knew . . . throughout his service under Captain North's command, he had never managed to save anyone from punishment, not even his own brother. To have gone back would have been merely to stand by and watch young Cochrane broken, powerless to intervene on his behalf so perhaps, as Admiral Lyons had said, he had made the right decision. He drew himself up and saluted and the Admiral, after glancing at him searchingly, dismissed him with the promise that he was to be sent for when the embarkation from Varna began.

CHAPTER EIGHT

I

TWELVE days later, Phillip received orders to join *Aga-memnon* and, when the dispatch steamer which had brought him from Constantinople dropped anchor in Kavarna Bay, he saw that the embarkation of the British Expeditionary Force had already begun. From then until 4th September it continued, as the 30,000 troops, with 2,000 horses and 54 guns were loaded on to the waiting transports, together with tents, stores, arms and equipment, in an open bay and impeded by a strong swell. Every officer and seaman in the British Fleet toiled unceasingly from dawn to dusk, under the personal supervision of Admiral Lyons and his Principal Officer of Transports, Captain Christie.

The embarkation was a masterpiece of efficient and even inspired organization ... the whole, Phillip realized, stemming from the man who had visualized and prepared for it so far-sightedly and who now, with tireless energy, set about putting his carefully thought out plans into operation. Admiral Dundas, with ten sail-of-the-line and a few small frigates, was cruising off Sebastopol, ready to intercept and, if necessary, do battle with the Russian Fleet should its commander decide to launch an attack on the convoy bearing the invasion force. Admiral Lyons was therefore in sole command of the embarkation and he was everywhere ... ashore, on foot or on horseback, in his barge rowing about the bay and even, at times, in *Agamemnon* using her among the crowded lines of shipping as he might have used a sheepdog to round up a straggling herd of sheep. Captain Mends, on whom fell responsibility for much of the detail involving the complex manoeuvring of over a hundred vessels, as well as command of his own, performed minor miracles of staff work and Phillip, acting as one of his assistants, was hardly able to snatch an hour's sleep, from one night to the next.

By 4th September the operation was successfully completed, the only losses being the tragic but seemingly inevitable deaths from cholera. The British flotilla formed up into six lines of fifteen ships, each line containing a division of the Army complete with its arms and equipment, and with a steamer to tow each pair of sailing ships. A small detachment of six transports, also in the tow of steamers, carried the medical department, siege train and reserve ammunition . . . the former cut to a minimum, owing to lack of space. For the same reason, the Heavy Cavalry Brigade, the ambulances and transport wagons and the pack horses and mules had to be left behind in Varna, to be brought on afterwards, when the steamers had discharged their present loads.

After a number of delays, the British convoy weighed anchor on the morning of 7th September, with the intention of joining up with the French and Turkish ships at the agreed rendezvous, forty miles N.W. of Cape Tarkan, the most westerly point on the Crimean peninsula. By ten thirty the ships of the convoy took up their respective stations and, in compact order, four cables' lengths separating each vessel from her next ahead and astern and the same distance between each of the six lines, put to sea. They made an impressive sight, Phillip thought, surveying the spectacle from *Agamemnon*'s poop, pride and excitement dispelling his weariness. The sun rose in a blue and cloudless sky, the contrary wind which had been responsible for the long delay dropped and, on board the transports, bands played and soldiers in their scarlet uniforms lined the decks, cheering as the steamers took them in tow.

Of the Russians there was no sign but the twenty-seven men-of-war composing the French and Turkish Fleets – in which the bulk of their troops were carried – were sighted on the morning of 8th, in company with Admiral Dundas' battle squadron, some thirty miles south of Serpent's

179

Island. The British convoy had no sooner joined up with them than a signal from Admiral Hamelin requested Lord Raglan and Admiral Dundas to board the *Ville de Paris* for a conference with Marshal St. Arnaud, the French Commander-in-Chief. After this had been answered, the conference was transferred to the *Caradoc* – the small, 2-gun dispatch steamer in which Lord Raglan was travelling – and Admiral Lyons, Admiral Bruat, Sir George Brown and General Canrobert also invited to attend.

'I do not like it,' Sir Edmund Lyons said uneasily, as he waited for his barge to be called away. 'A conference at this stage of the proceedings can only mean delay ... and delay is the one thing we cannot afford.'

When he returned to *Agamemnon* some hours later, he was unusually glum and despondent. 'The French want to change our landing place,' he told the officers who clustered about him. 'Now at the eleventh hour, when all was settled and agreed before we left Varna! Colonel Trochu, representing the Marshal – who is apparently too ill to leave his ship – is in favour of disembarking at Kaffa which, gentlemen, is tantamount to putting off the attack on Sebastopol until next year.'

There were shocked murmurs and Captain Mends asked incredulously, 'But surely, Admiral, Lord Raglan did not agree?'

'Indeed he did not,' Admiral Lyons assured him vehemently. 'Neither did Admiral Bruat or our own Commander-in-Chief ... although the second thoughts regarding Katcha are said to have originated with the Admirals. I asked "Which Admirals?" but, as might be expected, no one could tell me.' He sighed, in bitter frustration. 'After hours of fruitless discussion, the final decision as to where the disembarkation will take place has been left in Lord Raglan's hands and, before making his decision, his lordship intends to examine the coast for himself. Tomorrow morning, gentlemen, *Agamemnon* will sail in company with *Primauget*, carrying the French commanders, and *Caradoc*, carrying our own, for the purpose of selecting a landing place. It means a delay which may well prove disastrous, should the weather change but . . .' he spread his hands in a resigned gesture of helplessness and, turning abruptly on his heel, made for his cabin.

After a momentary hesitation, Captain Mends followed him.

It took almost three days to reach agreement on a site for the landing of the invasion force. While the rest of the vast convoy remained at anchor to await Lord Raglan's final decision, *Caradoc* sailed, with the Allied military and naval commanders on board, to make a reconnaissance of the Crimean coast. With *Agamemnon* standing off shore to protect her from molestation, the little dispatch steamer ventured close in to Sebastopol itself. Her appearance attracted no attention from the Russians and indeed, Phillip was later told by one of her officers, it seemed to go unnoticed, although she was near enough to hear the ringing of the church bells and to see quite clearly the Russian line-of-battle ships at anchor in the harbour. Having surveyed the coast first to the south and then to the north, from Balaclava to Eupatoria, *Caradoc* rejoined the Fleet on the morning of Monday, 11th September. The signal to weigh and set course for the Crimea came at noon, from which it was assumed that the British military commander had made his decision.

Sir Edmund Lyons, although he appeared to have recovered from his earlier depression, was evidently still uneasy when he returned to his flagship from the *Caradoc*. Dictating orders to his Secretary and to Phillip who, with his Flag-Lieutenant, was assisting him, the Admiral paused, a worried frown drawing his brows together.

'The landing is to be made – subject of course, to Marshal St. Arnaud's acquiescence – on the beach at the Old Fort in Kalamita Bay, in latitude 45° North,' he said slowly. 'This, in Lord Raglan's opinion, is the most eligible spot for the disembarkation of the Army. His lordship is also of the opinion that Eupatoria, which lies twenty miles to the north and is defenceless, should be occupied prior to the main landing. Of course, I have no criticism of his choice, save for its distance from our objective and the fact that water is likely to be in short supply ashore. The beach at the Old Fort is in no danger from dominating hills – for which reason his lordship rejected my suggestion for a landing at the mouth of the Katcha. In addition, there is deep water close inshore, so that our naval guns can cover the landing but ...' he stifled a sigh and turned to his Secretary. 'Let me see the map, Mr. Cleeve, if you please.'

Frederick Cleeve spread it out in front of him and still frowning, the Admiral indicated the place chosen for the landing. '*This* is what worries me, gentlemen. From where our invasion force is to be set ashore, four rivers will have to be crossed before the attack on Sebastopol can be launched. The Bulganak here, the Alma, the Katcha and the Balbec ...' he stabbed each name on the map. 'Each offers a natural line of defence to the enemy, each is dominated by adjacent hills and we have observed a large enemy encampment in the valley of the Alma ...' he talked on, his tone unusually bitter, and his listeners exchanged anxious glances with each other as the truth of his words sank in.

Finally, with a tired gesture, Admiral Lyons thrust the map away from him. 'Our task is to set the Army ashore,' he observed. 'And to support and supply it from the sea, as well as to evacuate any casualties it may suffer during the march on Sebastopol. This task we shall perform, so ... let us concentrate on what that will entail, shall we, gentlemen? Captain Mends drew up a plan for disembarking the expedition before we left Varna ... you have it there, Mr. Cleeve, have you not?'

'The plan is here, sir,' Cleeve assured him.

'Then write out the necessary orders from that and see that they are delivered in writing, as soon as we drop anchor at the point of disembarkation. I want every boat in the Fleet utilized and, when laden, they are to form line abreast by signal and advance in that order to the beach. About seven thousand men will thus be landed simultaneously and guns will be landed with the first contingent ... in case the enemy oppose the landing. Captain Dacres of *Sanspareil* will command the beach, assisted by Commander Heath of *Niger* and Commander Powell of *Vesuvius*.' The Admiral rose, smiling from one to the other of his small staff. 'You may have to lose yet another night's sleep over this but I want it done, gentlemen. When we anchor, I will arrange for Commander Heath to give you his assistance and I shall place Lieutenant Johnson in command of the first line of boats.' He added warmly, his hand on Cleeve's shoulder, 'You have worked magnificently, all of you, and I shall not forget what you have done.'

But, in spite of their efforts, the disembarkation was delayed. The convoy anchored off the ancient Ottoman town of Eupatoria on 13th September, instead of proceeding to the landing place. On orders from Admiral Dundas the ships remained at anchor until *Retribution* and *Vesuvius* had negotiated the surrender of the town and a strong detachment of Marines, under the command of Captain Brock, was landed from *Sidon* to occupy it. *Trojan*, with two French steam frigates, was dispatched to reconnoitre the Russian encampment at the mouth of the Alma and Phillip was conscious of an unexpected lump in his throat as he watched her departure.

Next morning at first light, to the intense relief of Admiral Lyons, the convoy again got under way and, led by *Agamemnon*, anchored off the Old Fort in Kalamita Bay two hours later. The weather continued fair and – although the covering force of a line-of-battle ships anchored two miles off-shore, so that their boats took some time to arrive alongside the transports – the disembarkation was begun with the boats of the convoy and its escort. No enemy disputed the landing ... a few Cossacks, keeping well out of range, observed what was going on but that was all. Once more the organizing genius and energy of Admiral Lyons and his Flag-Captain were responsible for the speed and smoothness with which the operation was conducted. The boats of the Fleet plied ceaselessly to and fro between the ships and the shore and, by sunset, the whole of the infantry had been landed, together with a proportion of the horses and upwards of a dozen guns.

Lord Raglan boarded *Agamemnon* and stayed on board throughout the day to watch the landing, frequently, in Phillip's hearing, expressing his admiration for the way in which the sailors worked.

'Your men are magnificent, Admiral,' he said, as he was about to make his departure. 'Regardless of danger, fatigue and, indeed, of every consideration but that of performing an arduous duty, they have overcome every obstacle and put my infantry ashore with the utmost expedition and safety.'

'God grant this weather may continue, my lord,' Admiral Lyons answered, with a smile. 'If it does, I will have all your cavalry and artillery on shore by this time tomorrow and the transports on their way back to Varna to bring up the rest.'

The weather, however, deteriorated during the night. After raining heavily, a southerly wind sprang up which caused a strong swell in the bay and rendering the landing of either cavalry or artillery an extremely difficult and hazardous undertaking and little could be accomplished that day. On 16th the swell diminished by mid-day and, by dint of great exertions on the part of every officer and man of the Fleet, most of the remaining guns and horses were landed. The work went on next day, beginning at three in the morning and ending at eight in the evening so that, by noon on 18th, everything had been landed. The weary bluejackets were about to pause in their labours when orders came to re-embark the tents, since the army had been unable to commandeer sufficient transport ashore to move them. The tents were followed by a number of infantry packs, which the men could not carry, and when these had been taken back to the ships, there came an urgent request for water, that on shore being brackish and undrinkable and the soldiers' canteens empty.

Tom Johnson, in command of *Agamemnon*'s boats, said unhappily to Phillip when this request was passed on to him,

'We shan't have finished, even when we have taken them their water, you know . . . the poor fellows are collapsing like flies from cholera and dysentery. Before nightfall I fear we shall be bringing them back to the ships in their hundreds – and God knows what we shall be able to do for them, if we *do* bring them back!'

His grim prophecy proved, unfortunately, to be correct. Throughout that night and all the next day the sick were brought back to the ships they had left so recently and in such high spirits and the naval surgeons, working round the clock, did what they could to alleviate their sufferings. Many died before they could be carried to the waiting boats and hundreds more died at the end of the short but agonizing journey.

In spite of these setbacks, however, the Allied armies began the march on Sebastopol on the morning of 19th September. The French were on the right of the line, next to the beach, then the Turks and the British on the left of the line, farthest away from the sea. The men-of-war and commissariat transports of the combined Fleets followed, keeping abreast of the French and standing as close in-shore as the depth of water would allow. Most of the empty transports and a number of steam frigates had been sent back to Varna for reinforcements and to embark the Heavy Cavalry Brigade but five French and three British steamships, including *Trojan*, were again sent ahead to reconnoitre the mouths of the Bulganak and Alma rivers. As before Phillip experienced a pang, as he watched his old ship steam past *Agamemnon* on her way to discharge her mission. He had been too much occupied with his staff work for Admiral Lyons to pay even the briefest of visits to *Trojan* during the disembarkation but, seeing her now and recognizing Martin Fox on her quarterdeck, he promised himself that he would do so at the first opportunity.

The report brought back, a few hours later, by the frigates was not encouraging. The Allied armies had crossed the Bulganak at noon, without meeting any opposition but the Russians, it seemed, were in great force on the left bank of the Alma. Dense masses of infantry had been observed in occupation of the precipitous range of hills overlooking the river, with cavalry in support. Along a two-mile front, artillery had been posted to cover the approaches to the river crossing points, from which it was evident that the Russians were preparing to dispute the Allied advance. No accurate estimate of their numbers could be made from the sea but forty-five to fifty thousand was the most general and all the reports agreed that the Russian position was one of formidable natural strength. The character of the terrain, with its steep ravines and folds in the ground, the high cliffs on the seaward side and the size and strength of the fortified redoubts and gun emplacements were, according to one French frigate commander, 'such as to render the enemy lines of defence well nigh impregnable to a frontal attack.'

On the morning of 20th, as the British and French line-of-battle ships lay at anchor off the river mouth, the Russian army could be seen quite plainly. Phillip watched their preparations for battle from *Agamemnon*'s mizzen-top to which, with several of her other officers, he climbed soon after dawn. The Russians were, as nearly as he could judge, some two and a half to three miles from the mouth of the Alma, which put them well beyond the range of the most powerful naval guns and meant, he realized with a sinking heart, that the navy would have to be spectators when the Allied armies attacked. That they intended to launch an attack became increasingly evident as the day wore on. Through his glass, he watched first the French and then the British form up in line of march, still maintaining the order they had adhered to the previous day. The French marched in their traditional diamond formation, to the right of the line, with the Turkish infantry in reserve. The British were in 'grand divisions', the Light Division leading, with skirmishers spread out in front, the main body of infantry marching in double columns, with a front of two divisions, and cavalry and horse artillery covering their left flank.

Even at that distance, although reduced to the stature of toy soldiers, they presented a heart-stirring spectacle to the watchers in the tops, on the yards and in the shrouds of the anchored ships. As the well ordered ranks, in their brilliant uniforms, moved slowly forward to cross the two miles of sloping ground which separated them from the River Alma, colours were unfurled, bugles sounded and the bright, early morning sunshine struck a myriad dazzling reflections from lance-tip and sabre, from bayonet and unsheathed sword. Men still fell out and there were frequent halts – including a lengthy one, at ten-thirty, when the whole host came to a standstill in order to eat their mid-day meal – but the advance was steady and purposeful. To the right of the line, the leading French division – General Bosquet's Zouaves, with the Turks and their artillery behind them – marched rapidly forward to the beat of drums, and eight light-draught French steamers led by *Vauban*, moved closer in-shore to support them.

The allied plan of action had been drawn up by Marshal St. Arnaud and its details made known to the Naval High Command in a dispatch that morning. Phillip had heard it discussed and was aware that Bosquet's role was to be an attempt to turn the Russian left flank. In order to do so, his division would have to ascend the sparsely defended but almost perpendicular cliffs on the north side of the river, close to its juncture with the sea, dragging their guns with them ... a feat possible only to his mountain-trained Zouaves. Their appearance on the heights was to be the signal for the remaining French divisions to launch an attack on the Russian centre, whilst the British were to endeavour to turn the right flank of the enemy, forcing the strongly held position on the hills to their front at the point of the bayonet.

At one-twenty the eight French frigates commenced to throw shells at the heights above the river mouth and, as three bells struck from *Agamemnon*'s deck, Phillip watched with bated breath as the first Brigade of Zouaves crossed the river and hurled themselves at the towering cliffs. Displaying an heroic disregard of danger and with the speed and agility of moutain goats, the Zouaves gained the clifftop, manhandling their heavy field guns up the steep track, the Russian sharp-shooters who had sought to contest their advance falling back before them. A force of cavalry, attempting to come to the support of their comrades, was scattered and driven back in confusion by accurate fire from *Vauban*'s bow guns. Her commander had brought her within a few cables' length of the shore and, as the opposition melted before them, the Zouaves pressed gallantly forward, a second wave following the first. It seemed to Phillip an incredibly short time afterwards that he saw the French tricolour waving triumphantly from the highest point on the cliffs but in fact, he saw, consulting his watch, it had taken over an hour to place it there . . . and lines of motionless blue and red bodies bore mute witness to the lives which the Zouaves' achievement had cost them.

Someone touched Phillip's arm and turning, he saw that it was Tom Johnson. 'Look!' Johnson pointed inland, to where the centre of the Allied line had begun to move forward. To the left, the British divisions had deployed into two parallel lines and those in the leading divisions were – evidently on orders from their Commander-in-Chief – casting themselves face downwards on the ground. They were under heavy fire from the Russian guns, without the means to retaliate, and watching them, Phillip marvelled at their disciplined steadiness.

'The French are going into the attack, it seems,' Tom Johnson said. 'Those are Canrobert's and Prince Napoleon's divisions, surely, about to ford the river?' Climbing higher up the ratlines, he swept his glass in a wide arc and then lowered it, looking at Phillip with a bewildered frown. 'But our men are lying down. Poor fellows, the Russian batteries have found their range . . . it must be a ghastly ordeal to have to lie still under that concentration of fire.'

It would be a still more ghastly ordeal, Phillip thought, when their turn came to advance to the attack. To the British front, on the north side of the river, rose a double line of heights . . . the first steep green hillocks, upon which densely packed squares of Russian infantry could be seen, the sun glinting on their bayonets. Behind and above rose a series of rocky plateaux on which gun batteries had been placed to command the whole of the flat, low-lying ground across which the British troops would have to advance, in order to reach and ford the river. Highest of all, steeper and more rugged, the crest of the hills held reserves of infantry and still more gun emplacements, whilst a dark mass of cavalry could just be discerned over to the left.

This was the position which the British Army was to carry at the point of the bayonet ... Phillip felt his mouth go dry. The Zouaves' attack had been valiant enough but they had met with comparatively little opposition, since obviously the Russians had believed the hundred-foot high cliffs they had scaled unassailable. The British soldiers would need more than valour to drive the enemy from the heights they held in such strength and depth ... he sighed, lowering his own glass. He had made many friends among them and he wondered sadly how many of his friends he would see again, if Marshal St. Arnaud's plan of action were followed exactly.

The two French divisions crossed to the south bank of the Alma but were soon pinned down by a withering fire from above. One of the two – Canrobert's by its position – finding a certain degree of protection from the over-hanging rocks which confronted them, made a brave effort to continue the difficult ascent. Horsemen could be seen, galloping back and forth, evidently aides-de-camp bringing news of their progress to the French Commander-in-Chief.

'Phillip ...' Tom Johnson's voice was strained. 'Our men are moving now.'

'Yes,' Phillip said, 'I see them.' A cheer went up from a little group of *Agamemnon*'s midshipmen clinging to the shrouds as they, too, observed the scarlet-clad ranks getting to their feet at last. But the fire they had endured so stoically had taken a heavy toll ... many of the men lay where they had crouched obediently an hour before, deaf now to the orders which bade them arise. The rest closed ranks and, in meticulous alignment, two deep and on a wide front, the leading British divisions began their advance. As they did so the enemy sharp-shooters, who had been sniping at them from a village on the south bank of the river, withdrew from it, leaving the village ablaze behind them. A thick pall of smoke rose from the burning houses and Phillip stifled an exclamation of dismay as he saw the line of advance broken.

Men were crossing the river to the left, under very heavy fire and the first wave to reach the high south bank and drag themselves on to it had lost all semblance of alignment. They were, however, swiftly followed by others and, still subjected to a murderous hail of grape and canister from above, the lines were reformed and the advance continued. To their rear, the following divisions reached the river and started to cross and among them Phillip could see the tall black bear-skins of the Guards and the bonnets of Sir Colin Campbell's Highland Brigade.

'They are going straight for the guns!' Tom Johnson shouted. 'My God, look at them ... did you ever see such steadiness?'

Two regiments, formed into squares facing east, remained on the river bank to challenge the advance of the Russian cavalry which was bearing down in a bid to turn the British left flank but the rest, pausing only to fire two rapid volleys, charged up the first green hillock and drove the Russian infantry back in confusion. Great gaps were torn in their ranks when the heavy guns in a well-entrenched redoubt above them opened fire, but the gaps were filled, as other men scrambled up the river bank to fill the places of those who had fallen. One by one the tightly packed Russian infantry squares guarding the lower slopes wavered and took flight, seeking the protection of their own guns, rather than face the cold steel of the British bayonets.

The straggling, irregular line of red-coated soldiers fought their way tenaciously upwards. They reached the first redoubt and dragged themselves on to the parapet ... a regimental Colour was planted there, to fly in brave defiance held aloft by the bodies of the men who had borne it so gallantly into the mouths of the guns. With the rest of his fellow-watchers, Phillip cheered spontaneously when the Russians were seen to be limbering up their guns and carrying them to the rear in panic-stricken flight.

The enemy reserves moved forward but they, too, unnerved by the dauntless steadiness of the British advance, failed to halt it. Nowhere more than two deep, the British line was hurled back and reformed, yet it did not break. As men were mown down in the terrible hail of shot and shell directed at them from point-blank range, there were always others to take their places and the advance continued. The smoke of battle was so thick about them that, for long moments at a time, Phillip had to strain his eyes to see them.

But then they were leaping over the top of the earthwork which had shielded a battery of a dozen heavy guns and their resounding cheers could be heard on board the ships, even above the continued roar of gunfire. This came from British guns now, as the horse artillery galloped up to unlimber their guns and direct a deadly infilading fire upon the fleeing Russians.

In the centre of the line, the French, too – hidden for a time by the high cliffs – had managed to gain their objective. The crest of the plateau they had so heroically assaulted was crowned now, Phillip saw, with the tricolour and Canrobert's field guns, brought up the steep hillside with such infinite labour, were opening fire on the enemy. By four o'clock the battle was over, the victory certain and the Russian army streaming in precipitate flight towards Sebastopol, leaving their thousands of dead and wounded behind them.

'It is over,' Tom Johnson said and expelled his breath in a deep sigh. 'And, whilst I know that it was a glorious victory for our armies, I pray to God I may never be called upon to witness its like again, Phillip. Certainly' – his mouth twisted into a wry grimace – 'not in the role of a spectator, from the masthead of my ship. The butcher's bill will be high, I fear. Well, let's report to the deck, shall we? There will be work for us to do now.' He started to descend and Phillip, flexing his cramped limbs, followed him at once. There would be much for the naval spectators to do now, he knew, in caring for the wounded and bringing them back to the ships. . . .

2

Admiral Lyons went swiftly to work, mobilizing all the resources at his command, so that immediate help might be given to the army where it was most needed. Captain Mends and Captain Dacres were sent ashore, with the Admiral's Secretary, Frederick Cleeve, to ascertain Lord Raglan's wishes in this regard. All the surgeons who could be spared from their ships were ordered to assist their military colleagues in the regimental hospitals and dressing stations on shore. Where no hut or other form of shelter could be found, tarpaulins were erected to serve as surgical bivouacs, where the doctors could work close to the battlefield. Although only a few hours of daylight remained, parties of seamen and marines were landed with hammocks, slung on oars, to serve as stretchers, and ordered to bring down as many wounded as they could.

Phillip took command of one of these parties and, having established *Agamemnon*'s two assistant-surgeons in an improvised operating theatre at the foot of the hill which the Light and Second Divisions had stormed, he and his party carried wounded fusiliers and guardsmen down to them for treatment. They worked for as long as the light lasted, sickened and appalled by the hideous carnage and soon the improvised operating theatre was filled to its limit and beyond with the mutilated bodies of the soldiers who had fought so well. The two surgeons amputated limbs, extracted Minié balls and dressed wounds, until their supplies of dressings were exhausted. Still the number of suffering men requiring their attention grew and, by the light of lanterns brought from the ship, they worked on, in shirtsleeves, the sweat — despite the chill of the night — half-blinding them as it poured down their white, exhausted faces.

There was no transport for the injured, save for the piti-
fully inadequate number of stretchers carried by the regimental bandsmen and the seamen's hammocks, slung on their
oars ... the ambulance wagons, together with all the British
Army's transport and pack horses, had been left behind in
Varna. The French, Phillip saw, as he plodded up and down
the steep hillside, had an extremely efficient ambulance service for their men, which was put into operation as soon as
the battle ended. For the unfortunate British no provision
had been made and, as well as dressings, the supplies of
brandy and even of water were rapidly used up. Men with
freshly amputated legs and arms were laid on beds of hay or
straw, their stumps roughly dressed with the same material
as their wretched bedding ... there was no further comfort
for them, unless a soft-hearted bluejacket parted with his
tobacco and pipe.

When day dawned, the wounded who had survived the
night and the agony of the surgeons' attentions, were carried
painfully on the shoulders of their naval comrades for the
five or six miles which separated them from the beach. Even
there, they had to wait for upwards of an hour for room in
one of the boats plying between ship and shore. Only the
boats of Admiral Lyons' over-taxed squadron were available to embark the wounded ... those of the battle squadron,
anchored two miles off-shore, were not sent in until repeated
appeals brought the grudging promise of a few.

Phillip, unshaven, filthy and feeling like a sleepwalker,
toiled all day with his stretcher party. None asked for relief,
none demanded food or a rest and, in spite of persistent
rumours that the Russian wounded had fired on or attempted to bayonet those who sought to aid them, his men,
he noticed, dealt as kindly and as gently with the Russians as
with their own countrymen. Scores of them were brought
down to the beach and once, towards dusk, finding a party of
Turks callously engaged in looting the Russian wounded, his
Marines angrily drove them off at the point of the bayonet.

''Tain't right, sir, is it?' a husky boatswain's mate observed, gesturing to the discomfited Turks, who had paused

to argue their case with some young Marines. 'Them Rooskies may be our enemies but when all's said and done, sir, the Turks is heathens, ain't they? And they're acting like heathens, I reckon.'

Phillip agreed grimly that they were. He felt sick and light-headed with fatigue and lack of food, nauseated by the ghastly picture presented, as the aftermath of war, by this blood-soaked hillside which had been so valiantly contested and its possession so hardly won. Most of all he was distressed by the pitiful inadequacy of the efforts made to help those who had fallen in the battle, his own included. He watched men, whom he and his party had carried down to the beach, die there in the hot sun, because there were insufficient boats to take them to the waiting ships . . . and he saw them die in agony, because there was nothing with which to alleviate their pain.

The wounded bled to death because there were no dressings to staunch the flow of blood from their wounds; they endured the hideous torment of amputation without even the gulp of rum or brandy that was usually given to deaden shock. Many, all too many, were left entirely without attention, because there were not enough skilled men to attend them. Cholera cases lay beside the men injured in battle, were loaded with them into the boats and on board the ships, so that the infection spread. . . . He wanted to weep but had no tears left, only a bitter anger that such things should be and he himself compelled to witness, without being able to prevent them.

At dusk, Phillip sent his party back to *Agamemnon* for much needed food and rest but, still haunted by the faces of the dead and dying, he stumbled back to the battlefield once more, armed with a flask of whisky and some water canteens he had managed to obtain from one of the boat commanders. With these, he wandered in a sort of daze among the wounded who still lay on the hillside – the majority Russians – now kneeling beside a groaning sufferer to hold a flask to his lips, now pausing to raise another for ease from the cramped position in which, probably, he had lain since he fell. Faint cries, begging him for water to quench their burning thirst, came from all sides and he answered as many as he could. There were others besides himself, he realized as he limped wearily on, many others engaged in the same task ... both military and naval officers, non-commissioned officers and men, each with a lantern and, he supposed, each moved by the same emotions of mingled pity and horror as himself.

Indeed, someone had told him that Lord Raglan had ridden over the field after the battle had ended, his face a mask of grief ... and it was said that, heedless of the urging of Marshal St. Arnaud, he had refused to continue in pursuit of the vanquished Russian army until the wounded had been cared for and the dead buried. From what he had seen and heard of the British Commander-in-Chief, Phillip thought, he had no reason to doubt that this was true. Lord Raglan was a gentle, compassionate man and it had been he who had decided to leave the ambulance wagons and the bulk of the British medical supplies in Varna to follow with the reinforcements ... a decision forced upon him by expediency which, inevitably, he must now bitterly regret.

Phillip sighed. A burial party, carrying picks and spades instead of muskets and accompanied by an army chaplain, stumped past and he stood aside to let them go by, not envying them their melancholy duty. His last water canteen was almost empty and only a few drops of whisky remained in his flask ... he was turning away, preparatory to retracing his steps to the beach in search of fresh supplies, when a voice called out to him hoarsely, in English.

'Water ... please, a drop of water, if you have it. I ... am parched.'

Phillip, startled, lifted his lantern and peered about him, trying to decide from which direction the voice had come. A number of Russian corpses were scattered on top of a spur of rising ground and one man moved as he approached, weakly lifting a hand to signal to him ... an officer, judging by the quality of his uniform. In response to the gesture, Phillip crossed to his side and bending over him, gently turned him over on to his back. Gold lace gleamed dully in the fitful lantern light from the *aiguillette* of an Imperial aide-de-camp, although the heavily braided green chasseur jacket was darkly stained with mud and blood. A tourniquet, fashioned from the cords of the wounded officer's sash, was roughly bound about his right sleeve but this had not entirely succeeded in controlling the haemorrhage from a shattered arm, so that the sleeve, too, was soaked in blood. Its owner, for all the pain he must have been enduring, addressed Phillip with formal courtesy, his English carefully correct and almost without accent.

'Forgive me, sir ... it was I who called out to you, in the hope that you might spare me a sip of water. I have lain here for a long time in the heat of the sun and the pangs of thirst have become very severe, otherwise I would not have troubled you.'

'It is no trouble.' Phillip knelt beside him, an arm about his shoulders, helping him into a semi-sitting position. He picked up the canteen, regretfully aware that it held little more now than the sip which the Russian officer had requested. 'Try to drink it slowly,' he warned. 'There is very little left, I am afraid.'

'Even that little will be welcome, sir,' the Russian assured him. 'I am deeply indebted to you.' He drank the water, savouring it and murmuring his thanks between each sip. He was of high rank, Phillip saw, but quite young, the face which looked gratefully up at him, when the water was done, a strong and not ill-favoured one, despite its pallor and the disfiguring growth of stubble on chin and cheeks. There was something vaguely familiar about that face but ... he frowned, his mind instinctively rejecting the possibility of so fantastic a coincidence. He was tired, he told himself, strained to the limit of his strength ... in any case, he had only glimpsed Prince Narishkin in the distance, many weeks ago, from *Tiger*'s blazing upper deck and the chances of his being able to recognize him now were slim in the extreme.

'I'll take you down to our boats,' he said, setting down the empty canteen, his voice, even to his own ears, sounding harsh and peremptory. The Russian officer moved his head, to eye him in puzzled surprise.

'It is kind of you but ... I cannot walk, even with your assistance, I fear. I broke a leg, when my horse fell with me. In any event, sir, we are at war, are we not? You gave me water ... I can expect no more of you than that.'

'You can expect medical attention, Colonel,' Phillip returned. 'And you shall receive it, if I can get you to my ship. Let me see if I can make you a trifle more comfortable and then I will go in search of help to carry you down to the beach. It will be light soon and our boats will be waiting there.'

Brushing aside the other's protests, he removed his own jacket and shirt and, with strips torn from the shirt, bound the broken leg securely to its fellow, using a musket as a splint, and fashioned a sling for the injured arm. The bleeding had ceased and he removed the tourniquet although the arm, he realized, was probably past saving. The Russian officer bore his ministrations stoically and again expressed his gratitude, when the bandaging was finished.

'You are indeed kind, sir. I had not expected such kindness from an enemy.'

'I owe my life to the kindness I received, in similar circumstances, from your countrymen, Colonel,' Philip said shortly. He saw the Russian's brows lift and then comprehension dawn in his eyes. 'Which is your ship, sir?' he asked.

'Her Majesty's ship *Agamemnon* ... flagship of Admiral Sir Edmund Lyons.'

'Ah, yes ... a fine ship, a very fine ship. But previous to your appointment to her ...' the dark eyes met Phillip's confidently. 'Surely you were with the *Tiger*, were you not?'

'I was, Colonel.' Phillip attempted to make his escape but the Russian grasped his arm. 'No, wait, please. Your name is Hazard, is it not ... Lieutenant Hazard, late of Her Majesty's steam frigate *Trojan*?'

'Yes, I am Lieutenant Hazard. But ...' even to himself,

Phillip could not have explained his reluctance to allow the other to identify himself. Whilst even the smallest doubt remained, he could be objective, could treat this man as he would have treated any other helpless and defeated enemy, with compassion, even with kindness but once he had admitted who he was then ... he freed his arm and rose. 'There are some soldiers over there,' he said. 'I will ask them for help. We should lose no time, for your sake, in getting you to a surgeon.' He hailed the soldiers – Highlanders, he saw, as they came nearer in response to his call, three stalwart privates of the 93rd, with a grey haired sergeant, all of them carrying water canteens.

'Yes, sir?' The sergeant halted in front of him, coming smartly to attention.

Phillip gestured to the wounded Russian. 'I should be obliged if you and your men would bear a hand here, Sergeant. I want to get this officer down to our boats.'

The sergeant hesitated, studying the Russian's uniform. 'A prisoner of importance wad he be, sir?'

'Of considerable importance. I believe that Admiral Lyons will want to talk to him.'

'Verra guid, sir. We'll tak' him doon tae the beach. We're owing the Navy a few favours, one way and anither, are we no', lads ... and the Admiral in particular.'

The soldiers deftly contrived a stretcher from their muskets and two jackets and, with touching gentleness, lifted their prisoner on to it and hoisted him on to their shoulders. They carried him carefully over the rough ground, pausing at intervals to let him rest and, when they did so, giving him sips of water from their canteens. He must, despite their care. have suffered a good deal but he did not complain, did not open his mouth, save to thank them. Phillip limped along with the sergeant, listening to his account of the battle, at pains to avoid further conversation with the wounded Russian although conscious, several times, of the other's dark eyes watching him in evident perplexity.

'My, yon Sir Colin Campbell ... that's a braw auld man for ye!' the sergeant said. He chuckled reminiscently. 'Our lads were wanting tae press forward, seeing the Guards likely tae steal a march on us and what does Sir Colin do but ride back tae us and mak' us tak' up oor dressing again. "Damn all this eagerness, 93rd," says he. "Ye'll gang in like soldiers o' the Hieland Brigade or you'll no' gang in at all." But then, sir, when we reached the top o' Kourgane Hill and the Scots Fusilier Guards were racing wi' us and the Grenadiers and Coldstreamers for tae be the first tae enter the Great Redoubt there, up leaps Sir Colin. "We'll hae nane but Hieland bonnets here!" shouts he and by heaven, sir, he was gie'n his way, for they yielded us the honour. And we were cheering him till oor lungs gave out ... ye must ha' heard us from on board your ship, sir.'

'We did, Sergeant,' Phillip confirmed. 'And we watched you on your way up the hill.'

'We've the Rooshians beaten, sir, man for man,' the sergeant told him. 'They were in yon great massed squares, ye ken, wi' bayonets facing us and if they'd held their ground, I doubt we could ha' broken them. But they started to run from the rear, sir, and then the panic seized them and the whole lot turned tail and made off before we'd a chance tae touch them wi' the bayonet. Our casualties were remarkably light, sir ... just fifteen killed and eighty-three wounded.'

'What are our total losses, do you know, Sergeant?'

The sergeant shrugged his broad shoulders. 'Our adjutant tell't me about fifteen hundred killed and wounded, sir ... and the French about twelve hundred. The Rooshians will ha' lost twice that, sir, I would think and in dead, why . . .' he frowned. 'The bodies were in the proportion of one o' ours tae six o' theirs, sir, as nearly as I could judge. And I'm no' sic a bad judge ... I've been in a burial party since dawn today, sir. 'Tis a gey pity, though, that we were not permitted tae follow up our victory and gang after them, the day after the battle. We would be in Sebastopol now, had Lord Raglan ordered us forward and left the Navy tae tak' care o' the wounded.'

Phillip wondered whether he was right but he did not argue. If the Allied armies had continued in pursuit of the

Russians, leaving the Fleets to evacuate the wounded and bury the dead, they might well, by this time, have been in possession of Sebastopol. On the other hand, had the Russian Fleet issued from its harbour and found the British and French ships at anchor, denuded of men, it might have been a different story . . . with the battle squadrons destroyed and the Russian Navy in command of the Black Sea, they would not have retained possession of Sebastopol for long.

They reached the beach as dawn was breaking. The soldiers set down their burden beside the other wounded who were waiting to be taken off to the ships and Phillip dismissed them, with grateful thanks. 'We'll awa' back and bring down one or twa more o' the puir devils,' the sergeant told him cheerfully. 'And then maybe we'll be on our way tae Sebastopol. Guid morning tae ye, sir . . . and guid luck tae ye!'

Phillip watched him and his little party out of sight. There were, as yet, no boats but he could see them putting off from the ships, including several from *Agamemnon* and he walked down to the water's edge to meet them. The first to arrive was commanded by Tom Johnson and he readily agreed to take off Phillip's prisoner.

'Are you coming back with your Russian Colonel, Phillip?' he asked. 'You look as if you could do with a meal and a few hour's sleep. That old wound in your leg is playing you up a bit, is it not?'

Phillip nodded wryly. 'Has the Admiral asked for me?'

'He asked where you were but didn't say he needed you.'

'Then if you would be kind enough to see that my prisoner receives medical attention as soon as possible, Tom, I'll be back in half an hour or so. Incidentally the Admiral may be interested in having a chat with him, when his wounds have been dressed . . . he's an aide-de-camp to Prince Menschikoff, I have reason to believe.'

Tom Johnson pursed his lips in a silent whistle.

'Quite a prize, then. Do you know his name?'

Phillip hesitated, 'Ask him,' he suggested. 'I'm afraid that

I omitted to do so. But I also believe that it was he who captured the *Tiger*.' He pointed to where the Russian Colonel was lying. 'That's him, over there. Green cavalry uniform, arm in a sling and a broken leg splinted to a Minié rifle . . . you can't mistake him.'

'Where are you going, Phillip? Surely it's time you allowed yourself some rest? You aren't fit yet and—'

Phillip cut him short. 'I see a boat putting off from *Trojan*, Tom. I'd like to pass the time of day with whoever's in command of her but I won't be long. Since you're kind enough to feel concern for me, I'll make your next trip back with you, I give you my word.'

'I'll hold you to it, Phillip,' Tom Johnson warned. He turned to his coxswain. 'Right, cox'un, I want two men with a stretcher to pick up a Russian Colonel who's lying over there . . .' he repeated Phillip's description. 'Handsomely now and careful with him, he's badly hurt.'

Tom Johnson's boat, with its cargo of wounded Russians, was on its way back to *Agamemnon* when the boat from *Trojan* grounded on the beach. To his delight, Phillip recognized Martin Fox in the sternsheets, with Midshipman O'Hara at the tiller. They both greeted him warmly and O'Hara wrung his hand with such vigour that he was compelled to cry for mercy.

'You don't know your own strength, Mr. O'Hara,' he said, with mock severity. 'But I take it, from your presence here in such rude health, that you suffered no ill-effects from your swim back from the poor *Tiger* two months ago?'

'None, sir,' O'Hara assured him. 'We all got back, except you and Able-seaman Lacey, sir. But . . .' he glanced uncertainly at Martin Fox and bit back whatever he had intended to say. 'I'll take charge of the shore party, sir,' he offered, 'if you would like to talk to Mr. Hazard.'

Fox hesitated, a wave of embarrassed colour surging into his cheeks. Then he took Phillip's arm and led him out of earshot of the boat's crew. 'You look ill, Phillip,' he said, his tone flat. 'Do you want to be burdened with a long story of our troubles?'

'Are they so many, Martin?'

Martin Fox nodded, his mouth tightly compressed. Phillip searched his face anxiously. Although healthily tanned, the younger man did not look himself. Indeed, he gave the impression of one who, whilst holding himself under iron control, was rapidly approaching the limit of his endurance and he had aged almost beyond recognition. Meeting Phillip's gaze, he smiled but the smile was forced and it lacked all amusement.

'Let's sit down, shall we?' he suggested. 'We can talk until the boat's loaded.' They walked together to the far end of the beach and sat down facing each other. 'Take a mouthful or two of this, Phillip,' Fox said, offering his flask. 'I brought it for the wounded but I think it will do you more good.'

The potent spirit eased Phillip's aching weariness. He lit a cigar, also provided by his companion, and they smoked for a few minutes in silence. 'You nearly died, while you were in Odessa, didn't you?' Fox said at last. 'Or so we heard but quite honestly, Phillip . . .' he emitted a deep sigh. 'This may sound a gross exaggeration but I'd gladly have changed places with you, not once but a hundred times. I'd change places with you now, limp and all.'

'As bad as that, is it?' Phillip echoed his sigh.

'Worse than it has ever been,' Martin Fox asserted grimly. 'The men are completely demoralized . . . sullen, resentful, bitter. Even the petty officers and Marines are disaffected, the rot has spread everywhere. Seventeen men deserted in Constantinople the last time we called there . . . we recovered eleven of them and each was given ten dozen lashes, from which two have since died. There's not an officer who has not requested a transfer but the Captain now refuses to put their requests forward. Anthony Cochrane is under open arrest, awaiting court martial . . . perhaps you heard?'

'Yes, Martin, I heard.'

Fox inhaled smoke. He went on, his voice harsh with bitterness, 'The trial hasn't yet taken place, so Cochrane has not been relieved of his duties. He has been on watch-and-watch

202

for five weeks ... Laidlaw has now joined him and most of the midshipmen are in a like case.'

'Cochrane is to be charged with insubordination, isn't he?' Phillip asked, frowning.

Martin Fox wearily inclined his head. 'We could all be court martialled on the same charge,' he confessed. 'Perhaps we all shall be, because we're at the end of our tether, Phillip. North is a sadist and ... to be frank, I think he's insane. We were badly hit by the cholera, when we returned to Kavarna in July, after a spell of blockading Sebastopol. At one time we had nearly eighty men down with it or dysentery, lying helpless in their hammocks. The Captain ordered the whole ship's company to turn out, at three bells in the Middle Watch, and he drummed to quarters for a practice alarm ... lying at anchor in Kavarna Bay! Even the wretched men who were sick were forced to turn out and, because they were longer about it than he considered they should have been, North ordered *all* hammocks stowed in the nettings. Cochrane had the watch and he refused to obey the order so ...' he spread his hands helplessly. 'So he has been charged with insubordination and he is living for the day when his trial takes place, for then he intends to tell the court what it is like to serve under the command of Captain Thomas North!'

Phillip asked sharply, 'Does North know this, Martin?'

Fox repeated his shrug. 'He must know ... but it does not appear to worry him. That's why I believe him to be insane. No man in his right mind could behave as he does and be so completely indifferent to the consequences. If the men weren't so cowed, I'd have expected an attempt on his life before this.' He smiled unhappily. 'I've even, in my more desperate moments, considered making one myself!'

Phillip stared at him in horrified disbelief. '*You*, Martin? But in heaven's name—'

'Oh, I haven't made it yet. Perhaps because I, too, am afraid of him.'

'I suppose you have considered petitioning the Commander-in-Chief, to have him removed from command?'.

'We've considered that,' Fox confessed gravely. 'Indeed,' we talk of little else. But it is a serious matter in wartime, Phillip, and if our petition failed, it could break us all. At present we've decided to give evidence in Cochrane's defence when he is brought to trial . . . we shall *all* give evidence, on oath, to the court. That must surely lead to an inquiry, don't you think?'

'I should think it must,' Phillip agreed, forcing his tired brain to review the possibilities. 'When is the trial?'

'We have not been told but presumably the war must be prosecuted first. In any event . . .' Fox spoke with bitter cynicism, 'we are virtually prisoners aboard *Trojan*, you know. No shore leave for anyone, no ship-to-ship visiting, save by the Captain, of course. Believe it or not, this is only the second time our boats have been sent ashore. I did not see you yesterday and, had we not met here by chance today, I should have been unable to pour out my woes to you as I have. And of what use to pour them out to anyone else? You, at least, will believe me.'

'Yes, Martin, I believe you. And I am sorry.' Phillip laid an affectionate hand on his friend's shoulder and gripped it hard. He was stunned by what Martin Fox had told him, sickened by it as, a short while ago, the sight of the battlefield of the Alma had sickened him. He hesitated, every instinct he possessed warning him against doing what, he knew, he would have to do. *Trojan* was his ship, the men his men . . . he breathed a resigned sigh and, hearing it, Martin Fox made to rise.

'I must go, Phillip. The boat will be loaded, I can't keep those poor devils of wounded waiting. But it has helped to talk to you and—'

'Martin, wait a moment.' Phillip clambered stiffly to his feet. He felt ill, his head aching unbearably and his throat dry but there was no escape. 'Would it help if I applied to be reappointed to *Trojan*? There may be nothing I can do but at least I could try.'

'For God's sake, Phillip . . .' Fox turned, every vestige of colour draining from his cheeks. 'You will be mad if you do!

Leave *Agamemnon* for *Trojan*, when you've made your escape? Don't be such an idiot!'

'Leaving the question of my sanity aside, Martin ... *would* it help?'

'You cannot possibly mean it—'

'I do mean it, I promise you.'

'Then come back,' Fox said huskily. He clasped Phillip's hand in both his own, a suspicious brightness in his eyes. 'From the very bottom of my heart, Phillip, I shall thank you if you do.'

They stood looking at each other for a long moment in silence and then walked back to the waiting boats together.

Tom Johnson's boat returned to the beach a few minutes after Martin Fox's had left it and he said, as Phillip joined him, 'Your prisoner was safely delivered into the surgeons' hands, Phillip ... he's probably lost his arm by now. I asked him his name, incidentally and ... you *did* capture quite a prize. He is Colonel Prince Andrei Narishkin, aide-de-camp to Prince Menschikoff, and the Admiral is very interested. We also have a General on board, General Karganoff, who is severely wounded. Both, I understand, are to be transferred tonight or tomorrow to a transport containing about five hundred other Russian wounded, which *Fury* will escort to Odessa.'

'Do you mean,' Phillip asked, surprised, 'that they are to be repatriated?'

'On the Admiral's orders,' Tom Johnson assured him. 'And as a mark of appreciation of the way in which *Tiger's* men – including yourself, of course – were treated by the Governor.' He smiled. 'Does that please you? I imagine it must.'

'Yes, indeed it does.' Phillip fumbled in the breast pocket of his jacket and his fingers closed about the emerald ring Mademoiselle Sophie had given him. He looked down at the beautiful thing, lying in its opened case and suddenly his expression relaxed. 'Will you do me a small favour, Tom?'

'Of course, if I can. What is it?'

Phillip passed him the ring. 'Give this to Colonel Prince Andrei Narishkin before he leaves the ship and tell him ... tell him that it belongs to his wife and that I'd like to restore it to her.'

'His *wife*? But surely you—'

'Don't ask me any questions, Tom. Just give it to him, will you please, like a good fellow?'

'Well ... if you wish. But I scent a mystery and, in any case, why can't you give it to him yourself? You are coming back to the ship, are you not?'

Phillip nodded. 'Yes ... but only for long enough to pack my gear and see the Admiral. I am going to ask to be re-appointed to *Trojan* and I don't think he will refuse me.'

Tom Johnson's jaw dropped. 'Are you mad, Phillip?' he demanded incredulously.

'Yes, perhaps I am,' Phillip conceded glumly. He glanced once more at the ring, seeing in memory Mademoiselle Sophie's small, sweet face and then, as Tom Johnson closed the case and thrust it into his pocket, the vision faded. It was the end of a dream, he thought, the only end this particular dream could have had ... the only one Mademoiselle Sophie would want it to have, in the circumstances. He was glad that a quirk of fate had enabled him to return her husband to her, as well as the ring because now, if that same unpredictable fate were to ordain that they should meet again, his conscience would be clear ... burdened only with the awareness that, for a little while, they had loved each other.

Admiral Lyons agreed to his request without demanding his reasons for making it and, within an hour, one of *Agamemnon*'s boats took him back to *Trojan*.

CHAPTER NINE

I

On 23rd September the Allied Armies reformed and marched down from the Heights of the Alma to continue their advance on Sebastopol. The Fleets made contact with them that evening at the mouth of the River Katcha, in order to land stores and provisions and take off the sick for transport to the Bosphorus.

To Phillip, the days immediately following his reappointment to his old ship were among the most frustrating that he had ever experienced. Captain North did not welcome his return and made no attempt to conceal the fact and the atmosphere on board *Trojan* was tense and unhappy, the men sullen and the officers dispirited and close to despair. As always – although fully informed, at Captains' conferences aboard the flagship, of what was going on – North kept his officers in ignorance of what he learned and his orders were issued without explanation and with a minimum of detail. Phillip, accustomed to being at Admiral Lyons' elbow when plans were made and discussed and aware – since he had written out so many of them – of the orders issued to the entire Fleet, found this deliberate refusal to tell him anything a source of increasing irritation. In common with the rest of *Trojan*'s officers, he was forbidden shore leave and given little opportunity to pay or receive visits from other ships in the squadron, so that he was cut off from contact with those who would willingly have shared their knowledge with him.

Tom Johnson, however, contrived to make an official call with orders from Admiral Lyons late in the evening of Sunday, 24th September, by which time the Armies were bivouacked less than four miles from their objective, on the Balbec River. From him, Phillip learnt that Captain Jones, of H.M.S. *Sampson* – who had been keeping Sebastopol under observation – had reported several changes in the position of the Russian line-of-battle ships at anchor in the harbour. The significance of these changes became apparent when Admiral Dundas stood off the port with his battle squadron and, under cover of *Britannia*'s guns, *Retribution* was sent close inshore to examine them.

'Yesterday there was a two-decker, flying an admiral's flag at the mizzen, in Artillery Creek ... looking as if she were about to put to sea,' Johnson said. 'But according to Captain Drummond's observations this morning, Phillip, the Russians have scuttled a large portion of their Fleet in order ...' his tone was indignant, 'In order to block the entrance of the harbour to us!'

'To block the entrance?' Phillip echoed incredulously.

'Captain Drummond told the Admiral that seven sail-of-the-line, most of them two-deckers, have been sunk between Fort Constantine and the fifty-gun battery on the north shore of Quarantine Bay,' Tom Johnson continued, still indignant. 'Their masts are more or less above water. Eight others, including a three-decker, are moored from east to west, inside the booms. Three of these are heeled over to give their guns greater elevation and enable them to sweep over the land to the northward. The rest are lying at the head of the harbour, with their guns covering its entrance and the Russians have reinforced their land defences to the north. A large octagonal fort, which is marked on our charts as the Star Fort, mounting at least forty guns, covers the Balbec River where the French would have to cross and they want a complete change of plan.'

'What sort of change of plan?' Phillip asked.

'A change of direction.' Johnson shrugged. 'Admiral Lyons, as you know, had envisaged sailing into the harbour with our combined battle squadrons, to engage the Russian Fleet at anchor, while the Armies launched a simultaneous asssault on land from the north. But now, of course, with the harbour entrance barred to us, that is impossible. So . . .' he sighed. 'There have been conferences all day, which the Admirals as well as the Generals have attended. And . . . I don't know this for certain, Phillip, but they say that Marshal St. Arnaud is so gravely ill that he is about to hand over command of the French Army to General Canrobert. Not that this will affect French policy since both, apparently, are now of the opinion that Sebastopol is unassailable from the north. They consider that, without support from the Fleets, an attack launched from their present position north of the Balbec River would be doomed to failure. So a flank march has been decided upon, it seems, by means of which the Armies will circle Sebastopol and launch their attack from the south.'

'But that will take days, Tom!' Phillip exclaimed. 'And, once they leave the coast, they'll be cut off from us completely.'

'Nevertheless that is what has been agreed,' Tom Johnson said positively. 'Reluctantly by Admiral Lyons, as you may imagine . . . but with the harbour entrance blocked, what can he do save agree? The orders I have just delivered to your commander are for the steam squadron to prepare to proceed to Balaclava and – escorting transports and the siege train – take possession of the harbour there and await the arrival of the armies on the completion of their march.'

Phillip pursed his lips in a silent whistle. 'When do we sail, have you any idea?'

'No.' Tom Johnson shook his head. 'But probably tomorrow. Frederick Maxse is to accompany Lord Raglan and bring back instructions from him. *Highflyer* or *Retribution* may be dispatched to reconnoitre Balaclava and also Kamiesch and Kazatch or Admiral Lyons may go himself, this hasn't yet been decided. But Maxse says that both the Admiral and Lord Raglan favour Balaclava as our base for the final assault on Sebastopol . . . it is a good harbour and, according to our reports, is undefended or virtually so. Well, I must go.' He held out his hand. 'Good luck, Phillip . . . I shall probably see you at Balaclava in a day or two.'

Tom Johnson proved to be right in this assumption and also regarding Marshal St. Arnaud's failing health. Next day General Canrobert assumed supreme command of the French land and sea forces. The Marshal – rumoured to be on the point of death – was carried on board the French battleship *Berthelot* for what was expected to be his last journey. He died four days later.

In the meantime, the Allied Armies struck inland on a compass bearing, so as to circle Sebastopol. It was a difficult march, over trackless, thickly wooded country but, in spite of this, the march was rapidly and succesfully accomplished. Apart from an encounter with the rearguard of a Russian division marching out of Sebastopol in the direction of Simpheropol, they met with little opposition and Sir George Cathcart's Fourth Division, left to guard the approaches to the Balbec, was unmolested. The Fleets remained off the mouth of the Katcha – save for a few steam frigates engaged on reconnaissance or on escort duty with transports on their way to the Bosphorus with sick and wounded – to await final instructions from Lord Raglan.

These arrived early on 26th September, brought by Frederick Maxse, after a hazardous ride on horseback and in darkness, across fifteen miles of enemy territory, and requested Sir Edmund Lyons to proceed forthwith to Balaclava with his squadron and the siege train, in order to co-operate with the Army. Once again, Phillip was indebted to Tom Johnson for this information and the story of Lieutenant Maxse's perilous ride ... North merely ordered him to get steam up and prepare to weigh under engines, on a signal from *Agamemnon*.

By noon, the steam squadron, accompanied by transports carrying stores and provisions for the Army and the heavy guns of the siege train, was off Balaclava. *Agamemnon* silenced the token resistance offered by an ancient Genoese fort on the cliffs with a single broadside and *Niger* went inside to take soundings. Next day, just as the first British troops were descending on the little town from the hills above Kadikoi, Admiral Lyons shifted his flag to the *Cara-*

doc, in order to go ashore to greet Lord Raglan. Captain Mends, with his usual consummate seamanship, brought *Agamemnon* into the small, land-locked harbour a few hours later and landed an advance guard of Royal Marines to assist in its defence.

At first sight, Phillip decided, Balaclava appeared to be an excellent choice for the British base. The soundings taken by *Niger* indicated that there was sufficient depth of water for even the largest ship to enter and secure to the quay while her stores were unloaded ... and *Agamemnon* had proved this, to resounding cheers from the troops on shore. The harbour, half a mile long and some three hundred yards in width, was an inlet of the sea, entered by a narrow opening and hemmed in by towering cliffs. It provided safe anchorage and shelter and was possessed of powerful natural defences. The town, a cluster of small wooden houses, was within seven miles of Sebastopol and its inhabitants, who were of Greek origin, were evidently not enamoured of their Russian rulers, for they welcomed the invaders warmly.

General Canrobert, however, after inspecting the place, decided that the harbour was too small to serve as a base for his forces as well as the British. After consultation with Lord Raglan, he waived the traditional French claim to the right of the line and chose the Bay of Kamiesch, with that of Kazatch, as the French base. These two roomy, sheltered bays were in the neighbourhood of Cape Kherson – closer to Sebastopol than Balaclava – with a comparatively easy road giving access to the plateau above. The two Armies swung round and established themselves on this plateau, known as the Kheronese Upland, the French left flank at Kamiesch Bay on the west and the British right resting on the River Tehernaya, eight miles to the east. Five hundred feet below them lay Sebastopol, seemingly at their mercy, defended by a few forts and earthworks and denuded of troops. Preparations for its capture began at once.

Admiral Lyons' small squadron, consisting of *Agamemnon, Highflyer, Niger, Trojan, Triton* and *Spitfire*, was soon hard at work unloading stores and provisions and clearing transports. The ships were moored with their bows across the river and their sterns secured to the shore and the small harbour became packed to capacity as more and more transports were towed in by steamers. *Sanspareil* and *Diamond* came in, to land reinforcements for the Marines defending the heights above the harbour and the remainder of the Heavy Cavalry Brigade arrived from Varna and was disembarked. Orders came to put the siege train ashore and the bluejackets engaged in this task worked with such a will that, by 2nd October, all save two of the heavy siege guns had been landed, together with supplies of shot, powder and shell.

It was then decided, at Lord Raglan's request, to land upwards of fifty naval guns to be worked by seamen from the Fleet and contingents from the battle squadron were sent to Balaclava by Admiral Dundas, to form a Naval Brigade. *Trojan* and *Firebrand* ferried them in, the battle squadron remaining at anchor off the Katcha River. Under the command of Captain Lushington of *Albion*, with Captain Peel of the *Diamond* as his second-in-command, this force consisted of thirty-eight officers and a thousand men, in addition to the twelve hundred Royal Marines already serving on shore.

Most of the naval guns – 32-pounders, weighing about 40 cwt. – were taken off the *Diamond* and the ship herself moored in the harbour to act as a reception centre for sick and wounded seamen. The rest of the guns were found by the other ships and included four 68-pounders from the *Terrible*, each weighing 95 cwt., and two of the *Beagle*'s huge, long range Lancasters, which were designed to throw a 90-pound shot. A hundred and fifty rounds of shot and thirty common shell, with powder in proportion, were landed initially for each gun and seventy rounds for each field piece.

It was a herculean task to move guns and ammunition from the harbour to the batteries being constructed on the plateau above. Bullock carts, wagons, Malta carts drawn by mules, horse limbers and even camels were requisitioned for

'Is it, sir . . . *is* it beyond your power? You've been on Admiral Lyons' staff. The Admiral would listen to you, if you went to him, sir, and—'

'We are at war, Mr. O'Hara,' Phillip was compelled to remind him. 'I cannot question the Admiral's orders or ask him to change them. *Trojan* is a frigate, with specific duties to perform and a crew of three hundred, every one of whom is required in order to work her at sea. If these men were allowed to volunteer for service with the Naval Brigade on shore, *Trojan* would cease to be an effective unit of the Fleet. The men would either have to be replaced or the ship left, like *Diamond*, in harbour . . . and we haven't so many steamers. She cannot be spared, Mr. O'Hara. None of the steam squadron *can* be spared, you must realize that.'

'Yes, sir, I do,' O'Hara conceded. 'But all the same . . .' his young voice was adult in its bitter disillusionment. 'I'd as soon see *Trojan* stripped of her guns and her crew and used, like *Diamond*, as a hulk for the reception of the sick and wounded than send these men back to her against their will.'

'No doubt you would,' Phillip returned. 'But that decision, Mr. O'Hara, is not for either of us to make, is it?'

'No, sir. Only the men have had as much as they can endure, you see, sir, and I am afraid, if they go back, that . . . well, that there may be trouble. I've heard them talking, sir. The Captain—'

'Belay that, Mr. O'Hara!' Phillip bade him sternly. 'And form up your working party at the double, if you please. Our orders are to rejoin the ship.'

'Aye, aye, sir,' the tall midshipman acknowledged flatly. The men formed up in response to his shouted command and, as dejected as they had been a week before, permitted him to march them down to the harbour and the boats that were waiting to take them back to *Trojan*. There was no singing, they marched in grim silence, the fiddler with his instrument under his arm. Conscious of an aching pity for them which he could not suppress, Phillip did his best to cheer them with the promise that he would report favourably on their conduct to the Captain.

O'Leary eyed him defiantly and then spat, with studied insolence, at his feet. 'Save your breath, sorr,' he advised. 'Sure, you'll just be wasting it, if you do onything o' the kind. Captain North will hear no good of us, whoever says it, wouldn't you know that?'

Phillip affected deafness and did not reprimand him. Back aboard *Trojan*, little seemed to have changed and the atmosphere was almost a tangible thing, whose brooding menace reached out to enfold him within a few minutes of his return. Anthony Cochrane, his face grey with fatigue, still wearily kept watch-and-watch, walking the quarterdeck like a ghost. The men of the Foretop Division, Phillip learnt, had had their grog stopped for lack of attention to duty. Two of the Port Watch were under arrest and awaiting sentence by the Captain for refusal to obey an order and Martin Fox reported three men down with cholera ... one of these the Captain's personal steward who, fearing his commander's wrath if he went off duty, had carried on until he collapsed.

'The Surgeon says the poor fellow's dying,' Fox stated. 'He was too far gone for medical aid when they brought him below.' He added feelingly. 'Needless to tell you, Phillip, I am unable to find a voluntary replacement for him.'

'And I,' Phillip told him, an edge to his voice, 'have had to refuse a request, from my entire shore party, for permission to volunteer for service with the Naval Brigade, rather than report back to this ship for duty.'

They exchanged unhappy glances. 'Why do you not tell the Captain that, when you report to him?' Fox suggested, cynically.

'How can I? No, I shall confine myself to praising them for the way they have worked on shore. They have been magnificent, Martin ... every man-jack went on until he dropped and not a grumble from any of them, no matter what they were called upon to do. That is the truth and it's what I intend to tell the Captain. Where is he, do you know?'

'He's dining below ... but I doubt if he'll believe you or

216

welcome the interruption. However ...' Martin Fox shrugged. 'I'd like to talk to you when you can spare me half an hour in private, Phillip. So would Mr. Burnaby. Perhaps you should see him first.'

'Burnaby?' Phillip frowned. 'What does he want?'

'I'd prefer him to tell you that himself. But don't let me keep you from the Captain, Phillip ... even though you'll be wasting your breath if you try to convince him that our men are anything but undisciplined scum. Recently ...' Fox's tone was more cynical than ever. 'Recently he has taken to describing them as mutinous scoundrels with, I fear, more truth than he knows.'

Phillip's mouth tightened ominously but he did not argue. O'Leary had also told him that he would be wasting his breath, he thought wearily, as he went in search of the Captain, and perhaps it was true. But he would have to try, he supposed, even if his attempt were doomed to failure and the Captain refused to listen to him.

North, who was finishing his meal, received him with no pretence of pleasure and listened to his favourable comments concerning the working party, a sceptical expression on his high-coloured, angular face.

'I unfortunately chanced to witness your party's return, Mr. Hazard,' he said, cutting Phillip's recital short. 'And the men's appearance was a disgrace to the ship. See that they all shave and change their shirts before they return to duty. Very well ...' he commenced moodily to pick his teeth with a silver-handled toothpick, eyeing his First Lieutenant coldly. 'You may carry on.'

'But, sir ... Captain North, I—'

'Can't you understand plain English, Mr. Hazard?'

'Yes, sir, of course. But I—'

'Leave me to finish my dinner in peace, devil take it!' North interrupted irritably. 'You may have got into the habit of dancing attendance on the Admiral whilst you were aboard *Agamemnon* and possibly he welcomed your attentions ... but I do not. I prefer my own company, is that clear?'

'Aye, aye, sir.' Phillip contained his rising temper with difficulty and prepared to accept this brusque dismissal. His hand was on the cabin door when Captain North called him back. 'Oh, there's a small matter which almost slipped my mind, Mr. Hazard. It concerns your brother.'

'My *brother*, sir?' Taken by surprise, Phillip halted and turned to face him, pale and startled. But he controlled himself. 'If you are referring to Able-Seaman Hazard, sir, he is a prisoner of war in Odessa. That is, he—'

'Able-Seaman Hazard, as you are pleased to call him, was brought back by the *Fury* a few days ago,' the Captain put in, a sneer in his voice. 'From Odessa ... although it seems, from what he told the *Fury*'s commander, that he was for a time in St. Petersburg, undergoing a course of studies at the Imperial Naval Academy. Presumably he proved an unsatisfactory student, for they returned him.' North paused, savouring his triumph. 'You look upset, Mr. Hazard.'

Making an almost visible effort not to betray his feelings, Phillip shook his head. 'No, sir, I ... I was surprised, that was all.'

The Captain smiled. 'Well, it may surprise you even more when I tell you that he will shortly be rejoining this ship. When he does, I will find suitable employment for him ... I want no more of this skulking in the chartroom and meals with the warrant officers. He is rated as an able-seaman, not a Master's assistant.'

'Yes, sir.' Phillip's thoughts were in turmoil and his mind reeling from the shock of what the Captain had told him. Graham ... back with the British Fleet, returning to *Trojan*? But why? Why in heaven's name had his brother left St. Petersburg and why had he played his cards so badly that North had been able to arrange for him to be drafted back to *Trojan*? In the final analysis, he thought ruefully, as he closed the door of the Captain's cabin behind him, Graham had, it would seem, behaved no less quixotically and certainly no less foolishly than he himself had behaved. . . .

'Excuse me, Mr. Hazard ... I'd appreciate a word with you, sir, if you have a few minutes.'

Phillip turned, recognizing Burnaby, the elderly Master, who had evidently been waiting for him to emerge from the Captain's quarters. He stifled his impatience and nodded.

'Yes, Mr. Burnaby, what can I do for you?'

'What I have to say is for your ears alone, Mr. Hazard,' the Master told him.

'Then come to my cabin.' Phillip led the way, the old man following silently at his heels. In the sanctuary of his small sleeping cabin, he waved his visitor to its only chair and poured him a tot of whisky from the bottle he kept there. Burnaby faced him squarely, glass in hand, his warning of impending trouble delivered with blunt honesty and with no attempt to prevaricate.

'I can't tell you what form the trouble will take, Mr. Hazard,' he said apologetically. 'But it is coming ... I can feel it and I've been too many years at sea to be mistaken. You develop a nose for these things, an instinct, if you like. Your health, sir!' He swallowed his whisky at a gulp and, with an odd little gesture of finality, set down his glass. 'That was all I wanted to say, Mr. Hazard. But I had to tell you because, unless something is done very soon, I'm afraid it may be too late. And ... you are the First Lieutenant, sir. It's for you to act.'

'Precisely what action,' Phillip asked, 'do you consider I ought to take, Mr. Burnaby?'

'That is for you to decide, Mr. Hazard. I cannot advise you, it is not my place.' Burnaby spoke with quiet dignity, his eyes on the worn rug at his feet.

Phillip searched the lined, leathery old face but it offered no clue to the Master's feelings. Could he, he wondered, count on Burnaby's support, no matter how drastic the action he might be compelled to take? Was this what the old man was trying to tell him – was a promise of support implicit in his warning? Or was he, by issuing the warning, simply covering himself in case things went wrong and the situation got out of hand? Burnaby had come up through the hawse-hole, from the lower deck; he was closer to the men than the other officers so did he, perhaps, know more than they did?

Phillip sighed. 'You may rely on my discretion, Mr. Burnaby,' he said at last. 'As, I trust, I may rely on yours?'

'Of course, sir. I'd not be here otherwise.'

'Good ... then let us be frank with each other, shall we?' Phillip forced a reassuring smile. 'You spoke of the possibility of trouble, Mr. Burnaby, but of what are you really afraid? That this ship's company may mutiny?'

Burnaby glanced across at him apprehensively, his composure visibly shaken. 'Mutiny is an ugly word, Mr. Hazard.'

'Call it whatever you wish. This is an ugly situation, is it not?'

'Yes, sir,' the Master conceded unhappily. 'And it is true that desperate men do resort to acts of violence that could lead to mutiny, if they can find no other remedy for their grievance. These men have a legitimate grievance, but ...' he broke off, eyeing Phillip warily as if uncertain whether, even now, he dare speak his mind with complete freedom.

'I invited you to be frank, Mr. Burnaby,' Phillip reminded him. 'We shall get nowhere unless you are, I fear.'

The Master inclined his grizzled head. 'Well, sir, as I told you when we were leaving Plymouth Sound, there's nothing wrong with this ship's company. They're good men, most of them but ...' he spoke with deep feeling, forgetful of his earlier caution. 'But they've been driven too hard, Mr. Hazard and for too long. There's a limit to what flesh and blood can stand and I'm afraid that some of them – the bolder spirits – have reached their limit now. They've suffered tyranny and injustice for a long time and they can't endure much more. They want to put an end to it, war or no war and ... they're looking to *you* to help them. If you

220

cannot, they'll take matters into their own hands without counting the cost.'

'Anything that I could do to remedy the situation would have to be done through official channels,' Phillip pointed out. 'Which takes time and there would be a risk – a very considerable risk – of failure.'

Burnaby did not pretend to misunderstand him. 'The men would wait, so long as they knew that something was being done, Mr. Hazard.'

'Would they trust me to do what was in their best interests, do you think?'

'They trust and respect you,' Burnaby said earnestly. 'The more so, since you came back. They all know that you were appointed to the flagship by Admiral Lyons, with a fine chance of gaining promotion if you stayed . . . and yet you chose to return to this ship. That is why they are looking to you to help them, Mr. Hazard. They will all be behind you, as well as the officers, I give you my word . . . if you act now. Well, sir?' There was a gleam in the faded blue eyes, as the old man looked up expectantly to meet Phillip's gaze. His own did not waver as he went on, choosing his words carefully, 'I'm no sea-lawyer, Mr. Hazard, but I do know that a legal remedy exists for a situation of this kind. I also know that it will need a brave man, a man with the courage of his convictions, to set the wheels in motion, because tyranny and oppression aren't easy charges to prove, not legally. But you'll know better than I do what the risks of failure are likely to be . . . you said yourself they'd be considerable. If you bring the charges, *you* would be taking the risks, sir.'

He had no illusions on that score, Phillip thought, with weary resignation. 'Yes, I'm aware of the probable consequences of failure, Mr. Burnaby,' he admitted, his voice strained. 'I've always been aware of them.'

'Yet you came back to the ship?'

'Yes, I came back,' Phillip agreed. But he had been a fool to do so, he told himself wretchedly . . . a stupid, quixotic fool, throwing away his chances of promotion and perhaps his whole career because – even if he succeeded in getting

North relieved of his command – he himself would be a marked man ever afterwards. Why, even this conversation with Burnaby might be held against him, if it ever got out, construed as a 'conspiracy injurious to naval discipline' yet ... he stiffened. The alternative to risking his own neck was to see his ship's company risk theirs by taking the law into their own hands which, in time of war, meant that few of them would escape hanging. But ... there was Anthony Cochrane. He had forgotten about Cochrane, whose trial by court martial was yet to come. If it took place soon and his own petition to the Commander-in-Chief, based on the evidence heard at Cochrane's trial, followed after it then. ...

'What about the court martial on Lieutenant Cochrane?' he asked, clutching at this straw of hope with an eagerness of which he was ashamed. 'When is it to be, Mr. Burnaby?'

'Captain North has withdrawn the charges, sir,' Burnaby told him flatly. 'He has decided to deal with Mr. Cochrane himself.'

So North suspected ... well, that was scarcely to be wondered at, Phillip supposed. Some whisper must have reached him as to the nature of Cochrane's defence and, realizing that the man he had accused would be supported by his brother officers North had taken steps to avoid the issue. He had seen his danger and ... Phillip frowned. This, of course, closed the door on his own faint hope of escape because it was now he, not Anthony Cochrane, who would have to make the counter-charges and prove them, if he could. A petition to the Commander-in-Chief to have North suspended on the face-saving medical grounds of insanity or mental incapacity would not be of the smallest use. He would have to apply for a court martial, with himself as accuser ... he would have to prefer charges against his commander which, by their very nature, would be extremely difficult to bring home. Such charges always were, since the basis of all naval discipline lay in the power vested in the captain of a ship of war ... the power of life and death, absolute power which those under his command disputed at their peril. The dividing line between a strict disciplinarian and a tyrant was a very thin one and the benefit of any doubt that existed was invariably given to the senior in rank by a naval court, because authority must always be upheld.

Feeling suddenly as if the jaws of a trap were closing about him, Phillip shivered.

'Well, sir ...' Burnaby rose. 'I will leave this matter in your hands.' There was a note of relief in his voice. 'There's no more to be said, is there?' He had obviously said all that he intended to say and, Phillip reflected, it was more than many others would have said, in his place ... but then old Burnaby, too, was a good man.

He nodded and they shook hands solemnly, as if to seal a pact. Within a few minutes of the Master's departure, Martin Fox and Duncan Laidlaw, both looking strained and anxious, presented themselves at the door of the cabin. Phillip ushered them in, guessing for what purpose they had come.

'Well, gentlemen ...' he remained standing. 'What is it?'

'You've talked to Mr. Burnaby, have you not?' Fox said, his voice low.

'Yes, I've talked to him.'

'And you've agreed to take action?'

Phillip studied their two grave faces in the dim light of the lantern which, hanging from the bulkhead above them, provided the cabin's sole illumination. 'Is it your considered belief that I *should* take action?' he asked quietly.

They both assented, without hesitation and Martin Fox added vehemently, 'Things cannot be allowed to go on as they are, Phillip. As responsible officers, with the welfare of the ship's company at heart, we must intervene and you, as First Lieutenant, are the proper person to take whatever steps are necessary.'

'I will do what I can, then,' Phillip promised. He gestured to his chest and the single chair and invited them to sit, thinking to lessen their tension. 'A drink?' he suggested. 'I have a bottle of whisky and you both look as if you could do with a tot. Martin?'

Fox thanked him but Laidlaw shook his head. 'I won't, sir, if you'll forgive me. I am due to relieve Mr. Cochrane of the watch in fifteen minutes. I only came because ... that is I—' he glanced at Martin Fox, who came swiftly to his rescue.

'We brought these papers for your approval, sir,' he announced formally and held out a large, unsealed manila envelope. 'Perhaps you would care to look through them, in case any of them may be of use to you.'

'What are they?' Phillip asked.

'The statements we prepared for Anthony Cochrane's defence,' Fox explained. 'Since the charges against him have been dropped, they can no longer be used for the purpose for which they were intended. We thought, however, that they might serve as a basis for you to work on and also as a guarantee of our united support for whatever action you deem it most expedient to take ... a petition to the Commander-in-Chief or an application for the Captain's trial by court martial. You'll find they are complete.'

Phillip subjected the contents of the envelope to a quick scrutiny. The statements, he realized, had been made by all officers of wardroom rank, each of whom had appended his signature to his own hand-written account of Captain North's system of command, as practised since his appointment to *Trojan*. The mates and senior midshipmen had signed a joint statement, which was brief and to the effect that they whole-heartedly supported and concurred with the evidence offered by their superiors.

'There's also this,' Fox said. He offered another document for Phillip's inspection. 'It is in the form of a letter addressed to you which, as you will see, we have all signed ... requesting you to take action on our behalf. We felt it would be a safeguard for you, should your motives be questioned and—'

'I do not require safeguards, least of all written ones,' Phillip objected. He glanced up from his perusal of the letter, looking from one to the other of his visitors with unconcealed dismay. 'But this is quite the most dangerous and incriminating document I have ever seen in my life! For God's sake, Martin, have you taken leave of your senses? Whatever possessed you to allow anything like this to be put into writing?'

'I'm sorry ... it was my idea to write it, I'm afraid,' Martin Fox admitted, crestfallen. 'I did not feel that it was fair or just to put you in a position where you had to take all the risks, none of us did. And besides—'

'I am grateful for your concern, my dear fellow.' Phillip assured him, his expression relaxing a little. 'But if it should fall into the wrong hands, this letter could be evidence of conspiracy ... proof of it, in fact. Study Article Nineteen of the Articles of War, which deals with the penalties for 'mutinous assembly'. This damned piece of paper could get us all broken!' He expelled his breath in an exasperated sigh, turning the letter over to read the last few signatures. They had meant well, he thought, but. ... 'You composed and signed this in the gunroom, I suppose? When ... today?'

Fox and Laidlaw exchanged uneasy glances. 'Yes, sir,' Laidlaw confessed, 'This evening, whilst you were talking to Mr. Burnaby. But surely there's no danger, we are *all* in agreement, we are all behind you, sir. That was what the letter was intended to prove ... and no one refused to sign it.'

'No one?'

'No, sir, no one. In any case, the Captain isn't on board. He had his gig called away as soon as he had finished dining and went to visit the Captain of *Fury*, I understand.'

In order to expedite the transfer of Able-Seaman Hazard, no doubt, Phillip told himself resignedly and wondered what sadistic motive had prompted North's action.

'Nevertheless, Mr. Laidlaw, this letter will have to be destroyed,' he said. 'I'd better burn it, I think.' He reached up for the lantern, the letter in his hand and hesitated, looking again at the signatures it bore. 'You assured me that no one refused to sign this but there is one name missing, surely? That of the Captain of Marines ... a rather significant omission.'

'Alex Murray is ashore with the harbour defence force,' Fox answered promptly. 'But he would have signed it if he had been on board, Phillip. He felt as the rest of us do and you'll find his statement with the others.'

'Who is in command of our Marines, then?' Phillip questioned. 'They're not all ashore, are they?'

Both officers shook their heads. 'We have a temporary replacement for Captain Murray,' Fox said. 'Lieutenant Smithson ... I don't believe you have met him, he joined us from the *Britannia* about a week ago. Since he's not a regular member of the ship's company, I did not suggest that he should sign the letter. But—'

'But he is aware of its existence, is he not?' An alarming suspicion was taking root in Phillip's mind and, try as he might, he was unable to dispel it. 'And presumably he also knows about these statements you prepared for Cochrane's defence?'

'I ...' Martin Fox reddened miserably. 'I'm not sure. I suppose he must know, we've talked about them in his presence. And ... I think he was with us this evening. Was he, Duncan, do you remember? He's young and very quiet and unobtrusive, one hardly notices if he's there or not.'

'He was there,' Duncan Laidlaw asserted. 'I remember because I had occasion to speak to him about relieving the after-magazine guard. But ... does it matter if he knows, Mr. Hazard? I mean, as Fox says, he's hardly more than a boy.'

'It may matter very much, I'm afraid.' Phillip made an effort to steady his voice. His brain was racing now, as he sought to assess the possible consequences of his brother officers' indiscretion. If young Lieutenant Smithson, true to the traditions of his Corps, had conceived it his duty to report all he had seen and heard that evening in the gunroom to the Captain, then there was no time to be lost. The letter was their greatest danger, it had to be destroyed ... he took down the lantern and started to open it, his fingers clumsy in their haste. 'Why did the Captain decide to withdraw the charges against Cochrane, Martin?' he demanded tensely. 'Do you know?'

Martin Fox shrugged. 'He gave no reason. But ... I suppose because he got wind of the fact that these statements were to be made at the court martial and realized that, if they were, Cochrane would be completely vindicated.'

'*How* did he get wind of the statements and of your intention to use them? Who could have told him, who *would* have told him ... unless it was Smithson?'

'Dear sweet heaven!' Fox groaned aloud. 'I have been a perfect imbecile, Phillip. None of *us* would have breathed a word, that goes without saying but Smithson ... yes, I suppose Smithson could have told him. He's young and inexperienced, he's only been with us for a few days and, if he imagined that he had stumbled on a hotbed of disaffection and intrigue, he might have gone to the Captain. He might even have believed it his duty to do so.'

'Exactly.' Phillip's tone was harsh. 'And if he did?'

They stared at each other in mute dismay. From the deck above came the shrilling of the boatswain's mates' whistles and a stentorian bellow, calling the side-party to muster and Laidlaw said, the colour draining from his cheeks, 'The Captain! He's returning aboard and—'

'Burn this, Martin,' Phillip ordered, thrusting the letter into Martin Fox's hand and gesturing to the lantern. 'Laidlaw, on deck with you at once. Take over the watch from Cochrane and delay things for as long as you can, to give us a chance to get rid of these statements.'

'Aye, aye, sir.' Galvanized into action, Laidlaw opened the door of the cabin, only to jump back with a startled exclamation an instant later. 'There are Marine sentries posted by the after-hatch, Mr. Hazard. Four of them and ...' he swallowed hard. 'Smithson is with them.'

'Carry on, Mr. Laidlaw,' Phillip bade him, suddenly calm now that the moment he had dreaded was upon them. 'Relieve the deck ... the Marine's won't stop you, they are coming for me. And Martin ... for pity's sake, get that letter burnt!'

227

Martin Fox held up the charred remains of the letter, his smile unsteady. 'It's burnt to ash, Phillip. But we'll never manage the statements now.'

'Then give them to me and get out, I beg you!'

'No.' Obstinately the younger man stood his ground. 'This is all my fault, the result of my crass stupidity. I'm not leaving you to face the music alone. Can't you see I—' he was interrupted by a peremptory rap on the door. It opened and a slim, pale faced youth in the uniform of the Royal Marines stood framed in the aperture. He saluted and said nervously, 'Lieutenant Hazard?'

'I am Lieutenant Hazard,' Phillip acknowledged. Laidlaw, he saw, was not with the Marine guard by the after-hatch, which meant that they had let him pass and he wished, now, that he had given him custody of the statements. But he had not been sure . . . he drew himself up, eyeing the young Marine officer sternly. 'What do you want?'

'I have orders to escort you to the Captain's quarters at once, sir,' the youngster told him.

'To escort me? Do you mean that you have orders to place me under arrest?' Phillip challenged. 'Is that why you have brought a guard with you?'

Lieutenant Smithson reddened in embarrassment. 'No, sir. That is I am to place you under arrest if you refuse to obey the Captain's command to report to him and to—'

Phillip cut him short. 'I have never in the past refused to obey the Captain's commands, Mr. Smithson. Why should you imagine that I am likely to do so now? I would point out to you that I am the First Lieutenant of this ship and that, when the Captain requires my presence, it is not necessary to send a file of Marines to ensure my compliance with his wishes.'

Smithson's flush deepened. He passed his tongue agitatedly over his lower lip and said, avoiding Phillip's coldly disapproving gaze, 'I beg your pardon, sir, but those were the Captain's instructions to me . . . I am only repeating them. I have been charged with other instructions, sir.'

'And they are . . .?'

'Mr. Fox is also to report to the Captain,' the young Marine officer returned. 'And I am to take possession of a number of statements, which Mr Fox delivered to you and . . . a letter, sir. I should be obliged if I might have these, so that I may take them to the Captain.'

From the deck above came the thud of running feet and Phillip heard another bellow from the Boatswain, calling the watch below to muster at their stations. Laidlaw had taken over the watch, then, his mind registered, and the shrilling of the side-party's pipes meant that the Captain's gig had come alongside . . . his mouth tightened. Captain North must have given young Smithson his instructions before leaving the ship, he thought. Now, on the Captain's return, they were being put into effect and evidently the Marine guard had been posted as soon as Martin Fox and Duncan Laidlaw had entered his cabin, to make certain that the statements – and that unfortunate letter – were not removed from it. Therefore it would not be the slightest use his denying the existence of the statements, Phillip decided. By themselves, without the letter, they were not evidence of conspiracy against *Trojan*'s officers but rather so damning an indictment of North's abuse of his command that he would not dare to have them made public. And even if he destroyed them, he could not destroy the men who had written them, could not erase from their minds the bitter memories which had led to their being willing to put their condemnation on paper.

Phillip's gaze went to the little heap of ash at Martin Fox's feet and, from this, to his face. He smiled in reassurance, and turned to the pink-cheeked young Marine officer. 'Suppose I refuse to give you the documents you ask for, Mr. Smithson . . . what then?'

'My orders are to search your cabin for them, sir. But . . .' Smithson's sharp eyes lit on the scattered papers and he pointed to them triumphantly. 'Those are the papers I am required to take to the Captain. Perhaps you will be so good as to give them to me, Mr. Hazard.'

229

'Certainly. There's an envelope for them somewhere, I believe. Ah . . . thank you, Mr. Fox.'

Gravely Martin Fox replaced the papers in their envelope and offered it to Smithson, who tucked it self-importantly beneath his scarlet-clad arm. 'And now the letter, sir, if you please.'

'Letter? There is no letter that I am aware of, Mr. Smithson,' Fox said.

'But there *was* a letter . . .' Smithson began. 'I informed the Captain that there was, I . . .' he bit back the words he had intended to say and reddened again, looking down at the ash as Fox stirred it gently with his foot.

'Would you care to have your men in to make a search for it?' Phillip invited dryly but, recognizing defeat, Smithson shook his head.

'No, sir, thank you. May I be permitted to escort you to the Captain's quarters now, gentlemen?'

Phillip led the way from his cabin, the Marines coming smartly to attention at the sight of him. On deck, he could hear Laidlaw's voice, shouting an order and, as he mounted the companion ladder leading to the upper deck, he saw Anthony Cochrane at its head, obviously waiting for him. They drew level and Cochrane said, his voice low but with a flash of his old, exuberant spirit, 'The Captain is back on board, sir. But he was taken ill . . . it was necessary to rig a bo'sun's chair to hoist him to the entry port, as we did once before, sir, if you remember.'

'I remember,' Phillip assured him. 'Where is the Captain now?'

'In his cabin, sir. I've passed the word for the Surgeon and, needless to tell you, I'm keeping my fingers crossed, in the hope that history may repeat itself. But you . . .' Cochrane's smile faded, as he glimpsed the escorting Marines. 'Mr. Hazard, are you under arrest, sir? Laidlaw said—'

'No.' Phillip shook his head. 'The Captain requires me to report to him but there is no need for concern, Mr. Cochrane. With the evidence available, I do not think I have anything to fear.'

'Are you sure, sir?' Cochrane asked wearily. 'He has your brother with him and . . .' he broke off, as Lieutenant Smithson reached the head of the companionway, with Martin Fox behind him. 'For the Lord's sake, be careful, sir,' he added softly and then, in obedience to Phillip's gesture, stood back to allow the little procession to pass him.

At the door of the Captain's day cabin, Smithson said, a note of unaccustomed authority in his voice, 'Permit me to make my report to the Captain before he sees you, Mr. Hazard.' Without waiting for Phillip's assent, he thrust past him, knocked on the door and went inside, closing the door behind him. Martin Fox swore under his breath. 'Insufferable young puppy! But no doubt those were his instructions.'

Phillip was silent, busy with his own not very pleasant thoughts. Cochrane had mentioned that Graham was with the Captain and, whilst this came as no surprise to him, he wondered uneasily what his brother's presence portended. Some form of moral blackmail, perhaps. North was not above bringing pressure to bear on him, with Graham as the scapegoat and . . . the door of the cabin burst open suddenly and Smithson thrust a pale and frightened face through it into the passageway.

'Mr. Hazard, could you come, sir, please,' he begged and now, instead of authority, his voice held panic. 'It's the Captain . . . he's very ill, sir, he . . . he cannot speak. I don't know what to do or . . . or what's wrong with him. I . . . his steward is with him and he seems to think that it's the cholera.' He choked, his lower lip trembling and added, a catch in his voice, 'The Surgeon ought to be called, sir.'

'Word has been passed for the Surgeon,' Phillip told him curtly. 'Control yourself, Mr. Smithson . . . and you may dismiss your men. They won't be needed any more but had better wait, I think.' He went into the cabin and through it to the sleeping cabin beyond. Fox hurrying after him.

Captain North lay on his cot, his normally florid face greyish-white and his body twisted in the all too familiar agonized writhing of a cholera attack. Phillip had seen too many cases of late not to recognize the disease for what it was and Graham bending over the swaying cot and attempting to spoon brandy between the tightly clenched teeth, looked up to meet his gaze with a wry grimace.

'It's an acute infection, Phillip. He won't last long.'

The steward, Phillip thought, the steward who had died, had also suffered an acute attack and he had served the Captain's meals, poured his wine and attended his person ... it was not hard to guess how North had contracted the disease.

'I'll go and hurry Surgeon Frazer,' Martin Fox volunteered. 'He's not a pretty sight, is he, like this?' He shuddered, as he turned away. 'My God, though ... it's a ghastly way for any man to die!'

Phillip was silent. He stood looking down into the twitching, unconscious face of the man who, for so long, had exercised the power of life and death aboard the ship he commanded. Seeing death written plainly on that face now, he was aware neither of triumph nor relief but only – strangely – of pity. The tyrant, stripped of his power to tyrannize, was no longer an awesome but a pathetic figure and the sadistic bully, robbed of his strength and of the trappings of authority, was just another man. And, as Fox had remarked a few moments before, it was a ghastly way for any man to die. Others had died like this, it was true ... thousands of others, seamen and soldiers, on shore, on board the line-of-battle ships, the frigates and the overcrowded transports and hospital ships. They had died on the battlefield of the Alma, on the march, beside the bivouac fires and even in far-off Varna, before the war had properly begun for them, before they had fired a shot. They were dying now, as North was dying, young men and old, cowards and heroes, men who had dreamed of military glory, boys who had wanted only to live and yet ... Phillip gave vent to a regretful sigh. Motioning Graham to stand aside, he took the brandy flask from his brother's unresisting hand.

'Let me ... it's the least I can do for him, after all.'

Graham flashed him a curious glance. 'Spare your pity, Phillip,' he advised. 'He was out to ruin us both, you know . . . and he'd have shown *us* precious little pity. You were to be charged with inciting the ship's company to mutiny and I with having treasonable dealings with the enemy . . . and I, until he brought me to trial, was to be employed as his personal steward. He had already given me a taste of what *that* would entail and I confess I did not relish it.'

Phillip, an arm behind the Captain's shoulders, raised him a little and succeeded in spooning a few drops of the brandy into his mouth. 'Why did you come back?' he asked bluntly.

'Because,' Graham returned, with equal bluntness, 'the enemy expected me to have treasonable dealings with them. Believe this or not but . . . I was offered command of a frigate in the Baltic!'

'I thought that was what you wanted?' Phillip challenged bitterly and regretted his bitterness an instant later, when he glimpsed the expression on his brother's face. 'I'm sorry, Graham. That was unjust.'

'No,' Graham denied. 'I confess I was tempted . . . seriously tempted. But my father wrote to me . . . after all these years, Phillip, the Old Man actually wrote to me. He wrote to Odessa and, by some miracle, the letter reached me in Petersburg. And he was pleased – actually *pleased* – because I'd chosen to serve as an A.B. in the British Navy! He said he "welcomed my patriotic and self-sacrificing decision" and somehow, in the light of those proud paternal words, I could hardly go back on my patriotic decision, could I?' He smiled without amusement, catching Phillip's eye. 'So I refused my captors' offer of a frigate and they dispatched me to Odessa once more – overland, an endless and exhausting journey – to await repatriation. I was fortunately just in time to meet the *Fury* when she entered the port, escorting a shipload of Russian wounded from the Alma. Poor devils! Barely half of them survived . . . they were in a simply appalling state, Phillip, their wounds dressed with hay or straw, when they were dressed at all. The Governor was horrified by what he termed an example of British barbarity and, I confess, I did not blame him.'

'Our own men were little better provided for, in the hospital ships which took them to the Bosphorus,' Phillip told him. 'We had few dressings, few medical supplies of any kind, far too few surgeons and no ambulances. But ...' he hesitated, wanting to ask about Prince Narishkin. 'There was a Russian officer on board that transport whom I ...' the Captain was seized by another violent convulsion and he broke off, setting down the brandy and gently lowering the unconscious man into a recumbent position. 'Bear a hand here, Graham, will you? I'm afraid he may fall out of his cot, if he struggles like this.'

'The Surgeon has come,' Graham said and Phillip expelled his breath tensely, thankful to yield his place at North's side to the new arrival.

Surgeon Fraser's examination was brief. He administered a draught of some concoction from a bottle he had brought with him and then, leaving his assistant to apply hot flannels to the patient's chest and abdomen, he drew Phillip aside.

'There is very little I can do for him, Mr. Hazard,' he said, his voice level and quite devoid of expression. 'Save to relieve his pain as much as it is possible to relieve it. He is too far gone and the infection too acute for there to be a hope of saving him. I give him, at the most, two hours.'

'Two hours, Doctor?' Phillip echoed dully.

The Surgeon nodded. 'You can do no good by remaining here. Leave him to us.'

'If you say so. But—'

Fraser laid a plump hand on his arm. 'We shall do everything we can. He'll suffer less than some of the poor fellows he turned from their hammocks for a practice alarm in Kavarna Bay, when the ship was at anchor in the midst of the Fleet. And less than your brother there was made to suffer, when he had him flogged, Mr. Hazard. I suggest, sir, that you put the past behind you because, in less than two hours' time, *you* will be in command of this ship.'

'In temporary command, Doctor,' Phillip amended.

'Long enough, let us hope, for you to put right the harm your predecessor did,' the Surgeon told him. '*My* statement was amongst those our young and over-conscientious Lieutenant of Marines was holding, with the intention of delivering them to the Captain, when I passed him on my way here. I told him to read them, I trust with your approval, in the belief that, if he did so, he would have a better understanding of the circumstances which cause hitherto reliable officers to rebel against their commanders ... even in the British Navy. It's a lesson he needs to learn, I think.'

Phillip supposed that it was. He took his leave of the Surgeon and, as Fraser returned to his patient, he glanced inquiringly at Graham. 'Are you coming?' he asked. 'There is nothing more for either of us to do here.'

To his surprise, his brother shook his head. 'I am the Captain's steward, Phillip. Not the most honourable appointment perhaps, but, until he relieves me of my duties, I'll carry them out, if you don't mind. *Trojan*'s new commander may have other ideas as to my suitability, of course.' He smiled, this time warmly and without cynicism. 'It's to be hoped he has but ... good luck to you, Phillip, in whatever the future may hold for you.'

'I shall need it,' Phillip returned soberly. 'My God, I shall need it, Graham!'

Graham's smile widened. 'You were, I believe, about to ask me a question concerning one of the officers aboard that transport the *Fury* brought to Odessa. Perhaps this letter will answer your question more fully than I can.' He took an envelope from his pocket and laid it in Phillip's outstretched hand. 'I was charged to give it to you. I expect you know by whom.'

'Yes, I know.'

'The Prince Narishkin survived,' Graham said. 'And had no complaint of his treatment at the hands of the barbaric British. But the letter will tell you about it.'

Phillip did not read the letter until he was alone in the privacy of his own cabin. It was very short.

'*I thank you,*' Mademoiselle Sophie had written, '*for restoring my husband to me, which is a debt I can never repay. But I shall not forget what I owe you and one day, perhaps, when this terrible war is over, I may be able to tell you of the joy and happiness your kind action has brought me . . .*'

He was reading the brief missive for the third time when Surgeon Fraser came to inform him of the Captain's death. . . .

CHAPTER TEN

I

The day following Captain North's death, Phillip was summoned aboard *Agamemnon* and, at Admiral Lyons' invitation, he gave an account of the events which had preceded his commander's fatal collapse. He held back nothing and, when he had done, the Admiral said distastefully, 'This is an unpleasant story, Phillip, and one, I think, that is best forgotten by all who have been concerned in it. I intend to forget everything you have told me when you leave this cabin and I suggest that you should endeavour to do the same. Those statements you have shown me should be destroyed.'

'Yes, sir. I'll be happy to destroy them, sir.'

'I imagine you will be ... although you yourself emerge with nothing but credit from the unfortunate affair. In view of this – and since there is no officer of post-rank available here to relieve you – I shall place you in temporary command of *Trojan*. You must understand, however, that the Commander-in-Chief may decide otherwise when we leave Balaclava to rejoin the Fleet.'

'Yes, sir,' Phillip acknowledged gratefully. 'I understand.'

'Good.' Admiral Lyons smiled, eyeing him kindly. 'Then go back to your command and do your best to rebuild the morale of your officers and men. In a day or so, I shall send Captain Mends to inspect your ship and, if his report is favourable, I shall recommend to Admiral Dundas that you remain in temporary command. If and when you are replaced, I'll be glad to re-appoint you to this ship.'

'Thank you very much indeed, sir.' Phillip was

momentarily bereft of words. 'I ... I'm deeply indebted to you, sir, for all the kindness you have shown me and—'

Sir Edmund brushed aside his thanks. 'Between ourselves, Phillip,' he went on, a gleam of excitement in his fine grey eyes, 'I am expecting orders to rejoin the battle squadron off the Katcha within the next three or four days. Lord Raglan, when I talked to him yesterday, informed me that he was writing to Admiral Dundas to request the co-operation of the Fleet and that General Canrobert was making a similar request to Admiral Hamelin. His lordship feels, as I do, that an attack on Sebastopol by sea will greatly facilitate his own and the French Army's assault by land. The land-based gun batteries are all expected to be ready to open fire by the sixteenth or seventeeth. If they can put out of action the forts which bar the Armies' way into the city and if we, at the same time, can contrive to knock out the harbour defences ... then Sebastopol should fall to us without, it is to be hoped, too heavy a loss of life.'

'That would be wonderful, sir,' Phillip agreed, catching his excitement. 'If it succeeds.'

'I see no reason why it should fail,' the Admiral said. 'For our part, we shall be pitting wooden ships against stone-built fortresses, it is true, and our reserves of ammunition have been depleted, as a result of having to supply the guns on shore. But we proved in the past, at Algiers and Acre, that engaging at close range, with a heavy concentration of gun power on our broadsides, could be extremely effective against sea-forts. And this is where our steam squadron will prove their usefulness, Phillip. I hope to persuade Admiral Dundas to send in his sail-of-the-line, each lashed alongside one of our steamers which, having towed her into a position from whence she can open effective fire on the forts, will remain there in readiness to haul her off, with the least possible delay, when the action is over. You see ...' he explained his tactical plan for the operation, detailing the positions of the various ships in precise terms so that Phillip, when he returned to *Trojan* was as enthusiastically optimistic concerning the chances of its success as the Admiral himself.

Three days later, Captain Mends inspected *Trojan* and expressed himself satisfied with the efficiency of the ship and her crew. On 15th October Admiral Lyons received his long awaited orders to rejoin the British Fleet and *Agamemnon* steamed majestically out of Balaclava Harbour, cheered by the Marine artillerymen on the heights above the harbour entrance. The rest of the steam squadron still in harbour – including *Trojan* – were ordered to follow her with all possible dispatch and, by the morning of 16th, all were at anchor off the mouth of the Katcha.

Excitement ran high and rumours were legion as the British and French Admirals conferred aboard *Mogador*. The French Commander-in-Chief was said to be opposed to Admiral Lyons' plan of attack and was believed to have suggested an alternative, to which neither Bruat, his own second-in-command, nor Lyons would agree. Phillip waited, with what patience he could muster and learned from Tom Johnson, who paid a hurried call on him during the afternoon, that Admiral Dundas had eventually and with great reluctance agreed to the French demands.

'Sir Edmund made it clear that the Admiral had very little choice – the French would have refused to join in the attack at all, if he had not acceded to their wishes,' Johnson explained. 'So . . . we are to go in at noon tomorrow, instead of at six-thirty, when the land-based guns are to open the bombardment. The French, in order that they may support their Army, are to form a line on the south side of the harbour, from Streletska Bay towards the centre of the entrance, where the Russian ships-of-the-line were sunk. Our own Fleet is to sweep round to the southward and come up in succession, so as to form on the French van and prolong the line to the north as far as it will reach . . . but in such a direction that the distance between our ships and the forts will not be less than eighteen hundred yards.' He shrugged disgustedly. '*Britannia* has apparently been allocated a position where she will be exposed to the fire of several batteries, with all save her lower deck guns out-ranged. And *Agamemnon*'s main target, Fort Constantine, is protected by an

239

extensive shoal so that, if we are to approach within effective range, as the Admiral wishes, we shall have to send a small steamer ahead of us, to take soundings and pilot us in! The *Circassia* is to be charged with this unenviable task. Ah, well, you'll be summoned to a Captain's conference soon, I expect, so that you will hear it all at first hand. But I can tell you now, Phillip . . . our Admiral is close to despair at the turn events have taken.'

Phillip found this to be no exaggeration when he joined the rest of the British naval commanders on board *Britannia* to receive his final orders. Long faces greeted him and the atmosphere, as the assembled officers studied a memorandum which Admiral Dundas had issued for their information, was gloomy and despondent. The senior Captains, when invited to state their views, without exception condemned the French plan of attack and the conference developed into a series of heated arguments, only interrupted by the arrival of Admiral Dundas, who made his appearance accompanied by Admiral Lyons and the Captain of the Fleet, Rear-Admiral Montagu Stopford.

The Commander-in-Chief looked about him and then called for silence. 'Gentlemen, I like this operation no more than you do,' he announced. 'Indeed, I confess to having the gravest possible doubts concerning it. Nevertheless, we are committed to putting into it our best endeavours, in order that we may assist the attack which – if all goes well – is to be launched by our troops on shore.'

He spoke quietly but with telling emphasis and, as he outlined details of the stations to be taken up by the various ships, there was complete and respectful silence. The sail-of-the-line were, as Admiral Lyons had originally suggested, to be towed into position by the steam-ships and he paused, for his Flag Captain to read out the order in which they were to do so. *Trojan* was not named and Phillip leaned forward, listening anxiously.

The Admiral went on, when the list had been read, still in the same quiet, unhurried voice, 'Whilst I am bound to co-operate, as agreed, with the French Fleet, gentlemen, I have decided to detach certain ships under the command of Admiral Lyons, which will form an inshore squadron and adhere to our original plan of attack. Admiral Lyons' squadron will consist of the following ships ... *Agamemnon*, flying his flag, with *Sanspareil, London* in the tow of *Niger, Albion* towed by *Firebrand, Arethusa* towed by *Triton, Circassia* acting as pilot and *Trojan* in reserve. This division of the Fleet will pay special attention to Fort Constantine, which mounts some ninety guns, fifty of which command the north side of the channel, here ...' he pointed to a chart hanging behind him. 'And the Wasp Fort on the cliffs here, which has twelve guns, mounted *en barbette*. Admiral Lyons will approach as close in as he may deem necessary for the purpose of engaging these forts effectively with the starboard broadsides of the ships under his command.'

There was a murmur of approval from the commanders of the ships he had named and the Admiral permitted himself a fleeting smile. 'All other instructions are set out in my memorandum but it should be clearly understood, gentlemen, that in an attack of this kind, ships may not be able to keep their exact stations. Therefore ...' he eyed them gravely. 'No one can do wrong who keeps up a well-directed fire upon the enemy ... is that clear?'

The Captains murmured their assent, their faces suddenly more cheerful, as the implications of Admiral Dundas' last words sank in.

The Admiral continued, 'You will appreciate that it will be impossible in the smoke for me to see all your ships, so I wish every Captain to consider his own position after he gets into action. If you find yourselves in particular danger of being dismasted or running on shore, the decision to haul off will be your own responsibility and you should take it, without waiting for a signal from me. When hauling off, keep well to the south-west so as not to be raked by the north side batteries. And finally, gentlemen, as a general rule, I do not wish more than fifty rounds from each gun to be fired. *Spitfire* is due from Constantinople with stores and ammunition and you will transfer all sick, together with spare topmasts and yards to *Vulcan*, which will remain at this anchorage. Clear for action at first light tomorrow morning. I expect to open our attack at noon. That is all . . . have you any questions to ask me before you return to your own ships?'

There were a number of questions, which the Admiral answered or referred to Admiral Lyons or the Captain of the Fleet and, when these had been dealt with, the conference broke up, Admiral Dundas taking courteous leave of his departing Captains.

The morning of 17th was calm and sultry and, as the day advanced, it became oppressively hot. Soon after daylight the land-based batteries opened fire, which was returned with spirit by the enemy. The ships of the Fleet were busy with their preparations for the coming bombardment, getting up powder and shot, taking down bulkheads, stowing hammocks, sanding decks and running out guns. By noon, all was in readiness, the steamers secured alongside the sailing ships and the men went to dinner. The signal to weigh came half an hour later.

True to his promise to the French, Admiral Dundas in *Britannia* led his main body in a long, southward sweep, which caused the expected delay in getting into position. When, at one o'clock, the French and Turkish Fleets were seen to be firing on the forts on the south side of the harbour entrance, he made a signal to Sir Edmund Lyons to proceed to engage those to the north. *Agamemnon*'s helm was at once put to starboard and, followed by the rest of the inshore squadron, she steamed boldly towards her target.

Phillip, on *Trojan*'s quarterdeck, felt his heart quicken its beat. This was the first time that he had ever commanded a ship in action and he knew, as the minutes ticked slowly by, the thrill and the isolation of command. *Trojan*'s role, as reserve, was to stand by ready to take the place of any ship of the squadron which was compelled to withdraw, or to answer a request for assistance, should one be made. From the weather hammock netting, he watched the little *Circassia* steam ahead of the flagship, sounding as she went and saw the guns of the Wasp Fort on the cliffs open up on her. She held her course and, astern of her, *Agamemnon* came within range of the guns of Fort Constantine, as well as those on the cliffs, and she was struck repeatedly, suffering some damage aloft. But she, too, held her course and – as he afterwards learnt – with only two foot of water under her keel, dropped anchor first at the stern and then forward, so as to bring her starboard broadside to bear on her target, which was now less than eight hundred yards distant.

Just as her Admiral had planned, Phillip thought admiringly, the very closeness at which *Agamemnon* was engaging the fort constituted her principal advantage ... the guns on the cliff-top could not be depressed sufficiently to fire on her and, as she discharged her first thunderous broadside at the fort's massive walls, he could scarcely forbear to cheer. *Sanspareil*, no less gallantly handled, followed the flagship's movements and anchored off her starboard quarter, adding the weight of her own formidable broadside to *Agamemnon*'s. Astern of the two leading ships, *London*, *Albion* and *Arethusa* were towed up to support them, swinging round so as to give the small steam frigates to which they were lashed the protection of their greater bulk.

It was a perfectly executed operation and, from two until two-thirty, the inshore squadron continued to throw shot at Fort Constantine whilst the rest of the British Fleet was still getting into position in line with the French and Turkish ships. At two-thirty *Britannia* opened fire with her lower deck guns at maximum elevation and the action became general. Shortly afterwards Phillip observed a heavy explosion inside Fort Constantine, which caused a temporary cessation of the enemy fire but this was soon resumed and the hulls, masts and yards of the attacking ships were struck by a stream of projectiles, the smoke of battle so thick that, at times, they were hidden by it.

At three-thirty *Albion*, engaging the cliff-top batteries of the Wasp Fort, was hit by a shell and, blazing fiercely, had to be towed out of the action, her crew taking refuge aboard

Firebrand, which had her in tow. Phillip was about to take *Trojan* in to fill her place when, to his dismay he saw first *London* and then *Arethusa* withdrawing from their stations, both under heavy and accurate fire from the Wasp and Telegraph batteries. *Sanspareil* had been compelled to alter her position, having evidently found her guns masked by *Agamemnon*, and, as she manoeuvred to bring her broadside to bear once more, the flagship was left alone and unsupported, every gun in Fort Constantine directed at her. Through the thick pall of smoke, Phillip saw tongues of flame leaping from her upper deck and, a moment later, one of her boats was lowered and, with an officer in the sternsheets, this started to row furiously in the direction of *Sanspareil* . . . no doubt in an attempt to request her to close the flagship again. Realizing that it would take her some time to do so, Phillip bade his quartermaster change course, intending to draw some of the heavy fire from the flagship if he could.

He succeeded almost too well in his intention. Hitherto at extreme range, as her orders demanded, *Trojan* had suffered little from the guns on shore but suddenly it was as if she had become the target for every piece of ordnance on the clifftop. Chain-shot tore through her rigging and she was hulled a dozen times before Phillip, peering vainly into the smoke, was able to bring his own guns to bear, and reply to the enemy cannonade with a series of rapid broadsides. He was heartened by the way his gunners worked, heartened, too, by the speed and courage with which the topmen, in instant response to his shouted order, set about clearing the tangled mass of spars and rigging which the Russian chain-shot had brought crashing down on the upper deck. A blaze, started on the forecastle by a hail of red-hot shot, was swiftly extinguished and he saw, as the pall of smoke parted momentarily, that the crew of *Agamemnon* had also succeeded in getting their blaze under control during the brief respite his arrival had won for them.

At his elbow, Martin Fox shouted that *Queen* and *Rodney* were bearing up in order to give the flagship their support and that *Sanspareil* was forging ahead with the same purpose. But, within a few minutes of receiving this news, Phillip saw to his dismay that *Queen* was blazing from stem to stern and she signalled shortly afterwards that she was hauling out of range. *Rodney*, in the tow of *Spiteful* kept heroically on, her Captain so determined to assist the flagship that he steered between her and *Sanspareil*, being compelled finally to let go his anchor in perilous proximity to *Agamemnon*'s bow. Her stern swung round and grounded on the shoal, which gripped her fast. In the gathering dusk, unaware of the fate which had befallen her would-be rescuer but finding *Rodney* close athwart her hawse, their jib-guys touching, *Agamemnon* slipped her bower anchor and steamed astern, so as to clear her and the approaching *Sanspareil*. She then made a sweep, with the evident intention of bringing her lower deck guns to bear on two Russian batteries which had been raking her continuously in her previous position and, once again, was temporarily hidden from Phillip's sight in the smoke. *Bellerophon* and *London* closed in and, in response to a signal from the latter, Phillip took up the station previously allocated to *Arethusa*.

It was now almost five o'clock and, as far as he could make out, there was no sign of the expected land assault on the city of Sebastopol. Had they, he wondered wearily, failed despite all their efforts? The walls of Fort Constantine were pitted and riddled with shot but the fire from its powerful guns continued unabated. Above them on the summit of the cliffs, the Wasp Fort, the Telegraph Battery and the guns mounted behind a recently completed earthwork, although wreathed in smoke, went on pouring out a hail of missiles, aimed at the British ships beneath them. On the south side of the harbour, the French and Turkish Fleets appeared to have fared no better and now, he saw, were withdrawing. He glimpsed *Terrible* to the north-east, flying the recall signal, evidently repeating that of the Commander-in-Chief and was about to obey it when Martin Fox gripped his arm.

'*Rodney*'s in trouble, sir. She's requesting assistance from a steamer. She . . . I think she's aground, sir.'

Phillip climbed the starboard hammock netting and

turned his glass on the stricken two-decker. *Spiteful*, he noticed, was still lashed to her port side, the little 6-gun steamer making valiant efforts to extricate her from her dangerous position. *Rodney* lay stern-on to Fort Constantine, keeping up a strong fire with such guns as she could use effectively but the Russian gunners had her range and were subjecting her to a merciless cannonade. On her forecastle, a party worked frantically to warp her off by means of her bower anchors, but she remained motionless, held fast by the stern on the shoal on which she had grounded.

Like the ill-fated *Tiger*, Phillip thought, reliving the scene in all its remembered horror. Other ships were flying the recall signal now and he saw *London* haul off, a fire blazing on her upper deck and her crew at the pumps, as *Niger* towed her clear. Obviously *Rodney*'s distress signal was hidden from them and he knew that *Trojan* would have to answer it.

'Mr. Fox ... we must get a tow rope across to her.'

'Aye, aye, sir.' Fox was at his side, alert, obedient, not questioning his decision. Phillip gave his orders with a calm that belied his inner anxiety for the safety of his ship and her crew. Once again *Trojan* steamed towards the guns of Fort Constantine, once again the chain-shot hurtled through her rigging but now, with *Rodney* in their sights, their fire was divided and the Russian gunners permitted the frigate to approach her objective comparatively unscathed.

'*Lynx* is with us, sir,' Martin Fox said. 'On our starboard bow ...' he pointed. 'And ... she's drawing their fire. Do you suppose she means to attempt a tow?'

Phillip studied the *Spiteful*'s small consort through his glass, saw her run up a signal and, reading it, nodded. 'Yes,' he confirmed, 'she means to and she may stand a better chance than we should, since she draws less water. So we had better reverse our roles, I think ... *we* will try to draw the enemy's fire, while she passes her tow-rope to *Rodney*. Make a signal to *Lynx*, if you please, to say that we will stand by her.'

'Aye, aye, sir,' Fox acknowledged.

'And put a man on the lead – a good man. I'm going as close in as I can and we don't want to run on to that shoal. Quartermaster....'

'Sir?'

Once again, Phillip found himself issuing his orders with a calm confidence he did not feel. It seemed to him as he brought *Trojan* in on her new course, to take the tiny *Lynx* twice as long to accomplish her mission as such an operation ought normally to take her, but as he watched her manoeuvre herself close in to *Rodney*'s bows, he did not betray his impatience or the fear he felt for his own ship. To all outward appearances, he was unworried and the men about him on *Trojan*'s quarterdeck drew confidence from his semblance of calm. Her main deck guns roared defiance, as she stood-in to the shore and dropped anchor so as to screen the rescue operation and only when *Rodney* was afloat again did the hard pressed guns' crews pause in their work to cheer. The most serious damage *Trojan* had suffered throughout the whole action came with the loss of her foremast, which crashed down in a welter of tangled rigging just as she was steaming out of range in the wake of *Rodney* and her two escorting steamers. Her total casualties, Phillip was amazed and thankful to learn, were one man killed and thirteen wounded.

The wreckage of the fore-mast had been cleared away by the time *Trojan* rejoined the inshore squadron and dusk was setting in as, with the main body of the British Fleet, the squadron set course for the anchorage off the mouth of the Katcha River. But it was not too dark for those on her quarterdeck to see the signal *Agamemnon* ran up as she steamed past.

'Signal from flagship reads *"Well done, Trojan ... congratulations to Commander"*,' Martin Fox announced proudly. He added, smiling at Phillip, 'That must mean you've won your promotion, sir. You'll be confirmed in command of *Trojan*.'

'No, my command is still only temporary,' Phillip reminded him. 'I shall not be promoted to post-rank, Martin, so they will have to give *Trojan* to someone else.'

'After the way you commanded her today?' his second-in-command objected. 'I take leave to doubt that, sir.'

Phillip sighed. Whatever happened, he thought, feeling suddenly very tired, he had commanded his ship in action and her crew had fulfilled his highest hopes of them. He wondered, recalling Mademoiselle Sophie's parting words to him, whether she knew and whether, across the miles that separated them now, she was sharing this moment with him, in her heart. Perhaps she was . . . the heart, she had said, did not forget and his had not forgotten. But . . . he turned back to Martin Fox.

'Mr. Fox, we'll splice the main brace, if you please, as soon as we drop anchor. And I should like the grog issue doubled, for all hands . . . if any men have earned it, these men have today.'

'Aye, aye, Commander Hazard,' Fox acknowledged, grinning hugely. And then, to Phillip's gratified surprise, all his officers gathered round him – Cochrane, Laidlaw and Sutherland, Burnaby the Master, the midshipmen and mates, even young Smithson of the Marines, wringing his hand and offering their congratulations.

Last of all came his brother Graham, the lead-line he had been using to sound *Trojan*'s way across the shoal water still in his grasp. They smiled at each other, without the need for words and Phillip turned away, his throat tight as, from the deck below, he heard his seamen cheering.

Another exciting adventure story at sea

RAMAGE AND THE FREEBOOTERS

by Dudley Pope

Lieutenant Lord Ramage is summoned to the Admiralty, where the First Lord gives him command of the *Triton* brig and three sealed despatches addressed to the admirals of Brest and Cadiz and in the Caribbean.

But the *Triton's* crew has mutinied: and Ramage sympathizes with some of the mutineers' complaints. He also knows that failure to deliver the despatches means he will be a convenient scapegoat for the Admiralty . . .

This, the third novel in the 'Ramage' series, is an enthralling story which captures all the mystery and danger of the Caribbean in Nelson's day.

'A fitting successor to C. S. Forester' – *Books and Bookmen*

0 552 08582 0 – 35p

An epic novel from the incomparable John Masters

THE ROCK

Gibraltar: a place, a fortress, an idea, a byword. In this skilful novel, John Masters has sought not only to re-create what it was like to live on The Rock at different periods throughout its turbulent past, but to provide the essential core of its history: why it has always been fought over, coveted, threatened by invaders.

This is the Gibraltar story. From the misty Palaeolithic dawn to the present day, we run the whole gamut of man's experience – even incest has its place – and if at times the violence seems gratuitous, we must remember that this is the way of the world. The Rock has seen it all, The Rock tells it all.

0 552 08832 3 – 50p

From CATHERINE COOKSON, *renowned for her ability to capture the flavour of the Northern scene and its people, past and present, comes*

THE GLASS VIRGIN

Annabella Lagrange was the only child of a wealthy family, owners of glass-works in the North-East of England. When Annabella was seven, she thought the world a delightful place to live in, and only occasionally wondered why her parents never took her beyond the gates of their magnificent country estate. When she was ten, she decided that the seclusion didn't really matter very much, because when she grew up she would marry her handsome cousin Stephen and never be lonely again. When she was eighteen, Annabella learned the circumstancs of her birth – and her entire world crashed around her.

0 552 08849 8 – 40p

THE INVITATION

When the Gallachers received an invitation from the Duke of Moorshire to attend his musical evening, Maggie was overwhelmed. Naturally, she did not see the invitation as the rock on which she was to perish; nor was she prepared for the reactions of her family. Her son Paul, daughter Elizabeth and daughter-in-law Arlette were as delighted as she was but the effect on Sam, Arlette's husband, was to bring his smouldering hate of his mother to flashpoint. Maggie herself, however, was to be prime mover of the downfall of the family she loved too dearly . . .

0 552 09035 2 – 35p

A SELECTION OF FINE READING
AVAILABLE IN CORGI BOOKS

Science Fiction

☐ 552 08925 7   **THE BEST FROM NEW WRITINGS IN S.F.**
ed. John Carnell 25p

☐ 552 09061 1   **LION OF COMARRE**   *Arthur C. Clarke* 30p

☐ 552 08942 7   **A WILDERNESS OF STARS**   *ed. William Nolan* 30p

☐ 552 08860 9   **VENUS PLUS X**   *Theodore Sturgeon* 25p

General

☐ 552 09009 3   **A RAP ON RACE**   *James Baldwin and Margaret Mead* 40p

☐ 552 08944 3   **BILLY CASPER'S 'MY MILLION-DOLLAR SHOTS'**   50p

☐ 552 08926 5   **S IS FOR SEX**   *Robert Chartham* 50p

☐ 552 98958 4   **THE ISLAND RACE Vol. 1**   *Winston S. Churchill* 125p

☐ 552 98959 2   **THE ISLAND RACE Vol. 2**   *Winston S. Churchill* 125p

☐ 552 09011 5   **GEHLEN: SPY OF THE CENTURY** (illustrated)
E. H. Cookridge 50p

☐ 552 08800 5   **CHARIOTS OF THE GODS?** (illustrated) *Erich von Daniken* 35p

☐ 552 07400 4   **MY LIFE AND LOVES**   *Frank Harris* 65p

☐ 552 98748 4   **MAKING LOVE** (Photographs)   *Walter Hartford* 85p

☐ 552 08992 3   **MASTERING WITCHCRAFT**   *Paul Huson* 35p

☐ 552 98862 6   **INVESTING IN GEORGIAN GLASS** (illustrated)
Ward Lloyd 125p

☐ 552 09062 X   **THE SENSUOUS MAN**   *"M"* 35p

☐ 552 08069 1   **THE OTHER VICTORIANS**   *Steven Marcus* 50p

☐ 552 09030 1   **BORN TO HEAL** (illustrated)   *Paul Miller* 35p

☐ 552 08010 1   **THE NAKED APE**   *Desmond Morris* 30p

☐ 552 09044 1   **SEX ENERGY**   *Robert S. de Ropp* 35p

☐ 552 09016 6   **GOLF TACTICS**   *Arnold Palmer* 45p

☐ 552 08880 3   **THE THIRTEENTH CANDLE**   *T. Lobsang Rampa* 35p

☐ 552 08974 5   **BRUCE TEGNER METHOD OF SELF DEFENCE**   40p

☐ 552 09059 X   **BEHIND THE MASK OF TUTANKHAMEN** *Barry Wynne* 35p

Western

☐ 552 08194 9	No. 44 THE WILDCATS	*J. T. Edson* 25p
☐ 552 08971 0	TO ARMS! TO ARMS IN DIXIE No. 68	*J. T. Edson* 25p
☐ 552 08972 9	THE SOUTH WILL RISE AGAIN No. 69	*J. T. Edson* 25p
☐ 552 08995 8	CATLOW	*Louis L'Amour* 25p
☐ 552 09027 1	SACKETT	*Louis L'Amour* 25p
☐ 552 09006 9	CALLAGHEN	*Louis L'Amour* 30p
☐ 552 09058 1	RIDE THE DARK TRAIL	*Louis L'Amour* 25p
☐ 552 09048 4	RIO GRANDE	*Louis Masterson* 25p
☐ 552 08990 7	RETURN TO ACTION No. 16	*Louis Masterson* 25p
☐ 552 09007 7	MONTE WALSH	*Jack Schaefer* 40p
☐ 552 09064 6	SUDDEN RIDES AGAIN	*Oliver Strange* 25p

Crime

☐ 552 09024 7	THE GALLOWS ARE WAITING	*John Creasey* 25p
☐ 552 09025 5	'WARE DANGER	*John Creasey* 25p
☐ 552 08640 1	RED FILE FOR CALLAN	*James Mitchell* 30p
☐ 552 08937 0	THE KNIVES OF JUSTICE	*Mildred Savage* 50p
☐ 552 09005 0	SONNTAG	*Michael Sinclair* 30p
☐ 552 08883 8	THE BIG KILL	*Mickey Spillane* 25p
☐ 552 09056 5	SHAFT	*Ernest Tidyman* 30p
☐ 552 09072 7	SHAFT'S BIG SCORE	*Frnest Tidyman* 30p

All these books are available at your bookshop or newsagent: or can be ordered direct rom the publisher. Just tick the titles you want and fill in the form below.

....

CORGI BOOKS, Cash Sales Department, P.O. Box 11, Falmouth, Cornwall.
Please send cheque or postal order. No currency, and allow 6p per book to cover the
cost of postage and packing in the U.K., and overseas.

NAME ....

ADDRESS ....

(OCT 72) ....